Deadly Secrets

Phillip Strang

BOOKS BY PHILLIP STRANG

DCI Isaac Cook Series
MURDER IS A TRICKY BUSINESS
MURDER HOUSE
MURDER IS ONLY A NUMBER
MURDER IN LITTLE VENICE
MURDER IS THE ONLY OPTION
MURDER IN NOTTING HILL
MURDER IN ROOM 346
MURDER OF A SILENT MAN
MURDER HAS NO GUILT
MURDER IN HYDE PARK
SIX YEARS TOO LATE
GRAVE PASSION
THE SLAYING OF JOE FOSTER
THE HERO'S FALL
THE VICAR'S CONFESSION
GUILTY UNTIL PROVEN INNOCENT
DEVIL HOUSE
MURDER WITHOUT REASON

DI Keith Tremayne Series
DEATH UNHOLY
DEATH AND THE ASSASSIN'S BLADE
DEATH AND THE LUCKY MAN
DEATH AT COOMBE FARM
DEATH BY A DEAD MAN'S HAND
DEATH IN THE VILLAGE
BURIAL MOUND
THE BODY IN THE DITCH
THE HORSE'S MOUTH
MONTFIELD'S MADNESS

Sergeant Natalie Campbell Series
DARK STREETS
PINCHGUT
ISLAND SHADOWS

Steve Case Series
HOSTAGE OF ISLAM
THE HABERMAN VIRUS
PRELUDE TO WAR

Standalone Books
MALIKA'S REVENGE
VERRALL'S NIGHTMARE

Copyright © 2024 Phillip Strang
Cover Design by Phillip Strang

All rights reserved. No part of this book may be reproduced, stored in a retrieval system, or transmitted in any form or by any means (electronic, mechanical, photocopying, recording or otherwise) without the prior written permission of the publisher, except by a reviewer who may quote brief passages in a review to be printed by a newspaper, magazine, or journal.

All characters appearing in this work are fictitious. Any resemblance to actual events, locales, or persons, living or dead, is coincidental.
All Rights Reserved.

This work is registered with the UK Copyright Service.
ISBN - 13: 9798345787823

Dedication

For Elli and Tais, who both had the perseverance to make me sit down and write

Chapter 1

Detective Chief Inspector Isaac Cook and Commander Richard Goddard watched the scene unfolding in the House of Lords on the television in Goddard's office. It was something they would not have believed; it was something that answered a lot of questions.

Nine weeks had passed since Commander Alwyn Davies had taken the credit for thwarting the terrorist attack in Whitehall, but not before one of the three suicide bombers had detonated his explosive vest, taking the lives of ten tourists.

It was subsequently revealed after the attack that Superintendent Seth Caddick had stationed people along Whitehall, at the entrance to Downing Street, close to the Cenotaph, and outside Horse Guards Parade. Two other suicide bombers had died in the vicinity, one from a shot fired by a police officer stationed outside the entrance to Downing Street and another by Caddick, who, without concern for his personal safety, had wrested the man to the ground and broken his neck. Caddick, for his actions, had been promoted to chief superintendent by a grateful Davies due to his exceptional policing.

It had been hailed by the media and the public that Davies' approach to policing and law enforcement was vital, and the attempts to remove the man had failed. The planned elevation of Goddard to New Scotland Yard had been scuppered, and Isaac's hold as the senior investigating officer in Homicide at Challis Street Police Station was tenuous.

Caddick's name had been mentioned in parliament, Davies had met with the King, and Angus MacTavish, who had fought to remove Davies, had retreated to his castle in Scotland.

Questions were still being asked as to why Davies had been threatened and that a new government, after the impending election, intended to instigate a Royal Commission into the orchestrated attempt to remove the best head of the London Metropolitan Police Force in the last fifty years.

Isaac and Goddard knew there was skullduggery, but they were powerless to act, as they had no evidence, only questions that begged answers.

Five weeks after the terrorist attack, the adopted son of Martin and Beverley Marshall, a middle-class family in Nottingham in the north of the country, stood in front of the media and announced his claim to the title of Lord Alsworthy.

However, Benjamin Marshall was no ordinary son. At the age of twenty-five, the fair-haired Caucasian had embraced Islam. He soon proved himself a gifted orator and an ardent supporter of the oppressed, the weak, and the needy.

Isaac and Goddard realised the significance of what Marshall had said, although his name had changed to Ibrahim Ali.

'In my hand,' Ali had said to the media, 'I have a birth certificate and proof that my birth parents were married, if only for a short time, and that I am their son. Due to the delicacy of what I am about to reveal, DNA has been obtained from their children and me.

'My mother was Marjorie Frobisher, a famous actress in this country, who was tragically run down by a speeding vehicle as she left a restaurant. My father was Lord Alsworthy, who was a prominent politician. The Alsworthy title is hereditary, and I claim it.'

Deadly Secrets

Ibrahim Ali's views were well known. He advocated Sharia and regarded Islam as the true religion. Even though Ali protested, proselytised, and was a passionate believer, he had never been convicted of a crime, which would have been one of the few avenues to have withheld his entry into the House of Lords.

Goddard phoned Lord Angus MacTavish, a former government whip, laird of his clan, and the driving force attempting to remove Commissioner Davies. He put it to the man straight. 'How many people died to keep Ibrahim Ali a secret?' Goddard asked.

MacTavish's response had been mute, and in typical politician fashion, he had procrastinated, refused to be drawn, and did not come to London for Ibrahim Ali's triumphant entry as he was brought into the House of Lords, dressed in traditional Arab clothing, encased in ermine robes which signified all that he despised.

***

Isaac Cook reflected on the events that had culminated in Ibrahim Ali entering the august chamber at the Palace of Westminster.

Due to heavy rain, it had been a quiet day in Whitehall when the attack occurred; otherwise, the death count would have been higher. Of the three suicide bombers that day, two had been radicalised, and the third had the intelligence of a nine-year-old child, although he was in his thirties.

MacTavish and Goddard met six days after Ali made his speech, not in MacTavish's former office with its wood panelling and leather chairs, but in a restaurant in Canary Wharf.

'Someone told him.' MacTavish said. 'It was not me and certainly wasn't the Alsworthys or Marjorie Frobisher's family.'

'They didn't know?'

'The only one was Lord Alsworthy, apart from me.'

'You condoned murder,' Goddard replied.

3

'Goddard, a decision was made, the only decision possible. Do you realise what Ibrahim Ali's elevation could mean?'

'Back then or now?'

'Does it matter? Ibrahim Ali, a British citizen, could use his title and subsequent wealth to wreak untold damage to this country. And what about the Alsworthy family? Alsworthy's daughter took on the mantle of head of the family. She lives in the mansion; she controls the wealth.'

Goddard did not believe MacTavish or approve of his lordship's nonchalant manner. MacTavish had been a hard-nosed politician, used to making decisions for his political party, and people had died due to those decisions.

'Someone told him, and then there was a terrorist attack. Soon after, Davies reasserts his authority as the Met's commissioner, and Caddick is promoted. Conspiracy or fact?'

'Someone struck a deal with Ibrahim Ali.'

'Are you suggesting that Davies would condone the death of innocent persons to secure his position, that he would allow crime to occur, and then, for him and his cronies to stamp it out. And that somehow Davies was working in unison with Ali?' Goddard asked although he and Isaac had figured out the answer.

'Innocent people died for the greater good, once before. Margaret Frobisher did not deserve to die. I expected you not to interfere, but your protégé, Cook, could not leave it alone.'

'Did you authorise Marjorie Frobisher's death?'

'Mark my words before you condemn the actions of the past,' MacTavish said. 'There will be changes in London we will not like. Idealism and a belief in the good of humankind are the fodder of movies and fairytales, but we, men of the world, know differently.'

Goddard finally had proof that Marjorie Frobisher's hit and run had not been an accident and why Robert Williams, her sometimes paramour, had been murdered. It was political dynamite, and if Davies had known of the terrorist attack in advance and used it to cement his position, it was something Goddard could not tolerate.

Marjorie Frobisher had died because she knew but would never reveal it. And the deputy prime minister, the father of the child, in league with his party's government whip, had conspired to pervert the course of justice. Goddard knew there was only one person he could tell.

'We're minor players,' Isaac Cook said as Goddard explained what he knew and what they surmised. 'MacTavish was on our side before, even if he was the villain.'

It was late in the evening in Commander Goddard's office. Outside, it was raining and cold.

Isaac had always been an idealist, and now, revealed in stark reality, that MacTavish admitted that persons had died to protect the secret.

Not only Marjorie Frobisher and Richard Williams, but Williams had killed his personal assistant, who knew more than she should. All three were killed at the altar of political necessity, and now, apparently, ten tourists, not to protect the secret but to have it revealed.

'We were powerless,' Goddard continued. 'Was MacTavish, right? What would have happened had the new Lord Alsworthy known of his parents back when Marjorie Frobisher was alive?'

'One thing we know is that ten people would not have died in a senseless act,' Isaac replied.

'The information about Marjorie Frobisher and Lord Alsworthy, their marriage and their child, was buried so deep that it should never have been found, yet Davies had.'

'He's not the person to dive into the archives to discover the truth, or is he?'

'Someone told him, and there's only one person who would have, only one person he could trust.'

'Caddick?' Isaac said. 'The man's slime, but that would require two qualities: the ability to find out the true story; the second is how to use it.'

5

'There is another. Someone would have had to strike a deal with Ibrahim Ali, that in exchange for the terrorist attack, Ali would have his birthright.'

'These are extremely complex agreements to put in place, and Caddick's no intellectual. I just don't think he's capable.'

'Davies must have known, but he wouldn't get his hands dirty – mud sticks.'

'But Davies would never have trusted Caddick with something this complex.'

'That is where we come in. Regardless of what we thought of Angus MacTavish before and what we think of him now, I'm inclined to give him my trust.'

'And forgive him for murder?' Isaac asked.

'No sitting on the fence on this one,' Goddard said. 'What we have in an emboldened Commissioner Davies, who condones murder if it cements his position. Can we have a criminal as the commissioner of the London Metropolitan Police?'

'No.'

'Agreed. Then, you and your department must discover what happened in the Horse Guards Parade. How did Caddick become involved, how did he know when the attack was to occur, and how did he know about the other two with their suicide vests?'

'What about the Counter Terrorism Command? Isn't that a job for them?'

'MacTavish is not well, getting old and tired. He doesn't have the influence he once had or know who he can trust. Counter Terrorism Command could be compromised. Anybody could.'

'He knows us.'

'Precisely. We will conduct our enquiries, investigate where we can pull in favours, communicate with persons we can trust.'

'Who can we trust?'

Deadly Secrets

'MacTavish has set up a meeting for you tomorrow, eight in the evening, and for Christ's sake, don't sleep with her.' Goddard said. 'Your favourite restaurant.'

***

Isaac was not sure how to react. It had been many years, and his relationship with Jess O'Neill had been damned due to his spending the night with Linda Harris. And there she was, sitting across from him in a small restaurant in Belgravia, the last place they had met. Soon after their night together, she had disappeared, and the investigations into the murders of Richard Williams and Sally Jenkins filed away, never to be solved.

'You killed Williams,' Isaac said.

The woman was older but no less beautiful. He had lusted after her before and felt guilt that he still did. This was a woman he could have committed to, and after she had disappeared, his only contact since then had been a late-night call to say goodbye.

'I did what was necessary,' Linda said. She was dressed in a loose-fitting blouse and denim jeans. She had put on weight, but not much. Men still turned to look at her, even in the restaurant. Isaac could not help but wonder what they would have thought of her if they knew she was a killer.

Goddard was willing to give MacTavish the benefit of the doubt, to believe that the man's actions and that of the beautiful assassin were justified for the greater good. Isaac was unsure if he could. He regretted that he had not explained why he was meeting a former lover to his wife, Jenny, and that the meeting felt like the prelude to romance when it was strictly professional.

'I don't think I can do this,' Isaac said. 'After…'

'After we slept together, or after I liquidated people?'

'Both.'

'I work for the British government. I do what I must, whether that's kill or love.'

'And if they gave you an order to kill me or Superintendent Goddard or Lord MacTavish?'

7

'That's not why we are meeting, is it?'

'I know that Marjorie Frobisher was important. I didn't know how important,' Isaac said.

'Lord MacTavish still has influence.'

'Your function?'

'I am an intermediary,' Linda replied.

'To nameless bureaucrats.'

'Isaac, there's been a leak, information which should never have come to light. The question is how?'

'And why?'

'We know why, Davies. We also know that Caddick set it up, but we have never regarded him as any more than a sycophantic buffoon.'

'Who's we? Are you merely an intermediary, or do you have access to the inner sanctum of this country's secret service?'

'I have access.'

'Can you trust them?'

'Can you trust Commissioner Davies? Can you trust Commander Goddard?' Linda said.

Isaac realised he was compromised.

'Why you?'

'Our previous relationship, Lord MacTavish, and I know the extent of the previous investigation into the disappearance of Marjorie Frobisher and the deaths.'

'You were responsible for a couple of them.'

'You've been advised by your commander not to allow your inherent decency to get in the way,' Linda said. 'I suggest you heed his advice. You cannot take a back seat on this. It's clear that Davies knew what Caddick was doing, even if he distances himself from it.'

'If we get close to the truth, Davies will throw Caddick to the wolves.'

'He can try, but who is the new Lord Alsworthy? If his position is threatened, he will fight tooth and nail. Until we have advice or proof to the contrary, we must assume that Ibrahim Ali has no compunction to kill, and he gave his people to Caddick as a reward, allowing Caddick to emerge a hero. Any threat to him, and he will take anyone down, including you and me.'

'You can disappear into the ether like you did before,' Isaac reminded Linda. 'Where did you go, by the way?'

'Asia, deep in.'

'Countries not on the tourist map.'

'No tourist would want to go where I did.'

Chapter 2

Linda Harris' presence caused difficulties for Isaac as to how he would tell Jenny that he was working with a former lover who killed people on order.

Goddard was aware of the situation. His advice was to work with the woman and be circumspect but never give her his unbridled trust.

Isaac's take was different. The woman was not only a killer, but she was highly trained, manipulative, and possibly more capable than him.

'Keep your friends close; your enemies, even closer,' Goddard said.

Isaac had made the only decision possible. He told Jenny about the woman, not the full details, only that they had a brief relationship and the woman worked for MI5. Jenny deserved to know that he had thrown in his lot with people who could never be trusted and were adept at spinning a tale and lying and killing.

'Is it important?' Jenny asked.

'The terrorist attack, Ibrahim Ali, and Caddick, the hero of the moment. I think it is.'

'But it's dangerous. Commissioner Davies is taking the glory, and Ibrahim Ali is in the House of Lords. These are persons with serious clout, and you are an insect to be squashed underfoot.'

'Someone must take the lead and root out the evil.'

'And then Goddard takes the glory, the same as Davies. You and Caddick are expendable. Goddard and Davies are men who play to win, and if that means that they have to say and do evil, it won't stop them.'

'I hope Commander Goddard is better than that,' Isaac said.

'The commander's right; you must take sides and not sit on the fence, but don't trust the man, don't trust this woman. Is she pretty?'

Isaac realised that with sterling advice came jealousy. He could not blame his wife.

'Yes, very,' Isaac said. 'I'm being honest with you. I'd prefer not to be working with her.'

'You have no option,' Jenny said.

***

Isacc revealed certain facts to his core team. He needed them onside and cognisant of the limited facts he would reveal.

Goddard had told him to be careful and that investigating Caddick and the commissioner would cause an adverse reaction from people who had to be regarded as exceptionally dangerous if it became known. Persons who would stop at nothing to achieve their twisted aim.

Mindful of Jenny's advice, which included her summation of Richard Goddard, Isaac knew he would need to be careful with the truth when talking to his team.

They were about to investigate a crime when there was no crime under investigation, only actions that pointed towards a heinous crime that might have been condoned by a police officer or officers. The question was, who could be trusted, who would take a neutral position, and who would side with the enemy.

Goddard had sided with Davies until he joined with MacTavish, but his lordship was ailing, old, overweight, and increasingly drunk. Isaac realised that Goddard had MacTavish, and for the moment, he had Goddard. That could change.

Isaac realised that lying low would have been the best approach and to adopt a wait-and-see attitude, but this time, it was a terrorist act, and there was mounting evidence that Davies knew of it and Caddick had been intimately involved. Yet, Caddick wasn't his own man; he didn't take action without tacit support from a superior, and that superior had to be Davies.

Isaac called Bridget Halloran into the office. He needed the best computer person in Challis Street.

The door was closed. 'I need you to go through the databases, do what you must, but find out what you can about a murder investigation that goes back a few years,' Isaac said.

'That would be accessible on your computer,' Bridget said.

'I need you, Sergeant Wendy Gladstone, and Inspector Larry Hill, to conduct enquiries and delve deep, but whatever the three of you do, I do not want this official. I do not want a folder on a laptop where it will be stored.'

'Can I ask why?'

'There is the possibility of a crime, frightening in its implication. I need persons I can trust and minimal questions asked.'

'Is this illegal? Or dangerous?'

'It could be both. Store any data you find deep where no one can find it. Make sure that no one knows you have retrieved it. Leave no evidence of what you have done. Can you do that?'

'It depends how complex it is. In Challis Street, or New Scotland Yard, or further afield?'

'New Scotland Yard, and further afield. Can you enter any database?'

'With time, but to remain invisible is not so easy. I might be able to cover my trail, but they will almost certainly know they have been hacked. Hacking's illegal. Is that what you are asking me to do?'

'Not yet. For now, gather all the information you can relating to the investigation into Marjorie Frobisher. The official reports are available. I need to know what else we do not know. See if you can find any interest from Caddick in the woman. Correlate it, look for anomalies, see if there are hidden files.'

'Are there?'

'There must be. I need to know how someone else knew of them, how they accessed them, and what they contained.'

Isaac considered the first step challenging. He had been a detective chief inspector for a long time. He had relied on Richard Goddard to look out for him, but the man had proven to be divisive and no longer worthy of his unqualified trust.

Linda Harris, he knew, could not be trusted, and if she was willing to tell the truth, how would he know that it was.

It needed someone incorruptible, unwilling to bend and snap under the relentless pressure of others, and that was him, Detective Chief Inspector Isaac Cook, the son of Jamaican immigrants. It was up to him to save the London Metropolitan Police.

He would support Caddick, Goddard, Davies, Linda Harris and whoever she represented while continuing to investigate, inveigle, and ultimately expose. If he succeeded, he would accept the accolades and reap the records, but if he faltered or failed, he would be denounced as a whistleblower, thrown out of the police force, humiliated, and possibly convicted of a crime, whether he had committed it or not, or even dead.

He spoke to Jenny that night after he had told Bridget which murder investigation to research.

***

'You can't do this on your own,' Jenny said. 'You need allies.'

'I have. My team,' Isaac replied.

It was late at night; the children were in bed. It was just the two of them, each with a glass of wine. Isaac felt invigorated, too long adopting a wait-and-see approach. Now, he was going for the jugular.

'Your team is not enough. Is there anyone you can trust? Someone senior?'

'Only one, and I can't be sure of her.'

'Another of your women?'

'Unfortunately, yes.'

'One hundred per cent, cross my heart and hope to die, certain that you can trust this person?'

'Avenue of last resort? There is no one, although I might have to trust her sometime in the future, but not now. I need more facts.'

'Don't trust Goddard,' Jenny reiterated what she had said the day before.

The following day, after an early start in the office, Wendy Gladstone was in Isaac's office.

'Remember Marjorie Frobisher?' Isaac said.

'I went to Malvern to look for her; then, she's killed in a hit and run, and then the driver is exonerated.'

'Then I don't need to tell you about Lord Alsworthy.'

'You believe it's suspicious, the woman dying, and then her son claiming the title.'

'Did she know what had become of him?'

'She knew she had borne a son to Alsworthy. It does not mean she knew where or who he was.'

'I need you to find out if she did and if there is any record. She was married. Did her husband know, and if he did, how did Caddick? The records of Ibrahim Ali's parentage would have been hidden deep, the Official Secrets Act would have dealt with it, and we know people died, who may have known or not. What we need to do is to eliminate the possible sources.'

'After so many years. It might be difficult to find some of them, and if I do, is this an official police enquiry? Do we have the necessary authorities?' Wendy asked.

'The answer is no. Do not discuss this with anyone else, not with Bridget or Larry Hill. For now, the three of you will work separately on different aspects of the investigation.

'Are you sure about this? You can't rely on Commander Goddard, or do you know that?'

'I'm sure. I need facts, preferably proven. I'm unsure how I will proceed after that. As for Commander Goddard, I prefer not to let him know what I'm doing for now. It might be pure folly, and nothing might come of it, but we spent a long time

Deadly Secrets

looking for that woman. We never knew why she had died or why others had. But now, we know, and it's suspect. Information that had been buried so deep, and then Ibrahim Ali has the information, and Caddick's acting the hero, and Commissioner Davies is untouchable.'

'Are you inferring there is a conspiracy? That the commissioner would allow people to die to serve the greater purpose, to keep him in his job?'

'Davies, if he was honest, would say that the death of a few compared to the life of many is a small price to pay.'

'I'm not condoning his actions if proven, but he might be right,' Wendy said.

'That argument has been used for a long time, back into prehistory. Wars have been fought over that premise; millions have died on the altar of that ideology. Davies might have committed a crime, so might have Caddick. What we need to know is the truth.'

'How will you use it, even if you have it? Do you believe the majority will welcome your revelation, and what about those who support Davies? What will they say and do? You are one person blowing in the wind. Your death would be a small cost to pay.'

'It's something I must do,' Isaac said.

***

Isaac pondered what he needed Inspector Larry Hill, who was in his forties, struggling to keep away from alcohol and wrestling with the demands of an ambitious wife, to do. Larry would be the more visible of the three, and if, as Isaac suspected, these people were dangerous, then he and Larry would most likely be the primary targets of any vengeance.

Initially, Larry had not been part of the investigation into the search for the missing woman, Marjorie Frobisher, and the subsequent deaths. Isaac had complained when Homicide had become involved in the search, not aware of the woman's significance.

Ibrahim Ali had finally answered that question.

Larry Hill's involvement in the earlier enquiry came when the second body, Richard Williams's personal assistant, Sally Jenkins, was discovered in his area of London. Williams was the executive producer of the soap opera that Marjorie Frobisher acted in, and Jess O'Neill became the producer. Isaac realised it had been many years since he had thought of her. He hoped their paths would not cross. Two former lovers appeared inevitable, and Jenny was taking it well, but a third would be chancing his luck.

After Larry's evident professionalism, he was offered a position in Homicide.

'Here's the deal,' Isaac said. 'We know why Marjorie Frobisher and the others died.'

'We do,' Larry said. 'What sort of people are they, to kill people to maintain a secret? Any better than the idiot who blew himself up?'

'No better, but they are our idiots. Caddick was too quick off the mark in Whitehall. How did he know where the terrorists would be.'

'Is this your theory?' Larry asked.

'Commander Goddard's initially, although where he got it from, I don't know.'

'MacTavish?'

'Regardless, it needs investigating.'

'Are you willing to put your hand in the hornet's nest and rile them?'

'I must, but I need people I can trust.'

'You can't trust anyone, not even me,' Larry said.

'Why not you?'

'This is too big for you, for us. Are you sure you want to do it? You'll be the lone crusader against the forces of hell. They will mow you down if you get in their way.'

'I've considered all possibilities,' Isaac said. 'Are you in or out?'

'I'm in, but we need to be careful. Have you told the others the full details of your plan?'

'I've told Bridget and Wendy snippets. I don't know who else we can trust or will capitulate.'

'Any of us will, even in Homicide, if our families are threatened. We're against people who work by a different rule book.'

'By no rule book,' Isaac corrected his inspector.

'What do you want me to do?'

'Linda Harris, remember her?'

'How could I forget. You and her…'

'She's back, making out that she's on our side. I need to know if she is. Find out where she lives, who she meets, and if you can, what she says.'

'Leave it with me,' Larry said.

'And don't talk to Bridget or Wendy about what we've just spoken. We might get together at some time as a group, but for now, give the pieces to me. I'll decide when you should know the whole.'

'It's you taking the risk. Your wife?'

'She understands the situation.'

Chapter 3

Isaac knew Goddard's involvement in internal politics had gone from a skill to disingenuous. Would he ever be able to trust again the man who had mentored him from constable to detective chief inspector? He thought not, but first, he needed to talk to MacTavish, a man he trusted even less.

'Cook,' the booming voice hollered. The two men met in the man's castle in Scotland. Isaac realised that if he claimed the airline ticket and the hire car through Homicide, Caddick would know. Instead, he purchased the plane ticket and the vehicle's cost with his credit card, hoping he could claim the money back on expenses later.

The two men sat down in a large, high-ceilinged room. On the walls were portraits of previous lairds; above an enormous fireplace, there were crossed swords. A roaring log fire was in full blaze, large enough to heat the room.

At the feet of the laird were a couple of wolfhounds. Two persons, dressed in the uniform of servant and butler, respectively, wheeled in a trolley. On the trolley, a bottle of whisky and two glasses. Also, a selection of food, which MacTavish had no trouble in taking more than he needed.

'We can't discuss on an empty stomach,' MacTavish said. Isaac regretted the Big Mac he had at the airport in Edinburgh. There was too much food on the trolley and too much whisky, but to refuse the laird's hospitality would be akin to an insult.

After two whiskies, where MacTavish had toasted the clan, and Isaac had toasted MacTavish, a third toast, where both had toasted the London Metropolitan Police.

Isaac could have said it would need more than a whisky to save it but did not.

'Eat up,' MacTavish said. 'You're worried, can't blame you. And you're concerned that Commander Goddard is hedging his bets, waiting to see how the cards fall, that sort of thing.'

'I am,' Isaac said as he helped himself to several savouries.

'You're right to be worried. Goddard's a good man, a competent police officer, but he's a political animal.'

'Is that a recommendation?'

'It's a reality. Cook, you're idealistic, highly competent, and a credit to the Met, but you wear your contempt as if it were a badge.'

'I'm not ashamed of it.'

'Nor should you be. Did Caddick know about the terrorist attack in advance? Before you answer, how did he know?'

'I don't know,' Isaac admitted.

'A fair answer. Are you determined to follow through with this? Have you considered the probabilities? Taking down a commissioner is not for the weak. No one is going to make this easy.'

'Will you?'

'I'm old, in poor health, and no longer have a prime minister's confidence.'

'Did you ever?'

'At the time. I had the PM's support because he needed me to keep his party in power. Regardless of the political party in power, they are all tarred with the same brush.'

'But you persevered to get Davies removed.'

'I did because I thought it was right.'

'Even if that means your political alienation.'

'Back then, I would not have considered it, but now, what have I got to lose? I've always known that Commander Goddard would sit on the fence, but he keeps me informed, not with everything, but enough. You realise I don't have any real power, only perceived.'

'Politics is a dirty game,' Isaac said.

'Too many vultures devouring the same beast. Some will go hungry, some die, and some get eaten.'

'Including Marjorie Frobisher?'

'I wondered when you would get around to that. That wasn't only political; it was a necessity. What will happen with Ibrahim Ali in the House of Lords?'

'Does he have any power?'

'Not political, but he has a platform. He cannot be denied the right to speak in the House of Lords, and the media will lap it up.'

'You could give him the Marjorie Frobisher treatment. It was murder, what happened to her.'

'She knew who her son was, and there she is, enjoying the adulation of the masses and getting drunk.'

'Wouldn't she have kept quiet?'

'What would happen when the adulation vanished, and her phone didn't ring? Would she have hit the talk shows with her little titbit?'

'It's probable,' Isaac admitted.

'It's not only probable, it's one hundred per cent certain. She contacted me after she had resurfaced. I knew her when she was young. I was a friend of the previous Lord Alsworthy at Eton.'

'Old school tie.'

'Don't knock it. The previous lord was a good man, but he had been as young as you once, the same as me. Linda Harris, still carrying a flame for her?'

'I'm married.'

'Married, not married, what does that matter? You were keen on her once; she was keen on you, but she had to get out of the country.'

'If I'm to deal with her, level with me. Who is she?'

'MI5, but you know that. Senior operative, undercover, dangerous.'

'To me?'

'If she was ordered, without question.'

'She killed Richard Williams.'

'Did she? Did she admit it to you?'

Deadly Secrets

'Not directly, told me she didn't, but I can't believe her, nor Commander Goddard, definitely not Caddick…'

'And me,' MacTavish said.

'And you. You knew about Marjorie Frobisher; you knew about Linda Harris and who she was and who she had killed.'

'I did. Would you have understood back then; do you now? Based on what you know now, was I right in my actions?'

'I believe you only delayed the problem in the interest of political expediency.'

'Chief Inspector, you are right. Decisions had to be made; I made mine. Now the decision is with you. What is the right decision? To do nothing? To do something? Or, to sit on the fence?'

'Procrastination would not have worked; sitting on the fence would have achieved nothing. I despise what you did.'

'Then prove me wrong.'

'You know what this will mean?'

'I do. Ibrahim Ali will react if threatened, and people will die. Davies will use all his wiles to remain in position, and Caddick is a man without morals. That man could fall into a cesspit and come out smelling of roses.'

'Only if Davies is covering his back.'

'There again, DCI, your naivety. Caddick will change sides in an instance, fly the banner of whoever he can profit from.'

'Including you?'

'Strange bedfellows, I would admit. I would suggest you remain a police officer. It's what you're good at. As a politician, you wouldn't last ten minutes.'

'Commander Goddard?'

'Work with him. He's a decent man; he knows right from wrong, Caddick doesn't.'

'Linda Harris?'

'Trust her. She's on your side for now. If that changes, I'll let you know.'

'Can I trust you?'

'You might not approve of what I've done or might do, but yes.'

'Who did you intend to be the next commissioner?'

'Mary Ayton. Does that surprise you?'

'She would have been my choice,' Isaac said.

'You know her from long ago. For a man as naïve as you are, I don't understand how you charm the women. A legend in the Met, so I'm told.'

'Nobody knows about the future commissioner. I suggest we keep that quiet.'

MacTavish poured another whisky for him and Isaac. 'Here's to success,' he said.

Isaac downed it in one go. He didn't feel good after the whiskies he had drunk. He was a worried man.

***

Since his return from Scotland, Isaac spent two days in the office, met with Commander Goddard, filed a couple of reports, and held off Caddick, whose appearance late in the afternoon on the second day was unwelcome. Isaac rarely despised people, but he did Caddick.

When Caddick walked into the office, Isaac could feel his skin crawl. This was an evil man with no depths to which he would not sink. Isaac was convinced he had been the driving force behind the terrorist attack that had killed ten and could have killed a lot more. The day could have been wholesale carnage, and Caddick, even though he had been lauded as a hero, had been there on the day at the exact location. How was still unclear. It was up to Homicide to find out.

He was unsure they were up to the task, although Linda Harris was. He phoned her, and they agreed to meet at the restaurant where they had met before.

'Commissioner Davies is instigating sweeping reforms for the London Met,' Caddick said as he sat on a chair in Isaac's office. He was dressed in an expensive suit; Isaac could tell by the cut of the fabric and the way it hung on the lugubrious man. Usually, the man looked unkempt, but not this time.

'And you're the instigator,' Isaac replied, aware of MacTavish's advice and Goddard's suggestion not to rile the beast until you have the whip to tame it.

'I am. In the next couple of months, every police officer will be interviewed, their medical status will be confirmed, not by a police doctor or someone friendly to Homicide, as well as their sobriety, age, and qualifications.'

'Their record as a police officer?'

'The commissioner is cognisant of that, but the new Met will not have a place for the has-beens, the derelicts, nor those who indulge in petty politics, make deals with criminals, and get drunk. Your sergeant is a disgrace; she should be shown the door.'

'Did you come here as an independent arbiter, or do you intend this exercise of the commissioner's to be a witch hunt?'

'Not a witch hunt. I need someone to work with me; you have credibility and are highly respected at the Yard. Even Davies is an admirer.'

'Strange way of showing it,' Isaac said.

'Work with me, an adviser to what we are setting up.'

'What's the carrot?'

'Promotion. Superintendent. This time next week if you work with me.'

'Otherwise?'

'I'll go through this department like a dose of salts. You'll be lucky to be left with more than a laptop and a printer.'

'That means closing down Homicide.'

'It means restructuring and centralising Homicide at another location. In a modern police force, most crimes are solved with technology.'

'In Homicide, we still regard that out on the street is important.'

'I'm not disputing that it is, but statistically, more can be achieved in the office.'

Isaac thought back to a previous case, Harold and Elizabeth Colson. If Caddick had been the senior investigating officer in Homicide, they would have been charged with the murder of David Grayling when they were innocent of the crime. Isaac knew he could not allow Caddick and Davies to succeed.

'I need more details; I need time,' Isaac said.

'You've got one month.'

'If I agree?'

'Promotion and this department is left alone. Isaac, don't play me or Davies for fools,' Caddick said.

'And don't treat me as an idiot. I know what you're trying to do. The only question is whether the commissioner is ultimately right.'

'Still in doubt after all that's happened?'

'Give me two weeks, not four, Seth,' Isaac said. 'I need you to update me further as to your plans.'

Isaac was not fooled for a moment. Caddick was determined to separate the cord that connected Isaac with Goddard. Divide and conquer, or was there more to it. The man had found out about Ibrahim Ali's birthright. Isaac was sure of that, but how? And if he had, and Davies had so much power, why bother with the small fry? Why concern himself with a chief inspector in Homicide at Challis Street.

Isaac realised that Seth Caddick's reasons were personal.

***

They met for the third time since her return at the same restaurant. Isaac realised by how she embraced him when they met on the street outside that she was available for romance. Isaac felt guilty, not that he intended the evening to be any other than cordial and for them to discuss the investigation, but because he had not told Jenny he was meeting again with the woman.

Linda ordered ravioli; Isaac ordered lasagne. Isaac felt uncomfortable and compromised, wanting her but knowing he

Deadly Secrets

could not. He knew that Linda was a unique person the first time he had met her, and if she had remained in London, if she had not been a murderer, they could have moved in together.

Was Linda Harris, Linda Harris? Was she the person who sat opposite him, or was she a construct, able to change her persona to fit the need?

'What are we doing here?' Isaac asked.

'I thought we were having a pleasant meal, for old times' sake,' Linda replied.

'You were going to research what you could with the leak.'

'The file was buried, and I've not seen it. Have you?'

'I haven't, but Seth Caddick might have, and Ibrahim Ali definitely has.'

'Or he was told by someone else.'

'It must be Caddick. Ibrahim Ali is a firebrand, but not necessarily a murderer.'

'Are you saying he might have been forced to commit the atrocity?'

'I don't know; I need to know,' Isaac said. 'Find this file. Where is it? How deep? Do you know who has accessed it? Does the file have a reference number?'

'It's there, but it's encrypted. Nobody could hack MI5.'

Isaac thought of Bridget but discounted it. Linda was right; MI5 would have the best encryption and firewalls. Even Bridget could not do that, and if there were to be charges laid against Caddick and Davies, illegally obtained information would be ruled invalid in a trial.

However, Isaac knew there had been no trial for the murder of Richard Williams, and he was sitting opposite the woman who had killed him. It concerned him that he still wanted the woman, whoever she was.'

'Is Linda your name? Can I trust you? I'm told I can.'

'Do you trust the person who told you that? Whom do you trust? Anybody? Maybe your wife. How about Mary Ayton?

25

You knew her once. She's had a spectacular career, the one you could have, but you went with Goddard; she went it alone.'

Isaac found it disconcerting. Whoever the woman was, Linda Harris was not only the beautiful femme-fatale but the beautiful assassin. And yes, Mary Ayton had achieved success on her terms.

'Not tonight, Isaac. If that's what you're worried about.'

'I'm not, Linda. Not any night. Whoever you are, we will continue to meet and discuss until…'

'Until you're sure of me. But you never will be. You only see what I want you to see or what I'm directed to. Don't trust anyone; run your investigation, make your own decisions, and find out who supports you, cautions, and opposes.'

'And those who support?'

'Those open in their support are the ones you must fear the most.'

Isaac left the restaurant disturbed, but not before Linda Harris had leant across the table, grabbed hold, and passionately kissed him. 'In case you don't remember,' she said.

Chapter 4

Disturbed by his meeting with Linda Harris, Isaac did not sleep well that night, going as far as to lie to Jenny when he got home and say that he had met with DCI Farley Grainger, who he considered a possible confidante.

As he hung his suit in the wardrobe, he smelled Linda's perfume. He hoped Jenny had not but thought she had as she turned away from him in bed.

The following morning, his breakfast wasn't waiting for him, his shirt hadn't been ironed, and there was no kiss when he left the house.

'Sorry,' he said as he left. 'It's not what you think. I'm forced to deal with the devil, unsure if they've repented. You are the only one I can trust, believe me.'

'I do,' Jenny said, 'but don't lie or try to cover up meeting with that woman. With your record, is there any woman you've not slept with?'

'I've got to meet another one.'

'Tell me afterwards. I'll try to understand, but don't expect me to be pleased.'

Isaac met with Larry, Wendy, and Bridget in Homicide, whom he trusted unequivocally. As before, he would meet them separately.

Larry was first.

'What do you have?' Isaac asked.

'Not as much as we would have hoped. I kept tabs on her the best I could and followed her after she left your assignation with her,' Larry replied. Isaac could tell that his night out included visiting a pub. 'She's cautious. She grabbed a taxi, and I followed. It stopped outside a house, a block of flats in Kensington. She went in; no way I could follow her.'

'You waited?'

'Eleven minutes. She then came out and walked two blocks before entering a house. This time, she did not come out.'

'Did she know you were following her?'

'I can't be sure. If she's as capable as you say, then she might have, or else, that's the normal pattern for someone who kills people for a living. Is she as good as you reckon?'

'Better,' Isaac said.

'And you slept with her?'

'Once. Is that important?'

'It could be. Why did she sleep with you? Apart from your charm.'

'I hoped it was because of that. However, with her, I can't be sure.'

'Commander Goddard told you to meet with her, correct?'

'Yes.'

'Then who told him about her?'

'I assumed MacTavish. That man's got his fingers in every pie. He knows what's going on.'

'Does he, still? You met with him, what do you reckon? Do you believe he has the influence he once had? Or has that mantle fallen to someone else?'

'How do you know I met MacTavish?'

'I'm a detective inspector in Homicide. It's my job to know; besides, you left a printout of the ticket in your waste paper bin.'

'And you checked?'

'Ever since Goddard became your best friend again. We're playing with fire; some will get singed, and others will be burned beyond recognition. If you want to play this soft shoe shuffle with the three of us, you won't get the best result.'

'Your safety depends on your non-involvement,' Isaac said.

'If you go down, we go down. If Caddick and Davies are in league with the devil, who now calls himself a lord and dons the ermine robe, then the death of ten tourists and a few jihadists is of little consequence. They would not hesitate to kill police officers and their families. Remember, these people do not think as we do.'

'Ibrahim Ali and his followers?'

'Who can be certain about Ali, but Caddick and Davies could be tarred with the same brush. DCI, are you sure this is not paranoia?' Larry said. 'Caddick's a bastard, and Davies has no intention of relinquishing his position. That does not make their actions criminal.'

'There are too many coincidences. How did Caddick find out about the intended targets that day? Where did Ibrahim Ali get the proof from? The result was a voice for Ali in the House of Lords, Davies receiving a commendation from the King, and Caddick, another promotion in the offing. I must decide how to play this, and I don't know if I trust anyone.'

'Trust us. Anyone else you can think of?'

'Two possibles, but they could be compromised.'

'Let me sound them out.'

'Anyone who could tail them, with no chance of being discovered. Linda Harris would pick up on you soon enough if she hasn't already, and Jenny's not happy with the situation.'

'Do you still fancy the woman?'

'Linda or Jenny?'

'Linda.'

'You saw her, what do you reckon?'

'Don't, whatever you do, don't. You'll be hung out to dry if you do.'

'Hung out if I don't. I'm...'

'We,' Larry corrected Isaac.

'We are going into places, confronting persons who might be saints or sinners. But we can't know which, not yet.'

'Don't you mean murderers?'

'They've killed before; they could kill again.'

'Further terrorist attacks? Do you think Ali would risk it? He was never on the radar before. Sure, he was vocal, but he was not regarded as dangerous. Can we believe he was behind what happened in Whitehall?'

'He must be. Would he have allowed it if he was given the key to the castle as a reward?'

'It's not a castle. Has he moved in?'

'Soon as he's kicked out his half-sister,' Isaac said.

***

Larry wasted little time in the office after meeting with Isaac. He knew of one person, Harry Hamilton, although most people referred to him as Harry the Snitch.

The two men met not far from Notting Hill, on the northern side of Regent's canal. Larry knew one thing, apart from the fact that the moniker 'snitch' had been given to the man twenty-six years previously when he had ratted on a gang of robbers, a gang he was a member of. A guard at the bank had been killed in a botched break-in, and Harry had turned Queen's evidence for a reduced sentence. The other three had served their sentences and been released.

The reason Harry Hamilton still walked the streets was that, along with his evidence, he had made it clear that the guard's death had been an accident and the man had accidentally shot himself with his own gun. Forensics confirmed Hamilton's statement that the man had been holding the weapon, as his fingerprints were on it. What Hamilton failed to reveal, and which Larry did not know, was that the guard had dropped the gun after he had punched him in the stomach, and it had slipped from the guard's hand and hit the ground with such force that it had fired the bullet, as the man was bent double. The trajectory was correct, and it had been an accident. And that Harry had bartered for a reduced sentence for him and the lesser burglary charge for the others.

He failed to inform the police that one of the others had intended to pick up the gun with the intent of shooting the guard.

Deadly Secrets

For his trouble, Harry, after eighteen months in the slammer, had walked out of the jail: the moniker, a derogatory reference to most, but to the criminal community, a term of endearment.

Larry knew some of the story. Not that it concerned him, as Harry Hamilton, since his time in prison, had not committed another crime

Hamilton was of medium height and medium build, and his hair had greyed over the years, although baldness had not affected him, even though he was over sixty. He was known to a select group of private investigators in London, who once would have used him to check on cheating spouses, who was screwing who, who would get the lion's share of the divorce settlement, but that had dried up with no-fault divorces. Since then, steady employment checking the movements and the peccadilloes of those applying for senior roles in prestigious companies. He had found a few involved in shady deals, more than a few with a mistress, and one who preferred to dress in women's clothing than the business suit required as a senior executive.

'It'll cost,' Harry said.

'We'll pay,' Larry replied.

'And this woman? Secret agent?'

Larry had to give some of the details that were known about the woman. He could not have the man going in empty-handed, unaware of what he was up against. Trailing an adulterer or someone involved in industrial or corporate espionage was not the same as someone who had been trained in the act of deception, seduction, and murder. Larry failed to mention the last one; he needed Harry; he didn't want him to refuse the job.

Larry handed over a sheet of paper. 'That's what we have: address, name, and a photo.'

'Any of them verifiable?'

'The photo is. That's your job. Find out what you can, and don't take unnecessary risks. We believe she's on our side, but we can't be sure. Deal with her, and then I'll have another.'

'She sounds as if she's quite a woman,' Harry said.

'She is, but don't underestimate her; don't be fooled by the veneer.'

***

Wendy Gladstone sat in Isaac's office. 'Linda Harris?' she asked, disturbing Isaac's thought process.

'She's available if you're asking,' Isaac replied. 'Any update on Marjorie Frobisher?'

'None. I've gone through what we have on the investigation, read the trial report of the taxi driver that mowed her down, not that I can find any record of his ever existing.'

'He did at the time. Are you saying that wasn't correct?'

'I'm saying what is there now. Either he wasn't a taxi driver, or his proof has been erased.'

'Not that difficult to do if someone was serious,' Isaac said. 'Any comment from Marjorie Frobisher's husband? What about her children? Their reaction after they found out that they had a half-brother.'

'I've not spoken to them yet. Her husband is still in the family home. The son and daughter are not.'

'Fancy a trip?'

'To visit the husband? Did we speak to him after her death?'

'We did not. The case was closed. We were told to back off and leave well alone.'

'And now, we'll be visible. Any ramifications?' Wendy asked.

'We can't hide in the shadows. Either we conduct this investigation professionally, or we leave alone.'

'It's not an investigation. No case has been opened, no reports submitted, no Commander Goddard. Are you sure about this, DCI?'

'I only know what must be done and hope for the best.'

'Linda Harris knows, you know that.'

Deadly Secrets

'I suspect she knows much more than us. We need clear, unambiguous facts. Linda won't give them to us. We move forward until we hit a brick wall, or it hits us.'

'This could be dangerous, delving into areas we are not conditioned or trained for.'

'Hold back if you're worried,' Isaac said.

'Don't worry about me. This is exciting, and what can they do to me? Caddick will have me hung out to dry if he takes over from you. What do I have? A pension and an old cat.'

'You've got Bridget.'

'Yes, Bridget. No doubt she will be hung even further.'

'Why?'

'She hacked MI5.'

'Hell, how did she do that?'

'I've no idea. She was up all last night. I went to bed, and she was still at the computer when I came down in the morning.'

The phone rang; Isaac answered.

'Yes,' he said. 'DCI Cook.'

'The alarm bells are ringing,' Goddard said. 'Anything to do with your department?'

'What alarm bells?'

'MacTavish is on the phone to me, gave me a hell of a blast, told me that I was running a sloppy police station and that it was for me to call off the hounds, to give it a couple of weeks, and to tell our hacker to remove all trace of their activities. Can it be traced back to us?'

'It's not us,' Isaac said. He knew that what Bridget had possibly done was a significant achievement and that she would have covered all traces of her activity.

'Lay low, don't say anything, do nothing, don't rattle the chain anymore that you must.'

'Is that a recommendation to do something, but not to be obvious?'

'Not from me, not officially.'

'MacTavish?'

33

'He's in defensive mode, so am I. If Davies gets wind of this, prepare for a visit.'

'Don't worry, we're leaving the office.'

Isaac turned to Wendy after Goddard hung up. Isaac could not be sure if the commander was covering his back or giving him tacit approval to continue. Whatever it was, he did not intend to stop. 'Get Bridget in here.'

'Update,' Isaac said. 'You hacked MI5.'

'I got through the first firewall. Hackers are always testing it. I thought I'd try it, not necessarily to search their database, but to understand if someone else might.'

'Are you saying that you didn't set the alarm off?'

'Not me. I'm not sure I can get any farther, but I'm telling you that someone might be able to get further with sufficient time, resources, and expertise.'

'Assuming that's correct,' Isaac said, 'it still raises the question why. If they wanted to access any information about Marjorie Frobisher and Ibrahim Ali, they would have had to know that something was amiss. Who would have known that?'

'How is more relevant,' Wendy said.

'I could check,' Bridget said.

'No, thanks. That's enough for today. Who would be capable? Who's the best hacker in the country?'

'Not this country, but overseas. Everyone's trying to hack the other. It's become an art form, and if this job ends, I could offer my services.'

'It's criminal,' Isaac advised Bridget.

'It depends on who you work for. I know about Linda Harris. I've read the reports. Is she a killer?'

'Yes, and very dangerous. You don't want to mess with her.'

Wendy couldn't help but smile. 'Someone did,' she said.

Isaac ignored the comment, but he could see the humour in it. He found that it calmed him down, an unexpected jocularity.

'Bridget, stay tight in the office, don't do anything besides routine administration. Wendy, we've got someone to see. Is he at home?'

'I've got someone watching him.'

***

The house in Belgravia had not changed; the man had. When his wife had been alive, Robert Avers was a sprightly sixty-eight-year-old, but now he was overweight, unshaven, and sullen. He was sitting in the far corner of the main room.

Isaac and Wendy had been let in by the housekeeper, a young woman in her twenties with a Spanish accent.

'Mr Avers,' Isaac said as he offered his hand, receiving a limp hand in response.

'Chief Inspector Cook. How many years?'

'Seven, at least,' Isaac replied. He knew the exact date but wanted to know if Avers did.

'And Sergeant Gladstone. Please take a seat. I assume this isn't social.'

'We need to know,' Isaac said.

'Not before Maria brings us some drinks. As you can see, I'm not well. Cancer, nothing can be done about it, not worth complaining, and sympathy is wasted on me.'

'I wasn't about to offer it. You were a vibrant man back then. How's life treated you since then.'

'Strange, isn't it. Marjorie and I did not have much in common, but we stuck together through thick and thin, and then she's gone. After that, I seemed to lose interest in life.'

Wendy didn't see it as strange. Her husband and her had been the same; too many shared memories and years together. 'Your children, Sam and Fiona?'

'Sam, I don't know where. The last I heard, he was overseas, scrounging off the locals and the tourists.'

'Penniless?'

'He has enough money, but he was always a disappointment. As for Fiona, remarkable. After her mother died, she devoted herself to me and to herself. Lost the weight she had, got an education, had some plastic surgery, and found herself a husband. Not one of those that Marjorie favoured, but a solid middle-class solicitor, lives north of London, comes here twice a week, and brings her children with her.'

'She was always close to you,' Isaac said.

'The child of a famous person; it's always hard for them. Sam didn't care, but he was always disreputable, but Fiona had promise.'

'You're aware of Ibrahim Ali,' Isaac said.

'I am now. It came as a shock.'

'You didn't know?'

'I knew that Marjorie had history. I knew there had been a brief marriage, but not who the man was. I didn't know about the child.'

'We knew there was a child, but not who he was, nor his significance.'

'You didn't pursue it after Marjorie died?'

'We were told to back off. No reason was given, only assumptions on our part.'

'You didn't believe the taxi driver, did you?'

'We weren't convinced, but our instructions were clear.'

'Then why are you here? Marjorie's dead; her son is in the House of Lords. What do you want from me?'

'The truth?'

'Apart from her sleeping with Richard Williams.'

'Yes.'

'I've just given you it. I wasn't the only man before we married, and Williams wasn't the only other man after we married. Neither of us was a saint, but I didn't know about the child.'

'Has Ibrahim Ali contacted you?'

'Not a whisper,' Avers said.

Chapter 5

Harry the Snitch had Linda Harris in view. He was on the phone to Larry.

'She's good,' Harry said.

'Does she know you're watching her?' Larry asked.

'She moves like a cat, takes short steps, light on her feet, and her eyes dart here and there.'

'Do any others do that when you're following?'

'I don't follow that many these days.'

'Before?'

'Back in the old days, when cheating spouses were all the rage. With a camera, scaling a wall, and peering through curtains. Nobody moves like this woman unless they are trained.'

'You weren't trained.'

'Who said I wasn't? I was in the army, reconnaissance. I did my bit.'

'Where?'

'No war on when I signed up, but I was trained. I'm telling you, this woman is good.'

'Apart from your admiration for the woman, what else can you tell me?'

'She uses burners.'

'Certain?'

'I saw her go into a shop, buy the cheapest phone, go outside, make a call, and then throw it in a bin.'

'You've got it?'

'Not me. There's one other thing. She met someone.'

'Male, female, young, old?'

'Male, forties, walks like you, flatfooted.'

'Are you saying he's a police officer? DCI Cook?'

'Similar height, twisted nose. I've seen your DCI, and he's a good-looking man. This one isn't.'

'Dark hair? Trying to grab the woman?'

'Not grabbing, but they look friendly.'

'Look on your phone. I've sent you a picture,' Larry said.

'That's him. A classy woman with that sleaze makes you think.'

It didn't need Larry to think. He knew what to do; he messaged his DCI.'

'After they met?' Larry asked Harry.

'They went into a hotel and came out two hours later. He had a smile on his face; she didn't. What do you reckon?'

'I reckon she using what we can't.'

'Half his luck. Your DCI, friendly with her?'

'They were, but that's not your problem, nor mine. What else?'

'You reckon she screws men to get information out of them?'

'Kills them as well, so be extremely careful. This woman is in a league of her own. She appears to have a soft spot for my DCI, but one order and he would be dead.'

'You didn't tell me this when I signed up. My rates have gone up.'

'Just bill us, Harry, but stay on her tail. A report at the end of the day, anytime, midnight if you must.'

'I can't do this alone, not twenty-four hours a day. I must sleep, spend time with my woman, and visit the bathroom. I need a relief.'

'I could help.'

'You couldn't. If you had trailed her before, she would have picked you. You're known. Mind you, can't blame whoever the flatfoot is. Does he have a name?'

'It's best if you don't know it. What about this help?'

'I've got someone. You need to trust me on this.'

'Do what you must. We need 24/7 for the next couple of days.'

***

Deadly Secrets

Isaac took the news of Linda Harris and Caddick cavorting badly. He did not want to take it personally, but he could not seem to shake the feeling that the trust he had once placed in her, and for which she had destroyed on instructions from her superiors, was one thing, but to sleep with the man he despised above all others, irked him more than it should.

He had made a stand to deal with Caddick and Davies, to flesh out whether MacTavish and Goddard were involved, but now, he regretted that he had bothered. Jenny was his bedrock; his team were loyal, but he needed someone more senior to rely on.

Commander Goddard was out of the office. MacTavish was in Scotland, apparently laid low with pneumonia and not taking calls, which sounded serious.

Detective Chief Inspector Farley Grainger was someone he had always trusted.

There was another person who might help, but as with Linda, he had a similar problem. Linda was bad enough, and now she was sleeping with Caddick, but Mary Ayton was one of Davies' team when the man had been battling to hold on to his position. They had seen each other at one function or another and passed each other in the corridor on the infrequent times he had been to headquarters, but it had been close to fifteen years since they had spoken more than five words to each other.

Farley Grainger and Isaac met. This time at New Scotland Yard. Isaac thought that visibility in the domain of the all-powerful, all-conquering Davies would not raise comment.

'Farley,' Isaac said after the two men grabbed coffee from a machine in the corridor. 'How's tricks? Not made commissioner yet?'

Camaraderie, an easy manner with each other, would ensure that those with big eyes and even more prominent ears would not take much notice of two men with similar rank, height, and temperament, except that one was black, and the other was white, not that skin colour had ever bothered Isaac.

'Not me. What is the latest?' Farley asked.

39

'What's your take on recent developments?'

The two men sat in Grainger's office, which Isaac had to admit was better than his at Challis Street. The view from his window was of a brick wall, whereas Grainger had a view of the River Thames.

'The commissioner's revelling in his new contract, another five years. You heard about the knighthood?'

'Not yet.'

'An announcement in a couple of weeks, if the rumours are true, and then the official anointing a few months later.'

'Has he exercised his increased powers?'

'He's not flexed it yet, but once he's got the contract and the official anointing by a grateful King, there'll be no stopping him.'

'Which means I'll be out, especially if he finds out…'

Grainger interrupted Isaac. 'You played Caddick the last time. Are you considering it again?'

'I'm unsure,' Isaac said. 'I don't know who to trust. Commander Goddard, Seth Caddick, or maybe I should prostrate myself at the feet of Alwyn Davies.'

'I would not recommend the last option. A few have tried it and feigned their love of the man, but only Caddick has pulled it off. What do you reckon it is that Davies sees in Caddick? The man's a walking liability and detested at the Yard.'

'Davies has no interest in Caddick's well-being, only in what he can do. Caddick has the man's back, does the dirty work, allows Davies to maintain distance, and when it's opportune, to claim the success.'

'The failures?'

'Hidden from view, or swept under the carpet.'

'It must be a big carpet,' Farley said.

'What do you know? Any reason not to tell me?'

'It depends on what you intend to do. Is Goddard with you on this?'

'I'm not sure. I'm uncertain that I should be considering anything. I've got a family to worry about, and societies gone from benign to hostile. Assassination or murder have become weapons. Don't you see it?'

'You haven't got a hope against Davies.'

'If I was?'

'Then, Isaac, I suggest you leave, and we sever our friendship.'

Isaac left disconsolate, aware that without allies or support, he could rely on, it would be better to just play the game and get the promotion Caddick had spoken of.

That night, when sleep did not come, he tried to read a book but threw it aside. He had thought of engaging Jenny in romance, but he wasn't in the mood for it, nor was she, after he had bared his soul and told her it was hopeless. Television offered no respite, only politicians and pundits. None were convincing, and the majority were negative in the extreme.

At four in the morning, he made a phone call he never thought he would make; he phoned Caddick. 'My office, eight-thirty in the morning.'

'You've come to your senses?' Caddick asked.

In the background, Isaac could hear a woman. 'You're not alone; sorry to disturb you.'

'Disturb, not me.'

'Yes, I recognise the voice,' Isaac said as he ended the conversation. He was at an emotional low, staring defeat in the face, a wife who had told him to decide but not destroy the marriage and to consider the children, and then there was a man that he despised sleeping with a woman he had once been fond of. How much worse could it get, he thought.

The following day, eight-thirty in the morning, Isaac was to find out.

Caddick leaned back in the chair, his arms behind his head and yawned. 'She's hot, your woman,' he said. 'Why did you give her away? She's still keen on you, and it's me who's screwing her. How does that feel, Isaac? The man you hate more than any other, screwing your woman?'

'Not my woman,' Isaac said, but he was confused. It was a conflict before, but now it was an issue he had to address. If it wasn't Caddick, it would have been easier.'

'What do you know about her?' Isaac asked.

'Not a lot. She's been helpful, that's all.'

'Where did you meet her?'

'At a function, one of those you used to get invited too, until you become holier than thou, believing you're a cut above the rest. I've seen the posters when you were a constable. You were the face of a new multicultural, multiethnic, reinvigorated police. Little did you know that the old guard would return, led by a plain-speaking Welshman, ably assisted by a sycophantic snivelling weasel.'

'Is that how you see yourself?'

'It's what you think, and yes, I am whatever you might think. One other thing, Goddard's transferring out of the building.'

'To where?'

'New Scotland Yard.'

'To do what?'

'To implement reforms.'

'What about you? I thought you had that honour?'

'I've been offered an irresistible opportunity that comes with a promotion. In future, it's Chief Superintendent Seth Caddick. It's got a nice ring to it, wouldn't you agree?'

'What did you have to do to earn that?'

'Hero of Whitehall, personally recommended by the man who will make the London Met strong again, Commissioner Alwyn Davies, one of the greatest police officers this country has known.'

'Do you believe that?'

'Goddard does. He had no alternative, nor do you.'

'What does that mean?'

'I'm replacing Goddard here in Challis Street. And you can't forget the slurs, the smart-arse comments, and the disrespect. In future, it's not Seth. It's either Chief Superintendent or Sir, got it?'

Isaac knew he was beaten. 'Yes,' he said. What he had long feared had come to fruition.

***

Nine days later, Caddick took his seat in Commander Goddard's office. By the time Goddard had travelled from Challis Street to New Scotland Yard, his rank had changed to Deputy Assistant Commissioner, which was only three ranks away from the position held by Davies. Isaac knew that his former mentor and friend had sold out.

Downstairs in reception, a notice was pinned up on the notice board.

For meritorious service and outstanding policing, Superintendent Seth Caddick has been promoted to Chief Superintendent and will take up his position at Challis Street as the senior officer in Homicide. No other changes are intended. Also, Deputy Assistant Commissioner Goddard will head up the much-needed reforms committee, reporting directly to Commissioner Davies.

Whatever Goddard had said or done, Isaac knew it was significant and that a Deputy Assistant Commissioner, if the chain of command was intact, should have reported to the Assistant Commissioner, then to the Deputy Commissioner, and then to the Commissioner.

On the third day, Isaac sat down with the deputy assistant commissioner. There was tension, and the once-assumed camaraderie no longer existed.

'Chief Inspector, I thought we should meet,' Goddard said. 'I know you are disturbed by recent events; however, you have brought this on yourself. I repeatedly told you that decisions needed to be made and that sidelining would not work.'

'Commissioner Davies?' Isaac replied.

'He is conscious of MacTavish's attempts to remove him from office. Regardless of your personal views, there are certain realities. If you wish to carry the cross alone, then I suggest you consider its weight. You will be out of a job and virtually unemployable.'

'How?'

'This vendetta against Chief Superintendent Seth Caddick has gone on long enough. I agree that we have both had reservations about the chief superintendent's competency, but he has proven himself, even if his manner and speech can sometimes be jarring to someone of your sensibilities. Even so, he has proven to the commissioner and me that he is a committed police officer, as you are, and he has my trust. I will give him all the assistance he requires in his new position, and I suggest you do.'

Defeated, despondent, and despairing, Isaac could only weakly reply. 'He has mine, Deputy Assistant Commissioner.'

'You might ask what I intend to do in my new position, DCI.'

'I know what was planned. Will you follow them, or do you have other reforms?'

'I will continue with what is in place, make changes as necessary, and commit to a six-month implementation plan. I suggest that you use that time wisely.'

'When will the first reform start?'

'It has. My promotion and Chief Superintendent Caddick's. You risk being removed from Homicide and transferred to an administrative role, something you're well equipped for. As to the staff in Homicide, those below agreed standards will be reassigned or retired. Do I make myself clear?'

'Crystal. Wendy Gladstone?'

'I realise you are sentimental about the sergeant, and her health has not been good. You have two months to resolve it with her, but she is eligible for early retirement. That will happen, as it will with Inspector Hill. The man's a hopeless alcoholic, as you well know. Regardless of admirable results from Homicide, there has been concern for the last two years that, under your tutelage, they have been slipping, there have been cost overruns, and the murders have taken too long to solve. Sure, there are times when knocking on doors and interviewing passers-by has value, which your inspector and your sergeant prefer, but with Forensics and the police database, most crimes can be solved in half the time.

'How long did it take to find Oksana Akimova when we investigated the murders of David Grayling and Barry Sorrell? Bridget Halloran found the woman in an instant.'

'Sergeant Gladstone took full responsibility for not detaining the woman at the murder scene. And why that case? What about Marjorie Frobisher and Ibrahim Ali?'

'Chief Inspector, drop it. It's past history, fait accompli, and even if Chief Superintendent Caddick is sleeping with Linda Harris, it's not your business, and you shouldn't act like a lovesick puppy. She ended the relationship and found another man. It's her decision.'

'Is it?' Isaac was attempting to see if breaking through to the man was possible. The man had mentored him, came to his wedding, made a speech, and wished the happy couple a long life and plenty of children. This was the man who had invited him around to his house many times to meet his wife and his children, and now, the man was a complete bastard.

'I believe that's all, Cook. I would appreciate it if you would give Chief Superintendent Caddick all the assistance he requires.'

Goddard held out his hand at the door as Isaac left. Isaac felt the firm hand and then the tensioning of the shake. Isaac thought it was a signal to hang on, to be careful, and to fight, but he wasn't sure.

Isaac responded curtly, thanked him for his leadership, wished him well, and left the room. The fight would continue, but its tactics would need to change.

Chapter 6

On the fourth day, as Isaac was leaving Homicide, his phone rang. 'Twenty minutes, you know where,' the voice said.

Isaac phoned Jenny, telling her he would be delayed for two or three hours.

'Is it?' Jenny asked.

'We spoke about this last night. It's a murder investigation.'

'Even so, I don't like it.'

'Nor do I.'

'Richard Goddard's right. You're out of your depth on this. You can't be a mouse in a nest of vipers. You either play their game, or you don't.'

As usual, a devastatingly attractive woman sat opposite him in the restaurant. They had chosen a seat at the rear, Linda's decision, not his.

Isaac had to admit he enjoyed the woman's company, but soiling herself with Caddick had taken the edge off his admiration and dulled her desirability.

The waitress looked over at them; Linda nodded in return; the staff knew their order before they sat down.

'Seth's full of himself and reckons he's got you on the run,' Linda said.

'Pillow talk?' Isaac replied.

Linda did not reply but but focussed on what she knew. 'I know that Seth and Ibrahim Ali are somehow intertwined. However, I can't even get Seth to reveal it all.'

'I know even less than you,' Isaac said.

'What I have,' Linda continued, 'and you should know, is that Seth met with Ibrahim Ali two days ago.'

'What was discussed?'

'I don't know. We've got a tail on him, day and night.'

'And me?'

'Not you, only Caddick and Ali. Ibrahim Ali's not a terrorist. We're certain of that.'
'He was behind the terrorist attack.'
'He was compromised. What we believe…'
'Who's we?' Isaac asked.
'My people, that's all I can tell you. I believe a carrot was dangled under Ali's nose, and he grabbed it.'
'It must have been a mighty big carrot.'
'We have known about Ibrahim Ali for a long time. We know an intermediary met with Caddick three weeks before that idiot killed ten people with a suicide vest. We have a photo of Caddick with Ibrahim Ali five days before the attack. The two of them shaking hands, Ali dressed in Western clothes, sunglasses, and a baseball cap.'
'What can you prove?'
'Nothing to the detail you want. Has Goddard deserted you?'
'I don't know.'
'Assume he has. The man's compromised, and he's playing a dangerous game. Taking on Davies is fraught with problems, and MacTavish died two hours ago. I needed you to know that before it is announced.'
'How did you know?'
'We have people everywhere. There is to be an official announcement in thirty-five minutes. The man was ill, multiple ailments, some of them self-induced.'
'I met him in Scotland. A heavy drinker.'
'And womaniser in his younger days. He would have given you a run for your money. Regardless, he's out of the picture. You need to place your trust in either me or Goddard. I'm not sure which one I'd go with, but I'm sure you have little faith in me.'
'What I'm doing is unofficial, and Caddick won't give me a minute's piece.'
'He will.'
'How?'

'We've got enough to get him convicted of fraud. A few years back, a building burnt down, six stories. Insurance claims were regarded as suspicious by the insurance company. Caddick muscled in and paid one of the accessors twenty thousand pounds, another thirty thousand to the head of the arson team. Caddick apparently got ninety thousand pounds from the property owner for his troubles.'

'You can prove this?'

'Watertight. It would hold up if Caddick was charged.'

'Which you don't want.'

'Nor do you. You've got leverage over the man. Don't use it, just remember it's there.'

'Are you expecting more from Caddick? Does he open up to you?'

'He does. He not sure who I work for, but Caddick's suspicious.'

'Are you sure? You must be in police reports from the time of Marjorie Frobisher,' Isaac said.

'If Davies is threatened, or you or someone else is closing in on him, the man will strike out and do what is necessary. Ali's implicated, and he could be forced to comply.'

'I read that Ibrahim Ali was smart. Surely, he can hold out against an onslaught from Caddick.'

'How?' Linda said. 'If Caddick threatens Ali, the man will throw it back in his face, reminding him that they set up the attack in Whitehall.'

'Would it? Caddick's good as passing the baton on to someone else.'

'And that someone else is?'

'Who do you think.'

'But how? I've never met Ali or committed a crime,' Isaac protested.

'Haven't you? What about the Swedish au pair that you bedded and then arrested. How many murders did she commit after you slept with her? Goddard hushed it up, but it's still on the

Deadly Secrets

record. And then there's Caddick, with his tongue hanging out. You're both easy targets.'

'Are you suggesting I trust Goddard?'

'He's a better bet than Caddick, better than me.'

'Why not you?'

'I respond to orders. Those orders for now are to assist you, to take down Davies if that is what is decided, to get rid of Caddick if I must, and to get Ibrahim Ali out of the House of Lords.'

'Why Davies? What has he done to MI5?'

'Davies is a law until himself and rubs his authority in the face of those he should be sucking up to. Ali's in debt to Caddick. Expose one; the others will fall. Not that Davies is an Islamist. He's Pentecostal and grew up in the valleys of Wales, a small coaling town. Strange bedfellows, they make.'

'No stranger than you and Caddick. It can't be much fun with that man. Why do this?'

'What do you mean, whore for my country? You would not understand. One day you might, but it won't be this day.'

***

Day five showed that instead of the investigation stalling, there was more activity, and more decisions needed to be made. Harry the Snitch was to divide surveillance with his offsider, allowing a more rigorous focus on Caddick and Linda Harris.

Isaac's conversations with the woman gave him optimism that he could continue with the investigation. A phone call from Deputy Assistant Commissioner Goddard at New Scotland Yard added weight to his optimism.

'Play it carefully,' Goddard said.

'After your reprimand?' Isaac replied.

Goddard was standing on the Embankment, looking out at the River Thames. He was not enjoying his new job and was not afraid to admit it to those he trusted.

'Walls have ears,' Goddard said. Isaac knew what he meant. If New Scotland Yard had walls with ears, did that mean Challis Street was bugged.

Isaac thought back two months, a weekend when Challis Street Police Station had a skeleton team of police officers confined on the ground floor. A dozen contractors were on the upper floor to remove asbestos found in the roof. A good time to install surveillance equipment. Was Challis Street bugged? Was Homicide?

'Why in your office? Why the reprimand?'

'I wanted us to be heard.'

'Phone calls can be monitored.'

'Not this call. I've got encryption on mine; it comes with the pay scale.'

'You must have had that before.'

'I did, and that's why I have kept our meetings to a minimum. I needed distance.'

'You're playing a dangerous game,' Isaac said.

'I play to win, something you would be well advised to consider. Linda Harris? Sleeping with her?'

'Caddick is.'

'I know that.'

Isaac was interested in how the deputy assistant commissioner knew, but he realised the man was running his race, whereas Isaac was following another. The spies were watching the spies; the police were watching the police. No one trusted the other, and everyone was jockeying for position. There was no clear winner, no one was in the lead, and no one had yet fallen. That occurred on day six.

***

The death of Robert Avers, Marjorie Frobisher's widower, came as a surprise to many, including Sam Avers, the wayward, lazy, and drug-addicted son.

Deadly Secrets

'I came to see how my father was,' Sam Avers said. 'He's not been well recently.'

Wendy had her opinion; Larry Hill had his. The two had arrived thirty-five minutes after the son had phoned emergency services, and judging by the state of Sam, unshaven, wearing torn clothes, barefooted, and glassy-eyed, it was a wonder he could have made the call.

'Clearly, you didn't murder him,' Larry said as he looked at the dead man. The crime scene investigators were in the house. Fiona Avers, Robert Avers' daughter, was on the way and expected to arrive within the hour.

'You were supposed to be overseas,' Wendy said. 'Living the life of a gigolo or was it a beach bum.' Sympathy should have been expected from the police, but they had met Sam Avers before. They knew Sam would be unmoved by his father's death, and he was only in the house for money.

'I was. Ryanair, thirty pounds each way, get a grand off my father, and back to my life in Spain.'

'Which you will the moment you get hold of his money.'

'No need to now. The man's dead. Fiona will want to give me my share as soon as possible to get me out of this house.'

'Fiona, from what we have been told, is a changed woman.'

'She used to have some life in her, ugly bitch that she was. But now, she's pretty as a peach, the ideal husband, and two children who say yes and please. Performing seals, that's what they are.'

'I would have said they were perfect children and that insulting your sister does you no credit. I can't see why Inspector Hill doesn't believe that you murdered your father for his money,' Wendy said.

'He didn't, Sergeant,' Larry said.

'Are you sure?' Wendy asked.

'Look at the body, the gunshot at point blank range. Check Sam's fingers; no sign of gunshot residue from the bullet.'

51

After hearing the discussion, one of the crime scene investigators came over and took hold of Sam Avers' hands. 'Give me a couple of minutes, but the inspector is correct.'

The CSI ran an infrared scanner over his clothes and hands. 'No, he didn't kill him,' he said.

'Your reaction when you came in?' Wendy asked. She had accused the man of murder; she needed to be restrained in her questioning for the next few minutes.

'I saw him there. I thought he was asleep, so I helped myself to one of his choice brandies and settled in. I didn't want to disturb him.'

'Time from entering the house to phoning emergency services.'

'How long does it take to drink half a bottle of the best brandy money can buy.'

'Mr Avers, your father has been murdered. This is no time for levity.'

'Don't expect me to show emotion. He hated me. The feeling was mutual. Our mother wasn't much better, and then we discovered she had birthed a mongrel. And her with her high and mighty graces, highfalutin friends, and their money. Fiona and I were treated like lepers in this house. Mind you, she got it worse than me, the ugly duckling my mother called her, and our father, telling Fiona how precious she was. Screw anything that moved, would Fiona, worse than our mother for that. And then, we find out that there is a bastard child, and he's in the House of Lords, living in a stately home and driving around in a Rolls Royce. Do you reckon he's entitled to a share of the inheritance?'

Wendy felt like hitting the man but held off. If her sons had disrespected her and her husband, they would have felt the back of her hand.

A noise at the front door, and in came Fiona. Wendy was startled. She remembered the ugly duckling; the description from Sam, even if derogatory, had been correct, but what entered the room, rushed over to her father and collapsed on the floor, tears rolling down her cheeks, was not a duckling, but a beautiful swan.

Deadly Secrets

It was what Robert Avers had said his daughter had become. He wasn't wrong.

'What are you doing here, Sam?' Fiona said when she stood up.

'I came to see our father.'

'For money, no doubt. You weren't to ever enter this house again. We had spoken about this. If you wanted money, you would come to me, and I would deal with it.'

Wendy took Fiona by the arm to another room, sat with her on a comfortable chair, and asked a young constable to get them something to drink.'

'Tea for me,' Fiona said. 'Who would do something like that?'

'We don't know, but we have our suspicions. When you're ready.'

'He didn't have long. I had asked him to come and stay with us, but he wouldn't hear of it. They were still devoted after all he and my mother went through, including her affairs. This house reminded him of her. It was a shock when we found out we had a half-brother. Have you met him?'

'Not yet,' Wendy said.

The constable returned. 'Sorry, no milk.'

'Thank you, milk's fattening,' Fiona said.

Wendy took a long look at the woman. She was slim, her hair was combed, her clothes were good quality, but not designer, and she wore make-up. This was the woman who, in a drunken frenzy, had sex with her mother's co-star on the soap opera until the mother had walked in with Richard Williams, the executive producer.

'You've changed,' Wendy said.

'Wised up. You don't know how difficult it is to have a celebrity parent, unable to follow in her footsteps. I tried to but couldn't act or sing; I was plain-looking and clumsy. They gave me parts because of my mother, but even then, they would not keep me long. After she died, it was my father and me. We had always got on well. I started to care for myself and had a few visits to a plastic surgeon. He took off the rough edges, lips and nose, liposuction, a great diet and exercise, even elocution lessons, and I ditched the men I hung around with.'

'It's a magical transformation.'

'I still can't act or sing, but it doesn't matter. My husband is a good man; our children are a credit to us. Amazing how one person can put you down and another can bring you up. I owe everything to my father, nothing to my mother. Are you sure he didn't kill himself? I know he was lonely, missed our mother, and had another two to three months to live.'

'There's no gun,' Wendy said.

Isaac drove to the house to find Avers' body being taken out, the CSIs moving from downstairs to upstairs, and Sam Avers in the garden at the back of the house, downing his second bottle of brandy.

Larry remained with the CSIs. Isaac knew he would be looking where the CSIs would not. He didn't think he would find anything.

'Good to see you again,' Fiona said as Isaac walked through to where the two women sat.

'Fiona, how are you? Not good, I would imagine,' Isaac said. He knew he had fumbled his response, taken aback by the change in the woman's appearance from the last time he had seen her.

'I was conditioned for his death, but not this. Do you know why?'

'We have a theory, but it's an impossible connection to make.'

The young constable said nothing, not pleased that she had joined the police to solve a crime, not to be a maid, as she handed another cup of tea to Isaac.

'It gets better, Constable,' Wendy said. 'Baptism of fire. Your first Homicide?'

'Yes, Sergeant.' The woman seemed pleased after Wendy had spoken to her.

'Fiona,' Isaac continued, 'did your father know about your mother's first marriage?'

'Nothing was ever said, although I would not have been surprised. After all, he knew about her lovers.'

'And accepted it.'

'Never accepted, tolerated. Both were driven personalities, yet they believed marriage was a life-long commitment, but you knew our mother, the sort of person she was. It was a shock when Ibrahim Ali announced that he was Lord Alsworthy.'

'Then came to you for a DNA check?'

'They did. Sam wasn't here, somewhere or other, getting drunk or laid or drugged. He's not changed; worse, to be honest. Our father could drink anyone under the table, but Sam's a bad drunk. No hope for him. He'll take his half of the inheritance and blow it on bad women, bad drugs, and then either broke or dead within five years.'

'And you?'

'We'll move in here, enrol our children in the best schools that money can buy.'

'Assuming your father knew, that doesn't mean he knew about the child,' Isaac said.

'Ibrahim Ali could have found out. Freedom of information, or something like that.'

'Buried deep. He might have tried, but he would not have succeeded.'

'I've read about him, unsure what to make of him. He's got our mother's eyes, and when you look at Sam when he's not drunk, you can see the similarities. Remarkable that one son of hers can be so different to the other.'

Wendy didn't think so. Ali's adopted parents, Martin and Beverley Marshall, were middle-class and lived in Nottingham. Benjamin, as he was called as a child, went to the local school, proved himself to be a good student, church every Sunday, and sang in the choir. He had not been told of his adoption until he was thirteen.

So far, the Marshalls have not been contacted. If they were, then the unofficial investigation into Ali and Caddick's relationship would become known, and then the hounds of hell would descend.

Time was of the essence, and Isaac thought they were chasing a red herring with Robert Avers, but it was a homicide and gave credibility to investigating Ibrahim Ali, a relative of the Avers family, reluctantly or not.

'Have you heard from his lordship?' Wendy asked.

'No. He's got the title; what are we to him?'

'That's a good point,' Isaac said. 'Your father, any enemies?'

'None at all. You knew him; you knew about our mother and Richard Williams.'

'Who was murdered,' Wendy reminded her.

'To keep the truth from being revealed?' Fiona asked.

Isaac went out into the garden. 'Did you know about your half-brother?'

Sam Avers looked up, bleary-eyed. 'I met him once, didn't know who he was.'

'Did he know who you were?'

Avers took another swig and vomited over a rose in the garden. Isaac grabbed hold of a watering can and threw the water over him. 'You can't do that,' Avers slurred.

'I can, and more, until you tell me what you know.'

Avers attempted to take hold of the bottle; Isaac moved it away. 'Not now, not until you talk.'

Isaac remembered Fiona's comment. *Look at Sam when he's not drunk; you can see the similarities.*

'It was in Spain six months ago, or maybe nine. I can't remember.'

'Forget the date. What happened?'

'I was cadging money off the tourists.'

'Which you did often.'

'Not often, but I was low on money, and the tourists are easy targets. Anyway, I'm in this restaurant. I know the owner, and sometimes we do this scam. If one of the patrons is drunk, bachelor parties are the best, he adds on a few pesetas.'

'Euros,' Isaac reminded him.

'Whatever. Anyway, he adds on a few Euros. And if they're really drunk, they hand over their card, and he scans it and adds on a few more, or a lot more.'

'Your job in this scam?'

'I pretend to be their friend, tell them where the women are, how easy they are, and I can take them there and get a discount.'

'The more you talk, the drunker they are, the more your partner pads their bill.'

'It isn't padding, what he does.'

'Robbery, more like. And the women?'

'It depends on how drunk the men are.'

'Why did you need your father's money?'

'My money, now he's dead, not that I killed him,' Sam Avers said.

Isaac handed him the bottle. 'One swig, no more.'

Avers took the swig and put the bottle on one side. 'Ali wasn't in Spain to follow his religion. The man was drinking, not as much as the others, but drunk enough. I go through the routine, sit beside him, and act as his greatest friend. Let's get out of here, I say. I know a place where the senoritas are lovely and willing.'

'His reaction?'

'I couldn't be sure if he was interested. He wasn't that friendly; he didn't smile or say much. It was one of his group. He looks over at the two of us. "Hey, you two could be twins,' he said.'

'Your response?'

'I didn't think much of it. People go to Spain, thinking it's heaven, and don't want to return home, but this man is persistent. And then, we're off to the women. I've got a good deal with them.'

'Money and extras?'

'You got it. I don't need to pretend with you. You know me from before. I'm the black sheep of the family, not like that stuck-up bitch of a sister.'

'Keep to the story,' Isaac reminded Avers.

'Anyway, the others in the group, there were four of them, they're into the women, but Ali stays with me. I told him about my mother, another bitch. How she used to be on the television. He wants my phone number and where I live.'

'You told him?'

'Only my mother's stage name. and an address in Spain. The others come out after they have spent time with the women. We are all having a great time; the women have the men's credit cards, and I keep talking. Ali might have realised the scam, but he doesn't care. One of the women gives me the eye, which lets me know to come back later in the evening.'

'Which you did?'

'I did. Two days later, I walked down the street close to my home. It's dark, two in the morning, and I'm set on by a couple of local thugs. Usually, they give me a wide berth.'

'You've got a deal going with them?'

'I have.'

'Burglary, car theft?'

'I supply a good time and information. The tourists want a good time; the thugs want information. What they do with it is neither my concern nor illegal.'

'The thugs? What's the relevance?'

'At the time, it made no sense. They took my money and a knife I always carried. They punched me in the gut, a fist to the face, and I'm unconscious. I wake up in the hospital, a doctor hovering over me. He bandages me, puts on some ointment, takes some blood, and puts it in a vial. He also ran a swag inside my mouth. I didn't think much about it until I read that my half-brother was telling the world he was the new Lord Alsworthy. That's when I realised what had happened in Spain.'

'You're lucky that's all that happened.'

'They must have thought my father knew something. But why now?' And what's the point? Ibrahim Ali got what he wanted. What importance are we?'

'None, I would have thought, but there must be a connection. Your plans?'

'I'll stay here for now. Fiona intends to cheat me out of my share, but I will not allow it.'

Chapter 7

Isaac's concern was that Caddick, in his desperation to get him and Goddard out of Challis Street, had stumbled on what Bridget had confirmed years before when Marjorie Frobisher had been the focus of a homicide investigation; that her death had been the result of a romantic liaison in her youth.

Bridget scoured every database file on her computer and the others in the department for thirty-six hours. Wendy stayed with her and checked every cupboard and filing cabinet, looking for a note or a paper, anything that could have been found by a devious police officer whose impending arrival in Challis Street was imminent.

In the end, Bridget declared. 'We're clean. It wasn't us.'

Isaac breathed a sigh of relief. It would have been embarrassing if Caddick had discovered the information from Homicide. However, that brought up another question. How did Caddick become involved?

Homicide was still operating under the radar, and Richard Goddard was keeping his distance. Sucking up to Davies, Isaac thought but decided to give the DAC the benefit of the doubt.

In Scotland, Edinburgh Cathedral had been packed for MacTavish's funeral. Goddard had attended, and so had the prime minister and the foreign secretary. Isaac had been invited but declined due to concern that his presence would have revealed an association between the dead man and him.

The prime minister had given a eulogy on behalf of the government; the previous prime minister had given another. MacTavish's coffin had been borne out of the cathedral by members of his clan, and the cortege had been led by a dozen men playing bagpipes. The great man was gone, and now, only Isaac and his team, and Richard Goddard, if he could be trusted, would continue to investigate and unravel the quagmire that was

Deadly Secrets

the London Metropolitan Police. Although, this time, they had a homicide.

The Forensic and Pathology reports were in. It clearly stated that Robert Avers had been shot at point-blank range by a .33 pistol. Forensics had confirmed that the make of the weapon was a Glock; Pathology confirmed that what Fiona Avers had said was correct and that Robert Avers had terminal cancer and was close to death.

The question remained as to why Ibrahim Ali needed Caddick and why he was involved in a terrorist attack.

Isaac put it to Larry. Bridget and Wendy were taking the day off after having worked all night the previous night. Isaac reckoned they had earned it.

'Why kill Robert Avers?' Isaac asked. 'We knew the man; what did you think of him?'

'I didn't know him well,' Larry said. 'If you remember, I wasn't a member of Homicide back then. I was at another station. I was the first at Sally Jenkins' flat when she died. You brought me into Homicide after the murder investigation was wrapped up.'

'Okay, point taken. It was Farhan Anwar who sat in your place back then, but he's in the north of the country, chief inspector now, and glad to be out of London.'

'The woman he married?'

'Aisha? She's practising law and has a couple of children. The past is best left where it belongs.'

They both knew what they were referring to, that Aisha had been studying law and selling herself to pay for her education. It had been why Anwar had transferred out of Homicide and gone north. Aisha's name had not come up at the trial into the murder of Charles Sutherland, the man she had been servicing not long before his death. Even so, a black mark registered against Anwar for his indiscretion with a witness would have damned Anwar's career. Goddard had shipped the man north with his woman and deleted the offending information from his record.

It had been a magnanimous act on Goddard's part, another reason to express confidence in the man.

'Are we convinced that Robert Avers died because of the connection between Marjorie Frobisher and Ibrahim Ali?' Larry asked.

'Too many coincidences. Do we believe Sam Avers? This similarity between him and Ibrahim Ali? Ali would have brushed it off as one of his drunken friends having a joke.'

'But he did not, not if the hospital in Spain is correct. And who was this doctor? Why put the blood into a vial and take a swab? The hospital would not have needed that unless Ali did. Money would have changed hands. Would a doctor have taken payment?'

'It depends on how much money. Everyone has a price.'

'Which means Ibrahim Ali wasn't in Spain on the off chance. He had prior knowledge, and the DNA check with Fiona was a subterfuge that Ali knew already.'

'Which still comes back to Caddick. Is he the conduit, but how? Apart from a few people, nobody else knew, and they're accounted for.'

'Accounted and confirmed. Would there be a reason for MacTavish to have told Caddick? Was the man double-dealing, playing us off against him and Davies?'

'But why?'

'It's too deep for me,' Isaac said.

***

Isaac tried for two days to contact DAC Goddard. The first day, he phoned twice, left a message three times, and emailed him once; the second day, he repeated the process, only instead of an email, which he realised could be hacked, he kept phoning, only to receive a busy tone, or a message telling him that the phone was switched off.

In frustration, Isaac arrived outside the man's house at eleven in the evening.

Deadly Secrets

Without support, the investigation into Caddick and Ali was dead in the water. One more day, and Isaac realised he would have no option but to apply for a transfer, and that, given the depth of intrigue, corruption and murder, nobody was safe, and that Caddick, if Davies was working with him, could shift the blame.

Isaac sat in the car for two hours. He was tired; he was hungry; he was fed up. Jenny would get her wish, he thought, and he would reluctantly forget the skills he had learnt, the promise of senior management in the Met, and become a country police officer, dealing with lost cats, cars driving the wrong way up the street, and drunks spilling out of the pub.

A tap on his window, the angry face of the DAC. 'DCI, don't blow this,' Goddard said after Isaac had lowered the driver's side window.

'I can't continue on my own,' Isaac said.

'Damn foolish, you chasing me. Don't you realise that I'm under suspicion?'

'You're on the right hand of God; why are they suspicious of you?'

'Why do you think I got the promotion? For services rendered, for experience, because I'm a good police officer? They knew I would not refuse. They have got their eye on me, probably checking my emails and monitoring my phone calls.'

'I thought you said your phone had encryption.'

'It doesn't mean that someone could not break the encryption. I'm neutered, unsure I can help. I gave you the nod in my office. I thought you understood. Isaac, you're letting your vendetta against Caddick become personal.'

'It is.'

'It isn't.' Goddard walked around and sat in the car's passenger seat. 'Caddick knows you're onto him.'

'How?'

'I don't know how, only that he is. Any idea?'

'That's why I needed to speak to you. Ibrahim Ali knew he was the child of Marjorie Frobisher and Lord Alsworthy before the attack in Whitehall.'
'Can you confirm this?'
'If you regard a drugged-out space cadet as a reliable witness.'
'Evidence?'
'Spain, Valencia, a hospital, a doctor. We have a description and a name.'
'Vague. How's your Spanish?'
'No better than my French.'
'Do you have anyone in Homicide?'
'Nobody. Besides, I don't want others to run the risk.'
'Tomorrow, send Bridget and Wendy to Spain.'
'Caddick?'
'If anyone asks, they are on sick leave, drunk too much, or have food poisoning. You can decide, but phone them and ensure they have tickets. Use your credit card, and send me the cost. I can get the money to you. Book them in for two days at a hotel close to the hospital. Don't tell Larry.'
'You know someone?'
'Retired police inspector, lives fifty kilometres away. Helps expats with visas and real estate.'

Goddard took out his phone and dialled. 'Gordon, I've got people coming down early tomorrow. Need a favour, a big favour. Are you up to it?'
'For you, anything.'
'I'll get Wendy Gladstone to phone you. She's a sergeant, also Bridget Halloran. Two days maximum, and be careful.'
'Dangerous?'
'Not yet, but it's important and it's unofficial.'

Goddard hung up and focussed on Isaac. 'Since you have disturbed my chance at sleep, here's the deal going forward. One SMS, and don't use a known phone, and just text *later*. If I get it, we'll meet here at eleven that evening.

Isaac had reason to believe that his mentor was still there for him. Goddard exited the car, and Isaac drove to Wendy and Bridget's home. He knocked on the door.

'This is unexpected, DCI,' Bridget said when she opened the door.

'It's important, you and Wendy.'

The two women sat down. Wendy made a cup of tea, although it should have been black coffee judging by the breath of the two women.

'Here's the deal. You are on a flight tomorrow at nine in the morning. Passports valid?'

'They are.'

'You'll be picked up at the airport on arrival. Your contact will arrange one night's accommodation. Wendy, you know about Sam Avers and the blood and the swab in Valencia.'

'I do.'

'Good. Tomorrow, you're both to call in sick.'

'Chief Superintendent Caddick?'

'Don't worry about him. He can blow hot and cold if he wants; it won't make any difference. If he's upstairs in Challis Street, we're all for the chop.'

'What are we sick with?' Bridget asked.

'Food poisoning, or you got violently drunk, which, given the state of you two now, is believable.'

'DAC Goddard?'

'He's set it up. You know what we need. Proof that Sam Avers was in that hospital, who the doctor was and why. Two days and back here, regardless. Your contact knows the lay of the land and speaks the language."

'Tickets?'

'DAC Goddard told me to buy them, but it might be best if you do it. Send me the receipt, not to my phone or email, but to another number, or wait until you return. You'll be paid within a couple of days.'

'Unofficial, strictest confidence?'

'Yes. When you get back, if anyone asks, although they shouldn't, you're to say you got so drunk and you decided to hell with it and took off. Unless we succeed, it won't matter what excuse you use.'

'You couldn't make it a week, DCI?' Wendy joked.

'Not this time. Once this is over, take two.'

'We'll buy tickets at the airport. That way, nobody needs to know,' Bridget said.

Isaac wrote a phone number on a piece of paper and handed it to Wendy. Phone this number upon arrival and pick up a SIM at the airport. Give him one hour to get to you. Gordon is your contact. He's a friend of the DAC. Tell him what he needs to know, and no more.'

***

Valencia was a long shot; Isaac knew that even before he sent Wendy and Bridget, and the most that could be hoped for was additional facts to fill in the blanks. It was terrorism they were pursuing, but the Counter Terrorism Command had closed its investigation into the attack in Whitehall or was doing so little; it didn't matter.

Isaac had not contacted them, not while Caddick was there, but he would now be sitting upstairs in Challis Street, ready to indulge in verbal fisticuffs with anyone who didn't jump to attention as he passed by or failed to show deference.

Isaac was struggling, but it was a losing battle. There was only so much he could take, and now Caddick was angry that two members of Homicide were out of the office when it should have been a full detachment to welcome him.

That afternoon, the summons came to meet with Caddick in his office, not from the man but from a personal assistant he had brought with him. Sandra Trent, pretty, petite, and with a soft voice, was chalk and cheese to the man she reported to.

Deadly Secrets

Isaac had no issues with the woman. She was not there to be an easy mark, and Caddick had chosen her well. Caddick's rough edges were visible; hers were not.

'DCI Cook, take a seat,' Caddick said. 'I've got a few plans for Challis Street.'

'Homicide?'

'You make it hard work for yourself, working with a team of incompetents. Your sergeant is a disgrace. How many days sick in the last year?'

'None, until now.'

'How many days was she not fit for duty, either due to a bad leg, a cold, or hungover? She's a drinker, isn't she?'

'Out of hours, she is.'

'And now she's sick, off for a couple of days, or is it longer?'

'Two days, I'm assured.'

'And you accept it, this malingering? This living with Bridget Halloran, what's that? Are they, you know?'

'Friends. Wendy lost her husband; Bridget kicked out her lover. Nothing more to it.'

'I'll take your word for it, not that I believe it. Hill, now there is a drunk. You can't deny it.'

'He's a fine police officer.'

'That's not an answer. He is an alcoholic.'

'He's a functioning alcoholic. Occasionally, he suffers a relapse, and sometimes, if he's working, meeting people, pressing the flesh, teasing information, he will have a few drinks.'

'He gets a pass?'

'He does.'

'That's to stop. I can't have my officers making fools of themselves. Your workload isn't too heavy currently, is it?'

'We have a homicide,' Isaac said.

'Minor. An old man. Are you sure it's not suicide?'

'There's no gun in the house. It's homicide, and we've known the man from a long time back.'

'Marjorie Frobisher, that case is dead and buried.'

'We don't know why Robert Avers died, not yet. It may have nothing to do with his wife, and we never knew why people she associated with had died. Officially told to leave alone.'

'I'm giving you the official authority to solve those murders,' Caddick said.

'Is that your decision? We followed orders, and the Official Secrets Act was slammed on us. We didn't like it then, and to reopen it might rile those who know the truth.'

'Do you?'

'Some of it. We can't prove it.'

'Now you can.'

'Who's made this decision?'

'Commissioner Davies believes in solving crimes, not hiding them. I'm giving you the authority. When the two women get back, tell one to hack whatever she can and the other to report for a medical. I'll not have old and invalid in my station.'

'Yes, Chief Superintendent.'

Isaac realised that Caddick reopening a closed investigation after it had been closed by the Official Secrets Act was concerning. As if the man knew what his department was doing and using his authority to stick his oar in and to stir.

'By the way. In three weeks, Sergeant Gladstone is out. You've not dealt with it. I've got a Sergeant Clough to replace her. We worked together at another station; good man, you'll like him,' Caddick said.

Isaac knew he would not.

Chapter 8

The following day, early as usual, when there was a murder investigation, Isaac and Larry Hill met in Isaac's office.

Isaac had a cursory look at the inbox on his laptop before Larry had arrived and saw a dozen emails from Caddick, three from Human Resources, one of which was a transfer for Wendy to traffic, another was for her to attend a medical.

Isaac realised that lodging a complaint would be pointless. Caddick's flag was flying high; he could do no wrong, and HR would not go against the new Chief Superintendent.

'You better watch yourself, Larry,' Isaac said when the men finally got down to business.

'Teetotal for the duration,' Larry replied.

'You don't reckon he'll last long?'

'Long enough to drive us crazy, and this is the furthest the man's got. How many times has he tried to get you out?'

'Three, maybe four, but he appears to have succeeded this time.'

'He hasn't, not yet. The man's sees himself as infallible, all-knowing, and invincible. He isn't a superhero. You'll not bring him down with Kryptonite.'

'What's his Achille's heel?' Isaac said.

'Good policing won't be enough this time.'

'Look at the facts. Caddick's with Davies and grovelling to the man. He moved into Counter Terrorism Command with no interview or announcement of an opening in the department and then shifted to Challis Street. Others are more qualified than Caddick, and Counter Terrorism is a prestigious place to make your mark, not Challis Street. Deputy Commissioner Ian Jephson had risen in the ranks due to his time there; he even took a bullet to the stomach, and the man was exceptionally proud of Counter Terrorism, made it what it is today, and a snivelling toad would have been the last person he would have allowed in.'

'Except, Caddick's not an ordinary snivelling toad but a person anointed by the man who can do no wrong. You have seen Davies' popularity, and it's mentioned that he's up for a Knighthood.'

'And he'll get it,' Isaac said.

'Can you trust Jephson?' Larry asked

'He's a good police officer, and there's no reason to believe he's corruptible, but approaching him? I don't think we can risk it. What we're doing is unofficial, apart from Robert Avers' murder. Any more on that?'

'Nothing more. Fiona's dealing with the funeral arrangements, contacting her lawyer and attempting to get her brother out of the house.'

'How? He's as much right as she has to be there.'

'Wendy had a chat with her before she called in sick. She's planning to put him in a hotel. Fiona's planning to move her family in, but not while Sam is soiling the place.

'Could he have killed him? After all, no love was lost between father and son, and Sam was in Spain scamming if he could, getting laid less often, and doing nothing. And now, he's got the money.'

'It still doesn't explain how. The man didn't pull the trigger, which means he would have got someone else to do it.'

'Which would require organisational skills. Scamming drunks out of their hard-earned cash is one thing. Pulling off the murder of his father in Belgravia is not so easy.

'And if he can kill one, would he try another?'

'Fiona? How much money does he need?'

'How much can he waste? Fiona's convinced he'll blow whatever he gets.'

Isaac closed his laptop. 'Not today,' he said. 'Caddick can stew, set up a disciplinary, transfer me to who knows where, but I'm not going to curtail what we're doing.'

'In for a penny, in for a pound,' Larry said. 'My wife will have to accept what I can afford, even if it's a council house. What's on your mind?'

Deadly Secrets

***

It was clear that Fiona Avers was more sensible than her brother. Isaac and Larry had been invited into her two-story house in a leafy suburb in a small town to the north of London.

'Fiona,' Isaac said, 'is there a possibility that your brother could have been responsible for your father's death?'

'He had no reason. He knows the terms of the will, or what he thinks they are,' Fiona replied.

'He said it was 50/50, you and him.'

'He can say what he wants. It's not what he knows. My father explained that he intended to change his will.'

'Does Sam know it has been changed, or does he believe it was an idle threat?'

'Sam wouldn't have been told, not officially, and where was he? The occasional phone call and his phone number changed every few months. I certainly never phoned him, and he never contacted me.'

'Then, he could have been under the illusion that he's to get half of your father's estate.'

'He might be, but he isn't.'

'What will he get?' Larry asked.

'He'll receive two hundred thousand pounds and the drinks cabinet, complete with the alcohol in it. My father thought that would be poetic, giving him what he loved the most.'

'The house?'

'That's mine. The title's already in my name.'

'Sam doesn't know this?'

'He will, in the next week when he's evicted.'

'Tough love,' Larry said.

'It's not love; it's justice.'

'So, Sam is still under the illusion that if he killed your father, he would get a lot more money. How much?'

'The house and the money, close to fifteen million pounds. He thought he would get half of that instead of two hundred thousand.'

'It's still a lot of money,' Larry said.

'Inspector, it is to most people, and I don't need the money. I'm glad to have the house, but I wouldn't have killed for it, and my father ensured it was mine.'

'How long ago was the title transferred?'

'Eight months. I have the paperwork if you want.'

'A copy,' Isaac said.

Fiona leant over, picked up a folder, and gave it to Isaac. 'Check it, it's legal.'

'Two hundred thousand pounds. When will your brother receive it?' Larry asked.

'Three days, the day he moves out.'

'After the funeral?'

'Before. There is a room booked at a hotel in Bayswater. He can take his women there.'

'How will the eviction occur?'

'The lawyer will read the will in the morning at the house. Sam will protest, and no doubt get abusive. There will be a bank account with full details once he signs acceptance of the situation. He will give an address to send the drinks cabinet, and then he will be given one hour to collect his belongings.'

'After that?'

'I've hired a security firm. They will ensure two persons stay in the house for as long as necessary. Once Sam has drunk or drugged himself into a stupor or left the country, they will remain at the house. We will move in within three weeks. The house will need professional cleaners to go through the place. I will take responsibility for my father's belongings.'

'The funeral?'

'Sam can attend. I will ensure he receives transport and suitable clothing instead of the rags he prefers. He will be sober, clean-shaven, his hair cut, and he will behave. Otherwise, he will not attend.'

Deadly Secrets

Isaac realised that the woman was as tough as the mother she despised.

***

Two women, who should have been at home recuperating from their recent bout of food poisoning – that was the reason they had given when they phoned in from the airport – were not sitting by a heater and sheltering from the rain but enjoying paella at a restaurant recommended by Gordon Upton.

Bridget and Wendy had arrived in Valencia on the first flight out of London. The tickets were expensive, more than they had budgeted, but they were not worried, as they were confident they would get the money back.

At the airport in Valencia, they purchased a couple of cheap phones with enough credit to last them for two days and to send messages to the UK, which they did not intend to do. They had seen the beach, felt the sun, and knew the city was for holidaying, not policing.

Upton, five years older than Wendy and thirteen years older than Bridget, knew that time was money and that a request from Goddard would be taken seriously.

'Ladies,' he said, as they drank a glass of the local wine, 'I've got a friend in administration at the hospital. He's checking.'

Even though he was older than the women, he looked younger, his skin tanned and taut from the sun and his daily swim. It was such a place the two women had thought to retire to more than once. Bridget thought the man was worth spending more time with, not officially, but personally. Wendy wished her well, but two days wasn't long enough. If they could, they should get back to England as soon as possible, as Caddick was now in charge, and she was to be transferred out. She had seen the official email, and Isaac messaged her using Jenny's phone.

Don't worry, the message said. She knew her DCI was right and had ultimate faith in him.

'How much do you know?' Bridget asked. Her function in Spain was to assist Wendy, but she thought that their DCI, pre-empting the arrival of Caddick, had wanted her out of the office, as the new Chief Superintendent would have been badgering her for report after report, and what he didn't have, he couldn't condemn.

Homicide was a well-oiled machine, and Bridgete sometimes usurped her position and took actions on initiative rather than command. And that the new man, if he attempted to sweep clean and use regulations and procedures to his advantage, would look for a needle in a haystack, which he might find. If Caddick's personal assistant was as good as Bridget had been told, she would check everything and find something that Caddick would use to his advantage. Even so, she wanted to return to London as soon as possible, regardless of Gordon Upton.

Bridget stayed behind at the hotel. Gordon and Wendy went to the hospital.

Gordon spoke to his contact and explained the situation in fluent Spanish until the woman, in her fifties and wearing a white hospital coat, spoke English with a heavy Spanish accent.

'Dr Montero,' she said. 'The patient was identified as Sam Avers, a city resident. An address was given.'

'Who accompanied him?'

'Two men. I've spoken to Dr Montero. He's unavailable, as he is operating today. However, what I can tell you is that, yes, he treated the man, who had received a savage beating, and that blood was taken, as well as saliva.'

'Why the blood and the saliva?'

'It was requested and paid for. There was no reason to refuse.'

Wendy wasn't sure about Spanish law, but she doubted whether it would have been allowed in England without the patient's consent, and Sam Avers hadn't given it.

'Were the police called?'

'In Valencia, late at night? No, they were not called, and what would they do. Forgive me, another English tourist, drunk on red wine, staggering around the city in the early hours. We have too many, I'm afraid.'

'The two men?'

'One was named Ben Marshall. He paid the bill. We have done nothing wrong.'

'The other man?'

'Dr Montero said he was dark, but he didn't speak. There is no more I can do to help you.'

It confirmed Sam Avers' story, but why Benjamin Marshall, aka Ibrahim Ali, and now Lord Alsworthy, had used one of his names made no sense.

Gordon explained it later that day. 'It's Spain; why should he care? Probably thought no one would come looking. Is he as bad as you say?'

'I've not said,' Wendy replied. 'We don't know. He's loud and opinionated but not stupid. He misjudged our resilience.'

'I don't need to know more. I've got a place for tonight. You and Bridget will love it.'

They did, seafood, fresh from the sea, washed down with copious amounts of wine. They were sick the following morning on the plane, but this time, there would be no time to recuperate. They would have time to go home, change their clothes, freshen up, and then report to Homicide. There would be an official meet and greet with their new Chief Superintendent. Neither woman was looking forward to that pleasure.

***

The official meet and greet was scheduled for 11 a.m. Wendy and Bridget arrived at Challis Street at eight forty-five. On their desks in Homicide, there were envelopes.

'What are these?' Wendy asked Isaac.

'They were there when I arrived this morning. I imagine it's the first salvo from upstairs.

Wendy looked over at Bridget and saw an ashen face. 'What is it?'

'Human Resources. We're to report to them on arrival for a medical.'

'Which I'll fail,' Wendy said. She knew that her DCI had kept the wolves at bay, but the wolf was in the building, and he had pounced.

'Comply,' Isaac said. 'Don't protest. We play this cool.'

Caddick's first act as chief superintendent was completed by two in the afternoon. Bridget would return to work, but Wendy, who had failed the strict medical, would be placed on paid leave until a resolution could be reached, or she would be permanently invalided.

Isaac and Larry sat with the two women at their house that night. Regardless of the night before in Valencia, both drank wine they had brought back from Spain.

'It's over,' Wendy said.

'It's just started,' Isaac replied. 'You don't need to come into the office. You've got a vehicle, a phone, and a warrant card. What's to stop you from continuing with your enquiries.'

'It's highly irregular.'

'So is making deals with terrorists and people dying. Are you up to it?'

'Afterwards?'

'It depends on who we can trust, but I reckon we can get you back. For how long, I wouldn't know. You failed the medical, and there is no way we can deny that it is time to hang up your baton.'

'It's my life. I wouldn't know how to retire,' Wendy said, taking another drink.

'We didn't get the trip,' Larry said. 'You could at least offer us a drink.'

'I believe we have a reason to celebrate,' Isaac said.

Larry could not see what there was to be cheerful about. Caddick had dealt with one person in Homicide, and there was another in his sight, but for now, Larry was enjoying a glass of Spanish wine.

***

For five days, Homicide was run ragged with demands from Caddick and requests for reports from Sandra Trent. She wanted performance reports, daily reports on what each department member had done and achieved, and reasons if they were not.

Isaac was in his right to complain, but to whom? Human Resources? They wouldn't be listening and wouldn't act, not with Caddick, who everyone knew had Commissioner Davies' support. Go against Caddick; you go against the commissioner.

It wasn't only Homicide that was getting the treatment. In New Scotland Yard, Farley Grainger, a person Isaac had attempted to place his trust in, was under pressure, as was the entire Met.

There had been a circular from Commissioner Davies. Everyone had seen it. A reduction in budgetary expenditure of ten per cent, a doubling of the arrest rate, no crime to remain unsolved for more than sixty days, and an intended reduction of five per cent in staffing numbers within three months, another five per cent in the subsequent six months, and another five by the end of the year.

Nobody knew how it was going to be achieved. In Challis Street, Homicide couldn't be managed without full staffing. Caddick's answer when Isaac had put it to the man. 'Do it. Don't procrastinate or make excuses for your people. You know your problem, don't you?'

'I'm sure you're going to tell me,' Isaac replied. The pressure at Challis Street was spilling into his relationship with Jenny when he got home at night, and they weren't talking, and now, the option of a regional police station was out of the question.

'Too soft. They see you as their friend. Make them your enemy; make them shake in their boots when you come into the office instead of bringing you homemade cakes. How is that sergeant of yours? Got her feet up, downing the wine, or is she upset?'

'Does it matter?'

'Not to me. She's not coming back. She'll get a payout, and she's got her superannuation and the other woman. Are you sure they aren't?'

'You asked that once before. No, they aren't, and if they are, what business is it of yours.'

'Chief Superintendent Caddick or Sir. I don't think you realise how much power I've got, Cook.'

'DCI or chief inspector,' Isaac replied.

'Get out of my office. This will go on your record. How's your health? Reckon you could pass a medical.'

'Is that a threat?' Isaac replied.

'What if it is? What can you do about it? Sandra's checking everything, and believe me, there are issues. Your inspector still getting drunk every night?'

'He's not drinking. You can't get him for that.'

'What about these miscellaneous payments. Bribes, payments to criminals, look the other way, scratch my back, I'll scratch yours.'

'Detective Inspector Larry Hill is an exemplary police officer. He gets results.'

'Yes, maybe, but we have an ethics committee. We do it their way, not yours. I'll grant you one thing, Bridget Halloran, she's good. Sandra can't find much wrong with her work.'

Isaac felt like saying that Sandra was no match for a person of Bridget's calibre but decided against it.

'You're dismissed, Chief Inspector Cook,' Caddick said. Isaac didn't like how the man had emphasised his title and name, almost spitting it across his table. Once again, he had got angry. He vowed not to do it again if he remained in charge of Homicide.

***

The man had been due to arrive at the end of the month, but as Wendy Gladstone was out of the office, the mysterious Sergeant Clough arrived early.

Bridget disliked the poorly presented man, dressed in a suit that smelled of mothballs, whose breath stank, and from what she could see, was allergic to toothpaste.

Isaac had known that Clough was a plant, but regardless of Caddick and the imposition of the man into Homicide, he wasn't going to accept Clough in his present condition.

'What's your background? Where do you hail from?' Isaac asked after he had shaken the man's clammy hand.

'North of the country, not far from Newcastle.'

'Homicide?'

'Up there, we did it all. They are a good bunch of guys and gals. Not the same here, I can see that.'

'Why are you here?'

'Short-staffed, poor results, and you need my expertise,' Clough replied. He was tall, Isaac's height, in his late forties. Arrogant, that much was obvious. Isaac knew Clough's style of policing: uncouth, brutal, and foul-mouthed. He looked more like a criminal than a police officer.

'Well, Sergeant Clough, this isn't north of the country nor close to Newcastle. This is London, Paddington, and we do things differently down here.'

'Caddick said you'd be difficult.'

The man was attempting to start a fight. It was a setup. One more action from Isaac and he would be suspended, and no doubt, where Clough had come from, a detective inspector was begging to get down south and show them how it's done.

Isaac picked up his phone and dialled. 'Five minutes, my office,' he said.

Eight minutes instead of five, a young woman in her early twenties came in.

'Beth,' Isaac said. 'You're Human Resources. I need you as a witness. Sergeant Clough arrived today, a replacement for

Sergeant Gladstone. I'm not willing to accept him in this condition. I need him here tomorrow. He is to be clean, his teeth are brushed, and he is not to smell. Is that clear?'

'You can't treat me like that, Cook,' Clough said.

'Chief Inspector Cook, to you. Beth, got it?'

'There'll be fireworks,' she said.

'Hey, Chief Inspector, she didn't say it,' Clough commented.

'Tomorrow, eight in the morning, sharp,' Isaac replied.

'To pass muster?'

'To work.'

As Clough left the department, Isaac could see Bridget on the phone. 'After you've told Wendy what just happened, get her to phone me,' he said.

***

'I'm outside Robert Avers' house,' Wendy said. 'Fiona phoned me. Today's the day when Sam gets evicted.

'Who else is there?'

'A truck for the drink's cabinet. A couple of heavies, they look to be security and a distinguished man in his sixties. That would be the lawyer who will give Sam the good news.'

'Fiona?'

'She's here. She knows I'm across the road. I told her not to acknowledge me.'

'Stay with it. Keep me posted.'

Isaac knew that allowing his sergeant to continue working undercover while on leave contravened every rule in the book, but these were exceptional circumstances, and the man he was gunning for was in the same building, up two flights of stairs.

Isaac asked Bridget to do two things and ensure no one saw her. With the department and the police station in flux, people would be taking sides, and the majority, with families to feed and mortgages to pay, would go with the strength of Caddick.

Isaac understood, but he could not allow those persons to deflect from what needed to be done. 'Check Clough. Find out who he is, where he's from, and if there's any dirt on the man.'

'What else?'

'You've got the footage of Whitehall. Check if he was there when that idiot blew himself up. Don't do that in the office.'

'And the day off sick, tomorrow?' Bridget joked.

'If this doesn't pan out, it'll be more than a day off.'

Wendy phoned again. 'The cabinet's coming out, closely followed by Sam Avers. He doesn't look happy.'

'Are you up to it?' Isaac asked.

'I can try, but I'm unsure what will come from it. If he's as angry as I imagine, he'll be off to the nearest pub.'

'Or the hotel that Fiona's booked him into. Does Fiona realise she's not to tell anyone about your presence at the house?'

'I've told her I'm undercover, and we are uncertain about her brother.'

'Who she doesn't care if we arrest or not,' Isaac said.

'Blood is thicker than water. I don't think we can assume that. He's her last direct relative, all that remains of Robert and Marjorie. We know she had it rough when she was young, and Sam had been the favourite of the mother, but now, the tables have turned.'

'Even so, his story checks out. What about Fiona's?'

'She is the will's executor; she could have coerced her father. We assume that he had voluntarily signed the changes to the will because we met him, and we've become impressed with Fiona. She's bettered herself, although Sam's been honest and told us about the scams.'

'And if Fiona's not truthful, my presence outside her house might cause problems?'

'It could. However, we continue. Stay with Sam, and if he nips into a pub, make sure he's settling in for a long evening of drinking. We assume he knows where the hotel is.'

'Not our problem,' Wendy said.

***

Harry the Snitch phoned Larry. The two men met at the agreed meeting point, Harry's favourite pub. On the wall were horseshoes and photos from a hundred years before. At the back of the bar, rows of bottles lined up, and a rotund little man with ruddy cheeks serving the drinks.

'Has she spotted you?' Larry asked.

'Not yet, but she will. She's good, real good. Attractive, as you said, and she's still messing around with that man you don't like.'

'You wouldn't, not if you met him.'

'What's her angle? Who is she?'

'Don't push your luck; just report. Anything else?'

'Each day, she goes out and meets another man. They walk along the Thames, near the Tower of London, and sometimes sit down and have a coffee. They look friendly.'

'How friendly?'

'More than colleagues. Low key, but I reckon they're an item, but even that might be a subterfuge.'

'Get a photo,' Larry said.

'How can I do that? She'll spot me if I carry a camera with a tripod and a telephoto lens.'

'Then organise someone else. We need to know who the man is.'

The answer to the question was answered later that day. Isaac met with Linda in Hyde Park, although not far enough away from a homeless man who shuffled by and looked over.

'Call them off,' Linda said. 'They've become tiresome, these people you have following me.'

'What are you up to?' Isaac replied. 'Why spend so much time with Caddick? The man's making our life miserable; can't you get him to smile?'

'I don't want him to smile, only to talk. He mentions you and knows about us. He wants you out, believes that I won't tell you.'

'He's not a fool. He knows what you're up to.'

'That's what I want. I want him to be edgy, to fear me, unable to stay away.'

'Besotted?'

'Not with love, with sex, something you could have had, but you chose your wife over me.'

'It was you that ran out after you killed Richard Williams. What was the point if Ibrahim Ali knows the truth now?'

'No point, but we can't find how Caddick knew. Until then, I'll take Caddick to paradise and back anytime he wants unless you want to take his place.'

'Take, yes, but I won't. Besides, what do I know that you don't already know? You seem to be one step ahead.'

'Not one, but two.'

'Which two?'

'The man you were told about, down by the Tower of London. He's someone I care for.'

'Do you know Harry the Snitch?'

'We do now. He's good, we can use him.'

'Yet, you sleep with Caddick.'

'Believe me, it's no pleasure. One day soon, you will understand why I killed Williams. There will be a decision to commit a crime to prevent another.'

'That's a contradiction, the fodder of fiction, to go back and kill Hitler before he rose to power,' Isaac said.

'Williams knew who Marjorie's child was. He had always known, as there were no secrets between him and Marjorie. He would never have revealed it, but Ibrahim Ali was looking for his mother. If he had got close enough and then scoured around, Williams would have become known, and then he would have told all he knew.'

'Why? Did Ibrahim Ali know that he was someone important? Is that possible?'

'The Marshalls knew. Not that they knew who, but they had been told that their adopted son came from a good bloodline. Ali never knew how good, but he was determined to find out. Williams would have talked. It was a risk we could not allow.'

'Why not kill Ibrahim Ali instead of Williams?'

'That was not my order. MacTavish might have known, but not me. Killing Ali, if he was responsible for Whitehall, I would enjoy; Williams, I did not.'

'Marjorie Frobisher?'

'I wasn't in the country, but she had to die; Ali didn't. Blissful ignorance was better.'

'And then, someone tells him that he is the son of Alsworthy.'

'More or less, something like that.'

'Something? What do you mean?'

'We think he might have known before Whitehall. We don't know how or why.'

Chapter 9

Wendy was no longer in the office but still working for Isaac. DAC Goddard's support was tentative and behind the scenes.

The two men met again, using the same procedure: an SMS, one word. They met up that night at eleven outside Goddard's house.

Isaac thought it was fraught with danger or, at the least, complication. If MI5 or Lord Alsworthy were curious about what was going on with Isaac and his team, or if Caddick was playing both sides against the other, wouldn't they keep a constant watch on him and his people? Harry the Snitch was hidden on the other side of the road from where Isaac met Goddard, who was now aiming for the commissioner's job.

'Avers?' Goddard asked.

'Robert Avers and Marjorie Frobisher's son is out of the house, in a hotel in the city's centre. From reports, he's spending his inheritance as fast as possible,' Isaac replied.

'Wine, women, and song?'

'Whisky, whores, and cocaine. He'll blow his money in six months and then find out that his friends are fair weather and the women aren't there for his charm. Fiona's moving in to the house, and there's security.'

'She might need it. Any ideas as to why Avers died? We always regarded him as a decent man married to a woman who revelled in her celebrity.'

'It has to do with Ibrahim Ali. Strange, I can't refer to him as Lord Alsworthy.'

'It's his alter ego that concerns us.'

'Which one? Benjamin Marshall or Ibrahim Ali? And where do you stand, DAC? I cannot run this on my own. It's unofficial, apart from Robert Avers. I don't know who I can trust, unsure if I can trust you.'

'I've walked a narrow path, unsure who has the strength.'

'Who will benefit your career? Is that what you are saying?'

'Change comes from above, not from Challis Street, and you know that. What is coming next doesn't excite me. What about Mary Ayton? You know her, DCI.'

Isaac remembered that the two had gone out together on four occasions and that he had cooled the relationship. He recollected that she was driven and that policing and rising to the top were more important than a long-term romance. And then, she married well, a barrister in the city. Two children in private schools, and through sheer grit and determination, she had worked her way into Commissioner Davies' inner circle.

Even so, Isaac trusted the woman.

'I do know her from a few years back. Are you suggesting we place trust in her?'

'Unofficially, you can approach her and see if she's responsive to the Isaac Cook charm.'

'Charm is one thing, power is another. She has upset more than a few people on the way to the top. Would she condone a criminal act or even embrace it if it advanced her career? Would you?'

Isaac knew he was stepping outside of the boundary that separated a chief inspector from a deputy assistant commissioner. He felt he had no option but to risk disfavour and censure, alienating the bond that had held between the two men irrevocably for over twenty years.

'I'll turn a blind eye to minor infractions, but this is more than that. If anyone would condone senseless murders of innocent persons in the name of their religion, then that person had no place in England.'

'But this is not religious fervour,' Isaac reminded Goddard.

'It might have been for the hapless individual who blew himself up. If Caddick is clearly the primary person here, and Ali and Davies offered a de facto and distant agreement, we are not

Deadly Secrets

dealing with people I could support, not even for a crack at the commissioner's office.'

'You've told me enough times not to sit on the fence, but that's what you're doing.'

'I am, and for good reason.'

'No reason is that good. Investigating terrorism in this city is for the Counter Terrorism Command. What are they doing about it?'

'The question is what Homicide, Challis Street, is doing.'

'With what? We're not chasing suicide bombers. Our focus, and I thought it to be yours, was to understand how Ibrahim Ali knew of his birthright and how Caddick was in the right place at the right time.'

'You're conducting an internal police investigation without the authority. It's a dangerous game. Isaac, I'm close to the action; I meet with Davies once or twice weekly. I can't be too open, and if it's known that we're meeting like this, there would be questions which I could not answer.'

'And a subsequent demotion?'

'A demotion at my seniority would be subject to enquiry. More likely a sideways promotion.'

'Regardless, what do I do? We need to talk to Ali about his adoptive parents. We need to be open.'

'And if you're open, everyone's ducking for cover. What about Linda Harris? Still sleeping with Caddick?'

'She is. MacTavish had contacts in MI5 before. He knew what she was up to and where she reported.'

'Do we? Is there anyone we can trust?'

'Nobody. Isaac, I'm afraid you might have reached a dead end,' Goddard said.

***

Isaac saw no option. He phoned Chief Superintendent Mary Ayton. Either she was on board, or any further enquiry was pointless, and he would have to accept that Wendy wasn't coming

87

back, that Larry would be out within the month, and he, within two.

Isaac visited Human Resources to commence the process of transferring out of Challis Street to another part of the country. After filling out the forms, he climbed the stairs to Caddick's office. As he entered the first of the doors, he handed the form to Sandra Trent, Caddick's PA. 'It would be appreciated if you could get DCS Caddick to approve.'

He then went down to Homicide and told Bridget and Larry what he intended. Horror was etched on their faces as he laid out the reasons for his decision and that the situation was hopeless. They should work with Caddick and give Sergeant Clough, Wendy's replacement, every assistance to bring him into the fold and make him one of their own instead of giving him the cold shoulder.

After that, Isaac met Harry the Snitch in a lane that branched off a narrow one-way street in a part of London where neither was likely to bump into anyone they knew.

'Slim, heavy coat, wearing trainers, gloves on his hands, bearded,' Harry said. 'He was outside the house when you arrived.'

'That doesn't make sense. How would he have known I was meeting up with the man?'

'He could have followed you one night, reckoned it was your poorly executed attempt at keeping it secret.'

'And then, once he knows the time and the place, he's there every night, rain, hail, or shine.'

'Something like that,' Harry said. 'They contacted me and offered me a freelance position."

'You've accepted?'

'They pay better than the police.'

'They kill better, too. Has Inspector Hill told you?'

'I don't need to be told. I've watched the woman you were messing around with.'

'Inspector Hill told you?'

'He had to. If you want a five-star service, give me as much detail as possible.'

'And that includes my personal life?'

'Hill said this was vital, and I was dealing with professionals. I needed to know how professional and how dangerous.'

'Were you told how dangerous? What were you told about Linda Harris?'

'Seductress, and very professional. Is there any more I should know?'

'She kills people to order. Were you told that?'

'Hill didn't mention it.'

'Does it make any difference?'

'It does, to you.'

'Don't underestimate her.'

'The man outside Goddard's knew someone was watching him. He didn't see me, but he would have sensed me.'

'How?'

'I sensed him before I saw him.'

***

One was a chief superintendent; the other was a chief inspector, although there was a time when both had been constables. Mary Ayton had risen higher than Isaac due to her determination not to be held back by an organisation that preached equality but often failed to practice it. Not that she was strident, but it had ensured that she was extra-focussed and driven, most days in the office until ten or eleven in the evening.

Isaac had felt prejudiced when he first joined the police, but Richard Goddard mentored and ensured his rise in the ranks until Commissioner Davies appeared. He had taken an instant dislike for Goddard and those he guided.

'It's been a long time,' Mary Ayton said.

'Long time,' Isaac replied.

They had dated for a while, but now, there was to be no relationship, and Isaac felt uncomfortable with the situation.

'I know why you're here,' the chief superintendent said.

'Do you?'

'I know about you and DAC Goddard, and you were friendly with Lord MacTavish. I also know that there are plans to unseat Commissioner Davies.'

'And that you were supporting the commissioner,' Isaac added.

'I continue to support him.'

They met in Ayton's office, her demand, which Isaac had reluctantly agreed to. He was out on a limb, struggling to know who he could trust and who he could not. The romance with the woman withered within a month, and even back then, he knew she was a political animal, the equal of Richard Goddard. Two people whose stars were in the ascendancy, and he, a chief inspector, who, within the next three months, would be transferred out of Challis Street, either with a promotion or not.

He trusted the chief superintendent as much as he trusted Linda Harris. He realised his record with women, apart from Jenny, who was pleased at leaving London, was woeful. And now, he was looking for support from a woman clearly in the metaphorical bed with Davies, communicating with Caddick, sidling up to Assistant Deputy Commissioner Alfie Wigg and Deputy Commissioner Ian Jephson.

It was then that Isaac realised that he had made a strategic error.

'Isaac, you've come here to see if I favour your cause. Is that correct?'

'I need to know where I stand. Before, there was MacTavish and DAC Goddard. Now, there is no one.'

'And that's the way it will stay. I will grant you one favour,' Mary Ayton said. 'This conversation will not be recorded, filmed, or mentioned by me. I suggest you do, likewise.'

It was a dismissal by the woman, and Isaac, remembering their time together as lovers, shook her hand and retreated. That

Deadly Secrets

night, he reflected on the change in the woman, from young and gentle to middle-aged and calculating.

The situation was untenable until the next day in Homicide. It was the first meeting of the new team. In Isaac's office, Larry Hill, Bridget, and Sergeant Clough.'

'Welcome,' Isaac said.

'After five days in the office,' Clough replied.

Isaac, who had shaken the man's hand the day he arrived, realised that Clough had no fear and no intent to defer to authority. A plant should be discreet, not openly confrontational, as if the man intended to rile, to get the reaction that Caddick had almost got once.

And if he, as the senior officer, reacted, swore, or waved a fist at the sergeant, it would be reported.

Isaac ignored Clough's remark. 'Robert Avers,' he said. 'What's the latest?'

'It seems I came at the right time.' Clough was determined to irritate.

After a short meeting, where it had been agreed to continue with the investigation into Robert Avers's death and for Larry and Clough to visit Sam Avers at his hotel.

Larry spoke to the manager, a gently-spoken woman from the West Country. Larry could see that gently-spoken belied a gritty determination. This was no pussy cat, as Clough was about to find out.

'Avers? Women?' Clough enquired. His manner was dismissive and to the point.

Larry thought it was no way to get cooperation, as the manager had not committed a crime.

'Sergeant Clough,' she said, looking at Clough. 'This is a prestige hotel, not a bordello. We are not concerned if the guests are respectable, and we do not complain if they have uninvited guests in their room, not if it's for a short visit, but two to three women every night, we will not accept. The inference you have made demeans this establishment, and I would remind you that we do not take kindly to aspersions, that we are any other than reputable and respectable.'

'No offence intended, none inferred from what I could see.'

Larry, conscious that Clough was a contradictory, aggressive police officer, took control of the conversation.

'We're aware of Sam Avers,' Larry said. 'We have had dealings with him before, but this is a homicide. We need to know where he is.'

'I've already had his sister here. She's paying for the hotel. She's explained that their father has died, and there is an investigation into his murder, and she would prefer he remained here. Supposedly, he would leave the country if we removed him.'

'Spain, probably.'

The two men left the manager and took the lift to the fourth floor, knocking on Avers' room. The door was opened by a scantily dressed woman.

'Avers?' Clough said.

'He's having a rest,' the woman said.

Larry could see why the manager was upset. The woman was not what Sam Aver could have afforded but what he preferred: tattooed, bright-red lipstick and dyed red hair. She also smelt, not of perfume but of marijuana.

Clough took a seat across from the woman. 'How much?' he asked.

'More than you can afford, Sergeant.'

Larry wasn't sure whether this was the man's style or an affectation designed to rile.

Clearly drunk, Sam took a seat next to the woman. 'What is it?' he said.

Larry wasn't willing to let Clough monopolise the conversation. 'A couple of questions,' he said.

'Okay. What do you have?'

'You've been advised of your inheritance?'

'For what it's worth, I have.'

'Do you intend to contest?'

Deadly Secrets

'What's the point. Fiona's got the money, and her husband is smart. Besides, it's more than I deserved. Maybe I'll get lucky and find money from somewhere else.'

'From where?' Clough asked.

Larry had to grant that Clough's question had relevance.

'In Spain. I've got friends; they'll help me.'

'Sam,' Larry said, 'you were scamming tourists in Spain, making enough for a place to live and to buy drink or drugs. Your sister is living in a multi-million-pound home. Don't insult our intelligence by telling us you have friends. The kind of money you believe you're worth doesn't come from honest graft. Nor does it come from scamming. You're here in the hotel. You've got willing women as long as you pay. Good food and drugs. Sam, what do you intend to do about your sister?'

'She'll pay more. She's not what you see. You think that woman who screwed Charles Sutherland that night in the house before he died isn't the same person you seem to trust now. Ask Fiona how she keeps the weight off and if she's faithful to her husband.'

'Are you saying she's still an easy lay?'

'I'm not saying she is, but someone murdered our father. It wasn't me; it could be her. Have you considered it? You checked me for gunshot residue. Did you check hers?'

'We did,' Larry said, although he hadn't read a report from the CSIs that stated it.

The one thing that Larry did notice on the day he spent out in the field with Clough was that the man showed more intelligence than he revealed with his slovenly speech and direct manner with Homicide's DCI.

'And you are?' Clough said, looking across at the woman.

'Delvene. I'm a friend,' the woman replied.

'Paid?' Larry asked.

'Sam looks after me. We've known each other for a long time.'

'That's not an answer.'

'He pays in kind. He's got money; he's got me. In Spain, he had neither, and if he stops looking after me, I leave.'

'Tell us about Sam,' Clough said.

Larry thought Clough was a man he could work with.

'Sam takes life as it comes. He's still good fun, unlike his tart of a sister.'

'Do you know Fiona?' Larry asked.

'It goes back a few years before she redeemed herself, lost weight, and married a boring man.'

'You knew the woman that we knew. The change in her is miraculous. Any reason why?'

'Fiona and Sam's mother, you know about her.'

'We do. Fiona hated her, and so did Sam. But then he hated both parents.'

Sam Avers picked up a bottle of whisky, poured two drinks, and gave one to Delvene before downing his in one gulp.

'His father, upright and hard-working, hated him. Not that you could blame him, as Sam is not likeable,' Delvene continued.

'A damning indictment, given that he's sitting next to you.'

'Sam knows what he is and what I am. There is no point in denying the obvious.'

Clough got up and walked into the bedroom. He came back after two minutes clutching a bag.

'That's mine,' Sam Avers said. 'Do you have a search warrant?'

'Not on me,' Clough said. 'Either you talk, or this will be used as evidence.'

Clough opened the top of the bag and showed Larry what he had found. Larry realised the importance of the bag's contents.

'Sam Avers,' Larry said. 'You're under arrest for the murder of Robert Avers.'

Chapter 10

At the police station, Sam Avers sat in one of the interview rooms. He was not a happy man. His sister had been informed and would arrive shortly.

Isaac realised that the evidence was not solid until Forensics checked the weapon found in Sam's bag. Delvene, Sam's woman, sat outside the interview room. She had changed her clothes from sexy to demure and wore jeans with a blouse and a pullover. The ensemble was completed with a heavy leather jacket. The lipstick had been removed, and the tattoos were covered.

Isaac regretted that Wendy was not in the office, as she would have been the person to interview Delvene, now formally identified as Delvene Drayton, a mother of two children, whose home address was listed as 128 Batty Street, Whitechapel. There were four convictions against her for soliciting, but they were sixteen years prior. She had spent a total of ten months in prison, but since then, she had been clean of any crime.

Wendy would have asked what the woman was doing now. Due to Larry and Clough being in the interview room, Isaac would talk to Delvene, conscious of what Wendy would have asked.

'Miss Drayton, there is reason to believe that Sam Avers is involved in a crime,' Isaac said.

'Delvene, not Miss, Mrs, or any other title.'

'Very well. Delvene, I'm told that you are a friend of Sam Avers. Is that correct?'

'Not when he was younger. I was friends with his sister. You know what she was.'

'We do.'

'Then that was me. She was the fat friend you dragged along back then, but now I would be dragged along.'

'Your children?'

'They spend most of their time with their father. They are well looked after and a credit to both of us.'

'Married to their father?'

'We were for twelve years. I remained faithful; he strayed.'

'Not uncommon.'

'We're friendly, and we meet up occasionally to discuss the children. Sometimes, I stay the night with him.'

'Admirable,' Isaac said. 'What else do I need to know?'

'Only this. I was a streetwalker in my teen and early twenties, became a heroin addict, nearly died from an OD, cleaned myself up, met my husband at the detox clinic, got pregnant and then got married.'

'After the divorce?'

'I had to work.'

'That's not answered the question.'

'It has, but you need the salacious details. I went back on the game, not on the street; too old for that, and I wasn't into drugs. I became an escort with a select clientele.'

'Sam's not select,' Isaac said.

'He might not look the best and would win awards for laziness. However, he is kind, and he treats me well. If he had no money, I would still meet with him, but I would not stay. I still contribute to my children's education and must pay my bills.'

'Do your children know what you do?'

'I hope not. They see me on the weekends, sometimes during the week, and during school holidays, and if there is a function at their school, I go with my former husband. You can regard me as a whore with morals. That is not what Sergeant Clough saw me as. He's not a good person, you know that. The sort of police officer that compromises women like me who are down on their luck and makes an offer; look after me; I'll look after you.'

Isaac didn't comment but agreed with the woman.

'Sam's in serious trouble. You know about his father, shot at point-blank range.'

'Sam told me that his sister had shafted him. Did she?'

'I can't answer that question.'

'I know that the relationship between Sam and his father was tense. I knew his mother. Not well, but Fiona introduced me once. She thought she was something special, which she was. My mother was excited when I told her I had met Marjorie Frobisher. What is it with people who get wrapped up in celebrity adoration? What do celebrities believe they have that gives them airs and graces.'

'My parent are into soap operas,' Isaac said, 'but they're retired now. I grew up without a television in the house.'

'All those murders, and then Fiona's mother dies. Is Sam's father's death something to do with them?'

'We believe it might be. We never saw you back then. Where were you?'

'At home, looking after my family. Fiona and I go way back before she fancied herself as an actor, and I found the street and heroin. We lost contact and bumped into each other after I was respectable.'

'Sam?'

'He hasn't changed.'

***

Clough, who had entered Homicide as a stooge of Caddick's and had been regarded as such, was proving himself to be a capable officer. It had been him that had walked into the bedroom and found the bag with the gun. A gun that Forensics identified as the murder weapon. The situation looked grim for Sam Avers as he leaned back on his chair.

'How do you plead, Mr Avers,' Larry Hill asked.

Avers had rejected legal assistance and claimed that his sister would look after him, whatever happened, and this was a stitch-up, and that the gun had been planted.

'Not guilty. I didn't kill my father, not that he had long to live, and I did believe I would get half of the inheritance. But Fiona and that husband of hers screwed me.'

'It was your father who signed the will, and he was mentally sound, able to make decisions against you if he wanted. And, to be honest, you're not a person who seems to want much. What is it with Delvene?'

'I've known her for a long time. She didn't want much to do with me before, but I didn't have money back then.'

'We are aware that there were other women in the hotel, raucous parties, and drug taking,' Clough said.

'A few friends, but the hotel wanted to evict me. Fiona fixed it so I could stay, subject to my behaviour.'

'Which doesn't come easy.'

'It didn't, not until I phoned Delvene.'

'How long in the hotel, assuming you remain in England?'

'Two, maybe three weeks. I've got a lawyer to see, to ask him if I can contest my father's will. Inspector Hill is probably right that I can't.'

'Which means you'll be broke in six months. Delvene will not want to know you then.'

'Easy come; easy go. I hadn't seen that gun for a long time, and you can't prove I did.'

'You're laid back,' Clough said. 'What makes you think that we will believe you? Either you or Delvene put the gun in the bag.'

'Or else Sergeant Clough put it there.'

'Which one do you reckon?' Larry asked. 'Accusing a police officer of putting the gun in your bag won't help your defence.'

'Inspector Hill, I take Mr Avers' comment as a personal insult,' Clough said.

Larry could see that Clough would not be averse to gingering a prosecution, planting evidence to ensure a conviction. But this was not petty theft. This was murder, and the subsequent trial would be rigorous. He could not believe that Clough would be so stupid as to plant a gun.

There was one other consideration, the charge of murder against Sam Avers would need to be changed to that of conspiracy to murder. Someone else had pulled the trigger. Avers had been checked at Robert Avers' home for gunshot residue, and none had been found.

The charge was changed, and Sam Avers would be held for twenty-four to forty-eight hours, pending further evidence.

Fiona Avers made a scene when she arrived at Challis Street Police Station, demanding to see her brother and phoning a lawyer to represent him. 'He's my brother, my only living relative. I'm damned if I'll see him hang.'

'It's a custodial sentence,' Isaac said. He had ended the conversation with Delvene, and now, due to Sam Avers as a potential conspirator, the murderer needed to be found. And that person could be Delvene, although Isaac could see another conspiracy. He thought it ludicrous, but it couldn't be dismissed. If he pursued it, it would put him in direct conflict with Caddick and Commissioner Alwyn Davies. He would need advice before he went down that rabbit hole.

'I know what it is,' Fiona replied.

'How do you believe the gun came to be in his possession?'

'I cannot. Possession, what do you mean? Was he holding the weapon?'

'It was in a bag in his hotel room.'

'With Delvene?'

'A friend of yours, according to her.'

'We were, sort of. Did she tell you I was the plain frump she used to drag around?'

'Words to that effect. Why did you go?' Isaac said.

'Why not? You know what I was, and Delvene would tolerate me if I paid. Sometimes I got the sloppy seconds.'

'The men she didn't want.'

'The men nobody wants, but then you know that. You were told the story about Charles Sutherland and me, naked and going for it on the couch, and then our mother comes in with Richard Williams.'

'Delvene and Sutherland?'

'Not with me around, and besides, my mother abhorred Delvene and would not let her in the house when her snooty nose-in-the-air friends were there. How many do you think turned up at her funeral?'

'It depends if the media were there with their cameras.'

'All of them were, but two weeks earlier, when she had died, how many came around to the house to see my father, to offer their condolences?'

'Not many.'

'Jess O'Neill came, and so did you and your sergeant. A couple of others from the production site where they made the program.'

'Richard Williams?'

'He was sympathetic. He was a decent man, better than my mother, and then he was murdered. Did you find out who did it?'

'We did.'

'Did you arrest them? That's a more relevant question.'

'We didn't.'

'Warned off? Don't answer.'

'You know the answer?'

'I knew there was a secret. I didn't know what it was, but it was big, and our father might have known or suspected.'

'Did Richard Williams?'

'It was a week before he died. Our father was away on business. My mother didn't care whether Sam and I knew. Sam's out somewhere, getting drunk, drugged, or both.

'It's late at night. I had stayed home, in my room. I hear them come up the stairs into my mother's bedroom. I had an upended glass to the wall between my room and there. I can hear everything: the heaving, the groaning, the bed springs as they get a workout. Afterwards, the two of them, my mother and Richard, talk.'

'What did they say?'

'The usual nonsense about eternal love and how she should have married him instead of my father. Not that she would have. Our father, even if he played up occasionally, what man doesn't, loves the cow. Richard Williams, you met him. He is attractive, wealthy, and good for my mother's career, but he's not the marrying kind.'

'Did you?'

'Once. I think he got a kick out of it, the dowdy daughter.'

'Did you tell your mother?'

'Never. And he never mentioned it. He was a gentleman, not a slag like my mother. Anyway, my mother talks about this secret. They don't mention names or what it is. I remember Richard saying there was more than one secret, but I never knew it. We all know that the first one was our half-brother.'

'What more did they say?'

'They went back to giving the bedsprings another workout. I hated that woman; I could have killed her for what she did to my father. I'll not let Sam be convicted of something he wouldn't have done.'

'Sibling love might not be enough,' Isaac said.

'It's not only that. Sam is weak and easily led. Our mother worshipped him and then rejected him when he needed her the most. She gave me security, good schools, and a comfortable home. It wasn't enough.'

'The night your mother died. How did you feel?'

'Is it wrong that I felt nothing?'

'It's unfortunate, and yes, we knew your parents. We preferred your father, but we should all love our parents.'

'I loved one, not the other. And that night, after she died, I sat up with our father while he told me about her, when they met, the love they had felt, and then fame had become a wedge between them.'

'How long before he got over her?'

'He never did. He started to whither after that, and then he got cancer, and then he was murdered. Not a good way to end a life.'

'Not good, but you've still not answered why your brother wouldn't have been involved.'

'Conspiracy requires a plan. Sam, as you've seen at the hotel, is determined to blow the money. I could understand if he blew half and kept the rest for a rainy day, but not our Sam. Six months, and he'll be begging me to help him out.'

'Will you?'

'I'll complain and tell him to get a job, to straighten himself out, but he won't. Then I'll give him the money.'

'You'll weaken?'

'I will not. Sam doesn't know there's a fund set aside for him to live off. He won't change, but my father knew that whatever he gave him, he would waste. This way, when he's desperate, he'll suffer for a few months, giving him a chance to dry out and to come off the drugs. And then, with a fresh injection of money, the cycle will repeat.'

'And you're certain he wasn't involved in your father's death?'

'Positive. Sam's not capable.'

Isaac would accept what Fiona had said, for now.

***

Delvene Drayton had come to the police station to support Sam Avers. However, the situation changed after Isaac spoke to Fiona Avers, and Delvene was now in the interview room.

'Delvene, how long were you in the hotel with Sam?' Larry asked.

'Five days, although I left on the third at around four in the afternoon and returned at ten in the evening.'

'The reason?' Clough asked.

'I went with my former husband to our son's school.'

'The reason?'

'Careers night. Our son wants to be a police officer. We met with a careers officer, who explained what was required and that the Met would pay his university fees and give him a salary.'

'Will your career affect his chances?' Larry asked.

'I don't see why it should. My crimes go back to before he was born. My son doesn't know the full details, except I had a rough patch when I was younger.'

'Does he know what you're doing now?'

'I hope not. People might be judgmental, but it doesn't change the fact that he'll be an asset to the police.'

Larry thought that it would be an issue, not necessarily thwarting his acceptance by the London Met, but in a police station, persons have access to databases, and someone might find out that the young man's mother had walked the streets and given random blowjobs to strangers for a fee.

Embarrassment, if not condemnation, and his promotional progress could be slowed. And now, his mother was in an interview room, and it would be recorded, and a report would be filed. The child would be damned by the actions of the parent.

'Delvene, we have a problem,' Clough said. 'There's Sam's bag. It's got a gun in it. It's the weapon that killed Robert Avers. The question is, how did it get there? Did you put it there, or did Sam bring it with him?'

'I didn't bring it. Where did you find it?'

'At the back of the wardrobe, far corner, behind a stack of clothes.'

'Then it can't have been me. I never used the wardrobe.'

'Why not?'

'I arrived with one set of clothes. Sam gave me money to buy some more downstairs as I needed them.'

'Which you put in the wardrobe.'

'I bought one dress, two bras, three panties, a skirt, and a blouse. When they were dirty, I cleaned them, but seeing that we didn't go out, apart from when I went to the school function, I've not worn them, other than the underwear. The other items are still wrapped and in the shop's bag.'

'Who else visited? Fiona?'

'Not Fiona. She disapproves of me, thinks I'm after Sam for his money.'

'Which he doesn't have.'

'He had enough to pay my daily rate. I don't need more than that, and I'm satisfied with my life and my children, even my former husband.'

'Who's married,' Larry said.

'He never remarried. The children live with him and visit me regularly. Inspector, you might want to paint me a wanton woman, but I'm not. If I'm not selling myself for good money to respectable men, I'm at home, worrying about my children.'

'Sam, respectable?'

'I've known him and his sister for a long time. And no, he isn't respectable, doesn't hold down a job, but he's his father's son, even if they didn't see eye to eye.'

'Okay,' Clough said. 'We accept that Sam Avers is a good man, and you didn't put the bag in the wardrobe. Who else came to the room? We were told about parties with friends and women. Who were the women?'

'Some came with the men; others were paid for. All of them were available.'

'Including you?'

'I came with the deal.'

'Then one of those who came to the party must be a murderer, but why? Why attempt to implicate Sam? What would they gain?'

'They wouldn't gain a conviction against Sam, that's for sure,' Delvene said.

'Why do you say that?' Larry asked.

'I assume the bag wasn't there when I moved in, but I cannot be certain. Someone has tried to shift the blame for the murder to Sam, but he's innocent. He told me that the first night. He needed company, and he had my phone number. It was more than sex; he genuinely wanted someone to talk to. He knew that I wouldn't say anything.'

'How did he know he could trust you?'

'It was long ago when Fiona was plain Jane, and I was out on the street, three nights a week.'

'Why not seven? That's the routine for most of the women.'

'I'm not most. For some reason, he trusted me.'

'Do you know why?'

'He was comfortable with people down on their luck. He saw those from affluence and prestige as false, especially his mother. He wanted his father to accept him, but Robert Avers bottled his emotions and told him to get off his backside and make something of themself. But that's not Sam. He's a weak person, easily led by others. Robert was the father he couldn't have; Sam was the son his mother didn't like.'

'She did when he was younger, took him to events, and left Fiona at home,' Larry said.

'Even so, he didn't want to go and would have preferred her at home, but she wouldn't do that, and Fiona couldn't speak to her mother. When he was seventeen, I was out with Fiona most nights, finding men, spending their money, and if we felt in the mood and they were drunk enough, Fiona would take one, and I'd take the other.'

'A good life?'

'No protection, sexually transmitted diseases, and disgust in the morning.'

'You or Fiona?'

'Both. Fiona wanted better, but she was plain; men didn't want her. As for me, I read mushy romance novels. The sort of thing we were doing and random men do not figure in the novels I read. I wanted better, but I couldn't find it. Anyway, one night, Sam comes out with us. He's seventeen. He's still an innocent in many ways. We go to this club. It's in Soho, down a few steps into a basement. It's dark, and there are women on the stage, and Fiona's soon drunk, and I'm not much better.'

'What happened?'

'We shouldn't have been there, and it's expensive. The girls on the stage are for hire, not just for putting on a show. We get up to leave, but there are these men, three of them. They want Fiona and me, but we don't want them. Sam, for once in his life, jumps up to defend our honour, but he's no match for them, and they've got the bill for us to pay, and we don't have enough. They give us a choice. Either we put on a show on the stage, the two of us, or we go round the back and, well, you know.'

'You had sex with the men. What about Sam?'

'He's trussed up in the corner. He sees what happens to Fiona and me.'

'How many men? How many times?'

'The three men, until they've had enough. We stagger out of there after a couple of hours. Fiona vomits on the ground after we get out of the place. Fiona's crying. Sam, for once in his life, takes charge. He gets a taxi, gets me home, takes me into my house, and explains to my parents that I had drunk too much, and he's to blame.'

'He was chivalrous.'

'My father beats him around the head and kicks him out. Fiona stays the night at my place. We find him outside the house in the morning, lying beside a rubbish bin. He defended our honour by taking the blame. He didn't tell anyone what had happened, and my parents never knew the truth, nor did Robert Avers. You remember things like that.'

'If he had told the truth?'

'The police would have become involved. My parents would have been asked to explain why they let their daughter come home in that condition. Fiona knew that her father would have reacted by contacting the police, and if they didn't do anything, he would have taken it upon himself to confront the men at the club, who were possibly killers. And then, there was her mother's career. Fiona didn't like her but didn't want her to become the butt of jokes and gossip.

'Sam, for all his faults, took the blame for the two of us, got beaten up by my father, and spent three days in the hospital. Sam had a group of friends, some who were violent. As useless as Sam is, he told them what had happened to his sister and her friend, and the men needed to be taught a lesson.'

'Are you saying that Sam and his friends killed them?'

'Sam could not hurt anyone, barely able to blow the skin off a rice pudding. But men, those who are violent and criminal and run clubs, do not mistreat women and get away with it. That was Sam's ethos.'

'A few do,' Larry said.

'Not to Sam, and apparently, it was the same with his friends. I knew one of them who went to the club with Sam, a perfect gentleman but rough. I went out with him for a while.'

'Did he know that Sam was referring to you and Fiona?'

'Sam never mentioned what he had organised to us, and we didn't ask, but there were rumours of what happened at the club.'

'Sam could be implicated,' Clough said. 'It's still murder, whether the victim is deserving or not.'

'Your testimony doesn't help Sam. Sure, he shows that he can be a decent person, but he has condoned murder. Why shouldn't he have done the same thing with his father?' Larry said.

'Sam talks a lot, rarely does anything about it. He did that one time for Fiona and me. That shows his character, not his guilt.'

It did to Larry and Clough.

Chapter 11

Wendy sat at home with an old cat on her lap. On the table was a glass of red wine. She glanced across at the envelope next to the wine bottle before picking up her phone and dialling. 'It's come,' she said.

Isaac arrived at the house within the hour and read the letter. 'It was bound to come sooner or later,' he said. 'What are your thoughts?'

'It's generous. I'm considering it.'

'With your superannuation, money won't be an issue.'

'A couple more years would have been good. Chief Superintendent Caddick has wanted me out for a long time.'

'Regardless, Homicide will not be the same.'

'I'm told Sergeant Clough's settling in.'

'He's experienced, but we can't be sure of him. After all, he came courtesy of DCS Caddick, and Caddick's PA, the lovely Sandra, is proving to be a handful.'

'Lovely?'

'Caddick's hatchet woman. Endless reports, a stickler for procedure, and Caddick would thwart us if he can.'

'Clough?'

'Competent, but he's Caddick's man. I can't be sure what the long-term plans are for him. It depends if you return or Larry Hill gets drunk. One more time, and he's out. Caddick's mentioned it, but I reckon Clough likes a drink or two.'

'Get Larry to get him drunk. See if Clough drops his guard and starts talking out of turn.'

Isaac thought the idea had validity, but it would be unprofessional, compromising a fellow officer. Even though he was using Wendy to work undercover, which would lead to disciplinary action if discovered.

Isaac realised that he could no longer use his sergeant, and for now, she would have to take it easy, drink her wine, and consider the unwanted but generous offer if she were to accept early retirement.

Two days later, the situation resolved itself. Human Resources told Isaac, and Caddick reaffirmed it. 'Wendy Gladstone can return to work while considering the offer,' he said.

Isaac was sure there was something amiss. Even so, he was glad to welcome her back into the fold.

Sam Avers moved out of the hotel. It had not been possible to tie him to the murder, apart from the gun, and Delvene Drayton had gone back to her place in Whitechapel.

Sam had been quizzed about the incident at the club but would not be drawn on it. Fiona would not comment, and Delvene, after Fiona had told her not to talk about it, would say no more.

The gun remained crucial. Sam's defence was that he had handled the weapon on his last visit to England when he had found it in a drawer while looking for a key to the drink cabinet. That meant that someone had known where the gun was, had used it to kill Robert, and then taken it, only to plant it in the hotel.

Delvene supplied a list of the people she knew; Sam provided another.

Wendy commented at the end of three days that she enjoyed working with Clough.

Nighttime in the office and early morning meetings were no longer confidential, as Clough would be there, as the man was in the office before Isaac in the morning, and often, he was the last to leave, and he was getting results.

Wendy and Clough had divided the list of those who had been in Sam's hotel room, including three women from an escort agency, a couple of Sam's friends, one of whom, Clough was sure, was one of the men who had visited the club and dealt with the three men who had abused the women. Bazza Perlikos was born in Sydney, Australia, to Greek parents. When he was five, they moved to London and opened a Greek restaurant. Bazza, an

Australian derivation of Barry, the name had stuck in London, would never be a restaurateur or even a cook in MacDonalds. The man was of low IQ, heavily built and tall.

'Sam's my friend, do anything for him,' Bazza said at Challis Street.

Wendy and Clough persevered, but the man continued to reply even after he had been told of the club, the address, and the approximate date when he and others had gone there. 'Sam's my friend, do anything for him.'

Bridget had checked and found out that the man had a record for brawling outside pubs, taking on all-comers, and had almost killed a man once over the price of a pint of beer. Sober, and in the police station, he was a gentle giant, but in a club, after he had been told what had happened to the women and sufficiently primed with alcohol, he would have been unstoppable.

Three names had come from the club: Guy Moreau, French, and the club's owner. A small man with a nasty reputation for mistreating the women who gyrated and turned tricks. A dreadlocked Jamaican, Rasta Devon, who spoke patois and claimed to have gone to school with Bob Marley. That was false, as the age difference between the reggae singer and Devon was a generation apart, but then the man wasn't sure what day of the week it was, constantly in a ganja-induced euphoria. He was a bouncer at the club and frightened whoever he met. The third man, Sergio Soares, claimed to be Brazilian but could not speak Portuguese, although he spoke English with a foreign accent. The night of the attack, Devon and Soares had been outside the club, vetting those going in. They should have been checking the ages of those entering but did not; they were more concerned with ensuring that the patrons had enough money to pay for the extortionately costly drinks, the cover charge, and the money to slip into the girls' bras and panties on the stage.

Only Devon had been found. The dreadlocks had gone, as had the ganja. He had found religion and was a pastor at a small church north of the city.

Deadly Secrets

Wendy and Clough met the man there. 'Three people, sixteen years ago,' Wendy said. 'A small man in his teens, a bad case of acne, and two women. One was well-spoken and plain-looking; the other spoke poorly, used bad language, dressed like a tart, and drank like a fish.'

'You expect me to remember back then? I'd like to help, but I'm not sure how I can. Spotty teens and drunken women, seen a thousand of them. What was I back then? Not much, just someone who didn't care who came in as long as they paid.'

'And if they didn't?'

'It was the manager. He was a hard man. If they came in, they had to understand the situation. He was there for the money. We would rough up the man if he didn't pay, get his address, and ensure he would return the next day with the money and interest. The women, the same routine; either they agreed to the deal and if they refused…'

'You would rape them,' Wendy said.

'Not rape, although I wouldn't have put it past the owner. I don't know why people came to the club. There were better places to go.'

'Was yours the roughest?'

'It was. The shows were more explicit, if you know what I mean.'

'And then you get religion. When was that?'

'I came from a religious family, but I had lapsed, embraced sin and carnality.'

'And raped two young and silly women?' Clough added. 'Devon, your holier than thou belief doesn't wash with us. You don't rape women if they don't pay. You give them an ultimatum. If they had reported you, the police would have arrested all of you, but the man, he doesn't do that because the women plead with him not to. And then, a few days or weeks later, a group of men come to the club. These are big men; one of them is bigger than you. They grab those who attacked the women, and beat them to a pulp, and probably kill them.'

'I wasn't there, and yes, we used to get tough men in occasionally, but we could handle them.'

'Not if there were four of five.'

Wendy and Clough were theorising, as they didn't know the numbers.

'What about the others? Moreau and Soares?'

'I've not seen them, not for a long time. The club is closed.'

***

Wendy visited Fiona Avers at her new home, the house she had grown up in as a child. She had come alone and left Clough, whom she found she liked, regardless of his rough manner and association with DS Caddick.

'It's been a long time,' Fiona said, giving Wendy a heartfelt hug.

'Your father?'

'Life goes on. We were close, and he was not well, but to die like that, that's hard.'

They were sitting on the couch that Fiona and Charles Sutherland had used when Fiona's mother and Richard Williams had caught them, with Sutherland rapidly pulling up his trousers and insulting Fiona.

Wendy hoped it had been cleaned since then.

'The gun in Sam's hotel. What did you think?'

'It wasn't Sam. He was with Delvene, not that we have kept in contact, although she was here yesterday.'

'To renew an old acquaintance?'

'We were polite and drank a bottle of wine together, but neither drank as much as we used to. She's made something of her life, although she's still selling herself, but more selective. I even paid for her to be with Sam.'

'Did you set it up?'

'Did she tell you that she had been to Spain a few times and had met up with Sam?'

'When he was scamming or flush with money?'

'With or without money?'

'Maybe she felt obliged because of what happened at that club,' Wendy said.

'Delvene told you. I wish she hadn't, as I prefer to forget that night. But then, she was trying to protect Sam, but why plant the gun there? It makes no sense.'

'Why try to implicate your brother? Unless your father's death and Sam are interrelated.'

'Sam wouldn't have harmed our father.'

Wendy wasn't convinced by the sentiment that Fiona continued to promote. Sam disliked their father intensely. Robert Avers had died, not from family strife, but from something he knew, and either Sam or Fiona, or both, knew what it was, and they weren't talking. Even the story about the club had a stench about it.

'We've spoken about your half-brother before, Fiona,' Wendy said. 'Is there more? Could it be a reason for your father's death and the gun in Sam's bag?'

Fiona finished her glass and poured another. 'I didn't want to say, not before.'

'You've met him?'

'Briefly. Not at this house, but a random encounter close to where we used to live. He was dressed in Western clothing. He was charming, and we spoke for about twenty minutes.'

'When was this?'

'Six weeks before he announced that he was the son of Lord Alsworthy and my mother. I never knew she had been married, but my father did.'

'Stay with your meeting him for now. Afterwards, we can talk about your father.'

'The person I met was Ben. I did not know when I met him, but then, on the television, I realised. There was no mistaking the man I had met. Sam is shorter, and besides their hair colour and height, there is a similarity.'

'Your reaction when he made the announcement?'

'Shock. I asked my father.'

'His response?'

'He said there was a child. It was before he met my mother, and we should accept the reality.'

'Which you did.'

'What else could we do? We found out from Sam that he had met the man in Spain, and that blood had been taken from Sam, and that Ben, or Ibrahim, had DNA, and it was proven.'

'Was there any further contact with the man?'

'I met with Gabrielle Alsworthy.'

'Why?'

'She wanted to meet me to ensure Ibrahim Ali was her half-brother.'

'That was known.'

'She was confused. She had inherited the estate but not the title. She was not bitter about the title but confused as to how she could be related to a radical Islamist. She wanted a shoulder to cry on.'

'Were you that shoulder?'

'She is two years older than me, landed gentry, aristocracy, cucumber sandwiches, horses, and fox hunting. The family have been members of the idle rich for generations.'

'You came from a wealthy family,' Wendy reminded Fiona.

'Our wealth came from graft and talent. It was not my talent, as I had none, but it was mainly from my mother. My mother may have had her faults, but was not a snob. The hon Gabrielle was. It was at their mansion. The place looked like Buckingham Palace, and inside, the painting of ancestors stretched back four hundred years. All we have got is a half-empty photograph album. She didn't think much of me; I didn't think much of her. And she thought even less of Sam.'

'She met him?'

'We were kindred spirits, placed in a situation that was hard to understand, and we were unsure how to deal with it. There would be more for her than for us, but changes would come. She paid for two tickets, and we went to Spain, where we found Sam scamming. Gabrielle wasn't shy in telling Sam what she thought of him. Words to the effect "If Ibrahim is anything like you, God help us".'

'How did Sam take the insult?'

'He laughed. Mind you, he was drunk. It did not help Gabrielle Alsworthy's impression of our family, nor the Marshalls.'

'She met with them?'

'I went with her. I was curious and a little confused.'

'What did you find?'

'Martin and Beverley Marshall, middle class. He runs an architectural firm on the outskirts of Nottingham; Beverley is a primary school teacher. Their house was small but neat and tidy. Martin was an enthusiastic gardener, and Beverley helped at a woman's refuge at the weekend. Ben was their only child, and they told us that they adopted him at six weeks of age, and they had never known who his parents were, only that they were married at the time of the birth but had divorced soon after, and due to circumstances, that could not be divulged, the child had been placed for adoption.

'They insisted that he had been a joy to them, and at the age of eighteen, he had moved out and shared a flat with a friend, and that he had lived with a girlfriend and had changed his religion to Islam, but never forgot their birthdays, and his newfound religion gave him what he had missed in life.'

'Which was?'

'According to Martin Marshall, he had found his roots, and whereas he loved Martin and Beverley, he loved Islam better.'

***

Jenny, Isaac's wife, was concerned, although Isaac had told her the situation, but not to the depth which would have worried her even more. She knew he was meeting with Linda Harris and Mary

Ayton, that Caddick was being difficult, that there was a plant in Homicide, and that her husband was worried.

She didn't realise how dangerous it might become, although she had been pleased when Isaac applied for a transfer, knowing that he didn't want to accept it, as he would have preferred Homicide and a promotion to superintendent, but she had explained that life wasn't about absolutes, and that compromise was often required.

Gabrielle Alsworthy, her husband, and their children had been moved out of the main building, an eighteen-century Georgian mansion, and into one of the houses on the estate, although it wasn't a worker's cottage, but a comfortable four bedroom two-storey house with a thatched roof, and a garden at the rear.

Her concern, if she was approached, would be to admit her distress that the mansion no longer flew the Union Jack and that the ballroom was now a Mosque, and there were five chants a day calling the faithful to prayer.

She had been brought up in the mansion and had met her half-brother, only to initially receive a rebuke and a request to dress modestly. Gabrielle Alsworthy and her husband argued constantly, and the children were irritable and nervous, and the strain of the situation was proving difficult.

On the strictest condition of total confidentiality by Gabrielle, and with the agreement of her DCI, Wendy drove to Gabrielle Alsworthy's home on a wet and windy Wednesday night. She found that Gabrielle Alsworthy's husband and children had driven one hundred miles north to his parent's house.

She met Gabrielle alone and would stay the night and drive back to Challis Street in the morning.

The two women shook hands. Wendy thanked Gabrielle for inviting her to stay the night. The two women sat in the house, large by London suburban standards but small compared to the mansion five hundred yards away.

Wendy had always been fond of dogs but could not warm to the two small dogs snapping at her feet.

Deadly Secrets

As Homicide saw it, Robert Avers's death allowed the department to conduct interviews with the relevant persons, even with Lord Alsworthy, although without evidence, that would prove more contentious and might alert persons who, for the time being, were best left ignorant of the situation.

The house was warm, and on the table in the dining room, a meal had been prepared. Wendy could not remember eating pheasant, but she enjoyed it, as she did the bottle of Chablis and the glass of port afterwards in the sitting room.

'Why?' Wendy asked.

'Why I asked you down here to spend the night. Is that the question?'

'It's two of them.'

Wendy felt cosy and wanted to sleep after the meal and the alcohol; Gabrielle Alsworthy did not, although the dogs had stopped pestering and were asleep on a cushion in the corner of the room.

'The first one is easy. You phoned me and asked if I would talk to you about my half-brother.'

'The second?'

'I assumed you do not want your visit not to be known by those at the main house.'

'It would be preferable, but Lord Alsworthy will be interviewed at some stage.'

'You'll not pin anything on him, even if you have doubts.'

'Why?'

'Have you met the man?' Gabrielle said as she reached for another bottle of wine.

'I met his mother, her husband, and their two children,' Wendy said. 'Tell me about Ibrahim Ali?'

'Polite, respectful, and attractive. He gave me this place to stay.'

'For how long?'

'Six months to one year. Money is not the issue, but with Ibrahim claiming the title, the bulk of the wealth goes to the eldest son, or in this case, the only son. To the other siblings, ten per cent of the estate. As I'm the only other child, I will receive that ten per cent. It is enough to live well. No need for you to worry about that.'

'I wasn't,' Wendy said.

'What have you been told about me?'

'Upper class, aristocratic, and possibly believe yourself to be superior to the daughter of a subsistence farmer in Yorkshire.' Wendy saw no reason to gild the lily or give platitudes when they were unnecessary.

'I would agree with the first two, not with the third. To be evicted from the family home is a humbling experience, and giving it over to a man whose views I cannot agree with is a slap in the face.'

'Islam?'

'Ibrahim believes in Sharia, and at the mansion, the women are covered. I'm not saying they are wrong if that is what they believe, but in the English countryside, traditions die hard; traditions he would disagree with. I fear that when we move from here, it will be many years before I return, if ever.'

'My ancestral home was a rundown farmhouse. There is not much I miss from there,' Wendy said.

'Another glass,' Gabrielle said. 'We've got a lot to cover, and I'm not sure all of it is good.'

One of the dogs got up and sniffed at Wendy's leg before rejoining the other.

The call to prayer could be heard; Gabrielle grimaced.

Ignoring the sound, Wendy pressed forward with her questions. 'You say you have more to tell me. Are they relevant to Robert Avers' death?'

'I believe so. My father was a lover of life. The deputy prime minister of this country. He had renounced the title to sit in the House of Commons but later reclaimed it. He could have become prime minister if there had been a party room split. However, we know that was thwarted at a general election, and he lost his seat.'

'That's the political process. I'm concerned about the death of Avers.'

'I'm coming to that,' Gabrielle said. 'My mother knew some of the secrets, if not all, but I was never told them as a child, and then, I was at boarding school, and after that, I went to university, doing what all of us did.'

'Drugs, drink and men?' Wendy said.

'None of the first, too much of the second, and too often with the third.'

'Not much different between the daughter of a subsistence farmer, no more than two pennies to rub together, and the daughter of a lord.'

'There isn't. Another drink?'

Wendy knew she shouldn't, but couldn't resist.

Gabrielle Alsworthy cried, and Wendy put her arm around the woman's shoulder to console her.

'It's so awful,' Gabrielle said, dabbing a handkerchief at her eyes.

'Can it be resolved?'

'I think it can.'

'How?'

'My father had other women before he married my mother.'

'After?'

'I don't know the details, but I must assume that Ibrahim was not the only child of my father's philandering.'

'Are you aware of his upbringing as Benjamin Marshall?' Wendy knew the answer; Fiona had told her. It was a test to see if Gabrielle would lie.

'Some of the history, although I met his parents. I went with Fiona Avers.'

'Benjamin had been a good son and student, maintaining contact with them even today. However, there is a concern that Robert Avers knew more than Fiona and her brother have told us. We became involved with the Avers before Marjorie, Ibrahim's mother, died.'

'I used to watch her on the television,' Gabrielle said. 'My mother would always turn on the television when she was on; hard to believe that our families are indirectly related.'

'Did your father comment when Marjorie was on the television?'

'Only to tell my mother to turn that rubbish off, but she never did.'

'Why the tears?' Wendy asked but couldn't imagine the upheaval she had experienced. She had been removed from the mansion to become a secondary figure beholden to a man who did not share her values. He had already stood up in the House of Lords and given an impassioned speech about the need for equality, the embracing of all religions, and Sharia.

'I don't trust him,' Gabrielle said.

'Any reason?'

'It was two days after his speech. My lawyers were still trying to determine if his claim was valid. Although he is the legitimate eldest son of my father, then primogeniture is applied, and the firstborn legitimate son inherits. All that history and tradition gone.'

'Unless he changes.'

'Why should he?'

'Wealth changes a person. Will Ibrahim Ali remain devout?'

'I've not seen any sign of it yet, and religion is not political.'

'Ibrahim came from a humble middle-class upbringing. He's enjoying the wealth and the prestige. Were you happier in that mansion than me in my little house?'

'Of course not. It's the perception, but people who pretended to be my friend before now treat me like a pariah. Sergeant, you don't have a lot of sympathy for me, do you?'

'I can sympathise with the person.'

'I can't blame you. We're an insidious lot. My mother died before my father. She told me, when I was twenty or twenty-one, that on my father's death, I might be in for a surprise.'

'Is that it?'

'I was young and silly, not concerned about a dusty mansion or the history and the tradition. I was at university, living with my boyfriend, preparing to backpack overseas. Money wasn't important as long as there was enough.'

'Your mother didn't elaborate?'

'If she had, I wasn't listening. I don't believe she would have known of Ibrahim, or if she had, she would have never acted like she did. My father was often away, either in London or overseas. My mother would have regarded that whatever he did away from here stayed there as long as he didn't bring it home. He never did.'

Wendy thought the woman was rambling. 'Focus, Gabrielle,' she said. 'Ibrahim, what do you know about him?'

'I've met him four times. Each time, he has been polite but firm. He surrounds himself with a core group of men. There are three or four women in the house. I sometimes see them walking around the gardens. One speaks English; the others might, but they do not or intend to talk to me if they can.'

'The one who speaks?'

'She's from up north. Her accent is unmistakable.'

'The women? Are they with Ibrahim?'

'If you mean, are they his wives, I've no idea. My conversation with her is polite and short. She said she liked the main house and felt sorry for me.'

'Heartfelt or false?'

'I believe she was genuine, and, as I've said, Ibrahim has always been polite but firm. I don't have an issue with the man; it's only what has happened to the Alsworthys.'

'The other women, I need specifics.'

'I don't have any,' Gabrielle said.

Chapter 12

Early the next morning, Isaac phoned Wendy, who had woken with a throbbing headache after the previous night with Gabrielle Alsworthy when the women had drunk three bottles of wine between them. Isaac explained the situation and that, due to Ibrahim Ali's relationship with the Avers, he was a person of interest and would be interviewed.

Wendy explained the situation to Gabrielle.

'I thought you wanted to maintain a distance from the man,' Gabrielle said.

'We must focus on Robert Avers' murder.'

'What had you expected to gain from me besides the injustice of my half-brother evicting me from the family home?'

Wendy could see a problem. Gabrielle had nothing to do with Avers' death, but Wendy's car was parked outside, and marching up to the main house and showing her warrant card might alter the relationship between the lord and his half-sister.

Wendy phoned Isaac and explained the situation. She did not want to be responsible for Ibrahim Ali evicting Gabrielle and her family from the house.'

'You're right, we have a problem,' Isaac replied.

'We can't continue like this, DCI,' Wendy said.

'With what?' Gabrielle, who had been nearby, asked.

Wendy ended the call and turned to Gabrielle. 'This murder is more complex than I'm at liberty to tell you.'

'I thought it was.'

'How?'

'We are not country yokels. Some of us are perceptive. Why don't you tell me what this is about, and I'll tell you what I know.'

Wendy phoned Isaac. 'I'll not be back this morning. Trust me.'

'Do what you think is necessary. Always remember discretion,' Isaac replied.

Gabrielle went into the kitchen and made breakfast for the two of them. It wasn't often that Wendy ate bacon and eggs, but this one time, she thought, hell to the restricted diet.

Afterwards, the two sat at a table in the kitchen.

'What is it?' Wendy asked.

'You're not the only police officer who's been down here,' Gabrielle said.

'They've spoken to you?'

'Not me. At the main house, one of those who was on television.'

'Which one?'

'The one who killed one of the men in Whitehall.'

'Chief Superintendent Caddick?'

'Yes, although I don't remember that he was a chief superintendent.'

'The full story, please.'

Wendy set her phone on the table. She intended to record what was said. She dialled Isaac and asked him to find a secure location where he would not be disturbed and no one could listen.

'It was early morning,' Gabrielle said. 'I usually take the dogs out for a walk. I wasn't looking for anything specifically; I was down by the entrance to the estate. A car goes by; the man waves at me. Nothing unusual, but I remembered the face. I realise it is related to what happened in Whitehall. I find him afterwards, lauded by the commissioner.'

'Davies,' Wendy said.

'That's it. Caddick drives to the main house, parks his car in front, and enters.'

'How long after before he came out?'

'The police occasionally came to the main house when I lived there, but I didn't know he was a police officer, just a person visiting.'

'Why would the police come to the house?'

'The usual. Our father was receptive to their visits, and the police wanted to maintain contact with those who supported them. Regardless, Caddick's at the house with Ibrahim. The husband of Ibrahim's birth mother is murdered, and then you are beating around the bush without saying what this is about. Why me? What do I know about the dead man? Level with me if you want my help.'

'What help could that be?' Wendy asked. Isaac did not like where the conversation was heading. To bring in a third party with an axe to grind had all the ingredients of an unholy mess.

'Let me tell you what I think,' Gabrielle said. 'Is your chief inspector still listening?'

'He is.'

'Good. Ibrahim had been brought up in a good family environment. He finds religion. He's genuine in his belief but gets it bad, like a born-again Christian. But Ibrahim's not born again; he's new to the religion. He sees strength in its values. He becomes vocal. Have you met him?'

'Not yet.'

'I have, and you warm to him. He's charming, intelligent, and, I believe, genuine. That he kicked me out of my home does not alter the fact.'

'That's magnanimous of you?'

'Not magnanimous, realistic. Ibrahim is an impressive person; never forget that. He's not a poorly educated, deluded fool. He believes this because he sees the religion as offering something that our modern Western society does not.'

'It doesn't explain Chief Superintendent Caddick,' Wendy said.

Isaac realised that as he listened to Lord Alsworthy's half-sister, she could be an asset to the investigation, but he was unsure how much should be revealed to her. And if Ibrahim Ali and Caddick had allowed innocent people to die, what would they do to her.

Or, armed with the knowledge that the London Met was investigating him, could the woman go to Ibrahim Ali and use it as a lever to strike a better deal for her and her family.

After all, the Alsworthys had a history stretching back to the English Civil War in the seventeenth century, and the Alsworthy estate had been bequeathed to the first Lord Alsworthy by a grateful King on the monarchy's restoration. The Alsworthy had enough skeletons in their family history, and to believe that Gabrielle Alsworthy was incapable of trickery and deception would be naïve.

'It does, and you know it,' Gabrielle said. 'And If I'm right, others would also. If they know you're sniffing around, it could get nasty.'

'Are you suggesting that Ibrahim could be violent?'

'I can only deal with the facts. Ibrahim's offered a choice. Either preach from a street corner or from the House of Lords. But it comes at a cost, and that cost means that people die. It's all to do with the relative merits. In a war, do you kill fifty to save five thousand? What decision would anyone make?'

'It's not a war.'

'Isn't it? What do you think is happening? The country is changing, whether for good or bad.'

'You would say for bad.'

'Would I, Wendy? That's a presumption based on my class, not on the person. Nothing is static. We must accept the transition but hopefully guide it. If Ibrahim is not involved, I will accept it, but this chief superintendent's visit to him clarifies that your visit to me is not to solve a murder but a fishing exercise, and I believe that I deserve the truth.'

Isaac messaged Wendy. *Let me talk.*

'Gabrielle, two hours,' Isaac said. 'I'll meet the two of you at your house.'

It would take one hour to drive, but Isaac did not intend to take his car. He would take Jenny's.

***

Sergeant Clough proved to be an asset to Homicide, and his service record – Bridget had obtained a copy – had shown that he was a cut above the rest as a police officer and that he and Larry Hill had damaged their careers with self-induced foolishness. Larry's weakness was alcohol; Clough's was gingering the evidence, and on two separate occasions, he had been caught out in a trial while giving evidence. The first had been eight years previously when he had read from his notes that on the night of the 3rd of July, he had observed the plaintiff acting suspiciously around the back of a chemist, which had later been robbed. The only problem was that there was no back to the chemist, and on the 3rd, the plaintiff had been seen two hundred miles away. The second time was more serious, proof that he had planted evidence on a charged man. Easily proven and aggressively criticised at the subsequent disciplinary.

Clough spent his time following through with Sam Avers; Larry concentrated on Fiona. Neither was getting very far in their respective focus.

Clough's work record from his previous police station showed that he had taken off three days in the last year due to illness and nineteen days of leave; none aligned with Whitehall. Yet, he was Caddick's man. The question was how and why Caddick had brought him in. It could not have been to strengthen Homicide and to move Wendy out, as she was back.

Another mystery was when Larry found Sam at Fiona's house, the two of them sitting comfortably in the room at the back of the house, on the couch that Fiona knew intimately.

'Sam needs our help,' Fiona said.

Larry wasn't sure what kind of help; after all, he had him pegged as the man behind his father's murder.

'What help?' Larry asked. 'He's hardly covered himself in glory.'

'He didn't put the gun in his bag,' Fiona said, 'but your Sergeant Clough is convinced he did. He's hassling Sam and calls him up, day and night, not giving him a minute's peace.'

Deadly Secrets

'He's a good officer,' Larry said. 'If Sam told us the truth, we would back off.'

'I am telling the truth,' Sam said.

'You're not, nor is your sister. We need a motive for your father's death, and the fact that he knew your mother had been married before, even if he did not know about the child, is not a motive. What did he know? Did he know the name of the father and its significance? It was powerful. Your mother appears to have, or she would not have died.'

'They said it was an accident.'

'It wasn't, not that there is any point in asking for the investigation to be reopened. Too long ago, the facts will have changed, and the evidence won't be there.'

'Richard Williams knew,' Fiona said, 'and Charles Sutherland knew something.'

'Did he tell you, here in this room, on that couch?' Larry realised he was raising the tempo, hopeful of a reaction.

'Not this couch. That's a terrible thing to say.'

'Fiona, you were a tart and screwed around. Charles Sutherland was a one-time lover. What about Richard Williams? Anyone else.'

'Richard, yes, once or twice. If he couldn't have my mother, I was second best.'

Richard William's second best, Larry knew, was his PA, Sally Jenkins, and then Linda Harris.

'The truth,' Larry said. 'Why did Williams have sex with you? You were mixed up, and nobody thought you desirable back then. Compared to your mother, you were nothing.'

Larry didn't enjoy insulting the woman, but he could see no other way to break through the mental wall that separated supposition from fact.

'Inspector, I would be within my rights to take offence to your comments, but unfortunately, they are true. Richard was like a dog on heat, always looking for the next woman. Not that he was that young, but you remember him, the Ferrari, and the manicured nails. He had better than me, better than my mother, but any port in a storm.'

'And you were the port?'

'A port conjures up a vision of something desirable. I was more of a dock, nothing exciting, and if my mother wasn't around, sometimes, he would take me. It's not only Sutherland that spent time with me on this couch.'

'Did Williams know who Ibrahim Ali was?'

'Isn't that what you thought when he died?'

'We had our theories but no name and no proof. The investigation was closed, not by us, but by others. And now, your father's death is either related to that or to something different, which makes no sense. Why kill him after everyone knows the reason for your mother's murder?'

It was the question that continued to hamper the investigation. No motive made sense other than Sam Avers had arranged for his father's murder to ensure his inheritance.

'Sergeant Clough's still correct in pressuring Sam,' Larry said.

'Why?'

'Because he knows who might have put the gun in the bag.'

'Delvene knows,' Sam said.

'And you knew?'

'All that I know is that it was my bag. I didn't take it to the hotel, nor did I put a gun in it. Delvene had brought the bag to the room.'

'How did she get hold of it?'

'On one of her visits to Spain. She borrowed it from me after she went crazy buying souvenirs for her family. The bag meant nothing to me; she was welcome to it.'

'But you didn't mention anything in the hotel.'

'Delvene's had it rough. I did not kill my father, nor did Delvene. Why she was covering for someone, I don't know, but I wasn't about to get her in trouble.'

'Either you're a saint or the most stupid person in London,' Larry said.

'I'm not a saint, but Delvene's a good person. I'm certain someone pressured her to put the gun in the bag.'

'What sort of trouble?'

'Ibrahim Ali trouble.'

'Do we need Sergeant Clough here?' Larry asked.

'I don't think so,' Fiona said. 'Inspector Hill, we know you. We feel comfortable with you, but your sergeant gives us the creeps. Who is he? Do you trust him?'

'Trust is an unusual word to use. Fiona, you've got something on your mind.'

'Nobody was tried for Richard's death, nor that of Sally Jenkins. What happened to the blonde one that came after? She disappeared, and then our mother died. Hit and run is still a crime, regardless if our mother was drunk, and then the taxi driver is acquitted.'

'Are you suggesting that the police were involved?'

'I am, given what we know now.'

'Which means your father knew something, and Delvene's planting the gun on Sam. Not much of a friend if she did.'

'Delvene's had a hard life, bettered herself, and her children are a credit to her, but she's selling herself. Prostitution is prostitution, no matter what fancy word you use to describe it. She's got children, the joy of her life, and she loves them dearly. They live with their father, who, if there was a scandal, might restrict Delvene's access.'

'Is that enough to frame Sam?'

'It would be for me,' Fiona said.

'Did your father?'

'Inspector, I'm telling the story. Don't play your games with me.'

'Apologies. It's for Sam to talk.'

Larry had not seen Sam take a drink since he had come into the house, but then he realised that the drink cabinet was not there, and Fiona no longer had alcohol in the house.

'It was in Spain,' Sam said, moving across the room and sitting in another chair. You know the story of how I came to be in the hospital and Ali getting a blood sample and a swab. Delvene was in Spain, staying with me. You weren't told that Ibrahim Ali, after leaving me in the hospital to recuperate, had visited Delvene. I don't know what was said or if they had spent time together. I only know that she didn't tell me and that Ali told me later.'

'What did he say?'

'It was a message on my phone. It might not have been him, but it had to be someone close to him. It said that I was not to mention the blood sample and the swab, that they knew where I lived in Spain, that my girlfriend, if she knew what was good for her, was not to go to the police, and that I owed him a favour.'

'Which means?'

'I don't know. He threatened me, and people had died. I didn't know who Ali was then, but we all did after his speech. But in time, we got used to it and carried on, that is, until our father died, and then you start thinking. Is it us next?'

'Did Delvene think this, as well?'

'She must have,' Sam said.

'What are your plans,' Larry asked.

'There's not much to be gained from me, although Delvene might be in trouble.'

'Why now? Why tell me this when I come to the house and find you with Fiona? You two don't exactly hit it off.'

'Sam's staying here until this is resolved.'

'As long as he doesn't drink.'

'Worse than prison,' Sam joked. 'I'm to become a model citizen.'

Larry knew that in the spirit of unity, and due to unknown danger, the siblings had formed a bond. It would not last.

Chapter 13

Isaac noticed the security camera as he drove into the Alsworthy estate. If the camera was there to monitor potential troublemakers coming in, then it was fine, but if it was more than that and had been set up for high-level surveillance, then not only would it note the car, it would scan the person inside, and then check their identity.

Regardless, Isaac knew they needed to push the envelope and hoped that good would triumph and support would come from an unexpected area. But even that was uncertain. DAC Goddard was playing it cool and remained supportive. Mary Ayton had been non-committal and not mentioned their previous relationship.

Isaac discounted his concerns and drove to Gabrielle Alsworthy's house. He thought the home attractive and welcoming, but it paled compared to the stately mansion he had seen.

Gabrielle shook Isaac's hand vigorously. Wendy had seen it before, the tall black man with a London accent. The woman swooned.

'Pleased to meet you,' Isaac said. 'I understand we have seen a mutual friend.' It was his sarcastic reference to Caddick.

'I'm not sure I would regard him as a friend. I saw the man once. It's not that I overthought about it at the time, but then I got to thinking.'

'As we have. I would appreciate your thoughts on the matter.'

The three sat in the sitting room. Some of the portraits on the walls were from the main house. The two dogs sniffed at Isaac's ankles, then went to their bed in the corner and lay down. Issac's family had a dog when he was young, but it was a mongrel that he had found wandering the streets. Even so, he was impressed by the honourable Gabrielle Alsworthy, who had found friendship in a sergeant whose opinion of those born with a silver spoon in their mouth was less than favourable.

'This man that I saw.'

'Chief Superintendent Caddick,' Isaac said.

'He drove up to the main house and went in. I can't tell you why,' Gabrielle said.

'You have a theory?'

'It's timing. A man blows himself up in Whitehall, ten persons are killed, and Caddick is there and kills another man with his bare hands, and another idiot is killed by the police.'

'That's well known. Wendy says you have more to offer.'

'Not on Whitehall. However, a few weeks later, Ibrahim gets up and makes a speech, saying that he's the legitimate son of my father and an actress.'

'The aristocracy and actresses are not unknown.'

'I don't have an issue with my father and a mistress, but this was before he married my mother. Ibrahim's legitimate; he takes the title and moves me out of the main house.'

'As is his legal right.'

'I'm bitter but not totally disconsolate, but then I see your chief superintendent up at the main house. It makes me start to think, and if I think, others must also.'

'They have. Expound your theory,' Isaac said, unsure where the conversation was heading and what it would alter.

'Ibrahim is compromised. He has the chance to become an ardent Islamist with the power of the masses, but it's a perceived power. He's offered the opportunity to gain that power and a pulpit from which to preach it. It's seductive, it's violent, it's irresistible.'

'He was not known for violence before. Would the title be that important?'

'Chief Inspector, believe me, it is. The establishment might abhor him, but he's one of them, and they are a dying breed. Deals will be done; support will be given if needed, and respect will be there.'

Deadly Secrets

'And you believe that the cost of ten innocent tourists would justify what he did to achieve all this.'

'It's not justification that we're discussing here. Innocent people die for the greater good. I'm not accusing Ibrahim of wrong, only pragmatism. He might regard it with disgust but would have seen the greater good if he's passionate enough.'

'How do we discover his thoughts and whether he will open up to us?'

'By talking to him.'

'We're Homicide, investigating the murder of Robert Avers, not to solve a mysterious and implausible conspiracy that a firebrand preacher, in league with a corrupt police officer and armed with the proof that he is a lord, would agree to the deaths of innocent people.'

'How do you think the first Lord Alsworthy was accorded the title by a grateful king,' Gabrielle said.

'By foul deeds,' Wendy said.

'History records the deed, not the truth. And if I'm right, who will remember? Chief Inspector, you have not driven down here, and your sergeant hasn't spent a pleasant twenty-four hours with me, believing I know something about Robert Avers. You are after Ibrahim, and I'm willing to help.'

'How?' Isaac said.

'I've spent a lifetime around the rich and the influential. I've met prime ministers, presidents, and even the monarch. I know how this works. I know who can be trusted and who can't. I even knew Lord MacTavish. I know how influential the man was, how he worked behind the scenes.'

'Did you trust him?'

'MacTavish, not totally. But he was passionate about this country.'

'Tell us about MacTavish, and yes, I knew him. I met with the man in Scotland not long before he died. What else did you know?'

'I know what depths a person will go to. My father might not have agreed to innocent people dying, but he had led men

133

into battle. He knew that the need of the majority was sometimes at the cost of the few. Ibrahim might be fighting another battle, but it would be equally important to him. He might have wrestled with his conscience, but ultimately, he made the only decision he could, and now, you're after him.'

'Would you have made the decision that Ibrahim had?'

'Not for his cause, but if this country was under threat, I would do what my father and his father and his father would have. I would have made the only decision possible.'

'There are some that believe this country is at war.'

'I'm not making that judgement. I'm postulating a scenario, even if Commissioner Davies has adopted a tough stance against criminality.'

'Do you approve of it?'

'I do, but it won't last. Eventually, people will become weary of it, and then it will be weakened at the edges; the police officers will tire of the increased workload, the courts will tire of the convictions, and the government will want to reduce the prison population. And then Ibrahim will be there, as is his right, slowly integrating into the House of Lords and affecting change, even if minor.'

'Our interest is not to create a revolution or to change society. Our interest is to uphold the law and arrest the wrongdoers. Yours, Gabrielle, is not the same as ours.'

'It is. Either you nip it in the bud, or it will fester and become a bigger sore. You need my help.'

It was an unexpected ally, and Isaac wasn't comfortable using the woman, but he had trusted persons with less reason than hers before. He knew he had no choice but to go with his gut feeling.

'Unfortunately, nobody is willing to address this openly, and it's becoming increasingly difficult to proceed. To talk to you about this is dangerous, not only for us but for you, as well.'

'Concern yourself with what's right. I'm not important,' Gabrielle said.

'Your motive?'

'I want what is mine. I want my old life back.'

'It appears that our reasons are not compatible,' Isaac said.

'Honesty, that's what you get from me. I need to take a side; I've chosen yours. Do you want my assistance, or don't you?'

Isaac realised a decision needed to be made. MacTavish was no longer available. Was there someone else? Could they be trusted? He had to decide, but first, it was important to make a phone call. There was only one person that he felt deserved his trust.

'I've got a potential ally,' Isaac said.

On the other end of the phone conversation, DAC Goddard listened as Isaac outlined the situation, hopeful that the DAC's encryption was working on his phone.

'Mary Ayton?' Goddard asked.

'Uncertain, sitting on the fence. She's too close to Davies to be considered at this time. I've put in for a transfer. Either I take it, or I continue. And if I continue, what chance is there? Will you become the commissioner?'

'There are still two persons in my way, Webb and Jepson; I'm a non-starter, although the odds are firming in my favour.'

'Are you still operating in the shadows? Can you be trusted if this goes pear-shaped?'

'Isaac, you exceed your authority, insulting me,' Goddard said.

'This is not an official enquiry. If it was, it should be with the Counter Terrorism Command, but Caddick's got them under his control, although they may have an opinion. Maybe one of them could give support.'

'Nobody will, not yet. Careers will be dashed if people show their true colours too soon; lives might be lost. You're on your own. I suggest you choose your friends carefully.'

'I can't be certain about Gabrielle Alsworthy. She is charming and knows everyone, including MacTavish. She's also got Ibrahim Ali's phone number and easy access to the man.'

'Who could be a killer.'

'He's not the killer, but there might be people at the house who could be.'

'Who you will need to confront at some stage. Any update on Avers' murder?'

'Inspector Hill's meeting with Delvene Drayton. She's met Ali.'

'Clough?'

'He's Caddick's man.'

'Decide based on what you're told, and then we'll discuss it. In the meantime, I'll check out the situation at New Scotland Yard.'

Isaac wasn't sure if Goddard would check, but he had made a decision. He would listen to Gabrielle Alsworthy, who had learnt at her father's feet and would regard persons as disposable in a just cause, as Ali might have, as Davies certainly did. But bringing down the head of the London Met was not for chief inspectors or deputy assistant commissioners. It would need someone more powerful than two career police officers.

While Isaac was talking to DAC Goddard, Gabrielle prepared a meal.

On Isaac's return, the three sat down to eat. The conversation at the table did not mention Ali or Caddick or the murder of ten tourists but kept to the mundane: the weather, the cost of living, what the new government would do for the country, or was it all too difficult to contemplate. Isaac kept to orange juice; Wendy drank one glass of red wine; Gabrielle drank water.

In the sitting room, after the meal, the three sat. Gabrielle sat on a sofa, and Isaac and Wendy sat on chairs on either side.

Outside, a car passed by on the narrow road at the front of the house. Wendy recognised the vehicle. 'It's Clough,' she said.

'Some of them up at the house are weird.' Gabrielle said.

'Threatening?'

'They look but don't speak.'

Deadly Secrets

There was no option but to ignore Clough and the main house. 'Who do you have, Gabrielle?' Isaac asked.

Nighttime was approaching fast, and he wanted to be back in London with Jenny that night, but with Clough at the main house, he was unsure if he could leave before the other man, and when he did, he would have to make sure that he took another route back home.

'Are you willing to trust me?' Gabrielle said.

'We have no option. Who do you have? Wendy, do you want to be part of this?'

'I'm finished as a police officer, either way. I'd rather go down fighting,' Wendy replied.

'What's the problem?' Gabrielle asked.

'Age and arthritis, accentuated by nicotine poisoning.'

Isaac thought it was a good analogy for her situation and that regardless of Caddick, her time within Homicide was limited, and it might be him who would tell her when her time was up. Until then, he would do what he could to keep her employed.

Using a person of unknown character and truthfulness was a risk he was prepared to take, knowing that this woman had met and knew those who wielded power in the country. Persons who would throw you to the wind if it served their greater purpose.

How much Davies knew was unknown, and whether he had authorised Caddick's actions. There would be no further debate whether Clough was involved in wrongdoing. He could not be trusted, but keeping him from becoming suspicious of Homicide would be impossible.

There needed to be a frontal assault, no more lurking in the shadows, but as a chief inspector, he did not have the clout or the ability to move forward, and at the first instance, he would be sidelined, transferred, or dead. The cost was too high, but he could not consider abandoning what he knew or believed.

'I've got someone you can talk to,' Gabrielle said. 'Lord Moxon.'

'The prime minister, when MacTavish was chief whip. He would have known about his deputy and Marjorie Frobisher.'

'It's unlikely.'

'Why?'

'Deniability. You can't lie if you don't know. The chief whip's function is to deal with such issues, provide a distance from the PM, and any implication of involvement. To cover the indiscretions of party members, to get them to resign if that's the only option, to ensure they're present in the chamber when there is an important vote.'

'We know of MacTavish's deviousness. We know that he had knowledge and would have agreed with the murder of one person. Are you certain about Moxon?'

'He's your only option. No one else can help. Are we in agreement with what happened, the chain of events?' Gabrielle asked.

'Can you be trusted? After all, you know how the system works. Your father was part of the establishment, and so were your forefathers, and if Ibrahim Ali's out of the way, you have plenty to gain. And if we fail, you will not antagonise your half-brother.'

'DCI Cook, do you hold onto antiquated rules of right and wrong? Do you believe those in power believe that man is inherently good?'

'It's a good Christian value.'

'This is not Christianity; the meek shall inherit the earth. This is war, and you're on the frontline. Either you shoot first, or you're dead. And will I play the game? Better than you. And if that means throwing you to the wolves, I will. I've everything to lose; Lord Moxon doesn't. Goddard, can you trust him?'

'I believe so.'

'Belief is not good enough. You need allies, powerful allies. You can't go this alone, and if I wasn't intent on reclaiming what is rightfully mine, we wouldn't be here discussing what to do. Anyone else?'

'Possibly someone close to Davies, but she's still sitting on the fence.'

'Isn't everyone. Why this crusade of yours?'

'Because it's right. Murders have been committed to protect persons in high office in the Met.'

'And in government. My father, for instance, and MacTavish knew it. He was right to allow the murder of Marjorie's lover and to ensure she died.'

'If Ibrahim Ali had known back then, ten tourists might not have died.'

'An assumption based on weak logic. People die, people live. That's how life is. The situation is now, and if Moxon knew, although I believe he would not, he's the only person with the necessary ability to assist.'

'Will he help?'

'I've already phoned him while you were outside. He expects you at four this afternoon. Go alone. Lord Moxon will have security close by. Phone before you arrive. I'll give you the number, and the main gate will open.'

'You're very thorough,' Isaac said.

'I'm an Alsworthy. We never give in without a fight. It's up to you, Detective Chief Inspector Cook, to decide whether you're a foot soldier or a general.'

Chapter 14

Lord Moxon lived well, but not as well as Ibrahim Ali. The main gate at Moxon's that swung open as Isaac approached did not lead to a long tree-lined driveway leading up to a Georgian mansion but to a two-storey red brick home of indifferent architecture.

There was no butler to answer the door; instead, Lord Moxon opened it himself.

Isaac shook the hand proffered and entered. It was the first time he had met MacTavish's prime minister, although he had met others.

Sprightly for his age and in his eighties, Isaac walked behind the man, up one flight of stairs and into a room at the end of a corridor.' My office,' Moxon said. 'I've spoken to Gabrielle, and she tells me we must talk.'

'If I can be honest…'

'You must be honest, Chief Inspector. You're not sure you can trust me, is that it?'

'I'm not sure I can trust Gabrielle Alsworthy, although I did place my trust in Angus MacTavish, and he abused it.'

'Gabrielle said you were idealistic.'

'I am, although I am determined to follow through on this.'

'A one-man retribution, even well-intentioned, will not get you far. You knew what had happened with those close to Marjorie Frobisher. Do you believe the same will not happen again?'

'I believe that it could be worse.'

'Last time, we were saving the government from embarrassment, but now, we are talking about an escalation in terrorist-related crimes, and how far Caddick will go?'

'How do you know about Caddick?' Isaac asked.

'Who do you think MacTavish confided in until his death?'

'You?'

'Do you still believe that people are inherently good and that evil is learnt?'

'It's a good belief to have.'

'It's foolish and dangerous. Now, we are not talking political, but criminal and violent. The situation has changed.'

'I'm here with you only after I met with Gabrielle,' Isaac said. He was tired of Moxon's posturing and the man's attempt to take control of the meeting rather than be an equal member.

'Gabrielle has my confidence, although her reason is not altruistic but self-interest,' Moxon replied.

'Lord MacTavish had a solution.'

'Did he? The situation is fluid. Commissioner Davies has become a law unto himself. And if Ibrahim Ali dies or lives, will there be more terrorist incidents? Will Davies' firm hand save the day? Will it become impossible to control him?'

'Are you saying he would be more willing to subvert the law to achieve his aims?'

'We can't be sure. We need to know whether he gave the green light. We deal with one person at a time or one issue.'

'My position in this?' Isaac asked.

'To bring down Davies.'

'What does Ibrahim Ali want? And what will he do to achieve it?' Isaac said.

'He will throw in his hand with Caddick and Davies if that suits his purpose.'

'No different to us?'

'Ours is the more honourable.'

'He's got faith on his side. What do we have?'

'Are you willing to take the next step?'

'Which is?'

'To bait the beast.'

'How?'

Isaac realised it had gone from theorising to skirting around the periphery and now to direct confrontation with the beast, to use Moxon's analogy. He was unsure what to think or do. To have a suspicion with no evidence other than dead persons and a new lord was not provable, and if it was generally known, the majority would think it fanciful.

How could it be explained or believed that the commissioner of the London Metropolitan Police was involved in crime and that he had approved a terrorist attack?

'By organising a meeting of the minds, to bring in the best people we can trust,' Moxon said.

'Who are they?'

'You are one. Gabrielle Alsworthy is another. DAC Goddard, does he have your trust? Anyone else you are willing to consider?'

'Four is enough for now,' Isaac said. 'We can bring in others later. Although, would you regard a sergeant as a member of this group?'

'If you trust her.'

'I do. Gabrielle will also vouch for her.'

***

Wendy had remained with Gabrielle, determined to watch the movements at the main house. To see if she could glimmer any idea as to the reason why Sergeant Clough was there.

Gabrielle thought it was a wasted effort and that she had a better idea. She left her house and walked to the main house. Before she had knocked on the door at the front of the house, it swung open. A man dressed in Arab clothing bowed to her, accorded her full respect, and invited her to sit in a room to the left of the expansive entry hall.

She didn't know what she was doing and why she was there. She felt fear, although Ibrahim Ali had never threatened her, nor had his guards. The women in the house were nowhere to be seen, and it was only outside that she had ever seen them, and apart from one of them, the others had never uttered a word in her presence.

A young man in his early twenties entered and placed a tray before her. 'The master will be with you soon,' he said. He was dressed as an English butler. Gabrielle wondered if Ali's newfound status and wealth had weakened the man's resolve. She drank the tea, ate the savouries, and waited. After what seemed an extraordinarily long time, Lord Alsworthy entered. He was not dressed in traditional flowing robes, like a latter-day Lawrence of Arabia, which had become Ali's garb since his transformation from impoverished zealot to English aristocracy. Instead, he was dressed in a navy suit of the finest cut.

'Sister, it is good to see you.' Ali said.

'And you, Ibrahim. Is life treating you well?'

'It is.'

Ali sat down and rang a small bell to one side of him. The butler reappeared with more tea and savouries.

'Tiffin, which I have discovered refers to a light tea-time meal. Remarkably, an English tradition that has come from Asia when the British Raj subjugated the peoples of India,' Ali continued.

'But you are now a Raj, or has that escaped you?'

'It has not. Outside influences can be allowed if they do not conflict. Gabrielle, you must not allow yourself to believe that I have changed. I grew up in Nottingham, where I was the adopted child of good people, Martin and Beverley Marshall. I know the class structure and what you, your father, and those in the House of Lords were responsible for. Their elitism, the old boys club, and the desire to keep the peasants down. I will not only work for my religion but for all people in this country who have been treated as serfs.'

'Does that mean the overthrow of democracy, the imposition of your will?'

'Not the overthrow, but reform.'

'Why are you telling me this?' Gabrielle asked.

'I tell you because you are my sister and can do nothing, and your intent to alter the status quo will be in vain.'

'Are you suggesting that I am?'

'Sister, I do not blame you for this, but I should warn you that it will come to nothing. Your current accommodation is because of who you are, not what you were, and I would caution you that any attempt to involve yourselves in my plans or what I intend to do will result in unforeseen consequences.'

'I've done nothing,' Gabrielle said.

'I don't think you have, but you see what has happened. My biological mother was murdered to protect the secret of my birth. What else might I discover if I look further?'

'Are you?' Gabrielle felt a chill, and although the words were softly spoken, they came from a dark place.

'Am I looking? Yes. I have checked on this family's history. It is enlightening that the Alsworthys, regarding what they had done in the past, would be revered, whereas I am scorned. I know what they think of me in Westminster, what the current government does, but they will learn to fear, and if they don't, they will learn to respect.'

'Is that your faith or the DNA that courses through you? You are an Alsworthy; the key to the golden chest is yours. Why do you want more?'

'Our father gave up the title to become a member of parliament. He saw the advantage of power.'

'Which you have now, but you want more.'

'What is the House of Lords but a rubber stamp for the government. Old men debate, believing that what they say is important and their titles mean something. It's in the House of Commons where the power lies. Where a man is a man, and he can affect change. The country is ready for me; I am ready for it.'

'The democratic process will not be subverted that easily,' Gabrielle said.

'Then it will be rendered impotent. The power is with the people. They need a leader. I am that leader, the cast-off child of a lord and an actress brought up in a loving middle-class household by good people, and then I embraced the one true religion, and I intend to take the message to the people of this country.'

'Is that why you are wearing a suit?'

'It is. The first day of my political campaign. The reason that I engaged the support of the police is to provide security.'

Gabrielle thought that might be a response to why Sergeant Clough was at the house. But if that was the case, why Clough, and with whose authority was he providing protection. The London Met had provisions for protecting persons of importance, and there were private security firms that would be adequate. Ibrahim Ali, the Lord Alsworthy, would not be deemed at risk from unwarranted violence and protest, and most people in the country, if they thought about him at all, would not have regarded him as contentious.

'I need to know how long I've got in the house you've given me?' Gabrielle asked. It was the question that she had thought suitable to justify her visiting her half-brother, but now, after he had outlined his vision for the future, it seemed of little importance.

'For as long as you like, but Gabrielle, please know this, I will not take kindly to you becoming involved in my business, nor will you watch who comes to the house. My brotherly love is conditional; it is finite, and my patience with you is running out. We are both the children of our father, but I have the added advantage that I am also the child of Marjorie Frobisher, a determined woman who did not allow anyone to get in her way,' Ali said.

***

Larry had been willing to work with Clough, but now, after being seen at Lord Alsworthy's mansion, the man was again sidelined. That one act was enough to demand a visit by Isaac to Caddick's office on the top floor of Challis Street Police Station.

'Sit down, Chief Inspector,' Chief Superintendent Caddick said.

Isaac looked around the office, which he had visited many times when DAC Goddard was the chief superintendent, and Caddick was an irritant. The office had changed, and the bookshelf where Goddard had kept his books and displayed his medals was gone. In its place was a bare wall. Goddard's leather chair remained, although Caddick was a minimalist, with little paperwork on his desk.

In the outer office, Sandra Trent beavered away. Isaac had seen the glances between her and Caddick, indicating that their relationship was more than professional.

Isaac considered the situation. Caddick was sleeping with Linda Harris, who worked for MI5. He was also involved with Sandra Trent. There was apparently a wife in the north of the country, although Caddick never mentioned her, and nobody asked or was interested. Caddick was the worst kind of police officer, and Isaac knew that the antagonism and dislike of the two men for each other were cutting, as a knife is through butter.

'Sergeant Clough believes that you are unwilling to work with him,' Caddick said, who had told Isaac to take a seat this time. On his previous audience, Isaac had remained standing.

'Inspector Hill regards him a skilled police officer, an asset to the department.'

'And you?'

'It takes time to integrate. Personalities need to adjust.'

'Which means?'

'Clough is blunt in his manner. Besides, we are too busy to spend time getting to know someone. We're not a social club. Clough did find the gun at the hotel where Sam Avers was staying. That was appreciated.'

'And you have not arrested Avers. Why?'

'He didn't kill the man. He was checked at the murder scene.'

'Sergeant Clough believes that Sam Avers is involved.'

Theories abounded, and previously, Issac, when he had joined the London Met, would have believed them to be conspiratorial, absurd, and just plain stupid. But now, sitting across from the chief superintendent and increasingly certain that the man had been involved in a heinous crime, Isaac found it hard to believe Caddick was that foolish. But Challis Street was not the place to accuse the man, to confront Clough, or accuse Sandra Trent, who might be innocent. Time was needed; time he did not have.

The grapevine at New Scotland Yard, which had been remarkably quiet for several months, was re-energising, and the topic of interest: Commissioner Alwyn Davies.

Isaac had made a few discrete enquiries and met with DCI Farley Grainger. The men went back a long way to the police academy, where Isaac had seduced more than his fair share, and Grainger had got drunk most nights. The men were to meet again. Isaac might raise some concerns, but he would not trust him. And even Mary Ayton had been a risk, but there had been no comebacks from their conversation.

Before Grainger, there was another person who was anxious to meet. 'Not for long,' she said.

Isaac wasn't pleased to see her, as Linda Harris always unnerved him, as though he was unfaithful to Jenny when he wasn't. He thought what harm was there in a takeaway coffee, sitting on a park bench.

'It's good to see you,' Linda said. 'I've broken up with Seth Caddick.'

'I thought the relationship was more than romantic,' Isaac replied. He intended to remain curt with the woman and not to give into a natural desire that could not be. He had thought there was a future with her once, but then she had killed a man and disappeared.

'No more can be gleaned from the man, and it had become dangerous for me to remain in his orbit.'

147

'Orbit? What does that mean? It seems an expansive term for Caddick, a man who justifies a small hole in the ground, not a planetary reference.'

'Orbit is the correct term. Seth's heavily involved. You have your suspicions, and ours are the same. We have been working to the same end.'

Isaac wanted to believe her but could not. 'Linda, how can I trust you? How many times have you lied to me?' he said.

'I've never lied, only failed to tell you the truth. There is a subtle difference.'

'Is there?'

'What I am telling you now is important. Believe it or not, Davies is coming under pressure. The man has a legion of distractors who disagree with his authoritarian, bullying style.'

'He can't be touched yet.'

'And we won't kill him. We've got enough martyrs, and killing a police commissioner will raise the hackles of the police, and it could lead to an orchestrated campaign to round up every criminal in the city, and where would that lead to?'

'To peace and harmony,' Isaac replied.

'To anarchy, and you know it. The issue is not when to remove him but how? He needs to be discredited.'

'And I'm to be the vessel that brings down the man? Why not others more prominent?'

'You're expendable, the same as I am. Those pulling the strings will not show their faces until it is safe for them to do so.'

'Like a general in a battle, overlooking the fighting below, only mingling with the troops when it's time to accept the surrender and to claim victory.'

'Except our generals will not be on a hill or atop a horse but in a stuffy office or parliament. We are the cannon fodder, soon to rise through the ranks if we get this right,' Linda said.

'Or dead,' Isaac replied. 'We could die in the battle, although the ultimate victory will be claimed by others. Why separate from Caddick if he's involved?'

Deadly Secrets

'I must stand back and observe, to strategise, to keep our masters informed, our people secure, and to stop the next attack.'

'Is there to be another?'

'It is inevitable. When and how, I don't know, but Caddick might. I have done what I can with the man. He's reprehensible, only interested in himself and his master. It was his idea, Whitehall.'

'Can you prove it?'

'We have an ally so deep that he cannot show himself or give us the proof.'

'Even if it will stop a further incident?'

'Even. Ibrahim Ali has found what can be done with a title and fear. He intends to use both.'

'Is any of this provable?'

'Not yet.'

'Then why not the Counter Terrorism Command?'

'Who are they? It only needs one person to talk.'

'I could say no,' Isaac said.

'You won't. Why do you think you've been chosen?'

'Why don't you use your people?'

'My people are not employed in the Met. You are. You are our eyes and ears.'

'And scapegoat if this goes wrong.'

'Hero, if it doesn't.'

'An unsung hero,' Isaac replied.

'Those who remain will know who you are. You do this for your country, for the London Metropolitan Police. You will not refuse.'

'I won't.'

'I was sorry that I left you the last time, you know that,' Linda said as she touched him on the arm. He wanted to touch her back but desisted. Sometimes, life gets in the way, and whereas she represented excitement and allure, she also represented trouble and death. He had made his choice. He would work with her, even if he did not trust her.

'We make our decisions, and sometimes others do it for us. It is too late, Linda, to change the past,' Isaac said.

They parted, with Linda walking off in one direction and he walking in another.

Chapter 15

Isaac had always considered Farley Grainger, a good police officer, but this time he found him churlish. The easy conversation, the gentle ribbing of the other, that one was putting on weight, the hair was starting to thin, and age was getting to us, was gone.

'Rumours, there's always rumours,' Grainger said in the confines of his office at New Scotland Yard. 'This place thrives on them, and Davies has done a good job in the last three months.'

Isaac had to agree that Davies had tempered the excesses of his previous authoritarian drive, and they were less confrontational. By and large, the populace was comfortable with them. Even Jenny had commented that London was not as bad as it was, and Isaac had paused his transfer request.

Isaac persisted with the strained conversation for twenty minutes before citing that he had another appointment.

As Isaac left, Grainger drew Isaac towards him. 'Something is going on. I don't know what it is, and I would advise you to tread carefully.'

'Are you still there?' Isaac whispered.

'Don't trust anybody; that's my advice,' Grainger said.

***

Isaac slept little that night; his mind was in turmoil, aware that the threat to him could threaten his wife and their young family. He mentally debated whether he should continue or prostrate himself at the feet of Caddick.

The answer was obvious, but the reality was not. He was a good man dedicated to good causes and good people. He couldn't be something he wasn't, and before, his conflict with the commissioner had been about law enforcement, but now it was about death, and Linda pulling back from Caddick was an indicator that it was to become violent, and people would die. Some of those people would be good, some would be bad, and some would be members of the London Metropolitan Police.

Sensing that her husband was troubled, Jenny tried to console him but realised she could not, other than to offer her support and give him her total confidence that things would work out for the best.

Isaac would have liked to respond to her support, but instead, he turned over in the bed and pretended to go to sleep.

In the morning, Jenny was up first. On the table was his breakfast. Most days, with children to look after, she would remain in bed for as long as she could, but not today.

'Thanks,' he said as he kissed her goodbye.

'It will be safe, won't it?' she asked.

'Of course. Nothing to worry about,' Isaac replied. Neither was convinced by his reply.

In the office, Isaac busied himself with a report, the third that week. Bureaucracy and endless reports were starting to irritate, and if not sent on time, a visit by Caddick's PA to remind, cajole, and say if it was not sent in the next hour, she would have to inform their chief superintendent, and you know what he will say. Issac did, but the two men's relationship would not last much longer. One would succeed, and the other would fail. But Isaac wasn't sure which he would be, and the team Moxon was forming had yet to meet.

Isaac called Larry into the office. 'Keep Clough occupied. Go and see Delvene Drayton, pressure her about what she was doing in Spain. She met Ibrahim Ali but never told us; there may be nothing to it. Don't take Clough. What can you give him to do?'

'A list of those at the party. He can follow through and interview those that he can find.'

'Even if he planted the gun,' Isaac said. 'You've considered the possibility?'

'I have, but it's hard to believe he would be that stupid,' Larry replied.

'Is it? What do we know of what is happening between that trio of reprobates?'

'Tweedledum, Tweedledee, and their friend?'

'I'll remember that. Davies, Caddick, and Clough. It's got a nice ring to it, although they were harmless characters in fiction. I don't regard our three as harmless.'

Isaac left the office with Wendy. He would tell her on the way that she was to become involved in something of great significance.

***

Larry arrived at Delvene Drayton's house in Whitechapel at ten minutes to ten in the morning. He had come alone, although before leaving the office, he had spoken to Clough and told the man that in the interests of efficiency, they would work separately for the next few days and for the sergeant to lock down who had placed the gun on Sam Avers.

Clough had thrown up brickbats that it was a pointless exercise, and some of the men invited to Sam's hotel room had brought other men and women, and the escorts had come through an agency, and they almost certainly used false names. Even so, Larry was firm. He wanted Clough out of the way. Larry knew his DCI was up to something but didn't want him involved. He had known his DCI for enough years not to take it personally, and taking Wendy Gladstone meant she knew. Why interested him, but he would not ask, and that, in time, he would find out what it was about.

Delvene's house was a small, neat, and tidy terrace in what was once working-class grime and grit but was now upwardly mobile junior executives and their families, apart from Delvene, whose income depended on the generosity of the men she slept with. He doubted if her neighbours would be concerned.

There was stillness in the house, although he could hear a television inside. Ironically, it was the soap in which Marjorie Frobisher acted. Around the back of the house, accessed via a narrow alleyway between two of the terraces, he found Delvene's back door ajar.

Reluctant to enter, he phoned emergency services and told them to get to the address with an ambulance. He then phoned Challis Street and organised four uniforms to get down to Whitechapel.

His approach was contrary to procedure, and he should have checked before calling out for people to come, but experience had told him when to react, which was one of those times.

He removed shoe protectors and nitrile gloves from his jacket pocket and put them on. He pushed the door and entered the kitchen. In the sink, there were dirty dishes. In the oven, the burnt remains of a cake. Thankfully, the oven had timed out. He walked through the hallway, checking the rooms to one side before ascending the narrow staircase. The more he entered the house, the stronger the smell.

In the bathroom, he found the reason. In the bath was Delvene Drayton's body. She was half undressed as though she was preparing to take a bath, which someone had ensured would be her last.

Larry could see that the woman had been held under and drowned, and judging by the smell and the putrid water, she had been dead for two to three days.

He phoned emergency services and Homicide. Five minutes later, he heard the ambulance arriving. He left the house and walked out to it. 'Too late, I'm afraid,' he said to the medic. 'It's a crime scene. The body cannot be removed until the crime scene investigators give permission.'

Seven minutes later, a police car from Challis Street arrived. They secured the area, established the crime scene, and prepared to deal with the inevitable questions from neighbours and those who always surfaced when there was a murder.

Deadly Secrets

The crime scene investigators took twenty-three minutes to send an advance team and another hour for the remaining team to arrive. Their response time was acceptable, as the body was not going anywhere in a hurry.

There was one other responsibility for Larry, a responsibility that Wendy was better at; to tell the next of kin.

The woman's death raised questions as to why, and even though she had been adamant that she had not planted the gun in Sam Avers' bag, it now had to be considered a possibility.

Sergeant Clough arrived at the house soon after the CSIs, and even though the man was suspect, there was work to do, interviewing people in the street, coordinating with the CSIs, and ensuring all procedures were followed. Even if he was Caddick's man, a confidante of Ibrahim Ali, and a possible murderer of the dead woman, he would not be able to shirk his duty at a murder scene.

Before he left the scene, Larry received a preliminary report from the lead crime scene investigator. 'Whoever the murderer was, they were careful to ensure no fingerprints, and there is little evidence of their presence. Also, the woman appears not to have struggled, although that might be due to shock at an unknown person entering the bathroom.'

'Which she might not have heard,' Larry said.

'If the water was running, and the murderer was stealthy, then no.'

'Male or female?'

'It's too early to tell. We believe the person had removed their shoes and walked through the house in socks. The stairs don't appear to creak, further lending weight to the argument that she had not heard the person.'

'And then, in the bathroom, half-undressed and in panic, easy enough to grab her and put in the bath and hold her head underwater.'

'We might find more, but it won't benefit you. We'll also need to get the fingerprints of others that might have come into this house.'

155

Larry left the CSI and Clough at the house and drove two miles to where Delvene's former husband and their children lived. He found the man at home and gave him the sad news. There was no other way to sugarcoat the death of a loved one other than to show his warrant card and to get the person to sit down or to take it standing up and tell them directly. Larry had done it many times, and it never got any easier.

'Leave it with me,' Jacob Drayton said. 'I will tell our children. Murder, is that it?'

'It is,' Larry replied.

'I could ask why, but you know what Delvene did.'

'We do. We have interviewed her about the murder of Robert Avers. Delvene was Fiona Avers' close friend when they were younger and a friend of Sam Avers.'

'I know them both. A long time ago. Sam was wild, and Fiona was a tart.'

'Sam Avers is still wild, Fiona is not. In fact, she has had a major transformation. Anything about Robert Avers we should know?'

'None. If you'll excuse me, I need to tell our children. When can we see Delvene?'

'You can see her within the next day or two to identify her. The children will not be allowed at this time.'

'We were close, all of us, but Delvene was Delvene. She couldn't help herself, and now it's got her killed.'

'We're uncertain that escorting is the reason. We will interview you at some stage,' Larry said.

***

Wendy, briefed by Isaac on the drive to meet with Lord Moxon and Gabrielle Alsworthy, was grateful for the trust placed in her and a little nervous at meeting the man who had once been the prime minister. Although, as usual, Wendy, with her Yorkshire accent and humble upbringing, hit it off with the man, as she had with Gabrielle.

'Let us consider the situation,' Moxon said. The four were seated in Lord Moxon's office. On one wall were photos of him with world leaders and celebrities he had met, including one of Marjorie Frobisher. Isaac thought the photo ironic, considering the chain of events she and Gabrielle's father had set in place.

'A terrorist act leads to Ibrahim Ali becoming Lord Alsworthy and Commissioner Davies cementing his position.' Isaac laid out his concerns and what he saw as the chain of events. 'The concern is that these are interrelated, which is now further affirmed by Chief Superintendent Seth Caddick's visit to the Alsworthy ancestral home. And, Sergeant Clough is brought into Homicide by Caddick to replace Sergeant Gladstone, on the pretence that she was not up to standard due to ill health.'

'The poor health is correct,' Wendy said.

'It might be,' Moxon continued, 'but summary removal from the department may not be conducive to a well-run police service. However, we know Commissioner Davies has a habit of such behaviour.'

'Caddick and Clough's visit to the Alsworthy mansion reinforces our belief that it was not policing, but collusion, and intended to ensure Commissioner Davies could not be unseated,' Isaac said.

'And it worked. So much so, the man is invincible, and nobody will go against him.'

'Not openly.'

'Precisely. Before continuing, it must be clear that what we intend comes with a certain risk. For us to investigate without due authority, which will not come at this point, may place us in a difficult position.'

'Or dead,' Wendy said.

Moxon looked over at Gabrielle. 'Your interest is personal. Are you willing to accept that there might be violence and that persons, including us, might be subject to it and possibly die? Is the good name of the Alsworthys that important?'

'An Alsworthy had fought and died in every major battle and war since the sixteenth century. This is my war, and I will fight and die if I must,' Gabrielle said.

'If Ibrahim Ali lives, regardless of whether he is guilty of a crime, he remains the Lord Alsworthy,' Isaac said. 'Are you prepared for that contingency?'

'I am. What do you want me to do?'

'That is the question that needs to be answered here today. We don't know, although we all have a few ideas.'

Isaac wasn't sure that the group did. He had been conducting a clandestine investigation utilising Larry Hill and Wendy Gladstone, and so far, they had little to go with other than indicators of wrongdoing, which could be regarded as consequential if he had not known Caddick for a long time.

'The most important item is to find out how Ali came to be told of his birthright,' Isaac said. 'Lord Moxon, I believe you can answer that question.'

'Unfortunately, I can't. I knew Alsworthy had a problem, as he was my deputy, but MacTavish dealt with it.'

'You didn't know?' Gabrielle asked.

'I didn't want to know. That was why we had MacTavish. All I knew was when MacTavish told me the matter had been resolved. Ibrahim Ali's statement as the legitimate child of Marjorie and Alsworthy came as a shock.'

'Marjorie?' Wendy queried.

'I knew her and met her at a few functions.'

'Which means she would have met Alsworthy at those functions.'

'From what I can remember, they spoke to each other, but no more than that. Easier for her than Gabrielle's father.'

'Why?' Gabrielle asked.

'Your father was a good friend of mine. He believed in this country and me but was useless at poker. You could read his hand by the expression on his face, but with Marjorie, although my memory of the events dims, he showed nothing.'

'Lord Moxon, we need to know if Ali's file was hacked or if it was given.' Isaac said.

'Isn't the more pertinent question, who would have known about it?' Moxon replied. 'Did Robert Avers?'

'He knew of the child but not the name. His and Marjorie's children did not know.'

'Except, as with everything related to this, nobody can be certain of anything. Is there anything that we are certain of?'

'Ten people died in Whitehall, and Davies is invincible.'

'And I'm out of my house,' Gabrielle said.

Isaac doubted if the woman's commitment was as solid as it should be, as double-crossing the group could lead to a better deal from Ali. Moxon trusted her, and for now, Isaac would accept the man's estimation. Moxon was ageing, probably not as sharp as he had been when younger. Would he have the fight or the need to see it through to completion, and had he read Gabrielle Alsworthy correctly?

'There is one person who knows the answer,' Moxon said. 'Someone you know only too well.'

'How do you know about her?' Isaac asked. 'And why would we trust her? She killed one of Marjorie's lovers.'

'Politics is dirty, and so is life. MacTavish would have said one died to protect the many, but he was wrong back then. We are right now, and if people are to die, we must make sure it's them and not us.'

'You could kill Davies. Linda could do that for you. She could get close enough.' Isaac realised he was bitter about the woman. It was an emotion he didn't like and did him no credit.

'I have obtained some of Lord MacTavish's papers,' Moxon said. 'They make for interesting reading. There is a file on you, Chief Inspector. From what I see here today, MacTavish's summation of you is telling and accurate: idealistic, single-minded, honest, decent, and a man to trust. Young and green, wet behind the ears, and will not understand that certain actions sometimes need to be taken, contrary to good governance and the law. Hopefully, he will broaden his thought processes in time. He can be trusted, even when he is not in agreement.'

'Accurate,' Isaac said. 'What does it say about DAC Goddard?'

'Competent, aggressively ambitious, surrounds himself with the best persons, and supports them without reservation. His only weakness is DCI Isaac Cook, an exemplary police officer whose naivety and morality make him rigid in his actions. On more than one occasion, he has covered Cook's involvement with various women, who were proven to be criminals.'

'Accurate.'

'There is another. You need to hear it: Linda Harris, an alias. Female, blonde, attractive. Seductress, assassin. Handle with care, but has a vulnerability.'

'Is that it?'

'There is more: She has formed an emotional attachment to DCI Cook. It has clouded her ability. She did not complete her assignment before she had been taken off the case and transferred overseas.'

'What was that assignment?'

'Marjorie Frobisher was weakening in her resolve to keep quiet about her son.'

'She was to kill the woman?'

'She was to kill both of you. It appears your charm saved your life, Chief Inspector.'

Isaac sat stunned, realising that if he had spent that last night with Linda, he might be dead. It felt like a kick to the stomach to hear that his life had hung in the balance and that, in the end, Linda had refused to follow orders.'

'How did Lord MacTavish know this?' Wendy asked.

'Marjorie confided in him that she was tired of the lie. She had known him for a long time, and she felt him to be a man she could trust, which was correct, except the secret was too important to reveal. Lord MacTavish signed off on you and Marjorie's death.'

'But why did I remain alive after Linda Harris refused?' Isaac asked.

'MacTavish cancelled the kill order against you. Marjorie's was paused, but then it was reinstated with her impending removal from the soap opera and increasing drunkenness.'

'Did Gabrielle's father know?'

'His views would not have been considered. MacTavish would not have asked him.'

'If he had,' Gabrielle said,' he would have agreed. My father had little time for dead emotion and even less time for the unwanted offspring of a childish love affair.'

'He married Marjorie,' Wendy said.

'An act of chivalry on his part, nothing more. We Alsworthys have our moments of decency, but for much of the time, we are total bastards.'

'As you are now, Gabrielle,' Moxon said.

'I am, and proud of it. Whatever needs to be done, I will do it.'

'Ibrahim Ali is an Alsworthy,' Wendy said. 'He has the same father as Gabrielle. He will do whatever is necessary.'

'There are ten tourists to prove it,' Isaac said. 'There could be more.'

'There won't,' Gabrielle said. 'If you think that I would be willing to allow him to sully the family name anymore, then you have not heard what I've just said.'

'You would kill him?'

'I would.'

'What you are suggesting,' Moxon said, 'is to subvert the law and for us to mete out justice?'

'Don't expect me to wait around indefinitely.'

'Linda Harris is not the only woman who kills,' Isaac said.

'She did because she had been told to; I will do it with pleasure.'

'The law won't protect you.'

'The truth will ensure that the Alsworthys continue, even without me. That will be my legacy, enough to remove us from the slur of that upstart, my half-brother.'

'We need to make the connection to Caddick,' Isaac said.

'Assume the connection exists,' Moxon said.

'How anyone knew that it existed is the question. The only persons alive were those in Homicide, Marjorie, MacTavish, Alsworthy, and you.'

'I didn't know,' Moxon said.

'MacTavish?'

'But why let Caddick know?'

'Gabrielle's father would not have told anyone.'

'My father would have wanted it silenced. Why did it take so long to kill her?' Gabrielle asked.

'We had her in a safe house for a while,' Wendy said. 'But she was unwilling to be confined, away from her adoring public. We couldn't hold her, and then she was everywhere, getting drunk on more than one occasion, and, yes, there was every reason to believe that she would start talking. We knew about a senior government member and the child but not the name. We deduced who the government member was later when he was referred to as the former lord.'

'Then Marjorie revealed it before she died. She must have told Robert Avers,' Isaac said. 'There can't be anyone else.'

'There can,' Wendy said. 'Fiona.'

'But why her? The two women hated each other.'

'Did they? Marjorie had the talent and beauty; Fiona did not, but they had a bond. Both were ambitious, but Fiona had no chance, and then, not long after her mother dies, Fiona transforms, cosmetic surgery to change her appearance, elocution, and deportment lessons to deal with her foul mouth and sloppy dress.'

'A great secret that she could have used it to her advantage. Her father would have given her anything, but how much did the change in Fiona cost? Would the father have paid, or would he understand? He loved his daughter the way she was; he would not have wanted her to change.'

'Are you saying she used that knowledge to extort money from someone?'

'I think I am. Would Lord Alsworthy have paid her?'

'My father had gone to great lengths to protect the secret, including murder. There is only one person from whom Fiona could have gotten money to keep her mouth shut.'

"Your mother,' Wendy said.

'My mother accepted my father's indiscretions if they did not become scandals. And what could be a bigger scandal than Marjorie Frobisher and Ibrahim Ali? It must be my mother; nothing else makes sense.'

'It still doesn't explain how Caddick came to know,' Moxon said.

'One step at a time,' Isaac said. 'Once we have Fiona's story, we will know how Caddick came to know. I suggest, Lord Moxon, that unless we have more to discuss, we end this meeting and meet in two days, the next time online.'

'I agree,' Moxon said.

'My mother is the reason for our greatest disgrace,' Gabrielle said. 'I can't say I'm surprised, the family she came from.'

Chapter 16

Since arriving at Delvene Drayton's house on the day her body had been discovered, Clough had organised four juniors to door knock, coordinated with the crime scene investigators, and found out from the next-door neighbour that Delvene was a good person, and a friend, apart from the stray men who turned up on her doorstep at odd hours.

The reason for the stray men was not given, but Clough realised that the woman had known but preferred not to say.

Larry took Delvene's former husband to the mortuary to identify Delvene. He had been accompanied by their eldest daughter, who was in her teens. She had been insistent and had remained calm throughout the ordeal. The pair, father and daughter, left with their arms wrapped around each other.

Larry returned to Delvene's house. It was the second day, and the CSIs had vacated the place. Outside the front door, a lone constable stood. Larry gave him the coffee he had bought for him. The constable was thankful, as standing outside a murder scene, rain, hail, or shine, was a daunting task, not made easier by persons shouting over the garden fence as to what was going on.

Larry contacted Isaac and told him that Clough was asking questions, more than he should, as to what their DCI was up to.

'It's about to hit the fan,' Isaac had replied.

'What it is, I still don't know. It's about time you levelled with me?'

'Not for now.' Isaac wanted to bring his inspector into his confidence, but the groundwork hadn't been completed, allies and foes remained fluid, and there would be a battle royale. There would be winners and losers, dead persons, heroes, and villains, and his inspector's ignorance of the details would give him some protection.

Larry wasn't happy to be kept in the dark but trusted his DCI. However, keeping Clough at bay was not that easy. Clough was in his late forties, five years older than Larry, and clearly more knowledgeable.

The following day, Larry and Clough met with Delvene's former husband. The man was in better humour than the day before. 'Judy's gone to school,' he said. 'No point for her to mope around here.'

Larry understood the sentiment.

'We need to understand your relationship with Delvene,' Clough said.

Larry regarded Clough suspiciously, masquerading as a humble sergeant when he was clearly something more. He only hoped that his DCI knew what he was doing. Larry felt a sense of foreboding.

Wendy's health had been a concern for a long time, as had his alcoholism. Yet, both remained in Homicide. One was working with their DCI, and another was babysitting a man who might be party to the terrorist attack in Whitehall and reporting back to Caddick, who would be updating Davies.

Babysitter or not, Larry would do his duty. Two murders, almost certainly interrelated, to solve. If Clough could assist, it would be conditional on the man having Homicide's trust. This proved difficult as the man started to badger the former husband.

'Did you know Delvene was a whore?' Clough asked.

'I knew that she met with men.'

'That's not an answer. She sold herself, a trollop, a common prostitute.'

The man stayed calm as the assault continued. 'She had sex with men for money. That is correct. However, Sergeant, I can't see that this is relevant.'

Larry disagreed with the man, but Clough became abrasive and angry, and his interrogation became flawed.

'Delvene was with Sam Avers at his hotel,' Larry said to stop Clough monopolising. 'She was sleeping with him, getting drunk with him, and probably taking drugs. She died because of

Sam, who she had spent time with in Spain. Is this known to you?'

'Our eldest daughter knows some of it, which is a concern. We did not approve of Delvene's behaviour, but it doesn't alter the fact that she was a good woman and cared for our children and me.'

'Were you still lovers?' Clough asked. 'After the men she had been with?'

'On occasion, but it was rare. Is this relevant? Delvene has been murdered. It wasn't me, but she met other men. It could be one of them.'

'Statistically, it's the nearest and dearest,' Larry said.

'Which would mean me?'

'It would.'

'Well, it wasn't. I knew about her and Sam, and I've known Fiona for a long time. Fiona and Delvene were great friends once.'

'We know that, but what damaged the friendship?'

'You've met Fiona; you knew her before. Do you think Fiona would want Delvene nearby, now that she's Mrs prim and proper?'

'Did you know about the club when they were younger? When Sam defended their honour?'

'Not the detail, although I know that Delvene and Fiona had been abused. Sam, for once in his miserable life, had been honourable and nearly got himself killed.'

'And then afterwards, a group of his friends went to the club and beat those involved to a pulp, and some of them were never seen again.'

'I heard that it was all.'

'Were you one of those friends?'

'I wasn't. And if they killed the men, it was what they deserved. The scum of the earth.'

'You condone murder for a good cause?' Clough asked.

'I never said that. I offered an opinion.'

'Time out,' Larry said.

The three men were in the former husband's house. Larry took Clough outside and spoke to him. 'We've got nothing against the man,' Larry said.

'You said it, statistically,' Clough responded. 'The man has got a teenage daughter. She's at a difficult age and knows what her mother is. She loves the mother, but the mother's a prostitute. How can a teenager not be influenced by the parent? Isn't it possible that the father kills the mother to protect the daughter from a bad influence?'

Larry realised that the focus on Caddick and Ibrahim Ali had clouded the investigation into Delvene's death and that Clough, not distracted by what he did not know, had hit on the possibility. The husband had been familiar with Delvene's house, and she wouldn't have been shocked if he had walked into the bathroom. She might have even welcomed his visit. Once there, he took the opportunity to remove a bad influence and held Delvene's head under the water.

'A cold fish if he had killed her. And then, what's changed? A mother who prostitutes herself; a father who murders her.'

'Crimes of passion are not always logical. He saw a chance to remove one influence. He hadn't considered the horror of the other.'

'Can we prove this?'

'Not if he continues to deny it.'

'Then what do you suggest?' Larry asked.

'Let me watch his movements for a few days. You can get Bridget to check out who owns Delvene's house and how much money is in her account.'

Larry could see the logic in Clough's argument. If Clough was a plant, he was good, and if he could reason a murder investigation, it would not be long before he realised what their DCI and Wendy were up to.

***

Caddick continued to tighten the screws. A new reporting procedure was implemented, and each person in the department was to give a detailed list of their activities for each day they worked.

Reporting had been tough before, but now it was to become tougher, and Sandra Trent, Caddick's efficient personal assistant, was to monitor that procedures were followed and that any person who adopted a cavalier attitude to reporting would need to think again.

Isaac took the news badly, had visited with Caddick, and debated with the man that policing is not nine to five, five days a week, but odd hours, extended hours, and flexibility was vital. Isaac knew the man understood, even with his limited intellect. It had been a wasted trip, and Caddick was dismissive of Isaac's protestations and made it clear that he was in charge, not the chief inspector.

Isaac thought of Chief Superintendent Mary Ayton, who was sweet and easy-going when they had a fling, but now the woman had a reputation for her abrasive style of people management. A style that seemed to suit Caddick.

Isaac did not like the situation. He had enjoyed policing when DAC Goddard had been a chief superintendent and in charge of Homicide, but that was the past, and there was nothing to be gained by believing it would return. There was to be more surveillance of Homicide and less opportunity to investigate Caddick and Davies and thwart another terrorist attack.

Or was there more to it? Did Davies want, and others encourage? Was the man a lone wolf, or was his Nero fiddling while Rome burnt?

Regardless of Isaac's qualms about Commissioner Davies in the past, he had never believed the man to be corrupt.

Lord Moxon was succinct when Isaac met with him later that day before the full impact of Caddick's latest efficiency drive kicked in.

'Davies runs the Met well. The crime figures are improved. Our concern is how he has held on to power,' Moxon said. 'It's a slippery slope. A police commissioner, unanswerable to his political masters, is no longer an employee of this country but a despot.'

'Do you believe he has aspirations above his current position?' Isaac asked. It was only the two men. Gabrielle Alsworthy was known to be out of the country for a few days, and Wendy was at home resting. The two men met in a neutral location.

Isaac had taken his car, not Jenny's, and Moxon had arrived in a chauffeur-driven Bentley. In the back room of a pub, the landlord greeted Moxon warmly, and they shook hands. Apart from the Bentley, those in the front of the pub would not know that a former prime minister was in the same building.

'I can't see why not. The man's capable of more. Our concern is how he intends to achieve it. If the rule of law is to be dispensed of when it's inconvenient, what do we have?'

'Anarchy,' Isaac said.

'Not anarchy, but control of the majority by a select few who find rules and regulations, corruption, and crimes, as flexible, and that the end justifies the means. We, our small group, do not agree.'

'You agreed with Marjorie Frobisher's death,' Isaac reminded him.

'Not at the time, oblivious of it. In retrospect, MacTavish was correct. Checks and balances, weighing up the greater good with the lesser bad. But Davies has gone beyond this. He has allowed a terrorist attack to strengthen his position. Can't you see the subtle difference?'

Isaac could not agree with Moxon. If ten people could die in Whitehall, more could die elsewhere, and the possibility for wholesale slaughter could occur. Society rested on a knife edge. One act of violence could cause friction. Multiple acts of violence, especially if perpetrated against ethnic or religious groups, could escalate in retribution and then anarchy, which the government might be incapable of controlling. And then civil war in the country's hotspots, which were tinder dry, ready for a match, and that Davies might light it.

Moxon was right; Isaac knew it. He just did not like it. Moxon drank gin while Isaac drank an indifferent white wine. He thought Bulgarian, or maybe it was Spanish, but he wasn't a connoisseur, and he did not intend to finish the glass.

'Where do we go from here?' Isaac asked.

'Where you were always going. Confront Fiona Avers if she's still alive.'

'She is.'

'For how much longer. If, as we surmise, she knew, then she would have used that knowledge to her advantage. Maybe she didn't, but Gabrielle is suspicious of her mother.'

'Do you trust Gabrielle?'

'Her father could be slippery, and he wanted my job. MacTavish knew I was best for the party. He dealt with the man.'

'He protected his secret.'

'And I got a promise that Gabrielle's father wouldn't challenge me. That was the agreement. I didn't know who the child was.'

'But you knew enough.'

'It was a tough year, the party was challenged, and our majority was getting weaker with every by-election. MacTavish told me that Alsworthy was involved in a scandal. I didn't want to know the details. MacTavish said he would deal with it, that Alsworthy would not cause dissent or challenge my leadership, and that in return, I would rubberstamp whatever action MacTavish thought appropriate.'

'Including murder?'

'Cook, we've been over this before. Don't keep harping on about it. You're worried about the future, and so am I. Past mistakes or past actions don't alter the present. Focus on what's in front of us, not behind. Decisions were made, and people died. Full stop. No more to say on the matter, but now, we have a commissioner who's tasted the power that he wields.

'Undoubtedly, he will use it for good, except we are concerned about what he will do for that good. You've got to get Fiona Avers to speak, thumbscrews if you must, or I've a few friends.'

'Who have thumbscrews?'

'Not rough-handed tactics, but they'll apply the pressure you won't. If Fiona Avers knew, there would still be a record, a possible letter or a document from Marjorie before her death. Was there an envelope given to Fiona at the reading of the will or to Robert, and what about Sam?'

'Sam would have sold the story. Forget him. It's either Robert or Fiona, but tell Robert, and he would have told Fiona.'

'And if it was only Fiona that knew?'

'She wouldn't have told her father. She worshipped the man; she wouldn't have been able to inflict further pain on him.'

'Then we're finished here. Still squeamish?'

'I am,' Isaac replied.

'Good man. If you're not, you're no better than that poor fool who blew himself up in Whitehall.'

Chapter 17

'I refute your accusation,' Fiona Avers said. 'What proof do you have that I knew of my mother's marriage to Alsworthy and their child?'

It had been hospitable when Isaac and Wendy had entered the house, although it should have been Challis Street Police Station. However, that was the haunt of Caddick, Sandra Trent, and Clough.

Sam Avers was not at home and had become bothersome, not abiding by occupancy rules and haggling for a larger slice of the inheritance. However, Fiona reiterated that she would not leave him to rot on the street, but she did not intend for her children to remain in her brother's company for too long.

'It's the reason your father died,' Wendy said.

'And if you're correct, that doesn't mean he would have told me.'

'Doesn't it? Your father was dying. He knew that, and so did you. He knows there is a great secret that, if revealed, would cause you stress, and then Ibrahim Ali would be here, either wanting to get to know his new-found family or to learn what his mother was like.'

'I don't think he would care, not from what I've seen of the man.'

'The former Benjamin Marshall might,' Isaac said. 'He grew up in a Christian family, and he keeps in contact with his adopted parents, sends them presents, and remembers their birthdays. It would only be natural for him to be curious.

'We know Delvene met Ali in Spain, but not what transpired, and now, she's dead. She would not have known Ibrahim Ali's significance in Spain unless Sam had told her. Although, if she already knew, that can only have come from you.'

'My father was too fond of me to subject me to that trauma, and he would not have trusted Sam with the front door key of the house if he could have avoided it, let alone a secret of that importance.'

'Did Sam steal from your parents?'

'When he was younger. So did I. My mother is hardly likely to have left any details of her unwanted son in this house.'

'Why? We believe Richard Williams knew, and Sally Jenkins had overheard a conversation between your mother and Williams. Too many coincidences, too many possibilities, and too much importance for it not to have leaked out.'

'Not from me. You know that Sam was coerced or forced into giving blood and a swab,' Fiona said.

'He was beaten and then taken to the hospital, hardly coercion. Ibrahim Ali's not averse to violence, and you used to hang around with shady characters when younger, and Delvene's not the vestal virgin.'

'Delvene was a friend when we were younger.'

'Then why did she die?' Isaac asked.

'Ask her husband. How do you think he feels with their children at an impressionable age. Do you think the neighbourhood where she lives doesn't know about her? And then, there's the school where the children attend. You can't sell yourself and expect that no one will know.'

'Has it become a problem? We've met the father, and Wendy's met the eldest daughter. I can't say we've seen any problems with them.'

'People do not air their dirty linen in public, and as for her and Ibrahim Ali, I know the story about what happened in Spain.'

'We've asked you about this before,' Wendy said, although she couldn't be sure if she had.

'Sam, you know about. Ibrahim Ali found out about my mother and Lord Alsworthy, the elder. Sam doesn't know, but he's the innocent abroad, unsuspecting, scamming drunken English tourists, and then, there's Ibrahim Ali and his group. They befriend Sam. Sam's on a high, making money, getting drunk, but then, later, he's accosted, beaten hard, and taken to the hospital. You've spoken to the doctor?'

'We have,' Isaac said.

'Sam tells Ibrahim about Delvene. Delvene receives a visit from Ali, although why doesn't make sense. Sam's oblivious about what's happened in the hospital, and he's hardly likely to go to the police. Do you think they would be interested in a drunken English expat who got a good thumping?'

'They would have thought he deserved it. It's unlikely they would have bothered to fill out a report.'

'Precisely,' Fiona said. 'I went out there once to visit him, or to be more correct, to get him into rehabilitation. He had overdosed, and he was unable to look after himself.'

'How did you know?'

'I pay a neighbour to keep a watch on him.'

'And arrest him or report him to the police.'

'Neither. The neighbour's job is hands-off, to keep me updated, and to ensure Sam gets home of a night, if not in a fit state, but, at least, vertical.'

'Which Sam did most nights?' Wendy asked.

'Most nights. Sam's not going to change, but he's my brother. I've already told you I will look after him as my father did. Too much money and Sam will be dead.'

'Where is he now?'

'Wherever it is, it doesn't involve drugs or alcohol.'

'You've got someone watching him?'

'I must, not only because he can't behave, but people have died due to Ibrahim Ali, including my parents.'

'And Richard Williams, Charles Sutherland, and Sally Jenkins,' Isaac reminded Fiona.

'Richard, I knew, but he was my mother's lover. Don't expect me to shed a tear over him, now or back then. I never met Sally Jenkins, another of Richard's easy women, and as for Sutherland, the less said, the better.'

Neither officer needed to recount the story of Fiona and Sutherland in flagrante delicto in the house when Marjorie and Richard had walked in.

'And Sam is a probability?'

'Delvene died, which means she must have known something. Sam is possible, and if the police are sniffing around and asking too many questions, then people die. Sam's an easy target. Delvene was smarter and in Spain at the same time as Ibrahim. Who knows what she had figured out. Maybe Ali warned her off.'

'She attempted to blackmail you with what she knew?' Isaac asked.

'Not blackmail, no mention of Spain or Ibrahim. As a friend, she asked if I would lend her money while she sold her house and bought somewhere cheaper.'

'She could have gone to the bank.'

'With what? I'm a whore, make good money, and you can trust me. Delvene had an income but no paperwork and didn't pay taxes. The banks would not have looked at her.'

'Did you agree to the loan?'

'While my father was alive, I had not. After he died and I had access to the money, I intended to help her, not with a loan, but with a cash payment.'

'Why so generous?' Wendy asked.

'Delvene helped me to look after Sam; she had once been a good friend, and we had been through a lot together.'

'There was a condition?' Isaac said.

'She would spend one month every two with Sam, wherever he was. Basically, to help me with Sam.'

'Did she agree?'

'I hadn't put the final offer to her. We were going to meet on the day she died.'

Isaac found it hard to believe Fiona Avers. Her demeanour was suspect, and she kept averting her eyes. He was convinced she knew more and was either frightened or complicit.

All the murders seemed to have a thread that went back to Ibrahim Ali. Isaac was sure he needed to be interviewed, but to do that would raise Caddick's hackles, put Clough on high alert, and allow Commissioner Davies to bring the wrath of hell onto Homicide.

***

The two men met late at night, not outside the DAC's house but in Goddard's office at New Scotland Yard. It was Goddard's suggestion to change the location. Isaac saw it as a positive sign.

It was seven in the evening, and the day shift had gone. The building was still a hive of activity, but on the top floor, it was relatively quiet, apart from Mary Ayton, two doors away, and Commissioner Davies at the far end of a long corridor.

'He's got Caddick in there with him,' Goddard said.

'And we're meeting here?' Isaac asked the obvious question.

'The commissioner is feeling the heat.'

'You're a sitting duck. The man will have you out if he thinks you're attempting to double-cross him.'

'My rank gives me protection. Removing me would require the commissioner to give me notice and for me to prepare a defence. He's not a dictator, and I'm not here for services rendered in his hour of need.'

'Aren't you? You were promoted.'

'I was promoted because Caddick wanted my position at Challis Street. You're the thorn in his side.'

'Why me?'

'Caddick's devious, dirty, and a low-performing police officer. He uses what talents he has to great advantage.'

'That doesn't answer the question?'

'I believe it does. Let me explain it to you,' Goddard said. 'Seth Caddick joins the police and fulfils a childhood ambition. He's keen, honest, and hard-working.'

'Did he?'

'I believe so. Anyhow, with the transition from child to adult and then to a police officer, the keenness dissipates, and he finds out that honesty is an overrated commodity, and the hard work isn't for him.'

'Supposition or proof.'

'Both. I obtained his performance report. A complete history of when he joined the police up until now.'

'Reliable.'

'The copy I obtained is. But getting back to why I'm here, and Caddick is giving you strife. Deep within the man is a streak of the idealistic young man who joined the police. He admires you. You are what he had wanted to be, but life hasn't turned out that way for him. He's sold his soul to the devil, and his future is dependent on that devil. His future is grim, and he has farther to fall than us.'

'Commissioner Davies?'

'The commissioner knows what Caddick is. The man was in a corner, fighting for his career and reputation. Caddick had the solution; Davies had Nelson's blind eye to look the other way while Caddick worked the solution.'

'Are you saying that Davies might not have known its ferocity?'

'He must have, as he was quick to take credit for the swift response of the police in Whitehall.'

'Which means he's equally to blame for the murders. Davies could go to prison if it's proved.'

'Isaac, Davies will not go to prison. Whatever is proved, he will be allowed to resign and to be accorded full honours.'

'A cover-up?'

'Of course, there will be. The reputation of the Met is at an all-time low. Can you imagine what it would be like if Davies were charged with a crime? Caddick will be protected, as he won't keep his mouth shut if he's not.'

'Which means he would become a liability if it's intended to sweep it under the carpet.'

'He might be expendable. No point pussyfooting around with this. This is wrongdoing at the highest level,' Goddard said.

'Not as high as when Linda Harris, on orders, killed.'

'The secret service killings are sanctioned at the highest level. Whatever way we look at it, it's a quagmire, and you're in the middle of it, and I'm throwing you a lifeline.'

'How? Is this why we're meeting in your office when our nemesis is up the end of the corridor.'

'My corridor,' Goddard said.

'Are you sure? How?'

'I intend to take it with your help.'

Isaac didn't like it. He had known the deputy assistant commissioner for a long time and knew the man to be a shrewd operator, able to navigate internal politics, but a frontal assault, baiting the bear, was dangerous, and people could die or be maimed or even worse, thrown to the masses, derided online, and ridiculed – a living death.

'I need to interview Ibrahim Ali. He's related to the Avers family. It's only logical that we should meet,' Isaac said.

'Which will rouse Caddick to action. Are you asking me for advice, or do you intend to do it?'

'I need you to inform the commissioner that Ibrahim Ali's under investigation and that Caddick's involved. Emphasise that you will protect the commissioner with your life and soul.'

'And that I'm the best friend he never had. Are you joking? Isaac. What you are asking is impossible. Davies will smell a rat.'

'He will, but you've given him forewarning. He can either sacrifice Caddick, or we'll take them both.'

'I'll need a stronger lever before I approach the man.'

'I'll get it,' Isaac said.

Chapter 18

Isaac had committed to DAC Goddard to provide further proof of Commissioner Davies' involvement. However, he had no idea how to progress, and if he had, Jenny would tell him that family was more important than honour and life was preferable to death.

Isaac knew that if direct confrontation with the forces of evil were to eventuate, then his family would need to be elsewhere than at the family home. Wendy was in his confidence, and he met with her the next day, away from the office, at a small Italian restaurant favoured by those at Challis Street. Open enough not to raise undue suspicion; private enough to hold a confidential conversation.

'I met with the DAC,' Isaac said. There was no need to mention which deputy assistant commissioner. There was only one as far as Homicide was concerned.

'Is he with you?'

'I trust him to do what he can, although the man's a survivor. However, I must go with him. Lord Moxon's an unknown, and Gabrielle Alsworthy is interested only in herself and her family. She could sell us out if she could strike a deal with Ibrahim Ali.'

'What lever could she have over the man? He's got the title, the wealth, and the influence.'

'He's also an upstart, and the establishment will protect him for now and deal aggressively with him if he threatens them. As much as Gabrielle wishes to regale us with her family heritage and how they fought and died in every war the British fought in the last four hundred years, she is devious and an opportunist. Her family is more important than crimes committed.'

'Lord Moxon?'

'It was Gabrielle who referred us to him, and he's past the age of active involvement. He's also cunning. We trust him because we must.'

'You owe it to Bridget and Inspector Hill to let them know what is planned.'

'That's the problem. I don't have a plan, just a collection of ideas leading to a solution, but Ibrahim Ali won't lie down and let us walk over him, nor will Caddick, and definitely not Davies.'

'Sandra Trent's smarter than Chief Superintendent Caddick, and Sergeant Clough's a fine police officer. Both will know soon enough what we're up to and then, you know what will happen,' Wendy said.

Isaac did. He had been shot before in the line of duty; he didn't want to experience it again, and this time, it wouldn't be an angry woman confronted on a moving train but a seasoned fighter armed with a rifle or one of Ali's people wearing a suicide vest.

That night, he told Jenny what might happen and that he was committed, regardless of the outcome. It was that night that she told him that she loved him and trusted him, but he was a bloody fool who would get himself killed.

It was one of the defining moments in a person's life when a decision needed to be made, whether to turn left or right at the intersection or to advance or retreat. It was something he could not avoid.

After a fitful night's sleep, he awoke to find her sitting on a chair on his side of the bed. 'Do what you must,' Jenny said. 'But, remember your family, and if you think we should leave here, give me sufficient warning. I'll either be a hero's wife or a fool's widow.'

'You'll be neither,' Isaac said. 'Whatever the outcome, everything will be hushed up.'

'As it was with Linda Harris. Have you seen her recently?'

'Not for some time. She was entertaining Caddick but supposedly is working behind the scenes.'

'Never trust her, even if you fancy her.'

Isaac wasn't sure what to say, and in the interest of marital harmony, he didn't reply.

Deadly Secrets

That morning, when he left for Challis Street, he knew that Jenny was concerned and that he was worried. He was not rolling a loaded dice but was supported by disparate persons who could not be trusted, taking on a group of persons, namely, Ibraham Ali, Seth Caddick, and Alwyn Davies, who had no such confusion. They were resolute and determined, and they would kill for survival.

If any of those he had placed tentative trust is weakened, or if they changed sides or were double agents, a term more akin to Linda Harris' employer, then there was no hope.

***

Homicide was not the place to update Bridget and Larry. He had kept them in the dark for as long as he could, but now, with a frontal attack pending, they needed to know what the situation was, what was likely to happen, and that if they were fearful and opposed to it, they were to distance themselves from Homicide, and to transfer out if that was the only option.

'We're with you,' Larry said.

This time, it wasn't a restaurant, but Interview Room 3, which was soundproofed and the door locked from the inside.

'It has serious ramifications,' Isaac said, 'but it's been brushed under the table, and Caddick's taking the credit for breaking the jihadist group behind it.'

'Only you don't believe he did,' Bridget said.

'Too many coincidences. It's one thing to blow yourself up in the name of your religion. It's another thing to organise it.'

'And how did Chief Superintendent Caddick happen to be there at the right time to apprehend two others after the first one had blown himself up,' Wendy asked.

'Are you saying that the chief superintendent is complicit?' Bridget asked.

'I can't prove it,' Isaac said. 'It's a supposition, based on a presumption, proven by Ibrahim Ali's elevation to the aristocracy and Commissioner Davies' resurrection to a position of undeniable strength.'

'Heady words,' Larry said. 'How do you intend to prove it, and if you do, how do you intend to enforce it?'

'I don't know, other than a frontal assault,' Isaac replied.

'Which you can't win. Won't they take action in the only way they know?'

'I expect them to. That's why we're here. I trust you more than any others. However, this might get violent, and people might die. I cannot ask any of you to take that risk.'

'I'm in, you know that,' Wendy said.

'So am I,' Bridget said. 'Don't expect me to take direct action, but I can scour the internet for whatever we need.'

'Then find out if there are any links with Ibrahim Ali to illegal activities in this country, no matter how obscure,' Isaac said.

'Do you believe Robert Avers and Delvene Drayton's deaths are related to Ibrahim Ali?' Larry asked.

'What's your thoughts on this?' Isaac asked.

'Avers, almost certainly, which places Sam Avers in a dangerous situation. Also, Fiona, if she's not careful or becomes too smart for her own good.'

'Delvene Drayton?'

'Probably, but I've not investigated her former husband fully. Apparently, they were on good terms, and the children were well-balanced, but they were at an impressionable age, and the mother was selling herself. He might have thought Delvene's death was preferable for their children.'

'Sergeant Clough?' Bridget asked.

'He's a good officer,' Larry said. 'Are you sure he's involved?'

'He was at Ali's mansion, that we know,' Isaac replied. 'Any reason why we shouldn't suspect him?'

'None that I can think of. That doesn't make him complicit in what Caddick might be up to. He might be a reluctant ally of the man.'

Deadly Secrets

'It can't be proven, one way or the other. Although, at some stage, we'll need to find out. I'll leave that up to you, Larry. In the interim, the three of you know what is afoot. I expect complete secrecy, and Larry, no talking to your wife about this.'

'Not with her friends, no chance,' Larry replied. 'I'm not sure she'd understand or care as long as she's got her exhilarating life.'

'Which she hasn't,' Wendy said. 'Is she still giving you grief?'

'Always, but we're fine, the usual husband and wife issues.'

The other three knew that Larry was not telling the truth. To his wife, money and the driving ambition of her husband were what she wanted. Larry had made it clear to her, even before they married, that he was a plodding police officer, happiest when chasing a villain, despondent when discussing the family's finances with his wife. He wasn't going to advance much further in the Met, and he knew it, and he was content, although his wife wanted a go-getter, a man of action, an accomplished businessman who brought in the money, and for her to spend it.

For him, a small house, the children at decent schools, and a holiday once a year, not in the Bahamas or the fanciest hotel, but budget and good.

'What do you want from us, DCI?' Larry asked.

'Your total confidence and support. I don't want you to be open with it, but I need to know that you're in agreement, and if the proverbial hits the fan, you are to deny vehemently any knowledge of what I'm telling you and to protect yourselves,' Isaac said.

'It sounds like a death wish,' Bridget said. 'If you're after martyrdom, you won't get it. It'll be buried so deep, it'll never see the light of day.'

'Linda Harris?' Wendy asked. 'Is she in on it?'

'I've no idea. She cannot be trusted, nor can those she works for.'

'Who are?'

'We know the title of the organisation, but not the people. That we will never know with any certainty.'

'Is there more?' Larry asked.

'Not for now. I need to meet with others while the department focuses on Avers and Delvene Drayton's deaths.'

Nobody left the room in an optimistic frame of mind.

***

Lord Moxon invited Isaac into his house after Isaac had phoned the next day so they could go over what was intended and how they would do it. Isaac also intended to further evaluate the man, cognisant that this was a former prime minister who had played politics dirty and wasn't averse to treachery. And now, the most treacherous action was in play, and Isaac couldn't be certain if Moxon was up to the task or if he would sell anybody and anything down the river if pressured.

Isaac didn't expect to see Gabrielle Alsworthy sitting in an armchair in the sitting room. He realised that the tete-a-tete with Moxon would not occur.

'Lord Moxon invited me,' Gabrielle said.

Isaac could see she was a fine-looking woman who had dressed for the occasion. Moxon wore a suit. Isaac recognised the Oxford University tie.

'I invited Gabrielle for a reason,' Moxon said. 'I realise you're not convinced we're committed to the fight ahead.'

Isaac saw no reason to deny it. After all, this was not a group meeting to discuss a minor issue but a matter of national importance. If people couldn't have trust in the police, then the country was moving increasingly faster down a slippery slope, where the rule of law was decided by the strongest, where the public morality was determined by the morally bankrupt, where the United Kingdom would not be the country his parents had migrated to and had come to love.

'Gabrielle is interested in reclaiming her position in society but is now ostracised due to her father's unfortunate dalliance with an actress,' Moxon added.

'She was no more than a schoolgirl back then, and he should have kept to his social class,' Gabrielle said.' Marjorie Frobisher should have known better.'

'You mean, my class,' Isaac said, reminding Moxon and Gabrielle that he was the son of Jamaican immigrants and Marjorie Frobisher was the child of parents in trade.

'More was expected of my father. And yes, I believe in the class structure and people knowing their place,' Gabrielle said, momentarily taken aback by Isaac's bluntness. 'That doesn't make me bad. I'm in it for myself. That makes me the most trustworthy. DCI, what's your objective? Are we to believe that an attractive, well-educated, and articulate man like yourself is willing to risk life and limb to pursue a noble cause?'

'I've known for a few years that there is an underlying corrupt governance of the London Metropolitan Police. I'm committed to law and order, but it needs a standard bearer and the current commissioner, isn't it.'

'Is that it?'

'Not totally. I opposed the last push for increased policing in London, but I played it calm, whereas others were more supportive of the commissioner and prospered. I saw internal politics at play, which I abhor. But now, a criminal activity of such depravity that they must be held accountable. Also, if one terrorist attack succeeded in cementing Davies' position as commissioner, would another occur if the man was threatened. Is he that devious to allow it?'

'I don't believe he is,' Moxon said. 'Davies is no fool. He might show favouritism and ensure his back is covered, but I can't accept direct involvement to protect his position in a heinous crime.'

'Except, as prime minister, you allowed intervention in another country's politics when that country threatened to withhold oil supplies.'

'That's not the same,' Moxon replied angrily.

'I can't agree,' Isaac had decided to raise the tempo to see if the truth would be revealed with anger. He knew why he was pursuing the matter but remained unsure of Moxon.

'You cannot confuse domestic and foreign policy.'

'I don't see why not. Your government's actions resulted in the death of how many people? Hundreds? Thousands? Or was it more?'

'Decisions are made in the national interest, and my government was responsible for the welfare of this country.'

'And you, Gabrielle, would sell your soul to regain what you've lost?'

'I'm still English and proud of it, whereas you…'

'An interloper from the colonies when an Englishman ruled with a firm hand, and the natives knew their place.'

'You are a police officer, dedicated to law and order, and about to get your head blown off.'

'Is what I said was correct, or did you decide that discretion was the better part of valour?'

'If you're trying to bait us, you're not doing a very good job,' Moxon intervened.

'I need to know where I stand, where my people stand. If we're about to get our heads blown off, to use Gabrielle's terminology, which is very apt, given the circumstances, I need to know that you've got our back. I'll be the most visible and the most likely to be harmed or killed defending this country. I've always known where Gabrielle stood, and there's a challenge for her. As for you, Lord Moxon, you must reengage with former friends and foes to pull in favours.'

'And how do you suggest I do that?'

'Tell them you're writing an update to your memoirs, something to do with the nation's current state, the future of democracy, how to become an integrated society, and to reinvigorate the passion people once had for the United Kingdom.'

'And if I do that?'

'You've got people who owe you favours. Pull them in. Find out who MacTavish contacted. We need to know who Linda Harris is. She works for people who state that they are there for the nation, but are they? Is there a hidden agenda?'

'Isaac, that would be easier for you. I kept my nose clean, and my deputy left it to MacTavish.'

'MacTavish must have kept records. Find them, analyse them, and let us know.'

'Let you know? Do you have anyone you can trust to take what I've got and check them?'

'I do,' Isaac said. He did not intend to reveal Bridget's name.

'Very well. However, any records will be at his castle in Scotland. Can you take it from there if I give you a lead and somewhere to look?'

'I can.'

'DCI, after you've been so horrible, nothing like your charming sergeant, do you expect me to ask for forgiveness?' Gabrielle said.

'I expect you to be seething,' Isaac said with a smile.

'I'll have you know that the Alsworthys do not cower easily.'

'I didn't expect them to.'

'What do you want from me?'

'I need you to engage with Ibrahim Ali if you can. Also, the women you see walking around, invite them in for tea. Gentle probing, attempt to gain their confidence.'

'There's only one that seems amenable.'

'Then, work with her, become her friend. No reason for you not to be. Are any of them Ali's women?'

'In the biblical sense?'

'He has an English wife, talk to her.'

'He could have more than one wife. That's how it works, isn't it.'

'I believe so, but we must build a better profile of his lordship: his weaknesses and strengths. Is his religious fervour wavering now he's been anointed in the House of Lords.'

'And if he regrets the murder of innocent people,' Gabrielle added.

'He wasn't regarded as violent. What convinced him to change? Was the carrot that big? Has he done what Lord Moxon so eloquently defended?'

'Ibrahim Ali might have agreed if his faith had been that strong. We must never underestimate the man. His appearances in the House of Lords have been impressive, and he is a skilful orator,' Moxon said.

'That's what I believe we should do,' Isaac said, 'but I'm a police officer, not a former prime minister or an aristocrat.'

'Isaac, you're a snob,' Gabrielle said.

'I'm not, but if you want someone who's disparaging of your class, then Wendy's your person.'

'Who is charming.'

'Gabrielle, enough,' Moxon said. 'You can't help that you were born with a silver spoon in your mouth.'

'Not silver, just bronze. Ali has got the silver, although he never knew it. Why did you allow people to die to protect the secret? Your government was threatened; was that sufficient reason?'

'I didn't know the details. I knew Ali's mother socially, but I never knew of her and your father. Not that I would have been shocked, but the election was tight, and a new government would not have been to your liking.'

'Lord Moxon, are you sure you're the son of an engineer and his wife?' Gabrielle jested. 'Are you certain there is no blue blood in there? You have the cunning of a cavalier, the background of a roundhead.'

Isaac knew his history of the English Civil War in the seventeenth century, when the Cavaliers, loyal to the King, fought the Roundheads, who supported the Parliamentarians. The Alsworthys were on the side of King Charles the First, who was executed in 1649. And that Moxon's ancestors had sided with the Roundheads.

'I wouldn't know,' Moxon replied.

'Regardless, I disproved of the government's intervention and the murder investigation being closed by the Official Secrets Act.' Isaac said.

'And the end of your short-lived romance with Linda Harris.'

'Who is she?' Gabrielle asked.

Isaac answered. 'She killed one person that we know of. She's back, and I've met her a few times. Apparently, she's interested in Ibrahim Ali and Caddick's activities, but we don't know who for and how much she knows.'

'Caddick might know more,' Moxon said. 'From what I know, he's taken off from where you left off, got his shoes under her bed.'

'And him in it. Besides, Linda's making herself scarce, supposedly working behind the scenes, although I don't know if we're aligned with her masters or working against them.'

'We don't know much,' Gabrielle said, 'and you intend to go blundering in, hope you strike gold, but run the risk of coming back with a dirty face and a knife in your back.'

'That about sums it up. Are you sure you're up to it, and don't give us "I'm an Alsworthy" guff. I know something of your history. Eustace Alsworthy, one of your ancestors?'

'How many times removed?' Gabrielle replied. 'I can't be held responsible for the sins of a forebear in Jamaica three hundred years ago.'

'What is being asked of you is critical, and we need total commitment, not platitudes. If you stick your hand in the fire, it might get burnt.'

'Full of witticisms, aren't you, DCI? I must preserve the good name of the Alsworthys. Ibrahim must go, and the status quo must be restored. The offspring of my father and a showgirl is not to my liking. The bastard influence must be removed.'

'He's not a bastard,' Moxon reminded Gabrielle.

'He is, to me. My father was soft, but I'm not. A pretty face, and he was away. No doubt there are a few other mongrels out there, but at least he didn't have the option to marry their mothers.'

'He was already married?' Isaac asked.

'Mother excused him and believed he had certain responsibilities and rights as Lord of the Manor.'

'An antiquated outlook on life,' Isaac said.

'It served my father well, and he did care for us. My mother might not have liked it, but theirs was not a match made in heaven, more an amalgamation of two families.'

'Your marriage?'

'An amalgamation of sorts, but I married for love; my mother married out of duty. The affection came later.'

Chapter 19

Bridget spent three days during the week and a large chunk of Sunday researching, compiling, cross-checking, and preparing a PowerPoint presentation and a written report on what she had found. It came to forty-two slides and one hundred-and-two pages of text. Once complete, Isaac phoned Lord Moxon, who organised a conference room in a building near where he lived. So far, Larry and Bridget did not know of the man.

A room at Challis Street was deemed too risky because either of the three recent imports could walk in. The meeting was to be on Tuesday, at nine in the evening, in an office block owned by a former colleague of Moxon.

Sergeant Clough, whom Isaac hoped wasn't involved in criminal activity, was planning to visit Delvene's parents. There did not seem much that they could add to their daughter's murder, as she had left home when she was fifteen and had not been back since then, other than a couple of times. They knew of her life, that she had bred good children, and that she sold her body to men with the money and the taste for that sort of woman, as Delvene's mother dispassionately referred to her daughter.

Clough was not expected to have fun at Delvene's childhood home. Sandra Trent was supposedly off work with a cold, or was it because she had been seen coming out of a hotel, followed fifteen minutes later by Caddick. Harry the Snitch had done his job well. Isaac had to admit that as much as he disliked Caddick, he had to credit him with good taste in women.

Bridget set up the presentation in the conference room using a slide projector and Zoom as agreed. Moxon had the code and would view the presentation and listen to those in the room but would not actively participate.

Isaac explained to those assembled that another person was following the presentation. Wendy knew who he was. 'For now, this person will remain unknown. You will be told when you need to know.'

'What we don't know can't be beaten out of us,' Larry jested.

'Hopefully, it will not come to that,' Isaac said.

Wendy knew it was possible that one, if not all, would suffer. She would accept her fate, regardless.

Larry was unsure if he would, but if asked, he would say yes; Bridget was under no illusion; heroics wasn't her forte.

Moxon listened and watched as Bridget went through the PowerPoint slides. He had his laptop open, and as she moved to the next slide, so did he. He had to admit to being impressed, which would have excited Bridget if she had known, as she had voted for the man at the election that his party had lost. This was not the day for formal introductions.

'We know his adoptive parents, Martin and Beverley Marshall. Benjamin Marshall's school records show above-average intelligence, and he had been accepted to Oxford University but did not attend. The Marshalls are Church of England, but rarely attended church services, although Beverley went to the Christmas service every year with a friend.

'There was a period of delinquency at thirteen, mainly shoplifting, for which he received a warning from the judge, a severe telling off from his parents, and respect from his fellow delinquents. At fifteen, he had a girlfriend. Her name is in the file. I have located her, and she is a teacher now, married with two children, and another is on the way.'

Wendy remembered herself at fifteen and that she had to thank a local farmer's son for her clumsy introduction to sex.

'Apart from that,' Bridget continued,' Benjamin Marshall showed no character flaws. He was a credit to the Marshalls, apart from the shoplifting. They had told him of his adoption when he was thirteen and that a request had been made by Benjamin, when he turned eighteen, to the relevant authorities as to his birth parents.'

'Which were unsuccessful,' Isaac said. 'We are aware that the Official Secrets Act was used, some would say, unscrupulously. Even so, if the birth parents had placed a restriction on the adopted child finding out their identities, then it would not need the overbearing arm of the government to suppress it.'

Moxon knew he was correct in not requesting a detailed briefing from MacTavish. Deniability in politics was all the better when it was the truth.

'If Benjamin Marshall had requested the identities of his parents at eighteen, this would have been before we were given the fool's errand of looking for his mother,' Isaac said.

'Which means,' Bridget continued, 'that a letter would have been sent to one or both parents. And likely, the father's name on a birth certificate might be missing.'

'I have proof, on the next slide, and a copy of Benjamin's request, and the date the adoption agency forwarded it to Marjorie, but not before they had transcribed it to an official letterhead, removing any reference to the person requesting the information.'

'You've got a record of this?' Larry asked.

'In the folder that I gave each of you. I don't need to remind those assembled here that their folder will not be left in a drawer in Homicide or, heaven forbid, on a desk. Do not leave it at Challis Street. Take it home, read through it meticulously, and then burn it. I will maintain a file, which can be referred to,' Bridget said.

'Bridget's right,' Isaac said. 'We can't be too careful. Could we be hacked, Bridget?' Isaac asked.

'Any database, any computer in the world, can be hacked with enough expertise. I don't think anyone in Challis Street will be able to hack it.'

'Linda Harris' employees could.'

'Which means if someone in Challis Street is talking to the woman or sleeping with her, as Caddick was, then yes, if they are given a lead on what to look for, even a website address and a code name. It would still be difficult.'

'We know Sandra Trent's spending time with Caddick,' Larry said. 'Any chance?'

'Sandra Trent is bright, articulate, efficient, and professional but not skilled with computers,' Bridget said.

'She wouldn't show you if she had,' Wendy said.

'I've seen her at her desk outside Chief Superintendent Caddick's office, fumbling with her laptop's keyboard. She doesn't touch type or have an instinctive affinity with computers. The chief superintendent is a one-finger typer with no analytical mind, which is necessary if hacking computers.'

'More like a bull in a china shop.'

Bridget continued. 'At nineteen, Benjamin, a capable young man, according to the headmaster at his last school, realised that something was lacking in his life, as though he didn't belong. He loved the Marshalls but did not understand certain facets. He consulted a psychologist, who met with the young man weekly for five months. The psychologist's reports, which are in your folders, showed that Benjamin was mentally stable and compassionate but a lost soul in a troubled world and that the impasse with the Marshalls was real. Martin and Beverley are solid citizens, content in other's company, not driven to pursue causes, and content to let life drift by. However, Benjamin was extroverted, gregarious, and well-read. During those five months with the psychologist, Benjamin read everything from Plato to Nietzsche. The psychologist also stated that Benjamin's ability to absorb what he read was impressive and that he could recite large chunks of each book verbatim if asked.'

'Which is handy if learning the Koran,' Larry said.

'Not only that, he read the Bible and studied Buddhism.'

'How did you get the psychologist's reports?' Isaac asked.

Bridget's curt reply. 'Don't ask.'

Moxon needed to comment, but Isaac ensured he was on mute. He had let the lord listen in, a sign of confidence in the man, but Isaac wasn't convinced that he had been open in his discussions with him and Gabrielle. The idea that MacTavish was a lone wolf, making decisions of life and death, without the tacit approval of his prime minister stretched belief and that Moxon, a micromanager as a politician, would have known more than he was letting on. Isaac had met a few politicians over the years and knew them to be devious.

'You've not mentioned his conversion,' Larry reminded Bridget.

'There is more before we get to that. Ben Marshall works in an engineering workshop in Nottingham, a ten-minute drive from the family home. At night and weekends, he's studying. He moves out of home and into a flat with another man his age. Nobby Clarke, born and bred northerner. The man's a drunk, but he's got the gift of the gab, and he starts bringing women to the flat. Benjamin joins Clarke in the debauchery. There are drugs, something that Benjamin flirted with, but he's not addicted to them, whereas Clarke soon is. Sodom and Gomorrah, according to the neighbour.'

'You've spoken to the neighbour?' Isaac asked.

'A complaint is raised, and the police knock on Benjamin and Clarke's door. Inside, the police find them and two women high on drugs and sex. It's a den of iniquity. The police file a report, but none of the four are charged. Apparently, if they arrested everyone under the age of twenty-one who was into random sex and drugs, they would not have enough cells to lock them up, more paperwork than they could imagine, and then the courts would take a lenient approach, fine them, and let them go. The police warned Benjamin and Clarke about the noise, wished the men luck, and left after looking at the women.'

'You seem to have found out a lot about the encounter with the police.'

'I phoned the police station in Nottingham, got hold of the neighbour's phone number and phoned the person who complained, a retired school teacher, who reckoned it was a common occurrence, and whereas he didn't begrudge young people getting up to mischief, enough was enough, and he needed his sleep, and he didn't need the whiff of marijuana, or to listen to the grunting and the groaning.'

'How long did Benjamin's cavorting last?' Wendy asked.

'Fifteen months. It was fractious. Clarke fancied Benjamin's girlfriend, who was sharing a room with Benjamin. Nobby's having a dry spell, and he's put on weight. The women don't find him desirable, and he resents the woman and reckons that Benjamin, in the spirit of equanimity, should share. Benjam's not into it, and there's a fight on the road outside the flat. The police, this time, act. The two men ended up in a cell, and the girlfriend locked herself in the flat. Both are charged with an affray, receive a stiff fine, and go their separate ways.'

'How do you know so much?'

'The neighbour's a busybody. I've confirmed the affray and the girlfriend's name.'

'Who is she? Do you know where she is?'

'I'm coming to it,' Bridget said. 'Benjamin and Siobhan Kelly set up house in the flat after Clarke moved out. She works for the local council and pays her share of the flat's rent. Benjamin is twenty-four, and the two are still together. He's forsaken drugs, is not drinking alcohol, and is either in bed with Siobhan or reading the Koran.'

'Islam wouldn't approve of the two living in sin,' Isaac said.

'They weren't. He had become a Muslim and married Siobhan. Her parents didn't attend the ceremony, although the Marshalls did. I believe that Siobhan is the woman Gabrielle Alsworthy speaks to briefly, except now, she's covered from head to toe.'

'Which she wasn't when she was in the flat with Benjamin.'

'She dressed modestly and didn't cover up, but there was no sign of a leg. She wore loose clothing and, most of the time, wore a hat. She was still working at the council, and Benjamin worked in the engineering workshop.'

'Siobhan's background?'

Deadly Secrets

'Her father is an accountant; her mother stayed at home to raise their daughter and two sons.'

'You've not spoken to them?' Wendy asked.

'I've only found the details. I would think that's a job for Wendy,' Bridget said.

'Except that would get back to Siobhan, who would relay it to Ibrahim Ali, who would sense a rat,' Isaac said.

Moxon made a note to phone Gabrielle after the meeting concluded.

'Which means,' Isaac said, 'that Ali embraced Islam out of a need in his life to belong and that he felt alienated from the Marshalls. Does that apply to Siobhan, who had no conflict but felt love for Benjamin, who changed in a way she couldn't have expected? Is she the dutiful wife, or is she frustrated with her situation? Does she revel in the title and want to become accepted in society and to flaunt her good luck to her friends in Nottingham, or is she as fervent as her husband?'

'Questions you will need to answer,' Bridget said. 'I've done the groundwork. It's up to you three to follow through.'

'We could use Clough,' Larry said.

'We don't know who he is,' Isaac reminded him.

'Except that he makes visits to Ibrahim Ali,' Wendy said.

'Which means what?' Larry asked.

'It means that he was there at the request of Seth Caddick,' Isaac said. 'And we know what that man is.'

'Do we? We know Clough was brought into the department by Chief Superintendent Caddick. That doesn't make him a plant, and so far, he's behaved impeccably.'

'Test him. Put him in an impossible position; see which way he jumps.'

'How can I do that?'

'Delvene Drayton? Did she die because of her association with the Avers family, or is it closer to home? What do you reckon?'

'It's to do with Ali, although we can't make the connection.'

197

'Then work with Clough, day and night, if you can. Postulate your theory with him that you believe that Delvene and Robert died because of Marjorie and her firstborn, and that suspicion must fall on the one person who has not been interviewed. Tell him to meet with Ibrahim Ali, and you go along. Observe the body language. Bait Clough with the attacks in Whitehall. Where was he? What did he know?'

'We're opening ourselves to trouble.'

'Good, the more, the better. The sooner we bring this to a head, the sooner we can all relax.'

'Six feet under is more relaxing than I need,' Larry said.

Isaac ignored the comment.

'What else, Bridget,' Isaac asked.

'Benjamin left his job and took to wearing traditional Arab robes. He's calling himself Ibrahim Ali and making a name for himself. He's fluent in Arabic, knows his Koran, and can recite large chunks. He's interviewed on local radio and regional television. He's rallying people to the cause and arguing eloquently that his belief is firm and there must be more integration of persons across all societies and religions. He meets with Christian leaders and sets up food vans for the homeless, clinics for the drug addicted, and the cost of hospital treatment for those at his Mosque who are incapable of paying. There's a begrudging acceptance of the man. He makes the holy trip to Saudi Arabia, to Mecca.'

'Where is Siobhan?'

'She's at home, pregnant, rarely venturing out of the house, and if she does, it's in the company of other women.'

'Are you saying she's not his only wife?'

'I cannot find any record to confirm. Only that out on the street, she is indistinguishable from the other women.'

'Wendy, make the phone call,' Isaac said. 'Sound out her parents. They may tell you more if they are antagonistic towards their daughter.'

'And it might blow our investigation.'

'Do it,' Isaac said, 'or this could go on ad infinitum. Is there any more?'

'Just one thing. I checked the police records at the station near Ibrahim Ali's previous house. He's known to them, not for anything criminal, but he's a person of note in the area. There's a file of who he speaks to, his activities, and who visits the house.'

'Surveillance of that level would not be conducted by the local police,' Isaac said.

'It wouldn't, except there's a special request that ends before the terrorist attack when Ibrahim Ali announces to the world that he is the son of Lord Alsworthy and claims the title.'

'How long did the surveillance last?'

'Eleven months.'

'Who requested it and why?'

'It came through official channels. I spoke to Inspector Naismith, who confirmed it. He also told me he met a woman three days after the request. He described her as blonde, attractive, and very pleasant.'

'Did he sleep with her?' Isaac asked but realised it was a stupid comment, not worthy of a chief inspector.

'I sent him a photo. I did not ask him how cosy they were.'

'Was it?'

'It was Linda Harris. She was conducting surveillance.'

'But why end the surveillance before the attack in Whitehall. Was it coincidental, or does it have significance?'

'Only one way to find out,' Wendy said. 'You're the only person who can get closer to her.'

'Not that close,' Isaac replied. 'I never knew the truth from her, even back then. Linda's the name we use. I'm certain it's not her true name.'

'She called herself Susan when she met the inspector,' Bridget said.

Chapter 20

Isaac intended it to be just him and Moxon, but at the last moment, he chose to take Wendy. Moxon, on his initiative, invited Gabrielle. Wendy sat in one corner of the main room. Isaac remained standing, and Gabrielle sat on a sofa. Lord Moxon stood with his back to an open fire.

'Wendy,' Moxon said, 'I listened to your friend, Bridget. I assume you realised that.'

'I did. Bridget and Inspector Hill do not know of you and Gabrielle, but DCI Cook realised they needed to understand the risks and pull out if they were uncomfortable.

'Isaac, do you want to tell Gabrielle what Bridget discovered?' Moxon said, who took a seat next to Gabrielle.

'Gabrielle, Ali has a wife,' Isaac said.

'Or four?' Gabrielle replied.

'We know of one, and that might be the woman you have spoken to. Before she married Ibrahim Ali, her name was Siobhan Kelly. They had been living together before he embraced Islam. There was a pregnancy, so we assume there must be a child.'

'Her background?'

'Middle class, white, Anglo-Saxon. Ali had issues in his teens when he realised that the Marshalls, who had brought him up well and whom he loved, were different to him. He sensed reality, the truth that was not given to him. If it had, people might still be alive, but that's history, and no reason to dwell on it.

'Also, Ali's wife is ostracised by her parents due to her marriage to Ali, but not because she had been living with Benjamin Marshall. The child's whereabouts, if it survived, is unknown, as there are no records of its existence.

'After inadvertently bumping into her, Wendy met Siobhan's mother in a supermarket. They got talking, and Wendy steered the conversation to their children. Wendy's were fine and getting on with life; Siobhan's mother told her how her daughter was lost to her, married to a man who was a total bastard, and she wished him dead. She did not know about a child.

'Which brings up the most difficult part for you, Gabrielle. Are you willing to do this?'

'To talk to the woman, of course, I am,' Gabrielle replied.

'It's not that easy. As Ali's wife, she might need her husband's permission to spend time with you alone. Siobhan might not be responsive. Remember, above all else, that you do not know the woman's history or English name and never mention that Wendy met with her mother.'

'We, Alsworthys, know our duty. I will not let you down,' Gabrielle said.

'For myself,' Moxon said. 'I have access to Lord MacTavish's papers.'

'How?' Isaac asked.

'MacTavish was the laird of his clan. They are of value to his family. They intend to correlate and file, to add them to the clan's history.'

'If they don't include his assent to Marjorie Frobisher being hit by a vehicle or Richard Williams being assassinated by Linda Harris.'

'Not in this century. In time, when nobody is alive to remember, then colourful events orchestrated by Angus MacTavish will embellish the man and the clan.'

'When are you going to Scotland?'

'Two days. I need someone to come with me.'

'I assume you want Bridget.'

'I couldn't think of anybody more qualified.' Moxon said. 'I believe we will need a week to complete, and the library at the castle will be at our disposal. They will provide accommodation.'

'Do they know why?'

'I've told MacTavish's eldest son, the current laird, that I'm updating my memoirs. I hope that is acceptable.'

'It might come out at a trial.'

'It won't. The Official Secrets Act will scupper any plans for it to be revealed. That, unfortunately, I agree with.'

***

Bridget listened without comment as Isaac explained that she would be going to Scotland with Lord Moxon, that she would be staying in a castle and would be working alongside his lordship as they went through Lord MacTavish's papers. The proverbial needle in a haystack might be there, and if it was, to keep it confidential and not send emails to Wendy or him. Phone calls were permissible, but text messages were not.

Gabrielle made the phone call and received an invite to the main house, as it was known. A quaint term for a mansion. It was a massive structure, with three storeys, eight bedrooms, a library with over five thousand books, some of them first editions and valuable, a dining room that could accommodate twenty-four persons at one sitting, numerous oil paintings, most of them extremely valuable, and the pictures of the Alsworthys, recent and ancient.

Gabrielle would not show nerves, nor would she shy away, but face the man, look him straight in the face, and tell him that she wanted to meet with his wife and for her to come down to her house and for them to drink tea, play cards, to laugh, to cry, and that she did not need a chaperone.

That was until Lord Ibrahim Alsworthy entered the sitting room. For once, she was dumbstruck. Instead of his robes or the ermine, the man wore a top hat and tails.

'So pleased to see you, sister,' Alsworthy said. 'I had hoped to see you. My wife has taken a shine to you and would like to be your friend.'

Gabrielle took a moment to compose herself. 'That would be delightful. How kind. I've seen her a few times, but she has been reluctant to talk. Why the change?'

'Life changes for us all. I'm off to Ascot.'

'Your wife?'

'She's not going. How are you with horses? I've considered buying a couple; maybe you could teach me to ride.'

'Ibrahim, is this a change in you, or are you embracing your societal position?'

'Not that dramatic a change, but the title accords me responsibilities, which I intend to honour, and for you, dear sister, to assist.'

'I'll do what I can, but don't believe I'm happy with you in the house.'

'Spoken like a true Alsworthy. Of course, you are not. Life had been good for you, but with traditional stiff upper lip, you'll survive.'

'Your wife?'

'She will be at your house within the hour.'

'Alone?'

'Alone. We have been together for a long time. She will tell you I am no threat and will not dishonour the family name.'

Although you might have already, Gabrielle thought. She did not like the change in the man, which caused her to wonder why he had agreed for her to meet with his wife. It was the first time he had referred to any woman by that title.

Regardless, one hour later, to the minute, there was a knock at the door. Gabrielle opened it to find Siobhan or Latifa, as Ali had referred to, standing there. This time, she was not covered from head to toe but modestly dressed, wearing a silk shalwar kameez. There was a scarf across her head. She was attractive and polite and spoke with a northern accent.

The two women sat down for tea. It was apparent that Siobhan, the name she preferred with Gabrielle, enjoyed the freedom.

'Ibrahim is a good man,' Siobhan said.

'Are you married? Your parents?' Gabrielle asked innocuous questions, unsure how far she could push or what she hoped to achieve. If Siobhan had married for love and continued to love her husband, despite or because of what he had become, how far could she push before the woman pulled away, tightened the scarf around her face, and left?

'To Ibrahim, although you know he wasn't born with that name. In fact, he doesn't know what his birth parents had called him, even if they did.'

Gabrielle did not know, either, and it had never been mentioned, only that his parents were married in a brief ceremony, and the birth registered. She thought the name wasn't important.

'I know most of it,' Gabrielle said. 'Your husband has had plenty of media coverage, especially after he became Lord Alsworthy and my half-brother.'

'Which you must hate.'

'It doesn't sit comfortably with me. I cannot deny that to you or to Ibrahim. He's well aware of my disdain, but I will accept the situation.'

'Until…'

'Time changes everything. How about you? You came from an English background, probably wore skimpy clothes, went dancing, got drunk, and made out with men.'

'I never drank, although I had no issue with it. I enjoyed dancing, and I met Ibrahim when I was still young. He's the only one I made out with. Gabrielle, you were thrown out of your house by my husband, who could evict you from this one. That must give you a reason to hate my husband.'

Gabrielle could hate what had happened to her and her family, but she did not feel the loathing for Ibrahim Ali that would have been expected, and now, with his wife casually chatting, she wondered if the subtle transformation she had seen with the man, reflected his changed circumstance. Would that mean Lord and Lady Alsworthy would become English aristocrats in the style society would accept?

She knew of Siobhan's child but remembered that Ali's wife had not been mentioned in the media, and to reveal that she knew might raise the hackles of the woman.

'Before you married Ibrahim, what was your life like?' Gabrielle asked.

'My parents disapproved when Ibrahim became a Muslim. We don't talk anymore.'

'Does that concern you?'

'Ibrahim is a good man, and I am with him. Ibrahim and I were poor, living in a little flat, and then we moved to a house, but it remained difficult. But now, we have the mansion, your mansion, and there is enough room for me to relax.'

'And pray.'

Gabrielle noticed that Siobhan had emptied the plate of biscuits in front of her. 'How about an English breakfast? How many years since you had one.'

'A long time. That would be lovely, but no bacon. Ibrahim would not forgive me if I ate pork.'

'Beef sausages, fried tomatoes, eggs, and baked beans. Okay, by you?'

'I'll help you prepare.'

Siobhan was a better cook in the kitchen than Gabrielle, who, as a child and then at the mansion, always had staff. However, since her relegation to the second child of a dead father, she no longer had the desire to have staff, apart from a local villager who came twice a week to do the washing, vacuum, and change the beds.

She had noticed that even with that woman, the respect she once had was diminished, and in the nearby village, at the shop where they always gave her credit and she never had to wait in line to be served, there was no credit, and no moving to the front of the queue. If she wanted to hate, it would be her father.

'Ibrahim used to love bacon before,' Siobhan said.

'When he was Benjamin. Why did he change? He had you, and you were in love with each other.'

'He felt he didn't belong with his parents and friends. Now, we know the reason. Gabrielle, you would not understand.'

'I did, at university.'

'You've never been confronted by it, believed that your position in society was sacrosanct and that people would deem to you, even in this enlightened age. Tradition dies hard, and those who regarded Ibrahim with disdain now fawn after him. He's been asked to open the village fete next month.'

'Which I did last year,' Gabrielle said, feeling a shiver up her spine.

'He's uncomfortable with it, but you've noticed the change.'

'I have. Is it permanent, or will he discard it later on? The glory and wealth seem important when you first get it, but then you get used to it. I never considered it before; I just accepted that the family lived in the big house and that it was holidays in the Caribbean.'

'My parents used to joke that if they won the lottery, it wouldn't change them. Not that they had the chance to prove it, as they never won anything.'

'People change, Siobhan. I've become humbler since I moved out of the mansion. People treat me differently. I'm not sure I miss what I had before, but I would take it back without hesitation. Does that make me a bad person?'

'Gabrielle, it makes you human.'

The two women sat at a table in the kitchen. Siobhan wanted to ask for bacon but did not. Gabrielle considered asking if she wanted something stronger than tea but realised that if she did and it got back to Ibrahim, it would cause friction.

'I was surprised that your husband agreed to let you come here. Aren't you the property of your husband?'

'Ibrahim is conflicted. He had never thought that our lives would change so much. He's unsure how to react.'

'I've seen other men.'

'Before, he would have told them what to do, but now, they control.'

'If he weakens, they will take control, and he will become a powerless figurehead.'

'His life would be protected. Without the title, they are nothing.'

'Will your husband allow us to become friends? Who are the other women?'

'He will if he does not change from what you see today. Although, how long before the others impose their will on me.'

'The other women?'

'One of them was born in this country to an Islamic family; the other two came from overseas, and their English is poor. Be careful what you say in front of them, and be careful of the other men.'

'Your parents?' Gabrielle asked. She thought she was pushing too hard, but now there was an added reason, she worried for the woman.'

'We rarely met even before Benjamin became Ibrahim and I became Latifa. After our marriage, I haven't spoken to them.'

'Even though you are titled.'

'They would be ambivalent to it.'

'Children?'

Siobhan held a handkerchief to her eyes. 'There was a beautiful girl, but she died at three months. It was tragic, and we both miss her, but she was ill from birth.'

'I'm sorry,' Gabrielle said.

'I need to go,' Siobhan said. As she left the house, she kissed and hugged Gabrielle. 'Be careful.'

'Careful with what?'

'You've been evicted from your home and your position. I've seen it with Ibrahim; the Alsworthy blood runs strongly in him. You will not rest until you reassert your position. I don't believe you understand what you are up against.'

Gabrielle was left on the doorstep, wondering if it was a warning or an observation. Whatever it was, it unnerved her. Siobhan had not been offered alcohol, but it was what Gabrielle needed to calm her nerves.

Chapter 21

Bridget took an early morning flight to Inverness, where she would meet Lord Moxon, who had flown up the day before. Due to the sensitivity of the intended purpose of the trip, it had been decided they would not meet in London nor travel on the same plane, although they had spoken on the phone. She was a little nervous at meeting the eminent man, but when they met, they had shaken hands, visited MacDonalds for breakfast, and hired a car.

The two drove to Loch Lochy and up the driveway to the laird MacTavish's castle. Loch Ness wasn't far away, but she did not intend to visit, as she didn't believe in the Loch Ness Monster, Bigfoot, and things that go bump in the night. Although that first night at the castle, when the wind howled through the trees outside her bedroom window and branches brushed against the panes, she wasn't so sure.

Moxon and Bridget dined with the new laird's family. In his forties, the laird wore a kilt as did Moxon, who Bridget knew wasn't Scottish, but as a former politician, he knew how to flatter important persons. Bridget wore a dress she had bought in a department store. Even so, the laird's wife complimented Bridget on her dress. Bridget's mother would have said good manners cost nothing and good breeding amounted to a lot, as exemplified by the laird's wife. On the walls were paintings of important figures and battles the clan had fought in, some of which they had lost. Above the enormous fireplace in the dining room, crossed swords and a shield.

For the main course, Haggis, the national dish of Scotland, which Bridget and Wendy had joked about eating on a planned vacation to Scotland. Sheep liver, heart, and lungs mixed with beef and oatmeal, seasoned with onion, cayenne pepper and spices, packed into a sheep's stomach and boiled.

She enjoyed the experience and complimented the laird and his wife for their hospitality and the meal. Although, on the planned trip, Wendy could eat Haggis. Bridget realised it was an acquired taste. However, she had no issue with the wines on the table, nor the toasts to the clan, to each other, and to the visit of Lord Moxon and Bridget Halloran, with the finest whisky in Scotland, according to the laird.

The next day, later than either Moxon or Bridget would have liked, as both had risen late due to the late night and the alcohol, they sat down to breakfast. Sausages, bacon, tomatoes, and eggs, washed down with tea. After breakfast, the two retreated to the library. Angus MacTavish's papers were on a bookshelf at the back of a large desk.

A local historian was coming in the next month to collate and add to the previous generations' collected works.

Bridget took one of the folders. 'Won't some of these contain sensitive information?' she asked his lordship.

'MacTavish was a stickler for keeping records. They would be here if he theorised, planned, or doodled. Anyone in high public office always keeps a detailed record of everything, no matter how insignificant.'

'In case there's a book in it,' Bridget said.

'There's always a book, and then, there are the speaking tours.'

'I read your memoir before I came.'

'Staggered by the eloquence or critical of my policies?'

'Some policies weren't to my favour, but you were eloquent.'

Moxon appreciated the honesty. He had met enough sycophants in his time. He could see why Bridget and Wendy were such great friends.

The first folder contained records of MacTavish's expenditure. It was dull and ceded nothing of relevance. The second was more informative as it contained notes taken in his time as a parliamentarian, including one that referred to Lord Moxon when he had been Chancellor of the Exchequer, in that the man was barely capable of adding two and two, and how in a month of Sundays could he be hoped to balance the budget. Moxon laughed out loud when Bridget read it to him.

The third folder, larger than the previous two, appeared promising, and the two sat down and read through its contents, page by page. They photocopied what was important, scanning the rest into Moxon's laptop. Lord Moxon believed that anything secretive or damning would add little to MacTavish's' illustrious history and might be concealed behind other books in the library or in a safe. He hoped they were not, which made Bridget think that his lordship had a similar hiding place at his house.

After all, in his memoirs, he had alluded to scandals which had besmirched his career, including the unceremonious dumping of a member of his party for exchanging political favours for sex with a well-known model, who was dealing with an obstructive regional council and not allowing her to extend her house at the rear.

Also, the embarrassment when it was revealed that the government had approved the shipping of weapons from an English manufacturer to a country that should not have been trusted with peashooters, saving eight hundred jobs in a marginal constituency, three weeks before an election after the previous member had died of a heart attack.

Four days had passed, and still, there was more to do. Lord Moxon, who was ageing, had taken to his bed and would need two days of complete rest before he could continue, which meant that Bridget was in the library alone. Every day, around eleven a.m., a maid would come in with coffee and a light snack. Bridget would break at one in the afternoon when the maid would return and leave another tray with a cooked meal.

At six in the evening, Bridget would be exhausted and go to her room, freshen up, and join the family in the sitting room, where there would be another meal. It would be informal. She had to admit that she enjoyed her time away from the office, especially with the MacTavish clan at the castle, who treated her with the greatest respect.

Deadly Secrets

On the seventh day, Lord Moxon returned to the library, but he sat in a leather-backed chair while Bridget continued at a reduced pace. She was running out of energy, and they had found nothing of substance except a cryptic note that mentioned that Alsworthy needed the chief whip's assistance.

All the folders had been checked, twelve in total, and a stack of papers, receipts, and a business card to a high-class gentleman's club that dispensed more than drinks.

Bridget had phoned Wendy, who confirmed that the club was notorious for the available women if you had the money, that Angus MacTavish was known there, and that discretion was paramount. When pressured by Wendy, they revealed that he stayed in the main room, sat in a corner, and drank whisky. The action occurred upstairs, but nobody would reveal if MacTavish had climbed the carpeted stairs. Wendy assumed he had.

Moxon knew there had to be more, but Bridget was unsure; besides, she had worn herself out. Further searching was beyond her, and she wondered if MacTavish was as devious as Lord Moxon. Regardless, she thought long and hard about what she would have done if she had been MacTavish. She could hack a website, access locked files, and encrypt documents she did not want anyone to access, but it was known that MacTavish did not have the necessary skills and that his secrets would be on paper and in folders.

It was the last day, and the two were booked on flights to London the next day. As when they had come up, they would not travel together, apart from the drive to Inverness.

Bridget took hold of her drink and walked around the library, looking at thousands of books.

She thought a book title might help, a reference to a secret or a hidden compartment, even a mystery novel, but that seemed even more unlikely than her other two thoughts. She started to doubt if it was a puzzle after two and a half hours, but she persevered, which she did long after the family had gone to sleep.

It was close to midnight, and the library was cold and uninviting. She had looked through nearly eighty books that day, skimmed and put them back. She had decided the last book would be an obscure reference book on Sir Robert Walpole, who was considered Britain's first prime minister. A small sheet of paper fell out as she opened the first page. On it, there was a sequence of numbers. It was late, but she roused Wendy from her slumber, who said she would be up on the first flight in the morning. She knew what the numbers meant.

Bridget took a copy of the paper, returned the original and the book to where she had taken them from and went to bed.

***

Wendy arrived mid-morning at the castle, briefly exchanging pleasantries with Lord Moxon as he left, a taxi to the airport, as he was beyond the capability to drive. In London, a government vehicle would pick him up and take him to a hospital for a couple of days while his condition was evaluated before he would return home. A nurse would stay with him at the house for as long as it was necessary, which to Wendy, on their brief encounter, she thought would not be for long.

The investigation into Davies' complicity in an illegal act had been thrown when MacTavish died. She hoped it would not happen again after Lord Moxon's death. He had become the backbone of the investigation, a dying man's attempt to leave his mark.

'I'll be fine,' Moxon said as Wendy hugged him. It was her first prime minister, and he was not even of her party, but he had charmed her.

'Apparently, I'm eating Haggis tonight,' Wendy said.

'I don't think Bridget was too fond of it, but she bravely finished it. Hopefully, you'll enjoy it more than her.'

'I will.'

As Moxon's taxi drove away, a large door opened, and Wendy entered the castle; a butler led her to the library, where she met an exhausted Bridget. The two women sat down; Bridget pulled a cord that hung from the ceiling. Five minutes later, a maid entered with more than enough sandwiches, cakes, and an extra-large teapot. Neither woman was going to be thirsty or hungry.

Bridget took the book from the shelf, laid it on the desk she and Lord Moxon had used, and opened it. She then took hold of the small piece of paper and gave it to Wendy. 'It's the combination of a safe,' she said.

'Which safe? I haven't found one here, so why hide it in a book? How was anyone meant to find it?'

'No one was. Lord MacTavish must have had a reason. Appropriate that it references a prime minister, considering that one just left.'

'I tried everything I could think of. Connotations of secret and code, and then, I thought of politics. That was my last book.

'Put it down to serendipity, or somewhere up there is looking out for us.'

Bridget wasn't certain about anyone above, but it seemed more than luck or serendipity. Bridget would like to have claimed that it was a skilful deduction that she had chanced on that book, but even so, she hadn't even thought of the possibility and that, at the last minute, she had snatched triumph from shattering defeat.

They would not ask the MacTavish family where the safe was. First, Bridget and Wendy would look for it. The family might have been concerned about what was in it if there was a safe. Bridget could understand their possible reticence.

The chief whip of his political party was there to deal with scandal and innuendo, to get members of the party out of trouble or to get them into trouble if they needed to be ousted. What was in the safe could still be politically damaging.

Wendy, who had been in stately homes before on other investigations, realised that old houses and castles had hidden secrets, concealed doors, interconnected tunnels, and stairways.

The castle was old, and parts were built in the fourteenth century. Back then, its purpose would have been defensive, a stronghold against a neighbouring clan or the English.

Wendy assumed the library was the most likely place because the paper had been found there. She had to admit that it was weak logic. Regardless, it proved to be successful. She pulled one book out after another on the top shelf on the wall nearest to the window. She found the safe. It was old and dusty with a combination on the front. She knew what the numbers on the paper meant. She had no idea how to use them.

'Yale, probably fifty to sixty years old. I have a combination, but I don't know how to open it,' Wendy said. She was on a movable ladder in the room. Her phone was on speaker.

'Who is it?' Bridget asked from down below.

'The best safecracker in London,' Wendy replied.

Bridget wasn't sure of the ethics of using a convicted criminal to open a safe, but these were unusual times.

Wendy followed the instructions meticulously, and the safe opened. She withdrew the contents. There were three folders, a computer disk, and a stack of notes.

Bridget laid them out on the desk. She could see they were relevant.

The first folder listed the names of members of parliament, with dates and a summary of their indiscretions. Some were financial, a few were criminal, but the majority were sexual. The last column had a date for when they had been resolved. They were not believed to be vital to the investigation, but a photocopy would be taken before returning the folder to the safe. The second folder showed that MacTavish had been claiming expenses on his house in London while living with his mistress five days a week at another address, returning to Scotland most weekends and for meetings of the clans and holidays or when it was the grouse-shooting season when he would organise a group of his nearest and dearest political friends and financial movers for the shooting, the eating, and the drinking.

There was evidence of a crime in the folder, but the man was dead, and as a crime, it would never have been prosecuted due to acute embarrassment to MacTavish and Moxon's political party. Yet again, photocopies would be taken before being returned to the safe.

The third folder showed more promise. It was bulging, and it referred to Lord Alsworthy, who had renounced his title to stand as a member of parliament, the title restored on his retirement, and that the removal of the title had not been correctly processed, but no one ever knew, and MacTavish had never mentioned it.

Bridget and Wendy sat down with the laird and his wife that night. A piper played 'Amazing Grace' on his bagpipes for the occasion.

Wendy ate her Haggis and declared that she loved it. The laird's wife knew she had not feigned her joy of the Haggis as Bridget had. That night, Bridget and Wendy joined them for a dram of whisky after the meal before retiring to their beds. They had two days to go through what they had found.

The next day, breakfast was delivered to them in the library. Wendy took the stack of loose papers and tidied them to ensure that the writing on each flowed from top to bottom. She then put them through the photocopier before handing them to Bridget, who put the originals in an evidence bag.

She would look at the copies later, but she had the originals from the third folder for now. She read through them and entered the salient facts into her laptop before putting them into another evidence bag.

'What does it say?' Wendy asked. Detailed analysis of documents was her friend's forte, not hers, and after standing up for too long, she had taken a seat and put her legs up on a stool. Outside was a constant drizzle, and a highland mist surrounded the castle. It would have been romantic with a lover, but it was cold and depressing in the library, and the room was dark until the butler came in and lit the fire.

Bridget worked tirelessly for two hours and thirty-five minutes before declaring. 'I could do with a drink. This time, Wendy pulled the cord. They gave their instructions. Fifteen minutes later, the maid returned, this time with a trolley. On it were a bottle of uncorked red wine, a selection of savouries, and hot meat pies with homemade tomato sauce.

Bridget took a fifteen-minute break for sustenance and a glass of wine; Wendy took sustenance and washed it down with three glasses before falling asleep.

Thirty minutes later, Bridget woke her friend to give her a summary. 'It's what we thought, apart from a couple of issues.'

'What are they?' Wendy asked.

'MacTavish was more involved than what we thought. He knew what Linda Harris intended to do, who she was, and who she reported to. He approved Robert Williams' liquidation. There was also a contingency to liquidate Marjorie Frobisher before her eventual death. He had held off on that, for what reason we do not know.'

'We do,' Wendy said. 'Marjorie was Alsworthy's first love. He would not have wanted her to die, and MacTavish did not want to get on the wrong side of Alsworthy. Good breeding for the aristocracy meant the broodmare had to be one of them, not the daughter of a man in trade. Alsworthy had reluctantly divorced Marjorie, not due to their youth but because of their disparate social status. Who knows how history would have turned out if people married for love, not status, wealth, or breeding.'

'There is something else, much more damming. It's four pages. It reports Ibrahim Ali's movements from his earliest religious utterings to when he became a lord. The report shows when Ali and Siobhan married, the child that died, his meetings, and the people he met. It appears that whoever prepared this report was aware of the likelihood of a terrorist attack.'

'Which means certain persons might have been abhorred but not surprised when it happened.' Wendy said.

'Not only that but certain locations and possible dates.'

'Who prepared it?'

'It's marked secret. There is no name, only proof that whatever was happening with Ibrahim Ali and his people, others were keeping a watch on them. What it means, I've no idea.'

Chapter 22

Bridget would stay at the castle for two more days. Before leaving, the current laird would be given a précised version of what had been discovered. The man was concerned but knew what his father had been and the power he had wielded.

Wendy returned to London on the next day's flight after the discovery.

Isaac had been updated over the phone but not by email. The report Wendy carried showed details of Marjorie and the previous Lord Alsworthy, a reference to a marriage, and a birth certificate of the young Alsworthy, who had been named James. It was the Marshalls who had named their newly adopted son, Benjamin, after Martin Marshall's father, who had died the previous year.

The disk proved harder to crack, and Bridget wished for the computing resources at Challis Street, but she could not use them for obvious reasons. Instead, she persevered, ensuring she had two backup copies before she tried. A disk drive was no longer a standard feature on a laptop, but she had not only brought a police-issue laptop but another from home, older, more basic, with less memory but still with a drive.

It was late that first night after Wendy had left that Bridget gained access. Bridget was impressed by what had been entered onto the disk. Sixty-four documents, eighteen Excel spreadsheets, and two PowerPoint presentations. Also of interest were eight photos, two showing a young MacTavish, an equally young Alsworthy, and an even younger Marjorie Frobisher.

Whether the two photos had any bearing on the investigation wasn't known. Angus MacTavish had met Marjorie socially, but that was thought to have been after she had become a celebrity. The pictures proved that not only had he known her before, but that he had met her around the age when she had

Deadly Secrets

become pregnant and had given birth to the current Lord Alsworthy.

Unfortunately, the three in the photos were dead; one had been murdered, another had died in his bed, and the third had been hit by a vehicle as she staggered out of a restaurant.

Bridget pulled the cord in the library and unlocked the door, an added precaution due to the sensitive nature of what she was finding. The maid came, on cue, and left Bridget, her lunch supplemented by a glass of red wine. The library was austere and gloomy; she needed something extra to keep going.

Wendy phoned every couple of hours, not to pry, but to cheer up her friend, who wanted to leave the castle and return home. Castles were draughty, the floors were cold, and the paintings on the walls were not of flowers or happy things but of battles and sour-faced ancestors.

The safe was closed, and the books that had covered it were replaced. Whether the current laird and his family knew of its existence was unknown. It was unlikely the contents would have interested them much if they had, but they did to Bridget.

The PowerPoint presentations were related to party business, a list of expenditures, and a list of claims against them. Bridget could see that some appeared to be rorts, which did not surprise her. Nobody believed their political leaders were incorruptible and only there to serve the people.

Of the sixty-four documents, the majority were of little importance. One of those remaining after Bridget sorted them was focused on Marjorie Frobisher and the child. It was dated three months after the birth, two months after the child's parents had divorced. The divorce had not been contested, and the procedure had been circumvented. Another document related to the death of Marjorie and the murders of the others in the original murder enquiry. The second page listed key persons, phone numbers, work addresses, and residential addresses. DCI Cook's was there, and so was Wendy's.

Also, there was a kill order for Isaac Cook.

Bridget phoned Isaac and told him what she had found and that she thought he should know, procedures aside and running the risk of being overheard.

Isaac's response. 'Is there a name?'

'We know the name. It was scheduled for the night that you walked away from her. Coitus Interruptus would have taken on a whole new meaning.'

Isaac felt sick and could taste the bile in his mouth. All to protect the deputy prime minister in a tough general election, which had not protected him from inglorious defeat along with his party.

Linda Harris had never denied that she would execute an order, but she had further stated that she felt a strong emotion for Isaac. Regardless, she would have killed him that night if they had not argued. Was that the reason they had parted after harsh words? Had she tried to protect him, knowing that her training and psyche would have completed the task.

Isaac had read that recruits to the Secret Service often came from unusual backgrounds and that a lack of emotion, a psychopathic nature, and an innate ability to inflict violence were commendable assets. He was interested in what was mentioned about the latest investigation, whether MacTavish knew more than he said he did, and whether he was using police officers to give him the proof. But what if they had the proof? Who would deal with it? Commissioner Davies? A grateful government when it had been revealed that the august police force was rotten to the core? Or did MacTavish intend to get the proof and then bury it? Was Caddick not the instigator of the attack in Whitehall but the instrument of MacTavish?

MacTavish was no longer alive, but Lord Moxon was. Was he there to complete what MacTavish had started, and for what purpose?

Bridget checked the remaining documents and the files. Some were relevant, but most were not. She did not intend to spend another day in the library and closed her laptop, ensuring that all that had been taken from the safe was in her bags and very secure.

Before she left the house that afternoon, she spent time with the laird's wife, thanked her profusely for her hospitality, and then drove to Inverness. There was a restaurant at the airport, and Haggis was on the menu. She chose fish and chips.

The next day, she would go to the office in the morning, ensure her administrative duties were current, and then go home and work from there.

***

On the third day of Bridget's return, and with her analysis complete of what she had obtained in Scotland, she returned to Homicide. She had been making the occasional visit but staying only long enough to divest as much of her routine work to other persons as possible. Isaac had made it clear that he wanted her to focus as much time as she could on the current semi-official murder enquiry. The department was using the deaths of Robert Avers and Delvene Drayton to allow Isaac and his inner team to follow through on the more important objective.

It was difficult and exceedingly frustrating, especially when Clough, due to his relentless pursuit of Delvene's murderer, walked into Homicide at ten-thirty-five of the second day after Bridget's return to announce that he had arrested the woman's husband and that he had a verbal confession.

Wendy worried for Delvene's children, Bridget worried about the extra work to prepare the documentation for the prosecution, and Isaac was concerned that if it was true, it would be one less excuse for him and the team to continue to investigate Caddick and Ibrahim Ali, which Isaac realised had become an obsession, in that he was allowing emotion to overrule his professionalism.

Isaac was not a man to hate, but he did Seth Caddick. It showed the last time the man had come into Homicide to inform Isaac that Clough had proved his worth and would be replacing

Sergeant Wendy Gladstone, who would stay in Homicide for another couple of months. She could then transfer to Transport if she wanted or be given a clerical position in the station, but not in Homicide, and then, at the end of the year, she could be given a rousing send-off, and that the commissioner would come and present her with an award for meritorious service.

Larry sat down with Clough in the interview room. It was just after one in the afternoon; the delay was due to the legal aid lawyer, who appeared to be a cut above the usual. The woman, who was in her forties, had read the relevant documentation given to her and been told about the confession, only to declare it invalid, and that she hoped they had a better case with more evidence before her client was forced to sit through the verbiage that she had seen and read.

Larry thought that the woman's approach was refreshing in that she was not willing to sit dumbfounded in the interview as two seasoned police officers attempted to play the good cop/bad cop routine with a hapless individual who was still grieving after his former wife's murder.

Clough would wait for the interview before presenting evidence that showed that Jacob Drayton, Delvene's former husband, had grieved in the bed of a woman two doors down from where he lived. He was divorced, but the woman had a husband who was at sea for extended periods, and if he knew what his wife was up to, there would be one more murder and a severe beating of another.

When Clough briefly spoke to her, Sal Winters said she would give Jacob an alibi. Clough doubted if she would stand up in a court, swear on a bible, and repeat it, as Clough had checked, and Sal's husband, apart from his time at sea, had spent five years in prison for grievous bodily harm.

Larry went through the formalities and asked those present to give their names and titles, in the case of him and Clough, and the legal aid, Nneka Suleman.

'I have a verbal confession,' Clough said.
'I did confess,' Jacob Drayton confirmed.

'Did you?' Nneka Suleman interjected. 'Was the confession coerced? Who else was present? Important questions that need answering. My client is under duress, with a wife to bury, two children to console, and a business that is on its last legs. Your confession, Sergeant, holds little weight.'

'I did kill her. How could I allow her to live? Our children were subject to merciless teasing.'

'In the playground?' Larry asked.

'In the classroom. It was the week before she died that my eldest came home and told me what they say at school.'

'Which was?'

'That Delvene was turning tricks with the headmaster.'

'True?'

'I confronted the man. He admitted to it.'

'The school board? What would they say?'

'I informed them that the headmaster, nine years as the head and another five as a science teacher, was banging my former wife. And I would have to consider changing schools.'

'Leave your daughter where she is, give it a few months, and it will be old news,' Clough said.

'Except now, my client has been coerced into a bogus confession for reasons I don't know, and you can't prove,' Nneka Suleman said.

'Your client is holding to his confession,' Clough said. 'He's willing to sign it.'

'Willing, he might be, but I have read the Forensic and the CSI's reports. There is no mention of my client being in Delvene Drayton's house on the night in question. A confession is one thing; a murder conviction is another, especially if my client rescinds his confession when he realises that he's made a fool of himself and wasted our valuable time.'

'You're being paid, Miss Suleman,' Larry said.

'There are far more deserving cases.'

Larry believed a legal aid lawyer of her calibre would be in demand.

'Your children, think of them before you sign,' the legal aid said. 'I'm uncomfortable witnessing a travesty of justice.'

'Your lawyer's given you a lead,' Larry said. 'If you confess, we will hold you in the station. A murder charge does not allow bail. Have you considered this?'

'I have.'

'He's bluffing,' Clough said. 'It's the other woman, two doors down. She killed Delvene, and Drayton is covering for her.'

Sal Winters, Jacob Drayton's lover, would need to be brought into the station, and then her husband would get to know that she was sleeping with the man. That was when Sal Winters would withdraw her alibi; Clough was sure of it.

Jacob Drayton reiterated his confession and gave details on how he had entered the house, climbed the stairs, and entered the bathroom without leaving clues.

***

Isaac read the relevant documentation that Bridget had gleaned from the contents of the safe. In black and white, there was irrefutable proof that Linda Harris was not only a seductress and an assassin but more senior than she had previously revealed, and now, the woman, who hadn't been seen for a month, was on the phone and wanting to meet. Isaac knew he should not agree, but armed with additional knowledge, it was important to confront her and see how she responded.

The night before, after Linda had phoned, he had told Jenny how the investigation was progressing and the possibilities of a conclusion. He did not mention the kill order.

Isaac and Linda met at a restaurant close to Buckingham Palace. Linda wore a short skirt and a skimpy blouse; Isaac wore a suit. She kissed him and put her arms around him.

'It's good to see you,' Linda said as they sat down.

Isaac looked at the menu; Linda looked at him. The situation was uncomfortable. 'Where have you been?' he asked.

'Involved on other issues.'

Deadly Secrets

'In this country?'
'For now.'
'Caddick?'
'He had served his usefulness.'
'That night, before Marjorie Frobisher died, we met and argued,' Isaac knew he had no option but to confront Linda about the kill order. 'Why did you leave?'
'I regretted it afterwards. I thought we would spend the night together.'
'I've seen the kill order,' Isaac said. 'Angus MacTavish showed me.'
Linda said nothing for a while and looked through her menu before calling over the waiter and ordering a bottle of their best champagne. Eventually, unable to avoid the question, she took hold of Isaac's hands. 'I wouldn't have done it.'
'Why? You follow orders.'
'It's what I am conditioned to do.'
'What orders do you have now? Was Caddick an order?'
'We're on the same side, Isaac. You're a one-man crusade, looking for allies, but Moxon's too old, and Gabrielle Alsworthy can't be trusted. It doesn't leave you with many options.'
Linda poured the champagne.
'What do you know? What can you tell me?'
'Ask a question,' Linda said as she poured her second glass.
'Nottingham, when you visited the Marshalls.'
'I was doing research. I used a different name.'
'Why? What is it with Ibrahim Ali? Is he under suspicion? Is there a kill order against his name?'
'We had a file on him before he gained the title. We knew who he was.'
'How?'
'Benjamin Marshall became a Muslim and prayed at his local Mosque. We are always interested in persons who, for no apparent reason, change their religion and then become an advocate for Sharia. MacTavish knew what he was dealing with,

225

and it wasn't just political, but it would have struck at the very heart of this country. He understood the implications, but you wouldn't. MacTavish was dirtier than most, and where I work is the dirtiest. It's surprising that Ali's still alive.'

'Why is he?'

'For the same reason that you are interested in him. We knew of Caddick and his relationship with Davies. There were too many coincidences to believe they were unrelated, and we have a record of Caddick meeting with Ibrahim Ali four weeks before the attack in Whitehall. We can prove that the first time Caddick put it to Ali, he had some information that would benefit him.'

'Where did this meeting take place?'

'At the house where he lived with Siobhan Kelly, or Latifa, as she calls herself now.'

'Gabrielle Alsworthy's met her,' Isaac said.

'So have I,' Linda replied. Isaac could see she had become tipsy. He hoped he would not have to fend her off.

'How?'

'We have maintained a closer watch on Ali since we became aware of his birthright. Caddick's meeting with him raised the level of interest a notch. It started to ring alarm bells.'

'Had you been watching Caddick?'

'We recorded those who visited the house or came out of the Mosque. We had a camera outside the house and people who monitored, if not 24/7. However, the more vocal Ibrahim Ali became, the more interested we became of Caddick. We have people running through the photos we retrieve, then using data recognition and putting a name to the image. Checks were made of friends, colleagues, people in his pocket who owed him a favour, and people he detested. You were on the last list.'

'Detest is an understatement.'

'Subtle pressure was applied to Williams, that Sally Jenkins knew more than she should and might talk. He took the bait and killed her.'

'Who supplied the bait?'

Deadly Secrets

'Marjorie. Williams would do anything for her, and as it turned out, including murder.'

'We have little in common,' Isaac said. 'You believe violent and reprehensible acts are acceptable for the greater good.'

'That's not why I am here. I need to tell you something,' Linda replied.

'From your masters or from yourself?' Isaac was aware that he was being harsh on the woman.

'Both. Listen carefully, and use it as advice. Seth Caddick is meeting at the Alsworthy mansion, but not always with Ibrahim Ali.'

'Then with whom? It would have been Ali initially to set up the attack in Whitehall.'

'He was the person to gain the most advantage. It does not mean he was responsible.'

'What are you saying?'

'He wanted the title and a platform to debate from.'

'If he moves to the lower house, he could achieve political power.' Linda said,

'Ibrahim Ali understands Britain and what we hold dear, but those he surrounds himself with do not.'

'Precisely, Isaac. If what we believe, then we must concede that Seth Caddick is no longer using Ali to ensure Davies' survival as commissioner but has gone rogue.'

'I can't believe that of Caddick. He's a contemptible bastard, but more violence makes no sense. What would be gained by it?'

'Caddick's not interested in what he might do, but what's in it for him.'

'Money?'

'What price will he accept?'

'We need to know who he's meeting with and what is discussed. That's a job for you. Will you accept it?' Linda said.

'You're the Secret Service, not me. I'm a police officer; I would have no chance.'

'Gabrielle Alsworthy might, and now, she's friends with Ibrahim Ali's wife.'

'Are you asking Gabrielle to risk her life?'

'I'm asking Ibrahim Ali's wife to risk hers. What are the woman's views?'

'According to Gabrielle, Siobhan believes in her husband but does talk about his ambition or wants.'

'Then, Siobhan Kelly is the dutiful wife of a man who has committed a terrible act. Does she know this?'

'She will not talk about it. Gabrielle and Siobhan, she prefers her Christian name when she's with Gabrielle, meet two or three times a week. Their conversations are friendly. Siobhan realises that Gabrielle will do anything to get back the mansion; Gabrielle knows that Siobhan is a good person who supports her husband without question.'

'If confronted with the truth?' Linda asked.

'What is the truth? Ali took the title. Does that mean he who sacrificed his men?'

'He has never acknowledged them as his people, and we know he had not met with them before. We have enough surveillance of Ali to know that the three men in Whitehall did not attend the same mosque as Ali.'

'It still doesn't make him innocent.'

'He must know that his claim to the title came from what happened in Whitehall.'

'Which means he should be abhorred of the cost.'

'Would he?' Linda asked.

'When the reward is so high, do men rationalise the crime? Did Ibrahim Ali accept what happened? But now, he's acting as an English gentleman, attending Royal Ascot, and hobnobbing with his fellow lords.'

'And weakening his position as a voice for his religion.'

'He's not preaching in the street, but the House of Lords. They need him.'

'As much as he needs them?'

'Then how to deradicalise him?' Linda said.

'Or how to remove him,' Isaac said. 'If he causes unnecessary trouble, crime or no crime, you can remove him.'
'If there is an order, I would.'

Chapter 23

'He might get up tomorrow if it's sunny, but he'll not walk. Lord Moxon, a friend of yours?' the nurse asked.

'I believe so,' Isaac said, although, as with MacTavish, what did he know of the man. Only that murder had been condoned by the British Government, even if their application had been left to others.

Isaac thought it unusual that the nurse would be interested in whether he was friends with the lord but subsequently discounted it and that, left in the house with an ageing man, she was desperate for conversation.

'Your visit, Isaac?' Moxon said as he lifted himself up and propped himself against the pillows behind him

'There's a job for Gabrielle; it could get her killed,' Isaac said.

'Is it that important?'

'Depends if we trust my source.'

'Linda Harris?' Moxon asked.

'How do you know?'

'I've still got friends in high places, a few others in dark places.'

'Which means MI5.'

'Do you know what we said? Seeing you are so well informed.'

'Not in the restaurant, but I know you met with her. I don't know what you discussed, but you're about to tell me.'

'I am. The focus has been on Ibrahim Ali.'

'I would have thought Chief Superintendent Caddick would be more relevant.'

'It is, and he's visited Ibrahim Ali's mansion several times. My source believes that Caddick might not be visiting Ali but someone else. That Caddick's not protecting his commissioner but feathering his nest.'

'You know Caddick better than anyone else. What do you reckon? Would he stoop that low?'

'My hatred of Caddick could be enough to cloud my judgement?'

'You need to tell Gabrielle and see if she's willing.'

'I've pre-empted your response,' Isaac said. 'She'll be here within the hour.'

'Linda Harris, do you trust her?'

'I want to. I only wish that what we were doing was official. I am meant to be investigating two homicides.'

'Which you are. Aren't they related to the current investigation?'

Isaac thought they were but could not be sure. Even so, he left Moxon's bedroom and went downstairs to the kitchen, where the nurse was sitting.

'A cup of tea,' she said.

'Who are you?' Isaac asked. He was still perturbed by his initial conversation with the woman.

'I am Lord Moxon's nurse and doctor. I'm also his niece. He's close to the end. I intend to make sure he's comfortable, but you, Chief Inspector, excite him when he needs complete rest.'

'He thrives on the challenge. Tell me about your uncle?'

'An ambitious man who rose to the highest political position in this country.'

'Which means I shouldn't trust him.'

'You can trust him if you're smart enough. Are you that smart?'

'Is that a warning?'

'Not a warning, just advice. Whatever your plan, he is two steps ahead of you.'

Isaac sat at the kitchen table, a mug of tea in his hand. Whoever the woman was, niece or not, he felt that if Moxon was two steps ahead, she was one step. The woman left the room; Isaac messaged Bridget.

Bridget texted back within five minutes, confirming that the nurse was a doctor, she was Moxon's niece, and that he had helped her financially through school and university after her father had died when she was young.

Upstairs, Moxon rested.

'How long are you staying?' Isaac asked on the niece's return.

'Three weeks, maybe four. I've taken leave to look after him.'

'After that?'

'Either he's better, at which time I will hand over to someone else, or he's no longer with us.'

'Which one is the most likely?'

'It depends on you. My uncle needs a cause, and you, DCI, are it. Care to tell me what it's about?'

'The less people that know, the better.'

'The less that could get hurt. I know it's something to do with Alsworthy, but that's it.'

'Then, I suggest you forget about it, look after his lordship, and don't get involved.'

'Which means it could be dangerous.'

'It's possible.'

'Uncle likes a good fight. You'll not stop him. He was fearless in politics.'

Isaac thought there was a good discussion to be had with the woman, who would probably understand his feelings about the current situation. However, secrecy was paramount, and the niece was an unknown.

Gabrielle Alsworthy arrived. She opened the front door without knocking and headed up the stairs. Isaac followed soon after.

Moxon was sitting in bed, clearly pleased to see Gabrielle. Isaac could see by his response that if Moxon had a cause, his health would improve, but MacTavish had a reason, and he had died.

'What is it?' Gabrielle asked.

Deadly Secrets

Moxon nodded towards the door. Isaac understood what he meant. Carefully, he opened the door and peered up and down the hallway, catching a door close two doors down.

'Who is she?' Isaac asked when he had taken a chair next to Moxon's bed.

'My niece. No doubt you have gleaned that from her.'

'I have.'

'I don't doubt her affection for me. However, she's ambitious, and I've not long to go. She wants this house and a place I own in London.'

'Is she entitled?' Gabrielle asked, who was sitting on the other side of the bed.

'There's a wayward son. I've cut him out of my will. He could lodge a claim, but I intend to give one of the properties to her and another to him. She wants more and thinks I'll give in to her by spending time here with me.'

'Will you?'

'Not yet, but if she had a lever, she'd use it, and you, DCI Cook, might have given it to her.'

'Would she speak to Ali or Caddick?' Isaac asked.

'She's not a traitor, but as I reach the end, she will pressure me to sign over both properties to her.'

'It's not affection if she would do that.'

'But it is. Politics is dirty, and she understands it better than most, learnt at the knee of a master. Even as a child. I admired her for her gall.'

'Then why not give it to her now?' Gabrielle asked.

'If I do, I disown my son, who is a wastrel. I don't want to do that, and I hope for a reconciliation before leaving this world. If I give her everything, he will know.'

'How?'

'He's my solicitor.'

'Not a wastrel, then.'

'He is. A brilliant legal mind, capable of much more, a seat in parliament, a probable prime minister. But what does he do? He marries a devious woman, who he adores but I detest.

233

And then she breeds a couple of layabouts. I want him to see the error of his ways and to leave her.'

'It's not your decision.'

'But it is. A weak man, easily led by a strong woman. If I give anything to him, he will give it to her.'

'Then nothing will change,' Gabrielle said. 'He's a man who wants to be led.'

Isaac suspected that Gabrielle's husband, who he had not met, was also weak.

'Can we speak here?' Isaac asked.

'Not here. Put me in a wheelchair and push me down to my office. It's soundproof.'

Isaac thought about asking why but realised it would have been a wasted question. Lord Moxon was a man who had committed divisive acts and had made contentious decisions. His office was where decisions of state had been made, where he and MacTavish and others had discussed openly without fear of censure.

In the office, Isaac outlined the situation. Lord Moxon listened while Gabrielle showed an increasing level of anxiety.

'You want me to spy on them,' Gabrielle said. 'Are you suggesting that Ibrahim might not be responsible for the attack in Whitehall?'

'He must have known, but the information I have received implicates others in the mansion. What do you know of them?'

'Apart from Siobhan and Ibrahim, I don't know anyone else. The butler dresses as you would expect, and I've only seen two other men in the house who appear to be his security. When he leaves the estate, they go with him, one in the car, another following behind in a back-up vehicle.'

'Are you sure about the numbers?'

'I'm not sure,' Gabrielle said. 'Frankly, I keep minimal contact with anyone other than Siobhan and Ibrahim. If I started pressuring Siobhan, it could backfire. I sense that she is uncomfortable with the situation, but she's devoted to her husband, even if she does not understand what he is.'

'It's hardly the reason to stay married to him,' Moxon said.

'I believe it is. Her husband has a strong personality, and regardless of his religious and political motivations, he's a man who would do well in life. A true Alsworthy, worthy of the name.'

'You sound as if you admire him,' Isaac said.

'I do. I also like him, even if he is the result of an unfortunate error by my father. I cannot deny that I enjoy his company, and Siobhan is a good person.'

Isaac wasn't sure if her faith in the two was well-founded. After all, the woman had come across as an aristocratic snob when Wendy had first met her, but now, Gabrielle, a woman born with a silver spoon in her mouth, was betraying her class and crediting those of a lower stratum with a credence that previously she would not have given.

'Siobhan's your best way to find out what is happening with Ibrahim Ali and his people,' Isaac said.

'If I do this, putting my head in the lion's mouth, what support will I have?'

'None. We can't be seen to be involved.'

'If I confront him, engage him in conversation, I need some guarantees.'

'Which means you will do it.'

'I will observe and report.'

'Which you do now. Are you sure they are not watching you?'

'I can't be sure. Ibrahim is tolerant, and he has changed. He no longer preaches from a pulpit, but only in the House of Lords.'

'Which is toothless, merely a rubber stamp for the lower house.'

'It's not toothless,' Moxon said. 'It's rare to vote contrary to the lower house or the prime minister, but it has been known to dissent.'

Isaac knew that Ali had attempted to include Sharia in the legal statute. Yet, Ali often dressed in Western clothing and opened the village fete, and Siobhan handed out prizes for the best cake, best dressed, and best horse, an event where Gabrielle would have once been the guest of honour.

'Of course, it won't,' Gabrielle said. 'And you want me to bait the man?'

'I want you to find out what you can. Tell us about the other men.'

'The butler speaks good English. He is polite and agreeable.'

'Which doesn't preclude him as a person of concern.'

'It does not. There are his two shadows. One is a burly man, swarthy, and glares at me.'

'He disapproves of you and the clothes you wear?'

'Which I do not intend to change. He's short but strong. I've seen him running around the estate of a morning before prayers.'

'The other one?'

'Tall, skinny, voluminous beard. He scares me more than the other. Piercing eyes, visually undressing me.'

'Any others?'

'There's an older man. I see him in the garden. I assume he is a handyman.'

'Or not?' Moxon said. 'What else about him?'

'He makes himself scarce when I visit the house.'

'Either he disapproves of you or does not want anyone to get a close look at him. Photos would help,' Isaac said.

'Happy snaps, are you joking.' Gabrielle reacted alarmingly. Isaac realised that asking her to take photos was stupid.

'Don't do anything,' Moxon said. 'I'll get you the photos, and then we can attempt recognition.'

Isaac knew that photos would soon be available. Isaac thought Bridget could identify the person on her laptop but realised that Linda Harris's organisation would be better equipped.

'I don't want to break my friendship with Siobhan,' Gabrielle said. 'She trusts me as long as I don't push.'

'How often do you meet?'

'Most days, although sometimes it's of a morning when she goes for a walk.'

'The other women?'

'Most of the time, she walks with them. One of them gives me the creep. The other two seem harmless, but I haven't seen them clearly. One is pregnant, I'm sure of that.'

'Ibrahim Ali?'

'Siobhan told me that she is his only woman, and he has been pressured to take another, as befits his status, but he will not.'

'His increasing Westernisation is concerning,' Moxon said. The man had got up from his wheelchair and supported himself with both hands resting on a table. Isaac thought he looked frailer standing up than when sitting down.

'How long for the photos and recognition?' Isaac asked.

'It depends if they can get a clear shot. Four, five days, maximum.'

'Until we know who we're dealing with, Gabrielle meets with Siobhan but does not attempt to contact Ali. If it's dangerous, then forewarned is forearmed.'

'I agree,' Gabrielle said.

Isaac feared for the woman. It was too dangerous to bait the beast, but there was no other option.

Chapter 24

Three of the four unknown men at the Alsworthy Mansion were identified four days later.

Isaac looked at the folder on his desk. It was eleven in the evening, and the police station was quiet. Upstairs, Caddick was absent, as was Sandra Trent. Harry the Snitch had reported that Sandra had a boyfriend in another part of the city, and Caddick had a wife, but she was not in London. Whether their respective partners knew of their philandering did not concern Isaac, only that they were not about to walk into his office.

Bridget had printed the documents and photos and placed them in a folder. She had not studied them in detail on Isaac's advice. 'What you don't know can't hurt you,' he had said.

As Isaac read through the contents of the folder, he could see that one of the men who was always close to Ali was dangerous and had a history of violence.

The agreeable and polite butler, Gabrielle's opinion of the man, was Egyptian, born in Cairo in 1988, who had come to England as a child with his mother and three siblings.

Atef Ezzat had excelled at school and had been regarded as low-risk until, at the age of fourteen, he had fallen in with a gang, who, apart from petty theft and mindless vandalism, had shown little interest in his religion, until his Imam had pulled the young Ezzat to one side, and taken him under his wing. With the Imam, he learnt of the wisdom of his religion and then, over fifteen months, of the Egyptian Muslim Brotherhood. A sensitive person, easily led by others, he rejected his gang and reengaged with fervour in his religion. It was then that the security services started to take note, especially after the vandalisation of a synagogue in another seaside city, ten miles to the east of Brighton. He had signed his name on the wall in red paint, either in exuberance, sheer stupidity, or pride in his graffitied handiwork.

Deadly Secrets

Arrested, he was cautioned by the local magistrate and given community service. For two years, no more had been heard from him until the bombing of another synagogue. This time, he did not leave his signature, nor had he planted the bomb. He had, however, been one of those who had planned it. His file at MI5 showed proof of his involvement, but it was insufficient for a prosecution.

The next time he appeared was when Gabrielle had seen him at the Alsworthy mansion five years later. Whether he was still potentially violent and an advocate for the Brotherhood was unknown. Isaac assumed the worst.

The second person in the file, described by Gabrielle as burly and swarthy, was identified as a Pakistani from the sprawling metropolis of Karachi, the largest city in the country. He had grown up in Clifton, close to the beach, and had come to England as a student at seventeen, graduating with degrees in English and Mathematics, although he had set up as a tailor in London, specialising in bespoke suits for the gentleman. There was no security rating against Faiz Shahid.

Gabrielle had described him as one of Ali's two bodyguards. Shahid's history indicated otherwise.

The third person, tall and thin, had been identified as Salim Raheef, born in Baghdad, Iraq, in 1981. University-educated, with no history of violence or radicalisation, he had taught Middle-Eastern History at the University of Birmingham for eleven years until he resigned over a dispute related to his promotion. He had registered a case against the university, that their unwillingness to appoint him as the head of the History Department was based on his faith, not on his merit. His complaint floundered when the university appointed another immigrant to the country, a coloured woman. He had not been heard for eighteen months until he was identified at the Alsworthy Mansion.

The old man, who spent time in the garden, tending to the flowers and pulling weeds, remained unidentified.

It was Gabrielle who resolved his identification. Due to the sensitivity of meeting at her house, she met with Wendy in London, in a small, out-of-the-way café.

'I didn't ask,' Gabrielle said after the two women met, and Wendy had ordered a cheesecake slice. Gabrielle ordered a small cream cake. Both agreed on a cappuccino. 'Siobhan came over to my house. We sat down and spoke about the estate. She told me that Ali had plans to install a swimming pool at the back of the house and that the old man, as Ali affectionately referred to the man, had been the person who had taught him Arabic and that he was a sage, of great wisdom in his religion.'

'Does he have a name?' Wendy asked.

Since leaving her house that morning, one of Harry the Snitch's trusted lieutenants had kept tabs on Gabrielle, not that she had been told. Harry would file a report to Larry if she had been followed.

'Abu Taleb,' Gabrielle said when Wendy asked about the old man. 'Siobhan told me.'

'Why?' Wendy asked.

'I asked her who the men were. I realised I was taking a risk, but it seemed important. Siobhan told me he speaks good English and prefers the garden to the mansion.'

***

Clough and Larry sat with Sal Winters, Jacob Drayton's lover. Nneke Suleman, the astute and capable legal aid lawyer who had represented Jacob, would act for the woman.

Once again, Interview Room number 3, Challis Street Police Station. There was new evidence. Outside, waiting, was Sal Winters' husband. She had covered the bruising on her face and the swollen eye with make-up. It was clear that he had arrived home to find proof of his wife's infidelity and had reacted.

Clough thought it appropriate; Larry thought it understandable.

'Your husband?' Clough asked.

Deadly Secrets

'He's always away, and I've no idea what he gets up to,' Sal Winters said. She wore a dark blue blouse, ripped jeans, and a pair of Adidas trainers. Larry thought the dark blue matched the bruising.

'You can press charges.'

'No charges. After Delvene's death, Jacob came over more often.'

'Is this relevant?' Nneke Suleman said.

'We're establishing the criteria,' Larry said. 'Your client's been beaten by her husband due to her affair with Jacob Drayton, the husband of a murdered woman. That gives us three potential murderers.'

'How do you figure that out?'

'Jacob, the most probable; Sal, jealous of Delvene, and Sal's husband out for revenge.'

'It's obvious that neither of my clients is responsible.'

'Which only leaves the man waiting outside. Why is he here, Sal?' Clough asked.

'Moral support.'

Larry knew that Jacob Drayton was more than a flirtation; he had seen the husband and knew Drayton. The returning seaman had the build of a wrestler, and when he had shaken Larry's hand, he had almost crushed it. This was a man used to heavy work and to violence. A man who would cheat on Sal, get drunk, and then fight. He was also a man who could murder.

'We have proof that you visited Delvene Drayton on three separate occasions,' Larry said.

'I was friendly with her. She knew about Jacob and me. Besides, she was in no position to criticise.'

'However, one of those visits was on the night she died, forty-five minutes earlier, if we agree that she died at approximately 10.30 p.m. The question is, why that late at night, and why did you have Jacob's key?'

'I took it from him. I was concerned that Delvene and Jacob might get back together.'

'Why would he do that?'

241

'For the children. The eldest is ridiculed at school. She wants to go to university and needs to get good grades. She needs to focus, and everyone is calling her mother a whore.'

'And you didn't want Jacob to forget you.'

'I would have divorced my husband and married him.'

'What would your husband have said if you attempted to divorce him?'

'Or do. I believe that is apparent.'

'Jacob agreed?'

'Not yet, but he will.'

'Because you know he killed Delvene? Or because you have removed your opponent for his affections? How would your marrying Jacob help his daughter concentrate? You would have been a worse diversion.'

'I wanted to tell Delvene to leave him alone.'

'Which she would have ignored. Is that why you killed her?'

Clough wasn't finished yet. 'Sal, you enter the house, leave little sign of your visit. Even the crime scene investigators were hard-pressed to find evidence, but we found a CCTV camera in a shop on the other side of the road, pointing straight across at Delvene's front door.

'My client needs a break,' Nneke Suleman said. 'Unsubstantiated invective serves no purpose and gives no credit to this police station. Further badgering of my client, who is clearly not well, will result in my lodging a formal complaint. Rest assured, I will pursue it.'

'We will break when your client has admitted her part.'

'Don't you mean murder? After all, that is what you are trying to pin on my client.'

'When did your husband return?' Clough added.

'One day ago,' Sal said.

Larry took out his phone and sent a message. He knew he would have the answer within five minutes.

Clough looked at Larry to take over from him; Larry gave him a nod, indicating that he was to continue and was doing a good job.

Nneke Suleman observed the exchange between the two men and realised that her client would come under further pressure and that procrastination and denial would not work. She had coached her client, but it would not be good enough. She knew of DCI Cook and his interrogating style, whereby he used his experience and intelligence to good use, but Inspector Hill and Sergeant Clough proved formidable. 'Thirty-minute break,' she said. 'I need to discuss it with my client.'

Larry knew she was in her rights. He would accede; there was enough time for Bridget to get back to him.

***

Clough and Larry took the opportunity to grab a bite to eat and coffee from the machine in the corridor on the ground floor. 'It's not great,' Clough said.

'Better than most, a lot worse than others,' Larry said, although he never understood the perpetual complaints about the police station's coffee, but thought it might be that his taste buds had been impaired by the copious amounts of beer he had drunk over the years.

Clough was a drinker, but he knew his limit. He would get close to it and then back off; Larry could not.

A sergeant had ordered a pizza and two coffees for the client and her lawyer. Nneke Suleman thought it was bland and tasted more of cardboard than food, but she still managed two slices. Sal Winters ate the remaining slices.

'Mrs Winters,' the lawyer said, 'you're in trouble. Jacob Drayton confessed to the murder, and neither I nor the police were convinced. In the end, without proof, and after he had sat in a cell for forty-eight hours, he was released, not before he withdrew his confession. He did it for you, didn't he?'

'He thought I had killed her.'

'Which you had. Don't answer that question.'
'It's an easy answer. I did not kill her.'
'But your husband could have?'
'Not if he's at sea,' Sal Winters said.
'Except he wasn't. Why are you trying to protect him.'
'I thought you were representing me.'
'I defend; I don't prosecute, and I don't tell tales. You're my concern, not your husband, who is a reprehensible bully who beats up women.'
'He's not a bully but a jealous man. If he wanted to beat me in anger, I'd not be here in this station. I would be in the hospital,' Sal Winters said.

Suleman, who had met Sal Winter's husband and Jacob Drayton, could see Sal's attraction for the polite and attractive Jacob instead of her brawling husband. She assumed the police knew that the man had been arrested in Thailand nine years previously and spent twenty-eight days in a prison cell for a brawl outside a Phuket Girlie Bar, in which one man had ended up seriously concussed and another with a fractured skull and a broken collar bone.

'Are you determined to deny your husband's involvement?' Suleman asked.

'My husband did not kill Delvene, although he might have Jacob if he had found him in bed with me,' Sal replied.

***

Brett, Sal's bruiser husband, paced up and down in the visitor's area before, in exasperation, he had retreated from the station and found a seat at the bar in the nearest pub. 'A pint of your best,' he said.

'English?' the barman replied.
'English, of course.'
'You look het up. A rough day?'

Three pints later and suitably primed, Brett Winters told the barman his life story as how he toiled around the world on container ships, only to come home to find that his wife, the love of his life, was screwing another man.

The barman consoled and counselled the man. He had heard variations of the story before, a hundred times. The disappointed, the angry, the jealous, the violent, when presented with a conundrum, which, in most cases, was a wife who did not respect the sanctity of the matrimonial bed, or else it was a wife who spent as though there was no tomorrow, and it had to be designer clothes, designer handbags, and designer shoes. If the husband could not provide for her, she would look elsewhere for another.

Seven pints down, after the barman had accepted the drunk's penance, and the drunk had received absolution, that it was not his fault, and women, they're all the same, Winters staggered out of the pub and headed back to the police station.

Sal had pleaded her case in the interview room, saying that she wasn't guilty, nor was her husband. Larry wrapped up the interview and declared the legal aid the winner.

Confronted outside the interview room, the drunken Brett took another swing at his wife, who ducked, the fist landing in Larry's stomach, who keeled over onto the floor.

'Winters, twenty-four hours to sober up,' Clough said. 'Or long enough to get you in front of a magistrate.'

Wendy drove Sal Winters home, enough time for the two women to talk without the intimidating atmosphere of a police station.

Larry Hill, nursing his sore stomach, knew that what Sal had said about her husband was correct; if he wanted to kill her, he would not have failed. Larry could not remember having been hit that hard before.

The message he had been waiting for on his phone was not used. It wasn't the message he expected, but confirmation that Brett Winters had not been in the UK on the day Delvene Drayton had died, as his ship had been at sea three days from landfall.

Brett Winters would not be interviewed, but the swing at his wife was a criminal offence. The magistrate would pass a sentence, although, on a recommendation from Homicide, a custodial sentence would not be advisable, although a stiff fine would.

Chapter 25

At the station, Clough believed it was either Jacob Drayton or Sal Winters who had murdered Delvene. Larry tended to agree, but there was still the complication that the CSIs had found little evidence in Delvene's house, and the only persons they could prove with any certainty in the residence were Delvene, Jacob, and their two children. The youngest child was thirteen, and Larry had met the youth, who played football for his school, was above average height, and had a forceful personality. He was not likely to be concerned about what anyone said at the school playground, which the school's headmistress confirmed. 'Anyone on the wrong side of him doesn't last long,' she admitted.

'Disciplinary for fighting in the schoolyard?'

'With Terry, not a chance. He waits until he's out of school. Then, he and a couple of his lieutenants grab the offender, pull him off the street, and then Terry Drayton gives the young man a swift belting.'

'A skilled intimidator, don't mess with me, or else,' Larry said.

'He's bright, a natural leader and football team captain. We won a regional championship last year.'

'You sound as though you respect him.'

'I don't condone his behaviour, but he has the wisdom to get the message out; don't mess with me, or you'll regret it.'

'His sister?'

'She's not at this school.'

'But he could protect her, get the word out that mess with my sister, you mess with me.'

'Not if her tormentors are female. Terry Drayton could go far in life, except…'

'His mother.'

'I've heard the rumours, and then, she's murdered, not that you'd know it from Terry.'

'No signs of emotion?'

'He was out of school for a week, and then he's back here, subdued for a few days, but the following weekend, out on the sports field, leading his side to victory.'

'Do you believe he didn't care for his mother?'

'I believe he did, but the young Drayton's not the type to show weakness in front of others.'

'School counselling?'

'It's available, but he wouldn't consider it. He maintains an emotional distance.'

Larry thought it unusual for the headmistress to be so flowing in her respect for the thirteen-year-old but did not think too deeply about it. He remembered when he was thirteen, brawls at school, even considered joining a gang at one stage until his father had collared him, sat him down, and read him the riot act. 'If ever you bring shame to this family, I'll hang you out to dry' A blunt man, a caring father, a loving husband, but a man who lacked ambition and the charisma to drive him any further forward than the manager of a food wholesaler. At least the family had not gone hungry.

Larry knew that was where he had got his approach to life, but where had Terry got his? Was it his mother who prostituted, or his father who had the charisma, but did he also have the violence? Sal Winters had been considered a possible murderer, even after Jacob Drayton had made the confession, but it was clear that he had confessed to protect another. But was it Sal Winters he had been protecting? Could it be Terry? It seemed unlikely; after all, at thirteen, he was wise for his age and did not have the anger for his mother or the shame. Was there another? Larry knew there was, but it seemed implausible and impossible to contemplate. There was only one way to find out the truth.

***

Wendy was given the onerous task of informing Jacob Drayton that his bullied daughter would need to accompany her to Challis Street Police Station, where she would be interviewed.

It was four on a Thursday afternoon, and Shelley Drayton had an important exam at school the following day. She also said that she intended to study until ten that evening and then spend another couple of hours cramming in the morning. Wendy felt for the young woman, but a murder took precedence.

Reluctantly, Wendy, who had commenced her career looking for truant children in Yorkshire and had the necessary sympathies, knew that justice could not be avoided because of a young woman's education.

Jacob Drayton accompanied his daughter to the police station. Nneke Suleman was on the way and would arrive within the hour. Drayton protested on the way to the station; Shelley Drayton did not speak, only holding her head low and avoiding all eye contact. Jacob had his arm around her shoulders. Wendy feared that a child, a family, would be torn asunder. She hoped she was wrong.

Larry and Wendy would conduct the interview. Larry, because of his knowledge of the two Drayton children; Wendy, because of her empathy with teenagers and that a female police officer would give some ease to Shelley Drayton. Interviewing minors brought into question the possibility of a pressured confession, intimidation, and the overly heavy-handed approach of the police. Nneke Suleman had been briefed before the interview and was cognisant of Larry's theory and Terry Drayton's headmistress's comments, and she already knew that Jacob Drayton had confessed to protect another.

The badgering of Shelley would cause the interview to be halted. Outside the interview room, a female police officer, skilled in counselling distraught children, who Wendy knew would not be as capable as she was, except this time she would be an interrogator, not a ministering angel.

Outside, her father remonstrated, accused the police of acting with malice, and that it was a vendetta against the family due to the mother having been a prostitute, and for him being a philanderer, and their son a bully. He had been informed of the headmistress's comments after she had phoned him to tell him that she had spoken to Inspector Larry Hill and that she had given his son a recommendation, even if it had pointed out flaws in the young man.

Wendy led off, informed Shelley of what their concerns were, and told her that her father had confessed to her mother's murder to protect another, who they were convinced was innocent of the crime.

Nneke Suleman watched carefully, ready to pounce if the police went too far and reverted to their usual pattern of intimidation.

'We can prove that you and your father had visited your mother,' Wendy said. 'There are signs that your brother had been in the house, but they are not as distinct as yours.'

'I visited Mum every few days.'

'Is it true that you were bullied because of your mother?' Larry asked.

'I was ashamed of what she did, but she was still my mother,' Shelley replied, her head still held low.'

'And it was affecting your schoolwork, and you intend to go to university, and you're at a fragile age.'

'It does, or it did, affect me. And yes, I want to go to university, but that's a couple of years, enough time to get the grades required. My mother had said she would stop and maybe move away. If she did, I would go with her.'

'Another school?'

'There is another if she moved close to it.'

'Did she tell you whether she would sell the house and how she intends to buy another?'

'She said she had a friend who would help.'

'Did you know this friend?'

'I didn't. Someone she had known as a child.'

'The friend's father was murdered. Did you know that?'

'I didn't.'

Deadly Secrets

'Her mother, as well, but that was a few years back. Her friend intended to help your mother financially.'

'Did you believe your mother?' Larry asked.

Nneke Suleman felt the need to speak. 'What you are offering is conjecture, not proof. Shelley has an important exam tomorrow, and if this is a fishing exercise and you are attempting to trip a young woman, unused to the wiles of serving police officers, it will be viewed as intimidation of a minor. I hope you are aware of this.'

Larry was aware; he did not intend to reconsider his approach to the young woman.

'With my mother, I couldn't be sure. She had sold herself for as long as I can remember, although I couldn't have known when I was a child.

'What age were you when you found out?' Wendy asked.

'Ten or eleven,' Shelley replied.

'What did you think?'

'I'm not sure I even understood, although when I reached thirteen or thereabouts, I did. Even then, I wasn't sure that I was upset; after all, there were girls in my class who were sleeping around, and I don't believe any over the age of fifteen at school were holding onto their virginity.'

'Were you?' Larry asked.

The legal aid reacted with alarm. 'That's an insulting accusation,' she said. 'I could report you for that.'

Larry knew it was reportable, but this was a homicide, not a kiddie's party. Tough questions need to be asked, even to a sensitive sixteen-year-old female.

'It's not an accusation, purely a question to ascertain a fact. Shelley must understand the question's sensitivity and the interview's depth.'

'I do,' Shelley said. 'Not that I would criticise the others, but because I understand my mother. She couldn't help herself.'

'And you were worried you might be the same,' Wendy asked.

'I am like my mother in many ways.'

'So, if she intended to give up her career, look after you and your brother, and possibly reunite with your father, you wouldn't believe her.'

'It's what I would have wanted, but I wouldn't have believed her.'

'Is that what she told you the night she died?' Larry asked.

'It was.'

'You argued,' Wendy asked.

'I need time with my client,' Nneke Suleman intervened.

Larry wasn't about to back off. 'Shelley, tell us about that night.'

The head lifted, and Shelley looked across the table at Larry. 'How would you like it if your mother was a whore, who had sex with my headmaster every month.'

'Did he? Why?'

'One of the girls, a year back, had called me names, the daughter of a bitch, the whore's bastard child, and who is your father. And much worse. I had grown tired of it, and one day, she was in the toilet block. It's just the two of us, and she starts up again. This time, I don't run away but stand my ground, take hold of her and smash her head against a sink and then against a wall. She collapses to the ground.'

'After that?' Wendy asked.

'I walk out and go to my next class. I felt nothing, only a sense of relief.'

'The young woman you attacked?' Larry asked.

'She was taken to hospital; she's still there, in a coma.'

'Can this be proved?'

'In the hospital, it can.'

'The headmaster?'

'He had seen me come out of the toilet block. He knew what had happened. He's a good man who protected me, and then, my mother, when told the story by me and by him, ensures that he's rewarded in the only way she knows how.'

'And once committed to a casual relationship, your mother knows he can never reveal the truth.'

Deadly Secrets

'You've proven that you're capable of violence,' Wendy said.

'If it's true,' the legal aid said.

'I was the school's star pupil,' Shelley continued. 'I needed that other school; I needed my mother to do it for me.'

'And then, that night at the house, you are trying to reason with your mother. She's had a few drinks, getting ready to take a bath, and making promises as to how it will be better, but you're not convinced, and then she attempts to put her arm around you. And the next minute, she's in the bath, her head is underwater, and you're holding her down. Is that how it was?

Nneke Suleman had her mouth open, ready to speak. She was not going to get a chance.

'There is no headmaster here, no father, or your brother in this room. It's just you. What's the truth?' Wendy said. She felt sick, almost ready to collapse. She had spent time with troubled adolescents as a junior police officer. And now, she was pushing for a confession from another. It was the worst moment of her career, but she could not stop. Murder is murder; justice is justice without fear or favour.

'I didn't know what I was doing. My mother was the same as those at the school, belittling me. I was angry, but I didn't want to kill her. I loved my mother.'

Larry said no more. He would let Wendy deal with the confession.

That night, Jacob Drayton would remain in the station, consoling his daughter, who would be held pending trial. This time, a Drayton confession would hold.

***

Since returning from Moxon's house, Gabrielle had once seen the other women that Siobhan spoke about at the Alsworthy estate. It was early morning, and she had said hello, only to receive a scant acknowledgement but no further communication. Gabrielle had pointed to a swan on the nearby river, but it did not move the women towards it for a closer look or elicit a response.

Isaac had warned Gabrielle against attempting to communicate with them further, as they might become suspicious or wary and would report back.

Siobhan visited Gabrielle late that day in the afternoon. She was dressed in Western clothes. 'We're going to the theatre,' she said. In her hand, she held a leash. At the other end of the leash, there was a small dog. 'Would you look after Button for a few hours.'

Gabrielle thought it to be one of the new designer breeds. 'No problems. Couldn't you have left your dog at the mansion?'

'They don't understand why the English are fascinated with ineffectual animals.

'Your husband, my brother?'

'He's not keen, bitten by an Alsatian when young, and still has the scar, but he doesn't mind Button.'

'Is he taking you to the theatre?'

'He is, last minute.'

'Western clothes?'

Gabrielle took the dog, put it on one of the chairs, and looked at her two dogs. 'Don't you dare,' she said, worried that the two would regard the third as a threat and react, which would be a lot of snarling but not much action.

She prepared a makeshift bed for the animal in the other room from a couple of old blankets. On her return, she realised she should not have bothered. Button, as with its mistress, was a natural at making friends.

Gabrielle phoned Lord Moxon and told him that Lord Alsworthy was showing increasing tendencies of reverting to his Western upbringing and they should focus on the other men. The only issue was which man and who was the most radical and likely to create further acts of violence. Preaching from a soapbox, proselytising from a pulpit, and standing up in the House of Lords were not crimes; physical action was.

The four met at Moxon's house, although there was an unexpected extra person this time. Isaac was wary and believed that his lordship had made an error of judgement. Linda Harris did not.

'I've known all along,' Linda said. As usual, she was dressed attractively. Isaac judged the clothes to be designer labels, meaning she had a large budget from her employer or significant bonuses for those she killed.

Isaac shifted in his seat. He could see proof that Moxon had powerful friends, friends who were capable of ordering government-sanctioned murder and, in Linda's case, committing them. His trust in Moxon had waned, even though it had only been tenuous.

Not that it worried Gabrielle Alsworthy, who would make a deal with anyone, trust everyone, trust no one, use and reject. Linda, he knew what she was, and Moxon was tarred with the same brush as MacTavish, and that these people were not interested in the London Metropolitan Police but were pursuing their own interests.

For Moxon, it would be the thrill of the chase; for Gabrielle, the restoration of her influence and the Alsworthy estate, and if that meant the death of Ibrahim Ali, the theatre-loving and horse-racing aficionado, so much the better. As for Linda, whatever her background, which Isaac assumed came from a troubled childhood, all that she wanted was to be wanted, to believe in a secretive organisation of old men and younger women who seduced and killed. Here, exposed, the gritty reality of a corrupt and sick society, degenerating while persons of importance made pronouncements, and the populace, either sucked it up, revolted, or held out their greedy hands for whatever they could get, no longer interested in a country that had once ruled a quarter the world.

'How? Why are you here?' Isaac asked.

'You know how,' Linda replied. 'Where the police fear to tread, we go. You need us as much as we need you, Isaac, and besides, I have further information for you.'

'Which is?'

'After a drink,' Moxon said. He picked up a small bell and rang it. Three minutes later, Moxon's niece walked in, holding a bottle of champagne.

'Good to see you, Chief Inspector,' she said.

Linda could see that the woman appreciated the suave, tall, attractive chief inspector as much as she did.

'How is his lordship?' Isaac asked.

'Much better. I reckon he'll live to a hundred.'

'I'll live until we wrap up this little exercise,' Moxon said.

'Little?' Isaac said.

'Comparatively,' Moxon replied. 'The prime minister of this great nation is obliged to make monumental decisions, to trust in others to do things, which, let's call them, aberrations, which, if debated in parliament, would cause a furore.'

'Such a decision exists now,' Linda said.

'How?' Isaac asked. He realised he was hostile. He had lost his temper several times with Caddick; he didn't want to lose it again in such august company, even if their halos had slipped. He needed to hold his ideals above theirs, which he regarded as in the gutter.

'We have Alsworthy's mansion surrounded by an impenetrable barrier.'

'Which makes no sense.'

'Not physical, but video and sound. All communications in and out are recorded, and there are listening devices in six locations around the place.'

'Which Ibrahim Ali or his fellow conspirators could find and would place Gabrielle in a difficult position, considering her friendship with Lord Alsworthy's wife.'

'One of his wives,' Linda said.

'Who are the others?' Gabrielle asked. 'Siobhan's not mentioned it.'

'Abu Taleb's daughter. We picked up Taleb and Ali arguing.'

'In English?'

'Arabic. Taleb agreed to teach Ali Arabic and mentor him on the condition that he marry his eldest daughter. We are certain that Ali is not sleeping with her and that it is an arranged marriage.'

'Which one of the women?' Gabrielle asked.

'Of the three women you have seen, she is the shortest. We know little about her, and we don't believe she speaks English.'

'You've heard them speak?'

'I haven't, but our people have the mansion covered.'

'Inside?'

'There are three devices. One in the main room, another in Ali and Siobhan's bedroom, and another in Taleb's room.'

'How did you do that?'

'Accept that we did. How is not important.'

'I believe we should accept Miss Harris' comments as valid and give her the floor to elucidate,' Moxon said.

Isaac got up, walked over to the door in the far corner, slowly turned the handle, and pulled it open quickly, only for the niece to tumble onto the floor. Isaac said nothing and returned to his seat.

'Sorry, curiosity killed the cat,' the woman said as she picked herself up.

Moxon raised himself from his seat, walked over to his niece, and slapped her face hard. 'Out of my house, now,' he said.

'Not before she's signed the Official Secrets Act,' Linda said. 'I should remind your niece, even if she knows it, that if one word of whatever she's heard in the house, tonight, or at any other time is repeated to another person or is loaded onto the internet, she will be arrested and prosecuted to the full extent of the law.'

Moxon sat down with a thud. 'Get me a doctor and that card on the mantle over the fireplace; give it to me.' Isaac obliged with the card, but it had to be the niece, as despised as she was, who administered first aid. Gabrielle phoned emergency services, although, by the time it arrived, it was too late; Moxon was dead.

The solicitor, who had prepared Moxon's will, whose name was on the card, would not have the opportunity to change it, which would have been Lord Moxon's final act that night. The niece, who, through her stupidity, had caused his death, would still receive her inheritance.

Chapter 26

Linda Harris was adamant the meeting could not be deferred regardless of Moxon's passing.

Three hours later, enough time for emergency services to determine that Moxon was dead, for his body to be taken to the morgue, and for Isaac to call for a couple of uniforms to secure the house, he, along with Linda and Gabrielle, met in the backroom of a local pub.

The niece had gone in the ambulance to the morgue. She would not be allowed to return to help herself to what she was about to inherit and rifle through Moxon's private papers, some of which might pertain to why the four in the room had met.

'Taleb is the key,' Linda said. She was sitting too close to Isaac, making him uncomfortable. He attempted to move his chair, but she kept following with hers. He was sure it was a game she enjoyed, toying with the mouse. Gabrielle, still upset over the death of Lord Moxon, a man she had known since childhood, observed but said nothing.

'Ibrahim Ali must have known about Whitehall,' Isaac said.

The mood in the room was subdued and not conducive to a frank and open discussion about what Linda had to reveal, but it would continue.

'You mentioned an argument,' Gabrielle said.

'Abu Taleb remonstrated with Ibrahim Ali about his treatment of his daughter, that he was not giving her the attention she deserved, and there were no grandchildren. Taleb admitted that she was no great beauty, but Ali had agreed to give her a child for what he had done for him.'

'Which was?'

'We don't have the specifics. Marriage for teaching someone to speak Arabic does not seem a great bargain, although assisting with Whitehall and further attacks would be.'

'Which you can't prove,' Isaac said.

'We have conducted exhaustive enquiries into the four men. Atef Ezzat, the butler, has a history, but not recent, and we've regarded him as low risk. Faiz Shahid appears benign. Salim Raheef, the Iraqi academic, shows no radical intent. We are prepared to give those three the benefit of the doubt.

'However, Abu Taleb is a different case. Egyptian, attended a madrassa as a child, is well-versed in the Koran, and is devout. He is regarded as a pragmatist, believing that jihad is the only way forward and that Allah will forgive.'

'Murder and mayhem?'

'Whatever is necessary.'

'How do you know all this?'

'We have people in his country of birth. Taleb is a secretive man and a nature lover, and in Egypt, he used the name Mostafa Sherif, among others.'

'What others?'

'They are not important. In Egypt, he was a senior member of the Muslim Brotherhood. His daughter suffers from vitiligo, a disease that causes loss of skin colour. We believe that hers is severe, that she has a cleft lip and palate, and her speech is affected. Taleb could have seen Ali as her redemption.'

'Did he organise the attack in Whitehall?'

'He would have been capable, but we have no proof, and Ibrahim Ali, even if he had doubts, would have known, in part, if not of the possible carnage.'

'Which makes him equally guilty.'

Isaac was confused. There had been MacTavish, then Lord Moxon, and now, it appeared as Linda Harris would be taking the lead role. He had come to trust MacTavish and had given begrudging acceptance to Lord Moxon, but Linda did not gel. He felt that the investigation, for which he had been the major instigator, had once again fallen into the proverbial hole in the ground.

It was Gabrielle who spoke next, echoing Isaac's thoughts. 'With Lord Moxon no longer with us, what now?'

'I do not have the authority or the expertise to take over from Lord Moxon,' Linda said.

'I know what you are capable of, but not who you are, what you are, and where you and your people stand concerning Ibrahim Ali,' Isaac said. 'I know you act against the national interest, yet you deny this. Marjorie Frobisher was killed because she held the secret to the identity of her and Alsworthy's child. An error of judgement was used to save Moxon's party at the upcoming election and keep Gabrielle's father out of the scandal sheets.'

'We're not flawless. Isaac, if it's a time for revealing hidden secrets, you have jeopardised your career on a couple of occasions with women you later arrested for murder.'

'What is it with you two?' Gabrielle asked.

'Three times,' Isaac corrected Linda. 'I spent the night with Linda, destroyed a relationship that was important to me, and then, Linda kills a person who knew of your father and Marjorie's child.'

'You both behave as though the romance hasn't ended.'

'Isaac's confusion allows his professional judgement to be clouded by his personal feelings.' Linda said.

Isaac did not want to believe what she had just said, but he could not deny it. Linda represented excitement and living on the edge; Jenny, whom he loved, represented stability. The lure of one excited more than the other.

'I need to know who we can rely on,' Isaac said. He was uncomfortable with the situation in the pub's backroom, as though they were rats scurrying in the dark. The terrorist attack needed a full enquiry at the highest level by the London Metropolitan Police and MI5, and without it, they were floundering, but who could be trusted.

'There is a meeting,' Linda said. 'Isaac will receive an invite; Gabrielle will not.'

'Why?' Gabrielle asked.

'You will maintain contact with Siobhan, stay friendly, but do not pressure.'

'Am I in danger?'

'Not immediately. For the next week, keep your family away from your house. Where are they now?'

'With my mother-in-law.'

'They are to remain there. They are not to venture far; if they do, they will be observed and protected.'

'Your people?'

'You haven't seen my people at the Alsworthy estate, but they are there.'

'Your people kill. Is that enough for Gabrielle?' Isaac asked.

'It will be. Gabrielle, you want your position restored,' Linda said. 'Does the Alsworthy blood course through your veins? Are you willing to place your life in jeopardy?'

'Mine, not my children.'

'What about Wendy and Siobhan?' Isaac asked.

'Siobhan cannot know, and we do not believe Ali would harm his wife, but the others might. Abu Taleb concerns us. Be prepared for any eventuality. Isaac's sergeant knows the risks; she will not falter.'

'My family?' Isaac asked.

'That can be resolved at the meeting,' Linda said.

***

Fiona Avers attended the funeral service and gave a eulogy for Delvene Drayton; Jacob Drayton gave a reading from the bible. Fiona spoke about how they had been friends for a long time, and she would miss her greatly. No one spoke of how Delvene had died, and Jacob had even managed a weak smile when Wendy, who had attended, offered her condolences. Delvene and Jacob's daughter was absent; no one mentioned her name.

It was a sad occasion, sadder than it should have been due to Shelley Drayton's matricide.

The usual get-together at the end of the service was dispensed with; no one was in the mood to remember Delvene,

Deadly Secrets

as that would have meant revisiting her death at the hands of her daughter. No one mentioned Sam Avers, who was back in Spain, spending whatever money he had from Robert Avers, confident that there would be more from his sister when needed.

There had been a concerted effort to keep Sam in London, but with no firm evidence that he was involved in his father's death, Homicide could not prevent him from leaving the country. Gordon Upton, who remained in Spain, would keep an eye on him and report if there was any reason for concern.

Clough, having proven himself to Larry, celebrated the solving of Delvene's murder with Larry at a pub one night, the two men arriving in Homicide the next day, blurry-eyed and with raspy voices. Isaac did not comment.

The two men focussed on Robert Avers's murder, the only investigation that Homicide had at the present time. Larry was aware of the other investigation but did not ask unnecessary questions, and certainly not when Clough was around. Sandra Trent made regular visits to the department, and apart from suspicion about the woman, Bridget had found an affinity with her due to her fastidious intent to document, to ensure the reports were submitted on time and were factual, correct, and there were no glaring grammatical errors.

Wendy, who disliked writing reports, did not agree with her best friend and said so on more than one occasion. Larry, who saw that time in the department as wasted, had received a warning from Isaac, on instruction from Caddick, that lax reporting was akin to poor policing and would not be tolerated in the new and revitalised Met.

Apart from sucking up to Commissioner Davies, Deputy Assistant Commissioner Goddard, was taking his responsibilities seriously, drafting new operating procedures, which were filtering throughout the Met, and people were complaining but complying, or else.

Isaac found that he was in the office more than he wanted, and promotion, if it ever came, would restrict him even more. He had to admit that the challenge that now confronted him, realising that there was a risk of danger, excited. So far, he had not told Jenny that the situation might worsen. He considered sending her and the children to his parents in Jamaica but discounted the idea. Danger existed there, and it was preferable to have them close by, in case.

Two days passed with little activity. Larry and Clough were out of the office most of the time, focussing on Robert Avers. That included visiting Fiona, whose family had moved into Robert and Marjorie's house. Larry had noticed that the chair Robert died in was missing, as was the couch where the younger Fiona had cavorted with Charles Sutherland.

'We're redecorating,' Fiona said. 'This house has too many memories for me, mostly bad, although some were good.'

The visit did not last long, as there were few questions to ask, only to rehash what had been discussed before. The person who had planted the murder weapon in the hotel room that Sam and Delvene had occupied was more important than asking pointless questions.

Delvene had been adamant that she had not planted the weapon, and Clough had denied his involvement, initially angry when it had been suggested.

Larry and Clough returned to the hotel and sat with the manager. 'I can't help you,' she said.

They knew someone could and that someone was important. Once again, the staff were interviewed, and there was a blanket denial from all of them.

Valerie Agbeko and Lilith Amenu, friends who had come over from Ghana sixteen years earlier, had cleaned the room. According to the manager, they had worked at the hotel for twelve years, were reliable and punctual, and had never stolen from any of the rooms.

Larry reminded the manager that it was not stealing that interested them but the murder weapon that had been found in the room. Why in the room still made no sense and only distracted from the investigation, in that valuable time was lost attempting to make the connection from Sam Avers to the murder when the man had not pulled the trigger.

Also, the manager had to be under suspicion, as did the under manager, a dignified upright man who dressed in a suit, always wore a bow tie, and affected the appearance of an English gentleman, even though he had come from Belarus, close to the Russian border, nine years earlier. Educated, he had entered the country legally, and there was an offer of a teaching position at a school to the west of London. Proficient in five languages, he was to join the language department, which intended to offer Russian as one of its subjects. But as the man had explained, the demand for Russian had not been as strong as expected, and whereas he could speak French, Italian, and Spanish, his Belarusian accent did not lend itself to Latin-derived languages.

'They wanted someone from those countries,' he had said, and eventually, he had drifted into working in the hotel. Larry thought him to be a bitter man.

Larry did not want to think the worst of his offsider, although the reason for the gun in Sam's room made no sense. To plant it there, smacked of ignorance and a poor understanding of the British legal system, and that a person is presumed innocent before a trial declares them guilty. Clough would have known that and could not have planted the weapon, or did he? Larry could not reason why.

Late that night, Homicide was quiet when Larry sat with Isaac. It wasn't often the two of them had an open discussion. The office dynamics had changed, and people were on edge, uncertain of the future. When Chief Superintendent Goddard was up on the top floor of Challis Street, people knew where they stood. With Caddick, Sandra Trent and Sergeant Clough, there was uncertainty, further complicated by their former DCS and his edicts about reform in the police service: more accountability, stricter reporting, and advancement based on merit coupled with the necessary academic qualification.

Larry admitted he was confused and that he and Clough had hit a brick wall. Isaac sympathised, as he also had issues to confront, which appeared insurmountable.

'It's the weapon,' Larry said. 'It's one thing to find out who planted it; it's another to figure out why. We know Sam did not shoot his father, and he hadn't put it in the bag in his hotel room.'

'Hadn't he? Are you sure?' Isaac said. Amidst all that he was wrestling with, he could see a fundamental error that Larry had alluded to. The meeting was cut short, and Larry was on a plane to Spain. Gordon Upton would pick him up at the airport upon arrival, and the two men would work together to find Sam Avers and bring him to a secure place where the three could talk.

***

Isaac entered Thames House in Millbank, London, at six-fifteen in the morning. It was originally used by Imperial Chemical Industries (ICI) as its head office, but since 1994, it has been the headquarters of the United Kingdom's Internal Security Service, commonly known as MI5.

It was his first time in the building. Inside the imposing entrance, a young woman, barely out of her teens, introduced herself, ensured Isaac had signed in and received a visitor's card to secure to his lapel before whisking him down a couple of corridors, into an elevator and up to the fourth floor, where she deposited him, for another even younger woman to walk ten metres before leaving him in a conference room. 'The others will be here shortly,' she said. 'Please help yourself to tea or coffee.'

In one corner of the room, there was coffee, tea, and orange juice on a table. He chose the juice and took a seat. He assumed it would be Linda who would enter first. He was surprised when it was Sergeant Clough.

The two men shook hands. Isaac was unsure what to say but cognisant that he had disparaged the man due to his association with Caddick.

Deadly Secrets

Linda came in second, threw her arms around Isaac, and kissed him. 'Welcome to my home,' she said.

Shortly after, a man and a woman. The man was in his fifties, and greying at the temples. His accent was received pronunciation, traditionally regarded as the most prestigious form of spoken English. The woman, dressed plainly in a grey business suit, did not go to Eton or Winchester College, male bastions for the sons of gentlemen, as she was neither male nor privately educated. Her accent was pure Scouse, the accent of Liverpool, the birthplace of the Beatles, in the north of England.

'Sir Godfrey Fairweather,' the man said as he shook Isaac's hand. 'Sheila Cudworth, the woman said as she followed Fairweather, who was clearly the more senior, as he sat at the head of the conference table.

'Chief Inspector, I suppose you have a few questions,' Fairweather said.

'More than a few. I'm unsure if I'm pleased to be here or not.'

'We've had a file on you since Marjorie Frobisher and Lord Alsworthy. We realise you did not approve of certain actions and that the investigations into the deaths of two had been effectively brushed under the table.'

'I still don't.'

'Admirable that you have maintained a strong moral and Christian ethic. Unfortunately, those we are dealing with here have neither. We will forestall them and remove them if necessary. We are not expecting you to agree, but we need to know if you will work with us.'

'Sergeant Clough?'

'Maybe you could answer DCI Cook's query,' Sheila Cudworth said, looking over at Clough.

'DCI Cook has long suspected me due to my involvement with Chief Superintendent Caddick. He was right to be suspicious but wrong in his deduction. I am a serving police officer and have known Caddick for a long time.'

'An undercover MI5 operative?'

'More of a sleeper. The police service has an element of corruption and people who do more harm than good. Caddick was always regarded as a low performer and unlikely to see through me. Only when he joined forces with Davies at the Met did I show more focus? To Caddick, I'm one of his loyalist supporters.'

'Sandra Trent, his PA.'

'And mistress. That has been going on for a few years. We have no issues with her, apart from her choice of bed mate. She is efficient, even if demanding.'

Isaac thought he saw Linda squirm at the mention of bed mate.

Clough continued. 'I initially went undercover on another case, attached myself to Caddick, and remained as a policeman.'

'Your function? The same as Linda's?'

'If you mean either of her admirable attributes, then no. I observe, inveigle, report, and advise. Most of the time, there is little for me to do, and for several years, I have chosen to remain a lackey of Caddick's.

'We knew that Caddick had met with Ibrahim Ali and that Davies' position was threatened. We don't know if Davies knew what Caddick was intending, or if he did, that ten people would die. Ibrahim Ali might not have known either, but that seems less likely.'

'I thought you knew everything; ears in every wall, eyes in every window.'

'To some extent. However, Davies' office is regularly checked for bugs and hidden cameras, standard procedure, and Caddick wasn't bugged, only watched when he met with Ali, who was then living in a house to the north of the city.'

'Then who informed Caddick that Ibrahim Ali had a claim on the Alsworthy title? It seems critical that we know.'

'Only someone who had known. There is no way that it would be anyone in MI5,' Fairweather said.

Isaac did not place great faith in Fairweather's statement. He had known of the organisation for too long to believe in the utterance of a senior person in MI5, who might be covering his back. He still didn't know who Linda was, and never would, and now to be confronted by Clough, another MI5 operative who spied on the Met. The depths the organisation would stoop to were unfathomable.

'Sir Godfrey, I'm afraid I cannot believe you or your operatives. I've seen too much of what you and your people are capable of,' Isaac said.

'Scepticism is fine, and yes, undercover in the London Met smacks of heavy-handed bureaucracy and Orwellian nightmare, but believe me, there is more that you don't see. Clough and Linda are two of our people. There are more in places where the police can't go.'

'In the Mosques?'

'Sometimes, we receive a snippet, an overheard conversation, or a zealot sounding off.'

'Abu Taleb?'

'He is a recent arrival in this country.'

'Does Ibrahim Ali's wife know? Why would you let the second wife and her father enter this country.'

'It must be assumed that she knows of the daughter and her marriage to Ibrahim Ali. We have nothing against her other than her loyalty to her husband,' Linda Harris said. 'Taleb was granted entry due to our concern that he was orchestrating terrorist activities in this country and others. It seemed better to have him somewhere we could keep a watch on him.'

'How do you know all this?'

'We are monitoring the mansion, and before that, we installed listening devices at Ali and his wife's house. It would be best to focus on how Caddick knew and who killed Avers. There is a tie between them.'

'Are you sure?'

'Clough can comment,' Sheila Cudworth said.

'Sam Avers didn't kill his father, but we already knew that,' Clough said.

Isaac struggled to believe that Clough was not the murderer, as it hadn't stopped Linda Harris from killing Richard Williams and then claiming it was justified. Had Robert Avers been deemed a liability? After all, MI5 had been responsible for his wife's death outside a restaurant.

Isaac did not intend to tell those in the room that his inspector was in Spain, following up on an angle that might solve who had killed Robert Avers. Although if they were as good as he thought they were, they would know.

'If he did not, who did? You've been working with Larry Hill. The two of you must have a theory.'

'We do. The reason you sent Larry to Spain. Sam's covering for his sister, who was not checked at the crime scene.'

'This spying on us by MI5 is not appreciated.'

'Nor was you using Harry the Snitch,' Linda said.

'You were keeping information from us, and now, we're expected to believe that we're a team and you intend to be open with us.'

'Subject to secrecy, we will be,' Fairweather said.

'That's the operative word, isn't it? That's why Marjorie Frobisher died in a hit and run; why Richard Williams was assassinated by Linda. I had even been targeted.'

'If you want to play with the big boys, follow their rules. DCI Cook. You were a loose cannon, and they sink ships. Linda was reprimanded for her error, allowing emotion to interfere with her order.'

'I don't want to play with these so-called big boys. I want to solve a murder, prevent a further terrorist attack, and bring Caddick to heel, except he seems to follow your rule book in that crime is justified if the cause is honourable. Killing innocent people to protect the former Lord Alsworthy cannot be excused, even if you say it's in the national interest.'

'The reason you're here, Chief Inspector,' Fairweather said. 'Abu Taleb is planning a further terrorist attack.'

'With Caddick's assistance and Ibrahim Ali?'

'Ali doesn't know; Caddick might.'

'What's the issue with the Met's Counter Terrorism Command?' Isaac asked.

'You're proven, they aren't, and Caddick's in with them. We need people who are dependable and honourable. Cook, you will do the right thing, regardless. You can't be bought.'

'But you can.'

'We act in the national interest, and sometimes that's dirty.'

Isaac had reservations. Was he willing to go with Fairweather and an organisation that had once deemed him disposable? Did he trust them, and if he didn't, what would be their response.

'MI5 does not work independently. You are answerable to the current government. What would you do if the government and their bureaucracy gave you instructions contrary to our discussion? Roll over and come to heel? Or will you, if ordered, protect Davies?' Isaac asked.

'Questions that cannot be answered. We will not allow another terrorist attack. Counter Terrorism Command is compromised, your commissioner is suspect, and Chief Superintendent Caddick has involved himself with the devil. Why, makes no sense.'

'Unless he's an independent operator, working to further strengthen the commissioner's hold on power,' Sheila Cudworth said.

'Apart from the commissioner wanting to remove me and Deputy Assistant Commissioner Goddard, who is now sucking up to him, the man has done a reasonable job. It's his use of crime and murder to achieve it that I can't condone. You have no issue with crime and murder if you believe it's in the national interest. Why are you not supporting the commissioner?'

'A fair question,' Fairweather said. 'We might still protect Davies. What concerns us is Caddick meeting with Taleb.'

'Another terrorist attack would not enhance Ali's position in the House of Lords.'

'Ibrahim Ali's resolve has weakened. The hardliners will reject him, possibly martyr him if it serves their cause.'

'Where?'

'We don't know. That's where you come in.'

'Sergeant Clough, what was he doing at Alsworthy's mansion?'

'I'm the messenger boy. Caddick thinks I'm with him.'

'You are if there is another attack.'

'Isaac, work with us,' Linda said.

'And if I don't? Another kill order?' Isaac replied.

Nobody contradicted him. Fairweather smiled; Sheila Cudworth looked away, and Sergeant Clough patted Isaac on the shoulder. 'Chief Inspector, you've got no option. Believe me, our hearts are in the right place, even if our brains aren't always.'

Isaac said no more and left the room. He was compromised, in league with the devil, but was it his devil? He didn't know.

Chapter 27

Gordon Upton realised that DCI Cook was desperate, and his message to him had been borne out of frustration. On picking up Larry at the airport in Valencia, the two had driven to where Sam Avers lived. It was early morning, and the man would not be out and about before early afternoon, and then only to a local restaurant, where he would eat paella and down two beers and a glass of sangria, teasers for the serious drinking later that night.

'He's flush with money,' Upton said. 'At his place or somewhere else? How do you want it? Violence involved? I only ask because the local police can be touchy with an English policeman muzzling in on their territory.'

'And if I am?' Larry replied.

'I need to know. No issue to clear it with the locals. Murderer, our Sam?'

'Almost a term of affection.'

'Not affection, but he is a colourful character. If he scams the English, the locals don't worry. Not much love is lost for the tourists coming here, jacking up the prices and taking all the rental real estate for their holidays.'

'I need answers, and I'm pretty certain that Sam, if sober, won't talk, and I don't want to heavy him. Drunk, would be best.'

'Then, we befriend him when he leaves later tonight.'

'After a few drinks. Can you guarantee his movements?'

'There are three places that we'll find him. He's been thrown out of a few others. The ugly face of the British expat is Sam Avers.'

The two men settled in at the restaurant while waiting for Avers. Larry was not hungry, as he had eaten before leaving home and on the plane. Upton treated himself to a slap-up feed. He was on expenses and intended to milk it for what it was worth.

At eleven thirty-five, close to midday, Sam walked in, looked at Larry and Upton, and retreated.

Upton got up from his seat, walked out of the restaurant, and shouted across the road. 'Avers, we know where you live. Join us, Hill's paying.'

Sam, as with Upton, could not resist the chance of a free feed, and in his case, even though it was early in the day, a chance to down a bottle of local wine.

'Inspector, why are you here?' Sam asked.

'I'm here for the truth.'

'Which you had in London. My sister has the house and the money; I've got the dregs.'

'And you're bitter?'

'It was unfair. We both suffered due to our mother and her celebrity lifestyle. Our father cut me out because of spite and his preferred child. I was always the black sheep; there was nothing wrong with that, but fair's fair, and he wasn't. Fiona whispered in his ear about what I was doing in Spain and what a waste of space I was.

'Hill, you knew her from before, the ugly duckling. But now, the swan, and who paid for it, our father. What did he give me? A kick up the arse.'

'You got the drinks cabinet,' Larry reminded him.

'That's all, and by the time it got to a friend's place, the removalists had taken half the bottles, and the friend had drunk the rest.'

'If you had received your fair share?' Upton asked, irritated by the man's moaning.

'I'd be in England, enjoying myself.'

'You'd be dead, Larry reminded him. 'Drink and drugs don't mix, and you would not hold back on either, given half the chance. The hotel that you and Delvene shacked up in, a den of iniquity, both of you high on drugs or passed out with alcoholic poisoning. Is that why you took the gun there, to protect your sister? We can prove you carried it into the hotel,' Larry said.

It seemed a reasonable ploy to use on a man who had just woken up and was downing his wine. If he could get Avers to make a mistake and admit his complicity, there would be no need for the heavy arm of the law later in the day.

Sam sat still for a few minutes before getting up and walking out. Larry wasn't giving up that easily and followed, putting his foot in the door to Sam's apartment. 'Not so fast,' Larry said.

'Careful,' Upton said, as he followed Larry in, 'the local police won't take kindly to a heavy-handed British police officer intimidating the locals.'

'He's not a local,' Larry responded.

'He is if it's a British police officer that's involved. They're sensitive about it here.'

'You get involved in Spain.'

'I've lived here long enough, speak the language, and have a private investigator's licence, none of which you have.'

'Then you square it with them. Sam's playing us for fools, and I'm not leaving this place until I've got the truth.' Larry knew he was pushing harder than he should. He was ready to use his fists to get the truth, realising that Upton would deal with the police and they wouldn't be interested in a foreigner who scammed tourists and gave their country a bad name.

Larry grabbed Avers by the collar and looked him in the face. 'The truth. This is not England. You have no rights and the right word in the wrong ear, and you'll be deported back to London. At least, you've got a chance of getting off the hook in Spain; in England, you won't. I'll see to that.'

Upton looked on in dismay, unsure what to say or do. Larry realised that he was losing control and that the heat in the apartment and the food he had eaten that morning, washed down with a glass of wine, as Avers had enjoyed breakfast at his expense, was affecting him. He felt sick and made a dash for the bathroom.

Five minutes later, Upton made the three of them a cup of tea.

'Get this down, you,' Upton said as he gave it to Larry. Avers sat quietly on a chair.

'Inspector, I didn't put the gun in the wardrobe, and it wasn't Delvene,' Avers said.

'Sorry about that,' Larry apologised. He had exceeded his authority, and an admission under duress, even in Spain, could impact an English trial. 'It was Fiona, wasn't it?'

'Easy for me to say it. I need protection.'

'It depends on what you need protecting from. What can Fiona do?'

'It's not Fiona. She doesn't know the truth.'

'But you do?'

Larry was suspicious of Avers' willingness to talk. Regardless, Avers had the truth; he wanted it.

The atmosphere in the apartment was tense. Avers was playing with his smartphone. Upton was anxious to be out of the place, and Larry was about to grab Avers by the collar again and threaten, something he had sometimes wanted to do in the interview room at Challis Street but never had.

'Upton,' Larry said, looking over at the man who stood in the small kitchen, 'Either Sam gives me the answer, or I'll take action. I reckon you should wise him up, either in English or Spanish. Otherwise, he'll have an accident on the way home tonight, and after that, the senoritas won't find him of much use, if you get what I mean.'

Upton replied. 'An admirable idea. Another English waster, debasing the Spanish women with their bad manners and body odour. I can arrange that. Today or tomorrow?'

'Time is of the essence. Later tonight, you rough him up, and then I can get around here in the morning before my flight and get the answers I want. Tell them not to mess him around the face; he needs that for talking. Below the belt, that should do.'

'Okay, Hill. You want the truth. I'll tell you who it was,' Avers said.

'Proof?'

Avers handed over his phone to Larry. There was an image. It was date-stamped and showed the Avers family home with a man standing outside the front door.

Deadly Secrets

'How did you take this photo?'

'I was hard up for cash. My father's not answering the phone, and Fiona's unwilling to ask him. I caught a flight, cadged a lift into the city, and walked to the house. I was about to go in when I saw him. I took a photo and left.'

'Why leave?'

'There was no need to see a warrant card. You wear it like a badge, the size 11 boots, the dark suit, the surly manner.'

'And when you realised that he had killed your father?'

'What could I do? You would not believe me. I did not kill him.'

'Why did he?'

'I didn't know until the two of you arrived at the hotel. And then he finds the gun he had brought with him.'

'Why haven't you told us before?'

'I've met Ibrahim Ali; I've met your sergeant. I don't trust any of you. And then Delvene's dead, and someone is wrapping up the loose ends. It's probably your sergeant, but I don't know, and I'm staying here in Spain.'

'I don't reckon here's safer,' Larry said.

'Not now, it isn't,' Avers agreed.

***

Confronted by conflicting stories, Isaac met with DAC Goddard. He had multiple people telling him they were on his side and could be trusted, but only one had looked after his career since he joined the police. Isaac still maintained faith that ultimately, in the final battle, Goddard would be there for him, even if he was holding a weapon against him and backing Davies to the hilt.

The location was Goddard's office, at the DAC's insistence. 'Open door creates less suspicion,' Goddard said.

'Is there suspicion?' Isaac asked as he looked around the office. A bookshelf with the DAC's legal books stood on one wall. On his desk were photos of his wife and children. On another wall, pictures of him with the prime minister, with Davies, even with Lord MacTavish, but none of him with Isaac.

If Goddard was playing a strategic game, he was playing it well.

'Always. The commissioner's not a man to rest easy.'

'Caddick?'

'They don't get together as much as they used to. It might be planned, or Davies is wary of Caddick, who is making a name for himself.'

'As what?'

'The man most likely to get hung out to dry. He's ruffling feathers around here and at Challis Street.'

'He's not bothered us as much as I expected.'

'Strategic, don't you get it?'

'Explain yourself.'

'Caddick is going for the soft underbelly. He's pressuring the weak, the inept and the incompetent. He'll weed them out, install stronger persons, show himself as a disciplinarian focussed on results, not people.'

'Human Resources will have something to say about it.'

'Will they?' Davies is keeping crime under control; Caddick is strengthening his power base, ensuring that he surrounds himself with good police officers, dependent on his largesse for career advancement.'

'Wouldn't it have made sense to keep the weak in place?'

'And then, he wouldn't get the desired results. I've moved out of Challis Street and jumped a few ranks. He probably reckons he can do the same.'

'Except he doesn't have your track record.'

'Does it matter? Davies is cementing his position. His latest crime initiative shows good results, murders down eight per cent, robberies down six per cent, and pickpocketing is down thirteen per cent.'

'Terrorism isn't, or soon won't be.'

'You have evidence?'

'Not yet, but I will soon.'

'And you trust Fairweather?' Goddard said.

It proved that his DAC knew what was happening while maintaining contact with Commissioner Davies.

'Clough has two masters, the Met and MI5. I'm not convinced that he's one of the good guys, reason to believe he murdered Robert Avers, and if he had, then he would have been instructed to commit the crime.'

'He doesn't have two masters. Nobody knew who he was until you found out at MI5. Did they expect you to keep quiet about it?'

'I've signed the Official Secrets Act. They didn't mention it, probably thought I'd blindly go on, sticking my nose in and rattling the chains.'

'They are not interested in general crime, and you're expendable. A terrorist attack would concern them, but you've got the box seat, but keep your hands off the woman?'

'I am.'

'Good. Here's the deal. Bring Larry Hill up to speed; swear him to confidence. Let him know what we're up against.'

'We? Is that the Royal "We", or is there someone else?' Isaac asked.

'The commissioner's making sounds.'

'Saving his skin, or is it more serious?'

'It's more likely he's reading the mood on the street and in the corridors of power. If he knew about Whitehall, he certainly would not want a repeat. If you believe there will be another attack, tell me. What I tell Davies depends on the situation.'

'Which means you might protect him.'

'It does.'

'Absolution for the death of innocent tourists. Can you condone that?' Isaac asked.

'Personally, I can't; professionally, I might. However, we must prevent another attack. We cannot discuss how the commissioner's crimes are resolved now. You can't have everything in one hit.'

For now, Isaac would accept the status quo and report to the DAC, who would inform MI5 and Davies accordingly, with what information he saw fit.

Chapter 28

It was clear that deals would be made, assurances would be given, and persons would be hung out to dry or charged with a crime. Failing those, some might die. Isaac felt more perturbed than he had since he had started on his one-man crusade. There would not be a clean end to the investigation, and it needed his mentor and friend, DAC Keith Goddard's deft hand and astute strategic manoeuvring to affect a satisfactory outcome.

Unbeknown to Isaac, Goddard made the first move the day after they had met in Goddard's office. Isaac did not know about this for another two days when he met again at MI5 in the same conference room. This time, he was surprised to find his DAC sitting there. Clough wasn't present, nor was Sheila Cudworth or Linda Harris.

'How long?' Isaac asked Goddard.

'I've known Sir Godfrey Fairweather since Homicide was instructed to look for Marjorie Frobisher.'

'As a double agent?'

'Isaac, you're owed an explanation.'

'A mighty big one. You were abhorred when MI5 shut down the investigation into the murder of Richard Williams.'

'And Sally Perkins,' Fairweather added.

'I raised my concerns at the highest level,' Goddard said, 'but my hands were tied, the same as yours. Sir Godfrey has admitted that mistakes were made and that the kill order on you was an error.'

'Are there to be more mistakes?' Isaac asked. He was remarkably calm, considering.

'We hope not,' Fairweather said. 'This is not a precise art. There are variables we don't yet know about.'

'And you want my people to fill in the blanks.'

'In part. You have a murder investigation. Is Robert Avers' murder relevant to our investigation?'

'According to the man's son, it was Clough who killed him, and regardless of your denial or admittance, I remain sceptical that you have told the truth.'

'And so you should. For the record, Clough did not kill Avers; the man was dead before he entered the house.'

'He entered. Who opened the door?'

'Clough did not need a key. Inspector Hill pried the truth out of Sam Avers in Spain, but how much do you trust the man?'

'Inspector Hill or Sam Avers?'

'Either, both.'

'I believe, Sir Godfrey, you've spent too long in the dirt not to recognise a good person, believing that everyone is inherently corrupt or malevolent, given a price.'

'They are,' Fairweather said, 'and Chief Inspector, you know it.'

Reluctantly, Isaac had to agree. 'I trust Inspector Hill, but not Sam Avers, who has made it an art form when scamming tourists in Spain.'

'We would agree; however, Clough did place the gun in the hotel room.'

'And you're now going to tell me that was another error.'

'I'm not. It was agreed when Clough saw the body and the gun on the ground.'

'The murderer?'

'We know who he is.'

'I believe Chief Inspector Cook deserves a full explanation,' Goddard said.

'Chief Inspector, you must understand that we monitor persons such as Ibrahim Ali. He is not the only one, and until Whitehall, he was regarded as low risk, more bluster than action, a firebrand, evoking the easily-led, but not regarded as a serious threat.'

'Did you know that Whitehall was a possibility?' Isaac asked. He had helped himself to another cup of tea from the table in the corner. He was hopeful the truth might be revealed, and he needed to be calm, not judgemental, but to listen, attempt to understand, and hopefully agree.

'Firstly, you need to understand the situation. We have around forty-three thousand extremists on MI5's watchlist. The majority are regarded as low risk, with a few being severe or critical. Threat levels are low, moderate, substantial, severe, or critical. London is currently at moderate; an attack is possible, but regarded as unlikely.'

'And yet, you had no inkling that Ibrahim Ali and Caddick were planning something?'

'Ibrahim Ali was a low risk; we monitored his movements, but not to the detail that we would have others. Even now, it is uncertain why Ali would agree to such an action or that Commissioner Davies would consider it.'

'Why cover up Robert Avers' murder?' Isaac asked the question again. 'And what are we to do with Clough?'

'You thought he was Caddick's stooge, which he is, but he's ours. We play a complex game, and we usually get it right. No one reports the terrorist acts we prevent or your admirable Counter Terrorism Command did before it was compromised by Caddick.'

'Caddick meeting with Ali must have sounded alarm bells.'

'We had no information of a possible attack, and we thought Caddick, who knew of Ali's birthright, was making a deal. Without proof, what could we do? We knew who Ali was. It was a precarious situation, not made easier by Caddick's closeness to the commissioner, whose position was at risk.'

'Which means that MI5 made a decision to support Davies.'

'Not support, but not to destabilise. Any weakness on his side regarding law and order would allow another extremist to chance his luck.'

'Are you committed to the truth and willing to allow the guilty to be charged and convicted? Or will it be another whitewash, swept under the carpet at MI5?'

'Not swept; maybe a light brush, but yes, Chief Inspector, in the national interest.'

Isaac understood the reality. Any investigation into Davies, Caddick, and Ali was conditional on other objectives: maintaining faith in the establishment, the legal system, the police, and those who held power in the country. An unequivocal cleansing of malaise would not occur. The populace would be told certain facts but not necessarily the whole truth. Isaac realised that he would have been shocked by the realisation once, but now he accepted it without prejudice.

However, this led to another reality, what did they have now? In London, crime was down, and there had been no repeats of what had happened in Whitehall. Rattling the sabre at Ali, and more likely, his father-in-law, Abu Taleb, might create such an incident, which would allow Davies to strengthen his position by acting against the wrongdoers, and that MI5, in the persona of Fairweather, would support the man.

Isaac realised that the die had been cast, and now, it was every man for himself. He wanted out, but he was too far entwined. He needed advice, but who could he trust. Goddard would have been the obvious choice, but his star was aligned with MI5, who kept the current prime minister informed. But Goddard had a shot at Davies' position if the man was removed. To reach such a giddy height would mean that Goddard was not only politically smart but also a shrewd and manipulative weasel who had used whoever and whatever to achieve his goal.

Fairweather continued, but not before patting DAC Goddard on the back, a subtle sign that Goddard and MI5 were one and the same and that bringing Davies to justice was not foremost in everyone's mind, nor was Caddick, and if Clough had killed Robert Avers, another crime would be buried deep in the files at MI5. 'Chief Inspector, we're united in the one cause,' he said.

Isaac knew the cause was always changing, and the outcome remained fluid. 'And if I state that I don't trust you, will my life be forfeit? Will Linda Harris be given the job?'

Deadly Secrets

'She's more likely to seduce you,' Goddard said.

Was it a subtle deflection from the DAC to Isaac to tell him to keep his counsel and not to further rile the beast? Was Goddard still with him? Isaac could not be sure. He was confused and could feel tiredness sweeping over him.

Fairweather and the organisation he represented were masters at deception and intrigue. A competent and hard-working chief inspector would not have the training, the wiles, or the impartiality they did.

Had Gabrielle Alsworthy, a thorn in the side of her half-brother, become an embarrassment or a threat?

The next day, Isaac drove out to Gabrielle Alsworthy's house, not bothering to choose a neutral location. The Alsworthy estate was monitored, and the movements in and out of the place were recorded. Isaac was certain he and his staff were under surveillance, their phone conversations monitored, and any attempt at subterfuge while trying to find out what was going on would be futile.

The previous night, one hour after the meeting had concluded at MI5, Isaac levelled with Jenny. If the family was in danger, then it was for his wife to know what was going on and the level of intrigue and possible criminality that might occur. To her credit, Jenny took the news calmly and drove the two hundred and twenty miles to her parents' home. There, she would stay with the children until there was clarity.

At Gabrielle's house, Isaac outlined what he knew and what he thought. He needed her to see that she was expendable, that people might die, and that the innocent would suffer more than the guilty.

'Don't worry about me. I'm an Alsworthy. I know how it works. Of course, deals will be made. Your nemesis, Caddick, will survive if Davies deems him important.'

'He's supported Davies for a long time. The commissioner owes him for that,' Isaac said.

'The commissioner owes him nothing. I've not met Caddick, but I know he would understand, and your Deputy

285

Assistant Commissioner Goddard will drop you if it's important. Do you still place your trust in him?'

Isaac had to consider the question. He realised that Gabrielle Alsworthy, Seth Caddick, Alwyn Davies, and Godfrey Fairweather would have no compunction to sacrifice anyone, if necessary, but he still considered Goddard to be redeemable and that a skerrick of decency remained. 'Yes, he will look out for me,' he said.

'He might prevent your death but not ensure your position. A posting to a remote location, your dismissal from the police force, possible criminal charges, blame you for Whitehall, might be acceptable to him.'

'Not to me, it wouldn't.'

'Why are you here?'

'To bring this to a head, to meet with Ibrahim Ali,' Isaac said. He was unsure why he said it because it made little sense. He thought that it was probably the realisation that he could trust no one other than Wendy Gladstone, Larry Hill, Bridget Halloran, and his wife, and none of them would impact the outcome.

'Then not through me, Chief Inspector. If you want to bait the lion, that is up to you. Have you checked this out with anyone else?'

'There's no one I can trust.'

'Trust Goddard, not because you have total faith in the man. In your desperation, you might be committing a fatal error, revealing what you know to the enemy, and what do you think those with Ibrahim will do to extract the truth?'

Isaac considered the visit wasted. He had hoped that Gabrielle would have been his way into the mansion, an informal meeting with his lordship, a chance to flesh out the man, to see if he was capable of terrorism, or if he was trapped in an impossible situation with no way out.

***

Deadly Secrets

The situation changed dramatically the next day, with an unexpected early morning return visit to Gabrielle Alsworthy's house. On arrival, Isaac met with Lord Alsworthy, who was comforting his wife, Siobhan, or Latifa, as she was known by the other women at the mansion.

Wendy was already on the scene, as were two constables from the local police station and a sloppily dressed inspector with his tie askew and hair uncombed. 'Lady Alsworthy found her,' he said. 'Last night, late, I would estimate.'

'State of the body? Identification proven? Why last night?' Isaac asked.

'Suffocation, lying on the floor. She had a bag over her head and a cable tie around her neck. It's Gabrielle Alsworthy. I'm a local lad, and I have known her since childhood. I went to the same preschool as her. From what I'm told, you knew her.'

'I did.'

'Body temperature, rigour mortis, discolouration of the skin. Down here, we don't have the luxury of forensics or pathology, not that we see many dead bodies, not if they've been murdered. Regardless, I am certain it's accurate. What's your interest in the woman?'

Isaac did not respond, considering that Lord and Lady Alsworthy were nearby, and two other women from the house stood at a distance. Interestingly, Isaac noted that none of the other men from the mansion were present, although Abu Taleb interested him the most.

Inside the house, two crime scene investigators were checking in the vicinity of the body, and a police photographer was taking shots of the murder scene. A pathologist was on the way to conduct a preliminary investigation. Time was of the essence, and a sense of urgency prevailed. Death had come to the Alsworthy estate.

Isaac took hold of Ibrahim Ali and moved him away from the immediate area. 'You're aware of what this means?' Isaac asked. He had wanted to meet the man and had been advised by Gabrielle to tread carefully, and now the man was standing next to him.

'Chief Inspector, you have misjudged the situation,' Ali said.

'How?'

'I'm sorry about Gabrielle, I truly am. I know she was uncomfortable with the situation, and I cannot blame her. She was the senior Alsworthy, and then I usurped her. I never knew, nor did my parents, who had raised me. I never knew either Marjorie Frobisher or Lord Alsworthy, but once I became aware of my heritage, I realised that the Alsworthy determination was in me, as it was in Gabrielle. She was a fighter, and so am I, and now, she's dead, and the truth must be revealed.'

'Here or at the police station?'

'Here. Time is of the essence.'

Isaac made a phone call. Wendy joined the two men soon after. 'My sergeant will record what we say,' Isaac said.

'Yes, Sergeant Gladstone, pleased to meet you,' Ali said. 'I've been aware of your regular visits to Gabrielle.'

A police car drew up at the house. Gabrielle Alsworthy's husband and two children got out of the back seat. A female police sergeant took them to one side and spoke to them before informing them that their house was a crime scene and they could not enter. However, the mansion was open, and they would go there. Siobhan accompanied them.

The interview warranted more than the three persons standing away from the murder house. It required an interview room with audio and video recording, but Ali was adamant that he would not leave the estate. The three moved to an outhouse nearby. Inside were several benches, and the interview commenced amongst lawnmowers and hedge clippers. Ibrahim Ali, the incumbent Lord Alsworthy, declined legal representation.

'Lord Alsworthy, is there a statement you wish to make?' Isaac asked.

'I believe so. Firstly, my heartfelt sorrow for Gabrielle's death. She was of my blood, the only person alive, and important to me. Our relationship was complex, but I believe we were friendly towards each other, and there was mutual admiration.'

'That we will accept,' Wendy said. 'From my conversations with her, I agree with those sentiments.'

'Regardless, Gabrielle Alsworthy has been murdered, and she, along with you, are aware that criminal actions have occurred in the past,' Isaac said.

'If you mean the terrorist attack in Whitehall, then I concur with your evaluation. The question arises about my involvement and how I learned of my birthright. Were they related, I'm sure, is a question you want to ask.'

'We have two murders, Gabrielle Alsworthy and Robert Avers. Both directly relate to you.'

'They do, obliquely. Chief Superintendent Caddick approached me at the house we occupied. He told me a story,' Ali continued. 'It was full on context, short on fact, almost a fairy tale, about how a small boy had been adopted out, and the truth of who he was had been kept from him, and that people had died to maintain that secret.'

Isaac realised that the man was no dummy and had a sharp intellect. Investigative tricks were not going to work.

'We know Caddick,' Isaac said. 'He's not a subtle man. Fairy tales would not be his forte.'

'Maybe not, and I was suspicious. You realise that my fervent rhetoric disturbed people, and the police had been to the house several times when I spoke in public. Someone would always record what I was saying.'

'You were controversial. An eloquent advocate for a cause that frightens people.'

'It should not, but we are not here for that. Before I continue, I should inform you that Abu Taleb is no longer at the main building.'

'Where is he?'

'He left before you arrived.'

'Did he kill Gabrielle? And if he did, why?'

'I believe you need to search your soul, Chief Inspector. You visited Gabrielle last night and tried to involve her in spying on me and the others in the main house?'

'I wasn't sure what I wanted of her, but I was concerned there would be a repeat of what happened in Whitehall.'

It seemed strange to Isaac that he was moving the investigation forward when MI5 had been monitoring the situation, and they had resources he did not, and the Counter Terrorism Command at New Scotland Yard were twiddling their thumbs. He was glad Jenny and the children were out of the city.

'Let me state that I did not initiate the actions in Whitehall. However, it was soon after that Caddick revealed my birthright. Decisions were made on my behalf without my agreement.'

'And you realised that the terrorist action and strengthening Commissioner Davies' position were the traded agreement.'

'Initially, I didn't, but soon after, I realised it was.'

'Yet, you said nothing.'

'Say what? I had no proof. I didn't know the man who blew himself up, nor the others who were arrested or killed. I'm innocent of the crime and a lord because of it. I took advantage of a heinous crime.'

'Who organised Whitehall?'

'Abu Taleb.'

'Who is not here. Once again, who killed Gabrielle and why?'

'Last night, after you left, Gabrielle came to the house. She told me she could not believe I was involved in Whitehall.'

'Foolish,' Wendy said. 'How could she be sure of how you would react?' Wendy said.

'She was an Alsworthy. She would not want the family name tainted by murder or terrorism. The family history is rich. She would not allow it to be sullied by my actions.'

'Are you saying she would have covered for you?'

'Not covered, but struck a deal to get me out of the mansion. I could keep the title; she would be the mistress of all she surveyed.'

'She attempted to bribe you.'

'It was commendable, and I might have acquiesced. After all, I enjoy the title, but I don't need the mansion, and I have enough money to buy another. As I said, I was fond of her; I wished her no ill.'

'She was murdered soon after,' Wendy reminded him.

'Not by me. We were overheard.'

'Who?'

'Atef Ezzat overhead, and on instructions from Taleb, killed Gabrielle.'

'To silence her or to control you?'

'Both.'

'Where are the other men?'

'They are not here.'

'We had Ezzat pegged as not involved in any crime.'

'He is the son of Taleb, the brother of my second wife. Well-educated, but he is his father's son. He did what he was told. He killed Gabrielle.'

'Sergeant Clough?'

'A minor functionary.'

'Siobhan?' Wendy asked.

'She doesn't know anything about this. I would have protected Gabrielle, but now it's too late. I will make a statement to you, the House of Lords, and the media. I will accept censure but not criminal charges. I have committed no crime.'

Isaac knew that any revelation that Ali would make would be subject to misinterpretation, criticism, or applause and that those who had killed in Whitehall, in the Avers house, and in Gabrielle's house might target him for elimination.

'I suggest you take further advice,' Isaac said. 'Any comment from you will be a rallying cry to some, dissension by others, and even if we accept that you are innocent of a murderous action, you took advantage of it to further your cause and to benefit you. Not criminal, but concealing a crime is.'

'Which I knew nothing about. Caddick approached me and gave me a story, which made no sense.'

'Yet, it did,' Wendy said. 'You wrestled with finding your birth parents, attempted to find out several times in the past. Back then, you found out nothing, but you sensed you were more than the child of good and honest middle-class persons.'

'Mum and Dad are good. They brought me up well, supported my decision to convert, and they love Siobhan.'

'Good taste, I would say, loving your wife. She is an admirable woman, but you, Lord Alsworthy, are a rat, preaching one thing, doing another. You knew what Caddick had; you approved of any action that would give you the title.' Wendy was angry. Gabrielle was dead, her family were in mourning, and Marjorie Frobisher died, as had others, and now, his lordship was offering platitudes as to how he was not involved.

Isaac understood the hostility, but he needed the man on his side. If they were to arrest him later, it would be with concrete evidence rather than emotional anger.

'Lord Alsworthy, where do we find the others?' Isaac asked.

'Taleb will have left the country. You won't find him.'

'His daughter might be able to.'

'He cares nothing for her. He wanted a grandson from me.'

'Who would be the heir to the Alsworthy fortune.'

'And the title.'

'Why not his son, Atef? Why not a son from him?'

'Atef had no interest in women; besides, it was the Alsworthy fortune Abu Taleb wanted.'

'Which would have meant disposing of you when the time was right.'

'Taleb was threatening, and the man had no issue with violence, whether directed at the innocent or myself,' Ali said.

'Robert Avers, what did he know?'

Deadly Secrets

'I don't know, only that he was Marjorie Frobisher's husband. What could he have known that would have been controversial?'

'Unless he could prove that Caddick and Taleb were in cahoots and that you were cognisant of what was planned in Whitehall. After all, you were the one who benefited.'

'Other than it would be brushed under the carpet, the same as my birthright was, as was my mother's death, and by the same people, by Godfrey Fairweather.'

'Has he been in contact with you?'

'At the House of Lords, soon after, I entered the place. He told me some of what had happened, and there was a suspicion that I was involved.'

'Which he could not prove but would have frightened you into compliance. You have been playing a dangerous game you can't hope to win. Where is Atef Ezzat?'

'I will give you an address,' Ali said. 'You can find him there.'

'Why so easy?'

'The man has served his purpose. You want a murderer, not an organiser, and besides, the son meant nothing to Taleb. His daughter was only useful as a vessel to preserve his name, and she will die barren.'

'I don't understand that the father could be so callous,' Wendy said.

'And that, Sergeant, is why you will fail. You ascribe certain values to people, believe that every person has inherent goodness, when, with Taleb, there is only evil.'

Isaac's only concern was if that evil existed in Ibrahim Ali.

Chapter 29

Ibrahim Ali was taking flak in the media. Conspiracy theories abounded. Increasing details were revealed that added further condemnation, in that not only was he married to Siobhan, but to the daughter of Abu Taleb, who was no longer a harmless old man.

Isaac thought the media were being hand-fed information by informed sources to discredit Lord Alsworthy, as the second wife wasn't generally known, and there was no way they would have known Abu Taleb's activities in the Middle East.

Isaac suspected Fairweather, and it wasn't helpful in a murder investigation to have MI5 creating conflict when what it required was rational and calm, not someone with a political or religious axe to grind.

Caddick had visited Homicide on several occasions; the first was to discover what was happening, to offer unqualified support, to let the team know he was right behind them, and to keep up the good work. The second time was more direct, as he informed Isaac that he was taking charge of the murder enquiries, which caused Isaac to remind Caddick that he had been at the Alsworthy estate on seven recorded occasions and three at the house where Ibrahim Ali had lived with Siobhan before his elevation to the peerage. As such, Seth Caddick was a person of interest and would not be taking control.

It had been the one highlight of the whole tawdry investigation into the events at Whitehall when Isaac escorted the man out of Homicide. The second and more dramatic was when Commissioner Davies removed Caddick from Challis Street and placed him on administrative leave pending further investigation.

Isaac felt more optimistic than he had for some time, and that the cause which he had championed for so long was coming to fruition, that the Met was to turn a corner, and to get back to real policing instead of political pondering, and using terrorism to strengthen the commissioner's position. DAC Goddard did not agree and advised him accordingly, realising that his chief inspector remained naïve, an admirable quality, but foolish in politics and policing.

Clough was still in Homicide after it had been revealed that he was an undercover MI5 operative. He sat on a chair to Larry's right. 'I removed the gun and planted it on Sam Avers. DCI Cook knows that and the reason why.'

'I don't,' Larry said. 'Isn't it about time someone levelled with me?'

'Tell him,' Clough said, looking over at Isaac.

'Sergeant Clough works with MI5,' Isaac said. 'He didn't kill Robert Avers. What Clough needs to explain is why he planted the gun on Sam. Also, how come he and Caddick are friends.'

'I don't believe either should cause concern.'

It did to Isaac.

'I've worked with Caddick over the years, and taken advantage of our relationship,' Clough continued.

'Because of Ibrahim Ali?' Larry asked.

'Long term, strategic. We knew that Caddick had been told of Marjorie Frobisher and Ali's father. We are uncertain how, but we accepted the fact.'

'It can only have come from your organisation,' Larry said.

'It might have, but I would not be privy to everything that happens. It might be best to regard me as a sleeper agent.'

To Isaac, sleeper agents were Russian spies, not police sergeants. It was not a good analogy from Clough.

'We believe Robert Avers knew and that Marjorie must have told him. How Caddick came to know is open to speculation. And then Davies is under pressure, and Caddick, a slimy individual at the best times, comes up with a plan.'

'Slimy enough for MI5?' Isaac sarcastically said.

'Slimy and secretive are requisite qualifications. Although, Caddick is a loud mouth, a man inclined to lose his temper and blurt out what should remain unspoken.'

'Is there more?'

'We've monitored Commissioner Davies for several years.'

'Since he exceeded his authority?'

'And to get it signed into law. There was concern about what he was doing, abuse of human rights, illegal actions conducted without the due process of the law.'

'Which I opposed,' Isaac said.

'That was known. DAC Goddard was partially in favour and went along with Davies, whereas you stuck your middle finger up at Caddick, which almost got you kicked out of the Met.'

'I wasn't.'

'Only because Goddard told Davies that removing you would cause people to talk, and questions would be asked. Remember, Goddard had MacTavish back then, and that man had power and knew how to use it, whereas Davies had cunning.'

'MacTavish dies, Moxon steps in, but he's an old man, and then he's dead, and I'm out on a limb,' Isaac said.

'You never were,' Clough said. 'We were monitoring, and Linda Harris was there, trying to get you into her bed, whisper sweet nothings over the pillow, and give you gentle reinforcement that she's with you and that there are others.'

'I rebuked her.'

'You were out of the scene, so she draws Caddick into her web of intrigue. The man starts talking, and then he's sleeping with her, and then he's got Pentothal in his system, and we have the full details of how Caddick worked with Abu Taleb to set up Whitehall.'

'To get to Taleb, Caddick must have gone through Ibrahim Ali.'

'Ali knows what Caddick's offering but doesn't know how to use it or if he should. Taleb advises him. In Ali's defence, he thought Taleb was a mentor and did not know the full extent of his activities in Egypt and throughout the Middle East.'

'He does now,' Isaac said.

'He does, but he's not sure how to progress. He's not involved with the incident at Whitehall, but he accepts his birthright. Now the man's doubting his faith and considering how to continue, but he's not going to give up the title.'

'Which makes him a target.'

'It does. Four of our operatives are always in the mansion with Lord Alsworthy.'

'Is he safe?'

'Safe enough. It depends on how we proceed from here.'

'We want the murderers of Gabrielle Alsworthy and Robert Avers.'

'One and the same, Atef Ezzat.'

'Where is he?'

Wendy, who had been listening at the door, spoke. 'He's holding up at a commercial premises five miles from here. I've been working with Bridget. He's with Faiz Shahid, the Pakistani tailor.'

'We didn't have him as involved,' Isaac said.

'He's not, but with Ezzat, you either obey or you're dead.'

'Are we giving an all-clear to Ibrahim Ali on his non-involvement?' Isaac asked.

'At this time,' Clough replied.

'Proof that Ezzat killed Robert Avers?' Isaac asked.

'He was there before me; his fingerprints were on the weapon,' Clough said.

'Which you wiped clean,' Larry reminded the man.

'I had our people check the weapon, clean it off, and then get me to plant it on Sam Avers.'

'Why, if he's guilty, were you protecting Ezzat?'

'Ezzat is expendable at a time of our choosing.'

'We need the man,' Isaac said.

297

'Fairweather said you might. If the man survives in a clean operation, he's yours. But let's make it clear, he's expendable, and so is Shahid if he gets in the line of fire.'

'Why are you protecting Ibrahim Ali?'

'You'll need to ask Fairweather or sweet talk Linda Harris.'

Isaac noticed the change in Clough from a competent police sergeant to an astute MI5 operative. There was a sarcasm, which, if he had been one of his team and not a plant, he would have taken him to one side and given him a verbal dressing down. As it was, he would say nothing and hope the man would soon be out of Challis Street.

Wendy could see that her DCI was angry. She wanted to tell Clough to button his lip, but she suspected there was more to the man than met the eye.

'Taleb, any chance we'll see him again?' Isaac asked, knowing that Clough would know and that he was Fairweather's mouthpiece.

'Unlikely. For now, concentrate on the immediate.'

'Which is?'

'To solve two murders and to waylay any plans that Taleb has set in place.'

'Which means we have to sweat Caddick,' Isaac said.

'He's all yours,' Clough said.

'I need your evidence file from MI5. Can you get us a copy?' Isaac asked.

'It will be available.'

Isaac phoned Goddard to tease him with some of what Clough had spoken about to see if he knew the full story. He did.

'Davies is pulling back, letting you have a clean shot at Caddick, throwing him to the wolves. One thing, we don't go after Davies, and if Caddick implicates him, document it, but don't write it up in an official report,' Goddard said.

'The man's off the hook?'

'Not off the hook. Others, higher than us, will decide about him. We still do not know the full scope of his involvement, and if Caddick's evidence is one hundred per cent, which it probably isn't, a lot would have been verbal instruction.'

***

Jenny was adamant after Isaac had phoned her that night, more upbeat than he had been for a long time, that she was returning home and unwilling to spend another night with her parents.

Ibrahim Ali stood before the glare of the cameras as he explained that the death of his sister had affected him and his wife greatly and that he was going to dedicate himself to mending bridges and healing rifts between his religion and that of others. And that he had been duped by a man he had thought to be his religious adviser and mentor, but who, it turned out, was a man committed to violence.

The questions came fast and furious, but Ali made his statement and retreated into the mansion. 'What now?' he asked Fairweather, who stood in one corner of the main room, off to the left side on entering the mansion. Isaac was in attendance. Linda Harris was not and had not been seen in the five days since Gabrielle's death. Her disappearance, supposedly on assignment according to Fairweather, was suspicious, but Isaac had always known she was mysterious, even before she had murdered Robert Williams.

'Wait and see,' Fairweather replied. 'Chief Inspector, is there anything you want to say?'

'Plenty. Regardless of his lordship's association with Taleb and the other three, there is the question of what he knows about Whitehall. Taleb was in this building, and Caddick visited the house where Ibrahim Ali lived with his wife. Tell us, here, off the record, when you came to know of the title and the attack in Whitehall.'

It was just the three men. Siobhan was with her parents, a hastily arranged reconciliation by Wendy, who had considered it was time to get Gabrielle's friend away from the trauma. How long Siobhan would stay with them was unknown. MI5 operatives, supplied by Fairweather, would function as household staff if they could, which was thought to be minimal. They were fully armed; their one instruction was to protect the life of Lord Alsworthy.

Isaac had been told by Goddard that the establishment was rallying behind the beleaguered lord, and whether he was guilty of a crime or not, whether his gullibility had allowed a terrorist attack, they were determined to limit the flack aimed at an archaic title and the House of Lords. Isaac also knew that if Lord Alsworthy's crimes or ignorance were too large to be rubbed out or brushed over, they would throw him to the wolves, as Davies had with Caddick.

'Caddick approached me at the house,' Ibrahim Ali said. 'It didn't happen often, but sometimes the police would come around. I never preached violence, but not all those who listened heeded my plea to be passive. I was born in the country, a Christian. I understood that most in the country are tolerant, but they abhor violence used as a means of validating a message. Integration occurs when people are tolerant of each other. Sir Godfrey and his people didn't believe me, suspicious of anyone they don't understand.'

'It extends beyond you, Lord Alsworthy,' Isaac said. 'They're suspicious of me, see me as lily-livered, and probably prefer others to me.'

'Which is correct, DCI,' Fairweather said, 'however, his lordship will be protected unless his crimes are so severe that they cannot be ignored. And you are right. Why did Lord Alsworthy not report his suspicions about Whitehall to the police?'

'Caddick was the police, and I knew he was close to the commissioner,' Ali replied. 'Who would be listening? Who could I trust?'

Isaac knew that Ibrahim Ali was all bluster and no substance and that the prize was too valuable. If he had a conscience about what had happened and his part in it, active or benign, it no longer concerned him.

'A weak excuse,' Fairweather said.

'Sir Godfrey might be inclined to downplay your part,' Isaac said. 'However, you knowingly concealed a crime. How do you plead?'

'I plead guilty, although I claim mitigating circumstances,' Ali replied.

Isaac looked over at Fairweather. 'Sir Godfrey, we must arrest the murderer of Gabrielle Alsworthy and Robert Avers. Will you allow this, or will it be hushed to protect the guilty?'

'By guilty, you mean me,' Ali queried.

The mood in the room was tense; three persons, none who trusted the others.

'Hopefully, your crime is stupidity and greed,' Isaac said. He was unsure where the meeting of the three was going or if it had ended. Besides, he wanted to be with Larry and Wendy, the Special Firearms Command, a couple of police dogs, a local police inspector and his sergeant, where Ezzat held them at bay.

Inside the building, Atef Ezzat was known to be armed and, in an act of defiance, had brandished it out of a broken window. Faiz Shahid's whereabouts were unclear, and he was regarded as an unwilling accomplice.

Using a megaphone, Larry had let it be known to the two men that Shahid's family were safe. He said no more, concerned that Shahid would attempt to get away from Ezzat, who would have no hesitancy in shooting Shahid.

Wendy spoke to the sergeant in charge of the Firearms Squad, who told her that once they were given the all-clear, they would attack at the rear of the building to cause Ezzat to focus his efforts there while at the front, two of his best, kitted in protective gear, would break down the front door with a ram, rush in, and take control. Also, in the hullabaloo, another three men would enter another door at the rear of the building. The dogs would follow soon after but would be kept out of the direct line of fire.

'Nothing to worry about,' the sergeant said.

Phone communication had been made, and Ezzat was on the phone to Wendy, who passed it over to Larry, who then passed the phone to the Special Firearms Command's sergeant. Larry was not a skilled negotiator and did not have the patience to speak to Ezzat and listen to his protestations and demands.

'Safe passage out of the country,' Ezzat said, 'or else, I'll take down Shahid and blow this place up.'

There had been no indication of explosive devices in the building, but it had to be considered viable. All persons in the adjoining buildings had been moved to a safe distance.

The discussion continued with the Firearms Squad attempting to gain further information on the explosives, their type, and what they were capable of. If it was a suicide belt, then Larry had no issue with Ezzat putting it on and blowing himself up but remembered that in Whitehall, ten others had died. If Shahid was truly innocent, then his death was not acceptable.

A car drew up to where the police were situated. Siobhan, who had hastily returned from her parents, got out of it with another woman, her face covered. 'Atef's wife,' Siobhan said, which was a surprise as, according to Ali, Ezzat was uninterested in women and would not give his father, Abu Taleb, a grandson.

'We didn't know he had a wife,' Wendy said.

'Nor did I,' Siobhan replied. 'Arranged marriage.'

'Your husband?'

'He's watching developments.'

'I thought you were with your parents.'

'I was, but I returned after I realised that Ibrahim's under suspicion. He is innocent, you know that.'

Wendy did not, but for now, she didn't care. The police sergeant handed Ezzat's wife the megaphone. She placed it on the bonnet of one of the vehicles and gestured that she didn't understand.

Siobhan took out her phone, made a call, and handed it to the woman.

Five minutes later, after the woman had spoken to Siobhan's husband, she picked up the megaphone and spoke in Arabic to Ezzat.

Deadly Secrets

Larry couldn't see how the woman, who was Ezzat's wife in name only, would have any success. He was right, and at the next instant, a shot was fired in the direction of the police.

It was a standoff and could take longer to resolve than expected. Larry was all for storming the building; Wendy thought it best to wait. Time and hunger would weaken the resolve of the most resolute.

It would be thirty-six hours before Ezzat left the building. He was not carrying any weapons, and, as instructed, he had stripped down to his underwear. Nobody was taking any chances with the man. Two officers, wearing protective gear, approached and handcuffed him. Ezzat was led away and placed in the back of a police vehicle.

There was no sound from the building. The full team positioned themselves at the front and the rear of the building, expecting there to be no resistance and that either Shahid was incapacitated or dead. Neither proved to be true, and as the officers moved through the building, ensuring maximum room-to-room caution, there was an explosion. Two officers were thrown back hard, one of them sustaining life-threatening injuries, the other, a couple of broken ribs and a severe concussion.

Shahid was dead, not with a suicide belt, but with a hand grenade. Like Taleb, the mild-mannered gardener, Shahid portrayed himself as a successful tailor instead of a jihadist.

At Challis Street, Ezzat sat in the interview room after he had been checked by a doctor and given clothing and food.

Atef Ezzat's English was good, but a translator had been procured due to the seriousness of the charges against the man. Also, a lawyer of Ezzat's choosing.

There were five in the interview room. Isaac and Larry, Atef Ezzat, Hamid Mehmood, Ezzat's lawyer, and the translator, Omar Richardson, the son of an Egyptian woman and an English engineer, who had been stationed in Egypt in the 1950s.

Isaac went through the formalities and observed that Mehmood communicated with Ezzat in Arabic.

303

'Mr Ezzat, you know what the charges are, the murder of Gabrielle Alsworthy and Robert Avers. How do you plead?'

'My client reserves the right to not enter a plea,' Mehmood said.

'His prerogative,' Isaac said. He sensed that Mehmood was capable and would defend his client vigorously.

Larry was conscious of the situation and not sure what to say. They were interviewing a man fuelled by religion, not by greed, anger, or wealth. He was the most dangerous of all, yet Shahid had blown himself up. Would Ezzat attempt to shift the blame, or would he believe that the death of two infidels was not a crime but a necessity?

'We have a witness that you entered Robert Aver's house in Belgravia and that you shot him and left,' Isaac continued. 'Do you deny this?'

'I do,' Ezzat said.

It was Sergeant Clough's word against Ezzat's. It was not a crime that could be proven, as Clough had not seen the man in Aver's house nor heard the gunshot, only witnessing the man leaving. It was proof enough for Fairweather's people; it was insufficient to secure a conviction in a murder trial.

'Gabrielle Alsworthy, why did you kill her?'

'I did not.'

'Did you like her?'

'Compared to my wife, yes. But women do not interest me, nor do men.'

Isaac and Larry knew that Ezzat's last statement was incorrect, but in the room with Hamid Mehmood, the man would not give the truth for fear of condemnation by his religion and possibly death for the sin of homosexuality.

'Gabrielle Alsworthy regarded you as a decent person, moderate in your belief, and an asset to Lord Alsworthy. How was she deceived?' Isaac asked.

'She was not deceived. My father is extreme in his views; I am not. He is responsible for Aver's death.'

Deadly Secrets

'But we have proof that you killed Gabrielle,' Larry said. He realised he had thrown in an innuendo cloaked in probability. He could see that Ezzat was not fazed in the police station, and the same impassiveness that he had shown as a butler showed in the interview room. Calm, collected, and not riled meant the man would not blurt the truth.

A police sergeant entered the room and beckoned Isaac. The interview was paused while Isaac phoned DAC Goddard, as requested.

'Release Atef Ezzat, no charges pending,' Goddard said.

'Is this Fairweather's doing?' Isaac replied. He was angry, aware that others were intervening in a police investigation for reasons that remained unclear.

'Taleb's throwing his weight around in Egypt, threatening to scupper our prime minister's visit to that country. And you know what that means?'

'I don't, other than we are allowing a murderer to go free.'

'He didn't kill Avers, Clough did.'

'How do you know this?'

'Ezzat visited the house and met with Avers. We believe that Avers was about to go public and reveal that he had told Ali six months before Caddick told him and that Whitehall if it was part of the deal, did not need to happen.'

'Which means?'

'That Whitehall, Caddick's involvement and Davies' resurrection were more complex than we previously thought.'

'Gabrielle Alsworthy?'

'Ezzat could be responsible, but now we know Faiz Shahid is also suspect.'

'Caddick?'

'Davies has deserted him.'

'Arrest?'

'What for?' Goddard said. 'If you bring Caddick into the station, ensure you have evidence. He's not going to fall for any fancy tricks. So far, he's on leave, still being paid, and apparently enjoying the company of Linda Harris, who's back in the country.'

The thought of the lovely Linda and the obnoxious Caddick cavorting troubled Isaac.

Isaac returned to the interview room and informed Atef Ezzat that there would be no more questions and that he could leave the police station without charge.

A transcript would be sent to all parties that day and for all to sign and return. Outside the interview room, Omar Richardson confirmed that the conversation between Ezzat and his lawyer was related to the murders and that the lawyer had advised his client to be factual, non-committal, and not to rise to the bait.

Chapter 30

Isaac was sure the murders of Gabrielle Alsworthy and Robert Avers would eventually be solved, and it was either Clough, regardless of Fairweather continuing to claim the man was innocent, or Atef Ezzat. Faiz Shahid was not regarded as Robert Avers' murderer, as he was heavy-set and would not have had the ability to enter the Avers' home, commit murder and get out without leaving evidence.

Gabrielle Alsworthy presented multiple possibilities. Firstly, there was Ezzat, then Shahid, although discounted for the same reason as Avers' death. Thirdly, one of the women, or even Taleb. Siobhan was discounted, as she, along with her husband, were not regarded as guilty, and even as teenagers, before Ali's conversion, they had not been in trouble with the police, apart from complaints from the neighbour in their small bedsit when they had first moved in for their raucous lovemaking.

Caddick remained the lynchpin, and now, the man's protection was gone, which made no sense to Isaac, as the man's downfall would react badly on the commissioner. Or, was that, yet again, adroit political posturing by the master tactician, Davies.

Regardless, in the spirit of magnanimity, Seth Caddick was invited into Homicide to discuss the recent murders and the terrorist attack in Whitehall. Isaac knew the man would lie, but he might say more if sufficiently rattled.

It was handshakes all round when Caddick entered at two in the afternoon. Some of those in Homicide were too friendly for Isaac's liking, although sucking up to the boss if he was to return was not unheard of.

'You want the truth,' Caddick said as he sat in Isaac's office.

'In the conference room. I want Inspector Larry Hill, Sergeant Wendy Gladstone, and I want it recorded,' Isaac replied.

'Whatever you want. I'm an open book.'

The four moved to the conference room, Isaac sitting across from Caddick. 'It might be best if you give us a summation of what you know, Chief Superintendent,' Isaac said.

'Very well,' Caddick replied. 'Cook, you've got this all wrong.'

'I've not said what it is, not yet.'

'You will. Before you do, let me give you some facts.'

Larry and Wendy sat still, not intending to speak, only to listen for the present.

'Has Commissioner Davies deserted you?' Isaac asked.

'First, the full story. I was working alongside the Counter Terrorism Command. Later, I took command. We monitored a lot of people in the city, and one of them was Ibrahim Ali. I contacted him, met him a few times, and realised he could be an asset.'

'How? He's not a traitor. What made you think he could be?'

'He was an Alsworthy. I knew that from Linda Harris, who contacted me. She told me who he was and that I could use the information as I saw fit.'

'Why tell you?'

'Probably because she knew you wouldn't do anything with it, saw you as too much of a prude to get your hands dirty.'

'When was this?'

'Eight months before Whitehall.'

'You were there.'

'I was, and yes, I knew something was brewing. Linda Harris was priming me, expecting me to talk to Ali and cut a deal with the man. Surprisingly, I don't think she and her people knew where it might lead to, only that it was political dynamite, and by rattling the chains, something might come of it.'

'Were you sleeping with her by then?' Wendy asked. She knew it was the question her DCI would want answered, even if he would not ask.

'Not then. DCI Cook would agree that there is more to her than meets the eye. Deep, very deep, and ruthless, handle with kid gloves.'

Isaac thought of an appropriate comment but did not speak.

'I had been fed the information,' Caddick continued, 'but what to do with it. I'm sure that Linda's people were fishing, and they realised that what they had was hot and that they had stuffed it up in the past. Killed a few people for good measure. I'm not sure why they picked me.'

'I do,' Isaac said.

'Well put, Cook. I didn't initially, but I thought I'd run with it. I told the commissioner I had something that might help him, although I didn't know how. He's under pressure; I'm under pressure. But the man's a fighter, and I'm a bastard. I visited Robert Avers and told him that he knew. He admitted that he did, and he reckoned that his wife had been murdered to keep it a secret. I read the reports of when she died and realised that Robert Avers was a man who let things ride, did not like confrontation, and had no intention of making what he had about his wife and the previous Lord Alsworthy public.'

'What did you tell him?'

'That I was looking into an old case where two murders remained unsolved. Not a lie. Besides, I wasn't sure what I was looking for or how to use it. I believe Linda had given it to me to see if I could figure out something. Ali was an irritant, although they needed to know if he would become more troublesome. They could not openly approach him, but I could.'

'You reported back?'

'Not often, but sometimes, I would meet with Linda, and it would be more of a chat about Ali than anything else. No formal reports; word of mouth suited them better. I told them that Ali was rational, committed to his religion, and non-violent. However, I had met Taleb. I knew nothing about him except that he made himself handy at Ali's house and gave the man religious instruction and Arabic lessons.'

'When did you discover that Taleb was a notorious and violent man?'

'Not till much later, not until just before Whitehall.'

'Are you trying to say that you weren't involved in a deal whereby Ali is told his birthright in exchange for a chance to prove that Davies was needed as the commissioner?'

'I am, not that I'm guiltless.'

'Why this frankness, and where does Sandra Perkins fit into this?' Wendy asked.

'I've committed no crime, although I will be offered up as the sacrificial lamb, cast asunder by the commissioner and Linda's people. I'm not the villain here, never have been.'

'You'll not find a shoulder to cry on here,' Isaac said.

'Only an honest man, DCI. No matter how much you despise me and how keen you are to see me out of Challis Street, either in prison or on the street, you won't do it unless I'm guilty of a crime. Cook, your decency and your integrity will not allow it.'

Isaac knew he would need to act within the law, aware that Caddick would occasionally ignore it, that MI5 saw it as optional, and that the commissioner would take advantage.

'Sandra Perkins?' Wendy asked again.

'She's not involved. I've known her for a long time. She is professional and can be demanding. No doubt, you have found her difficult at times.'

'We have no complaint about her.'

'She knows some of what I will tell you but not all.'

'What do you know about Clough?' Isaac asked.

'Competent, unambitious, gets results, the same as Inspector Hill.'

'And meeting with Ali and Taleb.'

'I kept in contact with Ali and met with Taleb. I had no idea about Whitehall, only that I had information, and Linda and Davies were using me as the go-between, allowing me to gain Ali's confidence.'

'You do realise we don't believe you,' Larry said. 'We know what you are and that you've been a pain in the rear end.'

'The situation's changed. Cook has gone this alone, and he thought MacTavish and Moxon would be there for him, and Goddard is predictable. Do you still trust him, Isaac?'

'More than you,' Isaac replied.

'Which means you don't. I can't say I blame you. You know that Goddard's figuring the numbers, making a play for Davies' job, not that he'll give it up that easily, not if I'm behind him.'

'Are you?'

'Do I continue to support Commissioner Davies? Of course, I do, even if he's thrown me to the wolves. Goddard's your man, and he plays the game almost as well as Davies.'

'Let's move forward,' Larry said. 'The two of you bickering about the most loyal is tedious.'

Isaac understood where Larry was coming from, although Caddick struggled with an inspector taking advantage of the situation to deride him.

'We have two murders to solve,' Larry said, not finished with belittling Caddick. 'Chief Superintendent Caddick, we believe you are as guilty as hell and knew about the Whitehall attack, as did the commissioner and Ali. The last two might be able to claim ignorance due to non-involvement on the day, but you were there. You killed a man, arrested others, and made yourself the hero of the day, whereas, in reality, you should be in prison. How do you plead?'

'Hill, be careful what you say,' Caddick reacted. 'You're on a knife's edge in this man's police force. Accusing a senior officer without proof is subject to disciplinary action, and I am demanding your resignation.'

'Which you won't get, as long as there are good people in senior management. You're the fall guy for Davies, and someone will pay for Whitehall. It might as well be you. You've got the history that proves to us that you are a conniving, sycophantic officer who will break the law if the prize is high enough, and it was very high after Whitehall. What was that medal? We all saw you shaking hands with the King. What would he say if he knew the truth?'

Caddick sat stunned, collecting his thoughts, before looking over at Isaac. 'Are you going to allow your inspector to talk to me that way?'

'He's got a point,' Isaac said. 'It's hardly the time for us to start trusting you.'

Caddick leaned back on his chair and folded his arms. 'If this is a hostile audience, I'll keep it to myself, let all of you burn.'

'That's more like it,' Isaac said. 'We're not fooled by your friendship or any platitudes you might care to offer up. We're not part of your team; we don't trust you, and I know that you will destroy anybody to protect Davies and yourself.'

'Do you want the truth? I knew about Whitehall and why I was there that day. I didn't plan it, and I certainly didn't expect people to die.'

'You knew in advance, but you didn't prevent it.'

'I knew that Ibrahim Ali wasn't interested in violence, even though he knew about his birthright. I couldn't trust him.'

'What about the other personnel in Counter Terrorism? Were any involved?'

'Davies is under threat, and I could see a way to protect him without their involvement. What needed to be done had to be unofficial, and I couldn't trust the people on Counter Terrorism.'

'Why? They had been there longer than you,' Isaac asked.

'Elementary, to quote Sherlock Holmes,' Caddick continued. 'I had been given the information about Ali and his parentage. It was hot, and I saw a way to help Davies, give him a stunning victory, and claim success in forestalling a terrorist attack.'

'You were winging it, hoping it would pan out. Caddick, you want us to believe this gibberish?'

'It's the truth. I had a hunch that Ali could be a potential ally to protect Davies and get me another promotion. I met with

Deadly Secrets

Ali several times and kept feeding him additional titbits. He wasn't keen on the idea, but Taleb was hovering in the background on my third visit. Ali said he was there to help him with his Arabic and religious studies. Why Ben Marshall, as he was called by his adoptive parents, wanted to be involved in another religion defies belief.'

'Some do,' Wendy said.

'I suppose so, but Marshall was no dummy, with a decent education and an attractive wife. He had it made or could have, but then he's got Taleb in his ear. On that third visit, I saw that Ali had spoken to Taleb. Ali is more interested and is asking me for details.'

'Which you gave.'

'I'd already told him that I had information which would be of great benefit to him, but I needed a mock incident, in which I would play a part, and Davies would go on the offensive, praise the London Metropolitan Police, and instigate harsher regulations, and round up a few of the more extreme. At Counter Terrorism, we have a list of names with the fervour but not the courage to do anything about it. Two bomb-making facilities are within walking distance of this police station. One is in a block of flats in Bayswater; the other is in a terraced house with a hedge at the front, flowers planted in the garden, and lace curtains. Taleb lived there. The man appreciates beauty almost as much as he appreciates death. Anyway, on the third visit, I give Ali a teaser and tell him I know his birth parents and that he's the legitimate heir to a fortune and a title. I don't give him too much, certainly not names.'

'How did he discover it was Marjorie Frobisher and Alsworthy?' Isaac asked.

'Not from me. What I believe is that Taleb started digging, took all that he could from Ali and his search for his parents, correlated that with significant persons who had died as he was getting close to the truth, and found out that his access to the records confirming Ali's birth was not available. Standard policing techniques if you have got a few facts to go on.

'Too vague, Caddick,' Isaac interrupted the man's flow. It sounded like Caddick was making up a story, hoping it would abate Homicide's interest and give him a way out. It wasn't going to work.

'It's the truth,' Caddick replied.

'Chief Superintendent,' Larry said. 'we've known you long. Don't expect us to accept you at face value. You have few redeeming features, and honesty isn't one of them. The truth will serve you better.'

'And if I don't give it to you, or can't?'

'Then you're damned,' Isaac said. 'With Davies under pressure and DAC Goddard pushing to take his position, there could be a travesty of justice, in that a chief superintendent could be charged with being culpable in an incident that claimed ten innocent lives.'

'Which would place the blame squarely on Davies' shoulders,' Caddick said. There was a nervousness about the man. Isaac was not about the waste the advantage.

Wendy was sitting upright; Larry was sensing the situation; Isaac was ready to pounce.'

'Chief Superintendent Caddick, when did you tell Ali about his parents?'

'I've already told you that. Eight months before Whitehall.'

'Which would tally with his trip to Spain and Sam Avers in the hospital,' Larry said.

'Classic mistake on your part,' Isaac said. 'You revealed the reward before it had been earned. You had no control over Ali, or was it Taleb? How could you trust them?'

'I would do anything to protect Alwyn Davies, the same as you would with Goddard. I misjudged the situation, and I was at Whitehall that day. I knew who the men were that Taleb had put in place. I didn't know that one of them was wearing a suicide vest and was ready to use it. That's the honest truth, so help me God.'

'You better hope he will. You committed a crime, regardless of your ignorance of the calibre of the people you were dealing with. How do you answer that?'

'I didn't know people would die.'

'Then why didn't you arrest the man before he blew himself up? Why focus on the others?'

'I did not know that man would be that close in. It was meant to be a thwarted terrorist incident, and then Davies could stand up with proof of the averted carnage, and then over the next few weeks, I would be highly visible in arresting others. He could claim that he was the man to lead the Met and that I was the hero.'

'Only that you killed one of Ali's men at Whitehall.'

'I realised after the first explosion that the others we had identified in the crowd might be armed. I acted in peril to my life. I was duped, the same as Ali was.'

'And once it's over, Ali keeps his head low before revealing that he's the child of Alsworthy and Marjorie Frobisher.'

'Yes, that's how it worked out.'

'Is there a police report of your involvement in this sordid farce?' Isaac asked.

'There is,' Caddick replied.

'Where is it?'

'Commissioner Davies has it.'

'Can we get a copy?'

'Due to its sensitivity and ongoing investigations, you can't.'

'You could be charged with aiding and abetting, conspiracy to commit a crime,' Isaac said.

'I won't, Cook, not until you've conferred with our masters.'

Isaac did not like how Caddick, after revealing his involvement but not his guilt, sneered as he spoke. With that, Caddick left his chair and walked out the door.

Isaac wondered if he had been set up by Caddick and that the feigned admissions by the man were there to deflect but not to convict.

Chapter 31

It took a phone call from Isaac to DAC Goddard, who then walked the distance to Commissioner Davies' office and informed him that Chief Superintendent Caddick had consorted with a known terrorist and had allowed a terrorist act to occur. And that it was probable that Caddick would be charged in the next few days.

'Hang the man out to dry,' Davies had exploded, according to the story relayed back to Isaac.

Isaac knew that Davies gave the only answer he could.

Regardless of his misgivings at the pre-emptive strike, Isaac visited the Counter Terrorism Command. He spoke to an impressive young woman, an inspector, who was acting as the head of the department, not because she had the age or the rank, but because she was regarded as not tainted or corrupted. Isaac also noticed the others in the department lounging around or trying to look busy.

That was until Chief Inspector Mary Ayton, one of Davies' closest supporters, came into the department and read them the riot act, saying that this was a serious investigation and everyone in the department was under suspicion. And if you don't want to be thrown out of the police or subject yourself to a criminal investigation for negligence before, during, and after the attack at Whitehall, they better get behind Inspector Fay Westley and DCI Isaac Cook and not give lip, but do their job.

It was a masterful performance, and as she left the office, she looked over at Isaac, winked, and made an inappropriate comment, which made him blush and Inspector Westley smile.

'Old friends? 'the inspector said.

'A long time ago,' Isaac replied.

'Your reputation precedes you, DCI. Quite the lady killer in your day. If it was a crime, you would still be in prison.'

Isaac had to admit he liked the sassy inspector, humour mixed with responsibility, a person who would do her job regardless of those who despised her.

Those who remained standoffish after Mary Ayton had left came around two hours later when Human Resources, in the personage of another woman, entered and gave everyone in the department a letter stating that the department was to be subject to a vigorous examination and that each person was to be placed on notice. Heads would fall unless actions were taken proving the department was viable.

Issac thought Mary Ayton and Human Resources overreacted and that Davies was fighting back, aiming to prove that he was tough on stamping out crime and he would not tolerate any other than the very best from his people.

***

It was the night that Jenny returned home, and Isaac was out of the house meeting with a former lover. Caddick had said Linda Harris was back, and Isaac had phoned her and received a reply. The conversation was short, and they agreed to meet, not at the usual meeting place, but at the Churchill Arms in Kensington, the favoured watering hole of Robert Avers when he had been alive.

Linda arrived prompt at seven in the evening; Isaac arrived ten minutes later. They sat at the rear of the pub, surrounded by memorabilia of the pub's namesake, press clippings from the Second World War, and assorted paraphernalia of England in the 40s, a less-troubled time in the nation's history, apart from a man in Germany who sent bombs over every night, instead of jihadists who only had to move from Bayswater to Whitehall.

Isaac and Linda ordered a meal and a bottle of wine. He could smell the perfume she wore the night they had slept together.

'Why?' Isaac asked.

Deadly Secrets

'Why am I back? Or why are we meeting?' Linda replied. He felt uncomfortable in the pub with her and would have preferred to leave, but he knew he couldn't.

The enquiry into Caddick weighed heavily on him, and he had nursed the investigation from its early days when support had been minimal until now when others were willing to take over, claim the glory, and receive the accolades. Not that glory or accolades figured high in his mind, but there was the suspicion that others would suppress the enquiry and that Caddick would be back in Challis Street and Davies would again be resurrected.

Isaac had no illusion that Davies played the same game with Caddick that DAC Goddard had played with him. Letting the junior ride the rocky road while the more senior stands back and observes, making their position apparent when needed.

The new-found admiration of Davies for Goddard and vice-versa was just that, transient, and each man was holding the other in check, especially after Deputy Commissioner Jepson, Davies' obvious successor, had suffered a heart attack and was unlikely to last for long and would not be resuming his duties at New Scotland Yard. This meant that Goddard, if he kept his nose clean and could demonstrate that he was the driving force behind dethroning Davies and confining Caddick to the dungeon, would be the obvious choice to become the next commissioner.

'Penny, for your thoughts,' Linda said.

Isaac realised he was not focused on the woman. It was for him to ask questions. 'Why are you back? Are you sleeping with Caddick again? It's not that it's any of my business, but the man's under investigation. He could be arrested.'

'I'm not sleeping with him, nor do I intend to. Regarding your investigation, I can confirm that Abu Taleb is in Cairo.'

'An arrest?'

'Not a chance. The man has the dirt on too many people in the Middle East for that.'

'Is it possible for him to contact his daughter?'

'Taleb, unlikely. The man has eight children in Egypt. The two in England are of no importance.'

319

'Then why is Atef Ezzat protected? I assume that was Fairweather's doing.'

'Ezzat's expendable; the trade deal in Egypt is not. Once the deal is made, he is yours.'

'Gabrielle Alsworthy, Robert Avers, ten tourists taking happy snaps with their iPhones? Are the murder enquiries into their deaths about to be swept under the table?'

'You've not mentioned two others.'

'Commissioner Davies and Caddick. Are you joking?'

'What do you think will happen if it's revealed that the commissioner of the London Metropolitan Police has been making deals with jihadists who subsequently killed ten people?' Linda said.

'A breakdown in law and order, abolition of parliament, new elections?' Isaac replied.

'Nothing that dramatic. Unrest, open slather for Taleb and his people.'

'Is this official, Linda? Are you relaying Fairweather's instruction to back off and leave it to MI5?'

'I'm just explaining what will happen. If you want a different outcome, you must take affirmative action.'

'Such as?'

'Off the record or on?'

'Either. What are you telling me? Did you get instructions before we met?'

'I did.'

'What you're about to tell me is advice on what I should do?'

'Only if you are brave enough or honest enough. Are you that incorruptible, Isaac, or is it a façade? Nobody could be that good.'

'Incorruptible, I believe so,' Isaac replied.

'Then this is what you need to do…'

'Sanctioned by Fairweather?'

'Suggested by Linda, who will deny all responsibility, not that you'll ever find me.'

'Fire away.'

'Arrest Ibrahim Ali, charge him with terrorism,' Linda said as she sat back on her chair.

'Without evidence?'

'There is evidence of Caddick's ramblings with Pentothal in his system. Also, a recording of when Caddick and Ali spoke at Ali's house. Caddick outlines what he has and is willing to hand it over, subject to certain reassurances.'

'A terrorist incident?'

'It wasn't specific, but it could have only been that. You need to sweat Ali and get him to confess. It doesn't mean he knew that people would die. It's unlikely that he gave the go-ahead for the attack.'

'Which you can't prove.'

'Nobody can.'

Isaac still believed Caddick was the organising force behind Whitehall and that he had set it up with Taleb's assistance and Davies' de facto acknowledgement. Proving any of it would be difficult.

Regardless, there was no more to say to Linda, no intention to linger and make a night of it, not with Jenny at home. The two parted, a perfunctory kiss on the cheek, and each walked away from the pub in different directions.

***

Isaac spent time with Larry Hill, Wendy Gladstone, and Bridget Halloran. The others in the department were to remain oblivious to what he intended to do. The offer for any or all three to take leave for the next week was on the table; none took it.

Isaac explained the course of action, the probable difficulties, and the attempts by Davies, Goddard, and Caddick to intervene. He told them that he was in receipt of a conversation that Linda Hill had with Caddick when the man was under the influence of a truth drug, which would render the conversation inadmissible in a court of law.

That bringing Ali into the station and charging him without hard evidence was foolish in the extreme and that, as a chief inspector, he could be out of Homicide and Challis Street within the week.

Larry said it would not happen to a competent chief inspector, and Wendy wished him well. He appreciated their confidence in him, but Isaac had determined after meeting with Linda, who would not have proffered a course of action unless it had come from Fairweather.

Isaac realised he would need to ride the flak until the troops rallied to his side, but he wondered if they would come in time. That night, he explained to Jenny that political intrigue, internal politics, and Islamic extremism were three complications that would not bring the matter to a head and that he had decided to take the initiative, come what may. Jenny tried to talk him out of it, but not because she believed he was not right but because it was dangerous.

Isaac explained that there was support, but they were laying low, waiting for him to take the initiative, and then they would be there offering full support. He said it; he did not believe it. He knew that if his actions did not provoke an appropriate response, sacrifices would be made, deals would be struck, and police officers would die.

Regardless, it was ten minutes after nine on a Thursday morning, with clouds overhead and a light drizzle, that Isaac drew up at the front door of the Alsworthy mansion.

Inside, Isaac formally arrested Lord Alsworthy, or Ibrahim Ali, as he was known. His security did not intervene but reached for their mobile phones. Isaac knew where they had phoned, and they were told not to take further action and to allow the police to make the arrest. Isaac saw it as a good omen.

Larry had accompanied Isaac, and he placed the handcuffs on Ibrahim Ali.

'I protest,' Ali said.

Isaac wanted to say, so do I, but did not. He was in no-man's land, unsure of his commitment. He knew he would not be

Deadly Secrets

going home that night and would not until he had the murderer of two people and a complete and accurate dossier outlining the activities of Caddick and the incident in Whitehall.

After that had been accomplished, he knew that Davies would need to make a statement, tender his resignation, or yet again, claim another victory.

Ali sat in the interview room at Challis Street; his wife, Siobhan, who had accompanied him to the station, waited outside. Wendy stayed with her.

Ali's lawyer was in the station. The man was known to Homicide, King's Counsel, and one of the best. He would be difficult to deal with due to the lack of hard evidence. Regardless, Isaac was determined. Goddard had been on the phone, informing Isaac that Davies was on the warpath, shouting in his office that heads would roll, and first of them would be that chief inspector you protect and that the man's a public nuisance.

Goddard said that Davies had been more explicit when he gave him a dressing down and that he had been served notice to vacate his office and to tell that damn fool, Cook, to release Lord Alsworthy immediately. Off the record, and at the end of the phone call, Goddard wished Isaac well, and I hope you know what you are doing.

Goddard was in contact with Fairweather, who kept in touch with Linda.

'Lord Alsworthy, we know that you knew of your birthright before Whitehall,' Isaac said.

'My client reserves the right to not answer,' the lawyer said.

'Agreed, but we have proof that he was in contact with Chief Superintendent Caddick and that it was Caddick who was at Whitehall on the day in question, killed one of his lordship's followers, and arrested others.'

'He wasn't a follower of mine,' Ali said. 'He was a believer, a jihadist. I had never seen him before.'

'He prayed at your Mosque.'

'A lot of people do. I do not remember him, even if he was there. I cannot be held responsible for what others do in the name of my faith.'

'You went to Spain and gained proof of who you were, but you did not use that information until after Whitehall. Was that the deal with Caddick? We have released Atef Ezzat.'

'Why?'

'On instructions. Powerful friends. Did you know he was Taleb's son?'

'I did. What difference does that make? I married Taleb's daughter. It does not explain why I'm here.'

'Your timing proves that you waited until after the terrorist attack in Whitehall. That is irrefutable.'

'Chief Inspector,' the lawyer said, 'that is circumstantial. There is no way you can make the connection. A statement by my client that he was the son of a lord and an actress does not imply any kind of deal. He would have needed to verify his birthright and taken legal advice, which he did, from me, ensuring that his claim on the title would be upheld, that he would be offered a seat in the House of Lords and that he could claim the inheritance, even though it has been given to his half-sister.'

'Can this be proved?'

'I have complete records.'

Isaac thought that he probably did, although if the records were fabrications, no judge would question the veracity of a King's Counsel.

'We know of your relationship with your sister,' Isaac said. 'Were you surprised when we arrested Ezzat for the murder of her and Robert Avers?'

'I never met Avers,' Ali said. 'As you well know. Gabrielle was a fine woman, and if I believe Atef Ezzat was capable of the crime, I would state it.'

'Yet, he lived in the mansion and acted as your butler.'

'A good butler who knew his place. What you want from me is a statement that he's guilty of murder.'

'Precisely.'

Deadly Secrets

'My client is not here to speculate on other persons. He is here because you arrested him on the charge of murder, of terrorism,' the lawyer said.

'That's fine, I'll answer,' Ali said. 'I suspected Abu Taleb was more than he made himself out to be. Not initially, but he tutored me in Arabic, and eventually, I could understand conversations he would have with others in the house or on the phone. I could pick up the nuance, the discussions about violence in a good cause.'

'What did you do?'

'Nothing. I never saw any physical proof. Most people say things they don't mean. Obviously, he did.'

'It's hardly a defence,' Larry said.

'Not a defence, a fact.'

'You meet Caddick, get to know the man, and he feeds you information. You agree to go along with him. Is this correct?' Isaac asked.

Ibrahim Ali's casual manner concerned Isaac, as did the lawyer's stern countenance. Isaac had arrested Ali, although the evidence was flimsy. He looked for a way forward, for the troops to rally, but so far, it was just him and Larry, aware that arresting a person for murder without concrete evidence was bound to cause trouble.

Trouble wasn't long coming. Another phone call from DAC Goddard. Isaac paused the interview and took the call. 'It's on the news,' Goddard said. 'Alsworthy's contemporaries are up in arms, arresting an aristocrat without proof.'

'How do they know we don't have proof,' Isaac replied.

'You don't. You have gone on a limb, but there is insufficient evidence. Commissioner Davies is calling for an enquiry, and Caddick's off the hook, and you are on it. Prepare for the repercussions. Damn foolish, this time, Isaac. I can't help you; my hands are tied.'

'Is this on speaker?' Isaac asked.

'Say what you want.'

325

Isaac understood Goddard. Davies was hovering over him, and the DAC was covering his back, venting his spleen on Isaac. On the one hand, to satisfy Davies; on the other, to warn Isaac to get his finger out, to bring Ali's interview to a close, and to get the man out of the station.

'I've got nothing on Ali, only suppositions, good suppositions which I can't prove, and he's got himself a KC, and the man's sharp.'

'Cook, do what you're told,' Goddard's voice was stern and commanding. Isaac hoped that Davies didn't see through the ploy.

In the interview room, Isaac, with renewed vigour, pressed the advantage and reminded Ali that terrorism was a serious crime and Homicide had proof that Ezzat had been in Robert Avers' house at the time the man had died and that Caddick had been in Whitehall.

He also reminded his lordship that if he had suspicions of Abu Taleb, he should have informed Caddick or notified the appropriate authorities.

'But I did,' Ali said.

Ibrahim Ali was on edge, and Isaac was hot under the collar. He wanted to grab his lordship and throttle the truth out of him. Ten people had died that day, and everyone was ducking for cover or offering up platitudes. As though no one cared about the ten, five who were English, up for a day trip from the West Country to see the sights, another three were from France, and two more from Estonia, a small country on the Baltic Sea.

'With whom?' Larry asked.

'I told Caddick.'

'Confirmation?'

'I wrote a letter, attached it to an email, ensured that it was received, and the email had been opened.'

'By Caddick?'

'Who else? There must be a record on your servers.'

'Is there a copy on your laptop?'

'At the mansion, there is.'

Deadly Secrets

'Did you speak to Caddick about it?'

'The next time I spoke to him. I told him that I believed Taleb was interested in what we talked about and that I suspected his motives.'

'Caddick's response?'

'He said he would look into it.'

'Which he didn't; otherwise, there would have been no attack. How long before Whitehall?'

'Three, four weeks. I can't remember the exact date, only that I told him, and then Caddick's meeting with Taleb at the mansion. Do you know what I reckon?' Ali said.

'Another attack. Taleb's out of the country. His son is free in England, and you have got Taleb's daughter. Are you sure you are not sleeping with her?' Isaac asked.

'I've got Siobhan. Why would I want Taleb's daughter?'

'To cement your relationship with the man, to prove that you are a devout Muslim and a good son-in-law.'

'None of which were needed,' Ali said. 'If I were you, I would investigate Caddick and find out what he knows.'

The arrest of Ali had been flawed, but Isaac knew it had been before he arrested the man. Lord Alsworthy would be released. Isaac knew those who offered de facto support had deserted him or were waiting their time.

He wrapped up the interview and informed Ali that he could leave. The lawyer's final comment. 'Unfortunately, DCI, you have made a serious error of judgement. I hope you realise that.'

Isaac did.

Chapter 32

A summons from Commissioner Davies was the last thing that Isaac expected, but the man had phoned and invited him to his office in New Scotland Yard.

Initially, Davies' conversation was terse until he said., 'Good work, Chief Inspector.'

Unsure what to say in reply and unsettled by the man's friendliness after the roasting he had received from Davies by way of DAC Goddard, Isaac initially fumbled, eventually offering up, 'Thank you, Sir.'

'I thought we should get together. One hour, alright by you?'

'Yes, sir, that's fine. Is there any reason?'

'Should there be a reason? You're one of the Met's finest chief inspectors, advising your commissioner. It's time for us to meet, chat, chew the fat, that sort of thing.'

Isaac was wary, as though Davies, increasingly pushed into a corner from which there would be no escape, was stretching out to the one person who could save him. Isaac thought the man was foolish to try it.

This time, he would not take advice from Goddard or anyone else about how to handle the man, and besides, who could he trust.

Isaac was confident he would not be taken in that easily if Davies aimed to sway him with eloquence, promotion, more money, or a lead on taking down Caddick and Ibrahim Ali.

On leaving Homicide, Wendy looked up from her desk. 'It looks grim, judging by the look on your face,' she said.

'That bad?' Isaac replied. 'Meeting with the devil does it to me every time.'

'It depends on the devil.'

'The worst kind, who is supposedly my new best friend.'

'Not the only best friend you are likely to have. The word is that New Scotland Yard is buzzing with rumours that Davies is on the way out.'

'Recent? Serious? Or just the usual gossip?'

'You're creating waves.'

'My name mentioned?'

'Indirectly. Some are talking and creating dissent; others are taking sides or keeping their heads down. Where do we go from here?'

'It depends on what the devil's got to say,' Isaac said as he left the office.

It was his second time in Davies' office; the first time had been three years earlier, when Davies was flexing his muscles, and Chief Superintendent Goddard, as he was back then, was causing the man aggravation. Then, it had been volatile, and he had felt uncomfortable while his senior officer was standing to attention and being shouted down.

This time, it was a firm handshake, polite conversation, and a warm smile. 'You're wondering why you're here, DCI,' Davies said.

'It's unexpected,' Isaac replied.

Davies' PA came in and left a selection of nibbles and a pot of coffee.

'Help yourself,' Davies said after the PA had left.

Isaac remained wary, unsure why the man was being friendly, although he realised Davies could affect one emotion while feeling another.

'Tell me, how's the investigation going?' Davies said.

'Commissioner, you've read the reports. You know our concern,' Isaac said.

'It's what happened in Whitehall that concerns you. Was Caddick involved? Did I know?'

'An honest answer from you would be appreciated. You're under pressure, Commissioner, a fair summation?'

'There's always someone after my position. Goddard reckons he's got a chance.'

'Has he?'

'Not yet. He's got the killer instinct and is willing to do whatever's necessary to get and hold, but you remain a weakness he will always support. You could have been a chief superintendent by now, but you play it by the book.'

'It's how I prefer to play it. Caddick's not my favourite person; apparently, he's yours.'

'He was, but he's careless, oversteps his mark on occasions, and believes that I'll be there to get him out of trouble, but not this time.'

'Does that mean you believe he knew of the suicide bomber and he could have stopped it?'

'He confided in me and told me he knew about Marjorie Frobisher and Lord Alsworthy. He did not say how he found out or from whom.'

'We have a shrewd idea, but everyone lies. With due respect, Commissioner, you could be lying.'

'I'll not convince you that I'm not. Besides, I have lied in the past and will again, but for now, you must consider how to progress.'

'Is this an offer to get me to drop it?'

'On the contrary. Caddick's in the thick of it. Some of it I can prove; some I cannot.'

'And you're willing to give it to me, conditional on something from me.'

'Your case is weak. You need my support, and yes, I need something.'

'What is it that you want?'

'Chief Inspector, I want what we talk about here off the record.'

'In return?'

'Caddick on a plate, proof that he organised Whitehall with Abu Taleb and with the approval of Ibrahim Ali.'

'Which means that Caddick gave you the details, which makes you equally guilty.'

'It does not. You will have to trust me at my word on this one.'

'How can I? Where did you get the proof? It could only have come from Caddick.'

'Sergeant Clough, what do you reckon to him?'

'I'm surprised you know him, Commissioner.'

'He's Caddick's man; Caddick's my man. It's a small world.'

'Are you telling me that you're in league with Fairweather?'

'Mild-mannered, able to leap tall buildings in a single bound, that Fairweather?'

'Is he more than he seems?' Isaac asked.

'The man acts like a government bureaucrat, but there's more to him than meets the eye. It was him that instructed Linda Harris to kill Robert Williams; it was him that organised the taxi driver to mow down Marjorie Frobisher, although I suspect you've figured that out.'

'Is Clough more than he seems? And if he is, why have you allowed him to remain a serving police officer? Is he a murderer?'

'Did he murder Robert Avers? That is what you want to ask, Chief Inspector.'

'It's a start.'

'How far do MI5's tentacles stretch?'

'Commissioner, you are speaking in riddles. I know my limitations, and committing murder in the name of Islam or national security is still murder. Fairweather does not believe that, nor do you, and that Caddick, with your agreement, did whatever was necessary to secure your position.'

'Chief Inspector, I can see why Caddick always admired you. You have characteristics that he wanted but never had.'

'Caddick had a strange way of showing his admiration.'

'Caddick has his positives, and I have rewarded him appropriately. And before you criticise, remember what Goddard has done for you. Caddick's crossed the Rubicon; he has committed errors and actions which I cannot cover, nor do I believe I should.'

'Yet, you knew about Whitehall.'

'I knew there was an increased risk of a terrorist attack, and the Counter Terrorism Command was working on it in conjunction with MI5. The suicide bomber was unexpected. The question is, did Caddick know in advance or not?'

'And did you, Commissioner? You have spent a long time trying to take DAC Goddard down, and Caddick's spent even longer trying, but DAC Goddard's close to taking this office from you, and you're willing to strike a deal with me, and, no doubt, offer me a promotion.'

Isaac did not trust the man, who had shown himself devious and a liar over the years. But now, there was a dilemma. The man was trapped and about to go down, but Isaac did not have enough evidence to wrap up any crime. The question was whether he accepted the compromise. He knew the answer, the only answer he could make.

'I agree,' Isaac said. 'Prove what you have.'

Isaac was surprised that Goddard hadn't made his presence known. It seemed important to understand why. 'Level with me, Commissioner, who knows about our meeting?'

'Everyone in the building, I would assume. The rumours are running strong. Apparently, there's a sweepstake in Fraud as to how long I will survive.'

'What are the odds?'

'100-1, that I'll last another six months. The consensus is that I'll be out of here in two.'

'Which one is nearer the reality?'

'It depends on you, Chief Inspector. For whatever reason, you've become the person calling the shots. Even Fairweather's hesitant to act unless you are in accordance.'

'Which means you're in communication with him.'

'I am.'

'Atef Ezzat?'

Deadly Secrets

'Another week, and you can arrest him. I assume you took his passport.'

'How? We released him on authority. We know where he is, but he could skip the country anytime.'

'Where do you think I got what I'm about to give you?'

'Which means you are working with Fairweather, and the two of you are willing to sacrifice your people to save your respective skins.'

'And so were Moxon and MacTavish. Do you think Gabrielle Alsworthy would not have sold you out or killed Ibrahim?'

'I knew what Gabrielle Alsworthy was. I know what you are. This could be a setup, a way to lay the blame at my feet.'

'I would sacrifice you, but then I would have to deal with Goddard. Fairweather's protecting you; it seems you have made an impression, or maybe Linda Harris has said a word in your favour. Cook, play this for what it's worth. Don't like it, but do it. You could be the Met's poster boy again.'

Davies opened a drawer in his desk and withdrew a manila folder. He then passed it over to Isaac.

'Who prepared this?' Isaac asked.

'Another of your women assisted in its preparation,' Davies replied. Isaac knew who he was referring to, Mary Ayton.

'Is she on your side?'

'She's on the side of whoever is likely to emerge victorious.'

Isaac felt sickened that the death of ten persons in Whitehall, Robert Avers, Delvene Drayton, and Robert Avers, was a game to men in power and that death meant little to them. Isaac realised that Davies was playing his trump card. He opened the folder and scanned through it. He could see conversations between Ibrahim Ali and Seth Caddick, Abu Taleb and Caddick, and Clough and Taleb. There were also photos. There was him meeting with Linda Harris, Caddick entering the hotel with Sandra Trent, another collection showing him entering the

333

building where he spent time with Linda, and even a photo of them in bed, vivid enough to blackmail the man.

'It's all on a database. That's for you to look at here but not to take with you,' Davies said.

'Clear proof that Fairweather gave you this,' Isaac said. 'It could be doctored?'

'It might be, and yes, it's what's been agreed and what will happen. The question is, do you want one murderer or two.'

'Avers and Gabrielle?'

'Clough killed Avers.'

'Ezzat shot at the police when we cornered him and Shahid.'

'He had to. If he had stood back and not acted, Shahid would have figured it out, made a phone call to Ezzat's father, and then, the games up and Ezzat's compromised.'

'Which means he could have killed Avers and Gabrielle, and that Clough has outlived his usefulness, and he's going to be charged with murder and possibly admit his guilt. But why would Clough kill Avers? What's the motive?'

'No motive needed. You can ask Fairweather or Linda Harris, but I believe that Avers, as he neared the end, had decided to tell what he knew.'

'What did he know?'

'That his wife had not died in a tragic accident, but that it had been meticulously planned and executed.'

'Without proof?'

'What proof was needed? Marjorie was frightened for her life, the reason she disappeared, the reason Homicide was instructed to look for her.'

'To save her, or to kill her?'

'Unknown by me. MacTavish would have known; Fairweather might have. It's complex, and it was a long time ago. No point in going there, only that Avers had his suspicions about her death. If he went public, the tabloids and the magazines would have been interested, the treasured star of a long-running soap opera.'

'And why are you giving this to me, considering that it's come from Fairweather. Mary Ayton might have assisted you, but the detail comes from the murky world of MI5, and Clough's one of them, and he's expendable.'

'Is he? Who knows how they work?'

Ten minutes later, Isaac left Davies' office. He knew one thing: he could not trust what Davies had said or the contents of the folder he had been shown. There was no one he could trust, not even DAC Goddard. Everyone was ducking for cover and avoiding any implication in the sordid saga.

As Isaac passed Chief Superintendent Mary Ayton's office, he could see her on the phone. She looked up briefly, smiled, and then looked away. Isaac could see Goddard's head behind a computer screen two offices down. Isaac knew Goddard was aware of him peering into the office but chose not to acknowledge him.

As he weaved his way down the building, eyes looked at him, but no one spoke. As if he was a pariah or the man who held everyone's fate in his hand. He realised he had more power in New Scotland Yard than the commissioner, who ruled by dint of authority, whereas he, a chief inspector, ruled by fear. It was an awesome responsibility; he was unsure what to do.

That night, he did not sleep.

Chapter 33

Sam Avers returned to England, not because he wanted to, and admitted to the reality when he walked into Challis Street Police Station. 'Persona non-gratis,' he said.

'Official?' Larry asked.

'Unofficial. The local police started to give me aggravation. Supposedly, one of the local women I used to send customers filed a complaint, a drunken football supporter, England vs Spain in Barcelona. This lout, Big Billy Thornton from Sheffield, has what he wants from the woman and then refuses to pay. The women in the place start remonstrating, and he responds by punching one and slapping another, even kicking one woman.'

'What happened to him?'

'A night in the jail, five hundred Euros fine, another five hundred to the women for medical treatment, and a police car to the airport.'

'You?'

'Same deal without the fine and told that if I come back, they will find a way to make me want to leave. They gave me seventy-two hours to deal with the apartment and pay my bills. On the dot, they were at my place and in the back seat of another police car on the way to the airport. I thought I'd come home and sponge off my sister.'

'You're still a suspect.'

'I didn't kill Delvene; I didn't kill my father, and you know it.'

'Not currently. We have two others lined up for it, but both are proving difficult to pin down.'

'Why?'

'One appears to be protected; the other is a police officer.'

'Clough, the bastard who put the gun in my room at the hotel?'

'Yes. What can you tell us about him? Had you met him before?'

'Never, miserable-looking bastard.'

Larry had to agree with Sam Aver's estimation of Clough, who was out of the police station, ostensibly on sick leave.

Caddick had stuck his head into Homicide once since Isaac had met with Davies. A few words between the men and no mention of the commissioner. After that, Caddick went to his office upstairs, emptied it of his personal contents, handed the key to Sandra Trent, and left the building.

Homicide saw it as a good sign that the man's support by the commissioner had finally severed and that the office was ready for their DCI to claim it.

Two days after the meeting with the commissioner, Isaac's usual demeanour was restored, especially after he had confided in Jenny about the bizarre meeting, and she had put her arms around him. 'It'll be fine. The family is behind you, come what may,' she said.

Determined to continue, Isaac was pleased to see Caddick gone but did not share the optimism that the others did.

Davies had given a press conference, made it clear that terrorism was high on his list and that no quarter would be spared in the relentless pursuit of those who wanted to bring the city to his knees.

One of the assembled media personnel had the temerity to ask about police corruption and collusion. She appeared to have facts but had been careful not to push the details and had allowed Davies to skirt over them. The woman had been tipped off, but by whom?

It was a question that should be answered, although the woman, who regarded her sources as sacrosanct, would not reveal it, not even under threat of prosecution. Not that it would stop a chief inspector, his back up against the wall, from trying.

Isaac occasionally met the woman at press conferences when he made a statement. Her questions at him, on those times, had been penetrating but fair. He phoned her and agreed to meet in her office.

Alexandra Marshall, tall, statuesque, with long blonde hair, was as attractive as she was competent. The two sat in her office, smaller than Isaac would have imagined, even smaller than his at Challis Street. 'Thanks for your time,' Isaac said.

'I know what you're after, DCI,' Alexandra replied. 'You know I can't tell you.'

Though it lacked detail, Davies's response to Alexandra Marshall's question was just enough for him to wrap up the press conference and leave. Yes, he was aware of the rumours, and there had been persons placed on leave, others suspended, and others drummed out of the Met.

Isaac did not expect the woman to respond, not in her office. Instead, her answer was non-committal. 'If, Chief Inspector, you're inferring that I would distort or ignore or even corrupt facts given to me in the interest of my career.'

Isaac sensed he had hit a raw nerve. 'This is what I will concede,' he said. 'Davies intends to strengthen his hand and is willing to take the brickbats along with the accolades.'

'Ethical journalism, that is what motivates me. A rare commodity, you would agree.'

'And I might be able to help you in exchange.'

'Commissioner Davies is no stranger to controversy or criticism. The man thrives on it, but you, Chief Inspector, play it by the book. What are you doing here?'

Isaac had to ask himself the very same question. Was it that he needed an ally, even from the most unlikely places. 'Whatever happens in the next few weeks, remember me, call me, and we can discuss what's happening,' Isaac replied.

'Tell me this, Chief Inspector, was the terrorist attack in Whitehall known by the police before it happened?'

'No comment,' Isaac replied.

'At least you did not lie. I phoned the commissioner and asked him the same question.'
'What did he say?'
'He lied; you did not.'

***

Aware that Alexandra Marshall knew more than she would reveal, Isaac met with DAC Goddard, going against his decision after meeting with Davies. As before, in the man's office. Skulking around in the corners was pointless; Goddard could not pretend he was busy this time.

'I've got a free hand but no support. I'm unsure who I can trust,' Isaac said as he sat. He was not concerned if Goddard was busy or about to go out. This time, DAC Goddard would stay and talk to him.

'Isaac, trust me, but you're doing this all wrong,' Goddard replied. 'You must be the catalyst to bring this out into the open. Can't you see it? People are battening down the hatches. Another month, and this will be old news, Davies will be on the offensive, Caddick will be redeemed, and you'll be back where you started.'

'Your suggestion?'
'Raise the heat.'
'I did that once before, and then you tell me to release Atef Ezzat.'
'I won't this time. Charge Clough with the murder of Robert Avers.'
'Even if Clough is innocent.'
'Does it matter? It's either Ezzat or Clough. Regardless, charge Ezzat with Gabrielle Alsworthy's murder.'
'For which we have no proof.'
'Resist anyone who wants to take you on.'
'Ibrahim Ali?'
'Leave him alone for the moment. Wait and see. If Ezzat's cornered, then he might start talking.'

Isaac left Goddard's office, not optimistic but charged with purpose. Back in Challis Street, he brought Larry and Wendy into his office, giving them clear instructions on what was required of them. Larry's was the easier task, as he knew where Clough was. Wendy's was more of a challenge, as she knew where Ezzat was, but he was surrounded by a group of men in a secure compound fifty miles from London.

'Ezzat first,' Isaac said. 'Take Inspector Hill and the Firearms Squad as a backup. Any resistance, use force.'

'Even though we can't prove Ezzat is guilty of either crime?' Wendy queried.

'Follow through, bring Ezzat into the station, and get Clough. The same again. If he resists, use force.'

'This is going to cause friction,' Larry said.

'That's the idea.'

'It's your career, DCI.'

'And yours. Are you with me on this?'

'We are,' Wendy said.

Thirty-six hours later, at nine in the evening, Wendy and Larry pulled up at the front gate to the compound. Larry beeped the car's horn. The gate opened enough for a burly man to come out and ask what they were doing there. Wendy answered. 'We've got a warrant for the arrest of Atef Ezzat.'

'He's not here,' the man replied. Larry could see the man had a gun under his jacket, and to the left of the gate, up high, a rifle barrel was pointing at them. He looked behind him and saw that the Firearms Squad had spotted the rifle and were prepared to respond if there was a shot fired at them or Larry and Wendy.

'We know he's here,' Wendy said. 'We have had a spotter watching this place for the last twenty-four hours. He went in; he has not come out, so I suggest you open that gate and let us in.'

'Or else?'

'He's wanted for murder. If you resist, you will be arrested.'

The gate opened, and four vehicles drove in.

Atef Ezzat stood at the entrance to the large house. He held a rifle.

Wendy got out of the vehicle and walked over to Ezzat. 'Atef Ezzat, I have a warrant for your arrest.'

'Are you sure about this?' Ezzat replied.

'I am. I suggest your people drop their weapons. We would not want a bloodbath here, would we?'

'This is my territory, not yours.'

Larry made a phone call. Five minutes later, another two police vehicles arrived outside the gate. One was a van, the other was a four-wheel drive; there was a total of five men, and they were heavily armed.

The instructions from Isaac had been clear; broker no dissent. Larry and Wendy knew that Isaac was exceeding his authority. They hoped he knew what he was doing, but they weren't sure.

A shot rang out as one of the men on the wall fired at one of the vehicles outside. Returning fire, one of the Firearms Squad in the compound returned fired and winged the man, who fell to the ground. Ezzat put his gun down and surrendered; his hands were handcuffed.

At Challis Street, Isaac received the news of the arrest.

Alexandra Marshall phoned Isaac five minutes later. 'I'm receiving reports of a gunfight,' she said.

'Does anyone else know?'

'Within the hour, everyone. What can you give me?'

'We have made an arrest. We have evidence that this person murdered Robert Avers and possibly Gabrielle Alsworthy.'

'You can't prove it.'

'Which means you are privy to certain information,' Isaac said. 'If you want my updates, you'll need to give me something in return.'

'Not yet. Chief Inspector, you're the most courageous police officer or a bloody fool. Which one are you?'

'Hopefully, neither, but it could be both.'

'We've arrested Atef Ezzat for murder,' he said.

341

'Who has got political connections overseas, and there's a trade deal, and you're jeopardising it. Bloody fool seems appropriate.'

'Or catalyst. What is your reaction? How are you going to report this?'

'Factually, for now, or do you have another idea?'

'In return for exclusivity?'

'Give me what you have before it becomes general knowledge.'

The call ended, and Isaac returned to what was happening in the station. Ezzat had arrived and was in Interview Room No. 1. His lawyer was parking his car, and the interrogation would commence in fifteen minutes.

Larry left the station. He would arrest Clough. He expected him to come quietly, which he did, but not without registering his anger. With a fellow officer, Larry dispensed with the handcuffs and sat in the back seat of a marked police car for the short trip to Challis Street Police Station.

Clough was in Interview Room 2; Ezzat was in Room 1. Commissioner Davies, who had been informed of the situation by Goddard, was hopping mad, accusing his DAC of gross disloyalty and that Cook was for the chop, and if Goddard didn't deal with it, he would.

Goddard said little, aware that his DCI could arrest whoever he wanted if there was evidence to ensure a conviction.

Goddard waited; Davies fumed; Fairweather watched with interest, and Caddick kept his head low.

Clough sat in the interview room, this time not as an interrogator but as an interrogatee. Isaac sat opposite; alongside him sat Wendy. It was thought that Larry's friendship with Clough would be counterproductive and that Clough would look to Larry for support. That benefit was denied him.

'Sergeant Clough, you've told us the chain of events that led you to be outside Robert Avers' house and that you saw Atef Ezzat leave.'

'I have,' Clough said.

Deadly Secrets

'The issue is who left first, you or Ezzat. Ezzat will claim he was not there, but you say he was. What interest would Robert Avers have been to you?

'I know my reason; Ezzat's I know, and so do you. What did Fairweather tell you? What did Linda Harris tell you?'

'Sergeant Clough, keep to the facts. You are in enough trouble as it is,' Wendy said. 'Planting evidence is a crime, and if you killed Avers, not only will it be a murder charge, but another for putting the gun in the wardrobe.'

'I was under instructions,'

'What instructions?' Isaac asked. 'Are you willing to sacrifice Sam Avers to protect Ezzat?'

'Ezzat's a killer; his father's another. Like father, like son. Taleb has influence, enough dirt on enough people to make them nervous. Nobody wants a loose cannon, and Taleb could be that if Ezzat is charged.'

'Which he will be if you are proven innocent.

'Clough, you're under suspicion of murder,' Isaac said. 'Your friends in high places will not be able to protect you. Straight answers to straight questions would be the best approach.'

'Cook, I've read your case file. I know about you and Caddick, the time you spent with Linda Harris, and those other women you dallied with. Straight answers didn't get you out of trouble before, only Deputy Assistant Commissioner Goddard. Who do you think is looking out for me?'

'Fairweather.'

'The whole damn MI5, that's who. They'll trump anything you've got to throw against me.'

Wendy didn't like the man's arrogance but knew Clough was stating the obvious. If they could cover up the murders of Marjorie Frobisher and Richard Williams, Robert Avers would present no trouble. An old man, in the last weeks of his life, takes a gun to the head and blows his brains out. Easily concocted, easy to believe, and the fickle public had no concerns when Robert had died, and even Marjorie's death had not troubled them for

343

more than a week, apart from one episode of the soap, where they had rolled the credits "In memory of Marjorie Frobisher".

Isaac did not want to discuss who had the greater support but thought it probably wasn't him. The question would be whether Davies had enough dirt on those out to remove him from office or enough political clout to stave off those after his office. Isaac knew that Davies would never be charged with a crime, bringing derision to the London Metropolitan Police and proving the innuendo that the force was rotten to the core.

'We have two homicides to solve, and your alibi is weak, non-existent, I would say.'

'I have no alibi, only my service record,' Clough replied. He had entered the nonchalant phase, leaning back on his chair, his arms crossed in front of him.

'It doesn't rule you out. What is it that Robert Avers knew?'

'How would I know, only that I was told to keep an eye on him.'

'Standing outside in the street. It doesn't seem likely that you and Ezzat decided to show up at the house simultaneously. Avers knew something. Could he have known that his wife had been murdered? Did he have additional information?'

'Even if he did, what use would it have been? The woman's long forgotten.'

'All of us in this room know Marjorie Frobisher was a professional hit.'

'I don't,' Clough said.

'Then we come back to why you and Ezzat were both at Avers's house on that fateful day. The man's close to the end, and apart from his daughter and a nurse, he barely interacts with anyone else.'

'Except he does. Ibrahim Ali visited him two days before his death.'

'You've not mentioned that before.'

'No reason to, nor did you ask.'

'You work for me, not Fairweather,' Isaac said.

Deadly Secrets

'I have two masters,' Clough said. 'I follow the more important.'

'Which is Fairweather.'

'Chief Inspector, you are not my master, nor is Caddick or Davies. I know what Fairweather is capable of, what I'm capable of. DCI, you're a boy in a man's world. No disrespect, but you hold to a "Boy's Own" belief of right and wrong. This is not fiction but fact.

'Ibrahim Ali wanted to know about his mother. After all, he had never met either parent, and he had been brought up to date by Gabrielle as to his father, but he had a natural curiosity to want to know about his mother. The two had met a dozen times, sometimes at Avers's house. And yes, Robert knew that his wife had been killed, told Ibrahim Ali at their last meeting, and gave him proof.'

'What kind of proof?'

'A video.'

'Which showed?'

'A fan of Marjorie's, who had seen her come out of the restaurant, drunk as a lord or a lord's first wife. The fan had an iPhone, and she recorded Marjorie coming out and then stepping out into the street, a car accelerating fast at her, irrefutable proof that it wasn't accidental and that the taxi had purposely sped up and swerved to the left as it reached her, killing her instantly.'

'How long had Avers had this video, and where is the fan?'

'He had it long before Ali had found out who he was.'

'You've seen the video?'

'It was in the house. Ezzat had been looking for it. Avers must have told Ali that his mother had been murdered.'

'Did it upset him?'

'It might have. After all, it was his birth mother. He could accept that she had died, but murder to prevent him from becoming the next Lord Alsworthy would have affected him badly, and now he had the title and the House of Lords to denounce those who had murdered his mother.'

'Old news.' Wendy said.

'Old,' Clough said, 'but still news. Extreme embarrassment for the police, serious questions about who was behind it.'

'Which would have brought into the picture Angus MacTavish, the previous prime minister, Moxon, and the police,' Isaac said.

'Not Fairweather,' Clough said. 'Blame would be passed from one to the other, political conniving would be used to protect the guilty.'

'But not the innocent.'

'Correct. I was at the house to get hold of the tape; Ezzat was there to get it as probable leverage against his lordship.'

'Abu Taleb?'

'Ibrahim Ali is committed to his religion, but he's not in favour of violence.'

'Who might not want it released,' Wendy said.

'It's unknown,' Clough said.

'Are you saying that Ezzat wanted it as leverage, which brings into question how he knew about it, and that you were retrieving it as a means to have leverage over Ali?'

'I was sent to retrieve, not to decide what to do with it, but I suspect our superiors, police and intelligence, wouldn't want the embarrassment if the tape was played on mainstream media. Too many questions, not enough convincing answers, and you, DCI Cook, would become part of it, the police officer who knew the truth about William's death, and then Marjorie's, and did nothing about it.'

'Official Secrets Act.'

'Do you think that will be an adequate defence?'

'I don't, and it would be the innocent who fall, not the guilty.'

'It might have been best if Taleb had taken it,' Clough said.

'How?' Wendy asked.

Deadly Secrets

'I found it, Ezzat did not. If he had, Taleb could have pressured Ali to use his influence to further Jihad and give his daughter a grandson who would one day be the next Lord Alsworthy. The tape was powerful, political dynamite. I assume that Ibrahim Ali would want to use it or to suppress that his mother had been murdered and his father had been complicit, although it's too deep for me. I could be wrong.'

'As soon as the child is born, Ali is expendable. Abu Taleb would become his legal guardian and the de facto Lord Alsworthy. A brilliant plan, if it had succeeded,' Isaac said.

'It didn't,' Clough said. 'I can produce the tape. Ask Fairweather or Linda if they will show it to you.'

It was not a confession from Clough, just another twist into solving the two homicides, but Isaac had to concede that Clough was probably telling the truth, or, at least, enough of it.

***

In another room, Atef Ezzat sat patiently. Gabrielle Alsworthy had regarded him as the most agreeable at the mansion and that he had performed his duties of butler impeccably.

Clough had left the building before Isaac and Larry commenced the interview with Ezzat, who did not complain about how long he had been waiting.

'Your father is Abu Taleb?' Isaac asked.

'He is an important man in his country,' Ezzat replied.

'He's also regarded as a man who uses violence.'

'Which you cannot prove, even if I was willing to admit its possibility.'

'Are you admitting it?' Larry asked, who could see a cat and mouse chase as he and Isaac put forward questions and facts, to which Ezzat would reply with a contradiction.

'I'm admitting to nothing. We are discussing the murder of two people. I thought one of those, Gabrielle Alsworthy, was pleasant, even if she had airs and graces due to her social position.'

347

'Robert Avers?'
'I found him dead and left.'
'And the tape?'
'I didn't find it,' Ezzat said.
Isaac breathed a sigh of relief. Ezzat had made an error in admitting that a tape existed.
'What was on the tape?'
'I don't know.'
'You've admitted to its existence, which means you must have received instructions. Those instructions either came from your father or Ibrahim Ali. Which one of the two?'
'I can't remember,' Ezzat replied.
Selective memory wasn't going to work, not this time. Ezzat was not going to leave the interview room, not until he had elucidated on the tape, its probable contents, and what he knew of the terrorist attack in Whitehall.
'Then let me elaborate,' Isaac said. 'The tape showed proof that Ali's mother had been murdered. Potentially embarrassing to some, political dynamite to others, a lever to others, namely, your father, who is a known jihadist and uses violence and murder to further his cause. And that he would have used that tape to force Ali to father a son with your sister and to be complicit in further terrorist attacks in London.'
'My father wanted a grandson. I wasn't going to give him one, but my sister could, but Ali won't go near her, not that I can blame him.'
'Why can't you blame him?'
'He had Siobhan; why would he want another.'
'She was in the way. Was there a plan to get rid of her?'
'Not by me. I couldn't do that, not to her.'
'But you could to Gabrielle. Why kill her? Why kill Avers? We have enough to keep you in custody until we get the proof, and why were you surrounded by heavily armed goons?'
'Protection.'
'Not in this country, not with guns.'

Deadly Secrets

'Your best defence is to work with us,' Isaac said. 'Also, we have the tape.'

'Ibrahim Ali is conflicted. Unsure of the way forward, seduced by Western affluence.'

'Aren't you? You've lived in this country for a long time and openly admit to your sexuality. In Egypt, openly gay?'

'Death, which my father would have granted me, but I was useful, could go places he couldn't, and I couldn't be disloyal to him?'

'Out of love or fear?'

'Out of respect.'

'You were released once before from this police station, but this time, no such phone call will come to make me let you go. I've got carte blanche now. Ezzat, either work for us or damn yourself. I'm beyond caring,' Isaac said.

Isaac picked up a large brown envelope that was on the table in front of him. The farce had lasted too long. It had been the night before when he had met Linda, a night he preferred to forget when she had lunged at him and drew him into a passionate embrace. It had been an out-of-the-way location, over an hour's drive from London. She had said it was important and not to tell anyone.

He had not told Jenny, although he intended to. The night had ended in disappointment for Linda and disgust for him in that he had not immediately pushed the woman away.

'Open this later,' she had said as she handed over the envelope. 'Choose your time carefully when all else has failed. It's not admissible; too many questions would be asked about where you obtained it.'

Sitting in front of Ezzat, Isaac opened the envelope, took a cursory look at its contents, and then placed them on the table.

Larry looked first and let out a gasping sound. 'You have copies?' he asked Isaac.

'I can always get more copies if we need them,' Isaac replied.

'These are enough. Ezzat, look at these, and tell us what you see,' Larry said as he pushed them over to Ezzat, who initially declined the offer but eventually succumbed.

'Damning,' Isaac said.

'How?' Ezzat replied. He was no longer sitting back, his arms crossed, but now, nervously sweating.

Isaac felt a sense of relief, a clear sign that Ezzat, who had remained free due to his father's influence and a pending trade deal, would not be able to use either now.

'How is not important,' Isaac said. 'It's proof.'

'It's a fake.'

It was not; Isaac knew that, although he didn't understand why he had not seen it before. But then, he realised that dealing with the secret service involved intrigue, dirty tricks, and a laissez-faire approach to murder. Ezzat had been important before; now he was not.

'We can't prove that you killed Avers, but we can prove this murder. Why?'

'Gabrielle was becoming nosey, always up at the mansion, listening into our conversations. She was recording some of them on her phone.'

'Ingenious,' Larry said. 'She could then get them transcripted and translated. She could have done that over the internet. Arabic?'

'It's unlikely that she ever heard anything important. Even so, my father cannot tolerate deception.'

'You killed her on your father's instruction?'

'I went to the house to remonstrate with her, to convince her it was folly and dangerous.'

'That's the first time. The photos are date stamped, and it's clearly you and Gabrielle at the door of her house.'

'She was determined and continued to do it. My father gave the instructions. I carried it out.'

'You can see the date stamped on one of the other photos. It's the day she was murdered. You're outside the house;

Deadly Secrets

the front door is open. She's smiling, so are you, but a bag is in your hand. The bag you placed over her head. It's undeniable.'

'How did you get these photos,' Ezzat asked again.

'The Alsworthy estate has been under surveillance. Other photos show Caddick and Clough, as well as your father. This is murder, and we have evidence. It's first-degree, and no phone calls will get you out this time. Are you willing to make a full confession?'

'There will be another phone call,' Ezzat replied. His posture had returned to what it had been previously, relaxed, his arms crossed in defiance.

Larry stayed with Ezzat while he wrote his confession and signed it. It was comprehensive; it would ensure that he would be found guilty and imprisoned for the murder of Gabrielle Alsworthy.

Outside the interview room, after Ezzat had been taken to the cells, Larry asked Isaac about what had just happened. 'Why did it take so long to get the photos?' Larry asked. 'After all, the woman was murdered two weeks ago.'

'Ezzat was protected due to the trade deal, or else, MI5 had another use for him, to work for them undercover, in exchange for immunity from the murder charge.'

'Why now?'

'You would need to ask them, but it's obvious they had no use for him, and he's compromised by association with his father. He was given to us, as is Clough.'

***

Ezzat continued to maintain that he had not killed Robert Avers. He had been given a meal, the chance of a shower, and a clean set of clothes, brought to the police station by Siobhan, accompanied by Ezzat's sister.

'Clough killed Robert Avers, I'm sure of that,' Ezzat said. Larry was sitting in the cell with him.

'Why?' Larry asked.

'My father always suspected the man, too skilled for an English police officer, more capable than a sergeant.'

'How?'

'My father recognised the skills. No one else did. What do you reckon to him?'

'We were always suspicious of him due to his association with Chief Superintendent Caddick.'

'Caddick's a bumbling fool. Useful, but the man had no moral compass, good or bad. My father believes in what he does. Caddick never did, only in the opportunity.'

'We can't prove he killed Avers, no photos this time.'

'Get me out of here, and I'll give you the proof.'

'A minor crime, I might, but this is murder, and you have confessed. I thought you liked Gabrielle.'

'You would not understand, but a son must obey the father, regardless of his abhorrence with what he must do.'

Larry thought it a lame excuse.

'At the mansion, my room has a phone in the top left-hand drawer. Check it,' Ezzat said. 'I was not outside the house. Listen and watch a recording on it.'

'Are you saying you were in Avers's house when Clough came in?'

'I am. I'll not get charged with two murders; one is enough, although I won't be there for long.'

'Did you talk to Avers?'

'I did, and I asked him for the tape. I was not violent with him, according to Ali's instructions. He would not tell me and asked me for a drink. I gave him one.'

'A sedative?'

'Strong enough to knock him out. I could hear the front door open; I hid in another room and watched through a gap in the unclosed door. Clough came in but couldn't wake him. He rifled through a few drawers, looked upstairs and down, and found what he wanted. Avers wakes up and goes for his gun, but he's weak and old. Easy for Clough to take it off him and then shoot him.'

Deadly Secrets

'And you've got a recording of this?'

'Enough to prove that he committed murder.'

Larry knew Clough would not confess, even if the tape's retrieval sealed Robert Avers' fate.

Larry and Wendy drove to the mansion, ensuring they had a search warrant, although it was unnecessary as Siobhan had shown them the room and left them to look for the phone. It was where Ezzat had said it would be. It was placed in an evidence bag. Forensics would download the recording and ensure it was transcripted and filed as evidence.

It was five in the afternoon before Sergeant Clough was formally charged with murder. As with Ezzat, he was arrogant and confident he would be released.

Isaac hoped he would not, but anything was possible when dealing with the Secret Service. His fate was uncertain. Clough had killed Avers, proving that Fairweather didn't want loose ends.

That left Caddick and Davies.

Isaac sat with DAC Goddard. The two met at Goddard's house. It was a Saturday evening, and both men's wives were in attendance.

Isaac had been a regular visitor in years gone by, but the relationship between mentor and mentee had soured as Goddard played internal politics, and Isaac had not.

After the meal, Goddard and Isaac went to another room, leaving the women to talk.

'What now?' Isaac asked.

'A serving police officer, charged with murder, doesn't reflect well on the Met,' Goddard replied. He held a glass of brandy, as did Isaac.

'Will it stand?'

'Fairweather's not going to protect him, and Davies will turn it to his advantage, weeding out the incompetent and the criminal.'

'Ezzat?'

'Fairweather considered him useful but will not intervene.'

353

'Ezzat believes his father can get him out.'

'Unlikely, although there might be behind-the-scenes discussions. Egypt does not have the clout.'

'It's impossible to comprehend that releasing a murderer for political or financial expediency would be considered.'

'Regardless, Caddick's the issue,' Goddard said. 'What can you prove?'

'Nothing, no solid evidence,' Isaac admitted.

'Ibrahim Ali might have known that Taleb was planning something, but Fairweather believes he was not involved in any crime. Ali might be a fervent advocate for his religion, but he is not a jihadist. There will be no further investigation of him at this time.'

'Which means he will be monitored.'

'Probably. We deal with crime, not national security. Ali has no crime to answer.'

'Caddick does.'

'Which you can't prove.'

'Fairweather might.'

'He might, but we don't know. Caddick's on extended leave and will not return to Challis Street. You are to be promoted to superintendent.'

'In Homicide?'

'Where else?'

'Who will take Caddick's position?'

'The positions will be amalgamated.'

'Your promotion?'

'Davies is under investigation, but there's no proof.'

'He might not have known the extent of the attack,' Isaac conceded.

'Caddick will be assigned a position out of London. Davies will hold on for now.'

'And you'll be working with Fairweather, strengthening your political alliances, sucking up to whoever you can.'

'Even Davies. I was always there for you, but I needed Davies to believe that I had changed and was there for him.'

'Did he believe you?'

'Never, but it was a pretence we both played. A pretence we will continue to play. I intend to take his position when he finally leaves, and he will not give up on bringing me to heel.'

The End

Phillip Strang

ALSO BY THE AUTHOR

DI Tremayne Thriller Series

Death Unholy – A DI Tremayne Thriller – Book 1

All that remained were the man's two legs and a chair full of greasy and fetid ash. Little did DI Keith Tremayne know that it was the beginning of a journey into the murky world of paganism and its ancient rituals. And it was going to get very dangerous.

'Do you believe in spontaneous human combustion?' Detective Inspector Keith Tremayne asked.

'Not me. I've read about it. Who hasn't?' Sergeant Clare Yarwood answered.

'I haven't,' Tremayne replied, which did not surprise his young sergeant. In the months they had been working together, she had come to realise that he was a man who had little interest in the world. When he had a cigarette in his mouth, a beer in his hand, and a murder to solve he was about the happiest she ever saw him, but even then, he was not one of life's most sociable people. And as for reading? The occasional police report, an early-morning newspaper, turned first to the racing results.

Death and the Assassin's Blade – A DI Tremayne Thriller – Book 2

It was meant to be high drama, not murder, but someone's switched the daggers. The man's death took place in plain view of two serving police officers.

Deadly Secrets

He was not meant to die; the daggers were only theatrical props, plastic and harmless. A summer's night, a production of Julius Caesar amongst the ruins of an Anglo-Saxon fort. Detective Inspector Tremayne is there with his sergeant, Clare Yarwood. In the assassination scene, Caesar collapses to the ground. Brutus defends his actions; Mark Antony rebukes him.

They're a disparate group, the amateur actors. One's an estate agent, another an accountant. And then there is the teenage school student, the gay man, the funeral director. And what about the women? They could be involved.

They've each got a secret, but which of those on the stage wanted Gordon Mason, the actor who had portrayed Caesar, dead?

Death and the Lucky Man – A DI Tremayne Thriller – Book 3

Sixty-eight million pounds and dead. Hardly the outcome expected for the luckiest man in England the day his lottery ticket was drawn out of the barrel. But then, Alan Winters' rags-to-riches story had never been conventional, and some had benefited, but others hadn't.

Death at Coombe Farm – A DI Tremayne Thriller – Book 4

A warring family. A disputed inheritance. A recipe for death.

If it hadn't been for the circumstances, Detective Inspector Keith Tremayne would have said the view was outstanding. Up high, overlooking the farmhouse in the valley below, the panoramic vista of Salisbury Plain stretching out beyond. The only problem was a body near where he stood with his sergeant, Clare Yarwood, and it wasn't a pleasant sight.

Phillip Strang

Death by a Dead Man's Hand – A DI Tremayne Thriller – Book 5

A flawed heist of forty gold bars from a security van late at night. One of the perpetrators is killed by his brother as they argue over what they have stolen.

Eighteen years later, the murderer, released after serving his sentence for his brother's murder, waits in a church for a man purporting to be the brother he killed. And then he is killed.

The threads stretch back a long way, and now more people are dying in the search for the missing gold bars.

Detective Inspector Tremayne, his health causing him concern, and Sergeant Clare Yarwood, still seeking romance, are pushed to the limit solving the murder, attempting to prevent more.

Death in the Village – A DI Tremayne Thriller – Book 6

Nobody liked Gloria Wiggins, a woman who regarded anyone who did not acquiesce to her jaundiced view of the world with disdain. James Baxter, the previous vicar, had been one of those, and her scurrilous outburst in the church one Sunday had hastened his death.

And now, years later, the woman was dead, hanging from a beam in her garage. Detective Inspector Tremayne and Sergeant Clare Yarwood had seen the body, interviewed the woman's acquaintances, and those who had hated her.

Burial Mound – A DI Tremayne Thriller – Book 7

A Bronze-Age burial mound close to Stonehenge. An archaeological excavation. What they were looking for was an ancient body and historical artefacts. They found the ancient

Deadly Secrets

body, but then they found another that's only been there for years, not centuries. And then the police became interested.

It's another case for Detective Inspector Tremayne and Sergeant Yarwood. The more recent body was the brother of the mayor of Salisbury.

Everything seems to point to the victim's brother, the mayor, the upright and serious-minded Clive Grantley. Tremayne's sure that it's him, but Clare Yarwood's not so sure.

But is her belief based on evidence or personal hope?

The Body in the Ditch – A DI Tremayne Thriller – Book 8

A group of children play. Not far away, in the ditch on the other side of the farmyard, lies the body of a troubled young woman.

The nearby village hides as many secrets as the community at the farm, a disparate group of people looking for an alternative to their previous torturous lives. Their leader, idealistic and benevolent, espouses love and kindness, and clearly, somebody's not following his dictate.

An old woman's death seems unrelated to the first, but is it? Is it part of the tangled web that connects the farm to the village?

Detective Inspector Tremayne and Sergeant Clare Yarwood soon discover that the village is anything but charming and picturesque. It's an incestuous hotbed of intrigue and wrongdoing. And what of the farm and those who live there. None of them can be ruled out, not yet.

The Horse's Mouth – A DI Tremayne Thriller – Book 9

Phillip Strang

A day at the races for Detective Inspector Tremayne, idyllic at the outset, soon changes. A horse is dead, the owner's daughter is found murdered, and Tremayne's there when the body is discovered.

The question is, was Tremayne set up, in the wrong place at the right time? He's the cast-iron alibi for one of the suspects, and he knows that one murder can lead to two, and more often than not to three.

The dead woman had a chequered history, though not as much as her father, and then a man commits suicide. Is he the murderer, or was his death the unfortunate consequence of a tragic love affair? And who was in the stable with the woman just before she died? More than one person could have killed her, and all of them have secrets they would rather not be known.

Tremayne's health is troubling him. Is what they are saying correct, that it is time for him to retire, to take it easy and put his feet up? But that's not his style, and he'll not give up on solving the murder.

Montfield's Madness – A DI Tremayne Thriller – Book 10

A day at the races for Detective Inspector Tremayne, idyllic at the Jacob Montfield, regarded by the majority as a homeless eccentric, a nuisance by a few, had pushed a supermarket trolley around the city for years.

However, one person regards him as a liability.

Eccentric was correct, a nuisance, for sure, mad, plenty thought that, but few knew the truth, that Montfield is a brilliant man, once a research scientist. And even less knew that detailed within a notebook hidden deep in the trolley, there is a new approach to the guidance of weapons and satellites—a radical improvement

Deadly Secrets

on the previous and it's worth a lot to some, power to others, accolades to another.

And for that, one cold night, he died at the hand of another. Inspector Tremayne and Sergeant Clare Yarwood are on the case, but so are others, and soon they're warned off. Only Tremayne doesn't listen, not when he's got his teeth into the investigation, and his sergeant, equally resolute, won't either. It's not only their careers on the line, but their lives.

DCI Isaac Cook Thriller Series

Murder is a Tricky Business – A DCI Cook Thriller – Book 1

A television actress is missing, and DCI Isaac Cook, the Senior Investigation Officer of the Murder Investigation Team at Challis Street Police Station in London, is searching for her.

Why has he been taken away from more important crimes to search for the woman? It's not the first time she's gone missing, so why does everyone assume she's been murdered?

There's a secret; that much is certain, but who knows it? The missing woman? The executive producer? His eavesdropping assistant? Or the actor who portrayed her fictional brother in the TV soap opera?

Murder House – A DCI Cook Thriller – Book 2

A corpse in the fireplace of an old house. It's been there for thirty years, but who is it?

It's murder, but who is the victim and what connection does the body have to the house's previous owners. What is the motive? And why is the body in a fireplace? It was bound to be discovered eventually but was that what the murderer wanted? The main suspects are all old and dying or already dead.

Isaac Cook and his team have their work cut out, trying to put the pieces together. Those who know are not talking because of an old-fashioned belief that a family's dirty laundry should not be aired in public and never to a policeman – even if that means the murderer is never brought to justice!

Murder is Only a Number – A DCI Cook Thriller – Book 3

Before she left, she carved a number in blood on his chest. But why the number 2 if this was her first murder?

The woman prowls the streets of London. Her targets are men who have wronged her. Or have they? And why is she keeping count?

DCI Cook and his team finally know who she is, but not before she's murdered four men. The whole team are looking for her, but the woman keeps disappearing in plain sight. The pressure's on to stop her, but she's always one step ahead.

And this time, DCS Goddard can't protect his protégé, Isaac Cook, from the wrath of the new commissioner at the Met.

Murder in Little Venice – A DCI Cook Thriller – Book 4

A dismembered corpse floats in the canal in Little Venice, an upmarket tourist haven in London. Its identity is unknown, but what is its significance?

DCI Isaac Cook is baffled about why it's there. Is it gang-related, or is it something more?

Whatever the reason, it's clearly a warning, and Isaac and his team are sure it's not the last body that they'll have to deal with.

Murder is the Only Option – A DCI Cook Thriller – Book 5

A man thought to be long dead returns to exact revenge against those who had blighted his life. His only concern is to protect his wife and daughter. He will stop at nothing to achieve his aim.

'Big Greg, I never expected to see you around here at this time of night.'

'I've told you enough times.'

'I've no idea what you're talking about,' Robertson replied. He looked up at the man, only to see a metal pole coming down at him. Robertson fell down, cracking his head against a concrete kerb.

Two vagrants, no more than twenty feet away, did not stir and did not even look in the direction of the noise. If they had, they would have seen a dead body, another man walking away.

Murder in Notting Hill – A DCI Cook Thriller – Book 6

One murderer, two bodies, two locations, and the murders have been committed within an hour of each other.

They're separated by a couple of miles, and neither woman has anything in common with the other. One is young and wealthy, the daughter of a famous man; the other is poor, hardworking and unknown.

Isaac Cook and his team at Challis Street Police Station are baffled about why they've been killed. There must be a connection, but what is it?

Murder in Room 346 – A DCI Cook Thriller – Book 7

'Coitus interruptus, that's what it is,' Detective Chief Inspector Isaac Cook said. In a downmarket hotel in Bayswater, on the bed lay the naked bodies of a man and a woman.

'Bullet in the head's not the way to go,' Larry Hill, Isaac Cook's detective inspector, said. He had not expected such a flippant comment from his senior, not when they were standing near to two people who had, apparently in the final throes of passion, succumbed to what appeared to be a professional assassination.

'You know this will be all over the media within the hour,' Isaac said.

'James Holden, moral crusader, a proponent of the sanctity of the marital bed, man and wife. It's bound to be.'

Murder of a Silent Man – A DCI Cook Thriller – Book 8

A murdered recluse. A property empire. A disinherited family. All the ingredients for murder.

No one gave much credence to the man when he was alive. In fact, most people never knew who he was, although those who had lived in the area for many years recognised the tired-looking and shabbily-dressed man as he shuffled along, regular as clockwork on a Thursday afternoon at seven in the evening to the local off-licence.

It was always the same: a bottle of whisky, premium brand, and a packet of cigarettes. He paid his money over the counter, took hold of his plastic bag containing his purchases, and then walked back down the road with the same rhythmic shuffle.

Murder has no Guilt – A DCI Cook Thriller – Book 9

No one knows who the target was or why, but there are eight dead. The men seem the most likely perpetrators, or could have it been one of the two women, the attractive Gillian Dickenson, or even the celebrity-obsessed Sal Maynard?

There's a gang war brewing, and if there are deaths, it doesn't matter to them as long as it's not their death. But to Detective Chief Inspector Isaac Cook, it's his area of London, and it does matter.

It's dirty and unpredictable. Initially, the West Indian gangs held sway, but a more vicious Romanian gangster had usurped them. And now he's being marginalised by the Russians. And the leader of the most vicious Russian mafia organisation is in London, and he's got money and influence, the ear of those in power.

Murder in Hyde Park – A DCI Cook Thriller – Book 10

An early-morning jogger is murdered in Hyde Park. It's in the centre of London, but no one saw him enter the park, no one saw him die.

He carries no identification, only a water-logged phone. As the pieces unravel, it's clear that the dead man had a history of deception.

Is the murderer one of those that loved him? Or was it someone with a vengeance?

It's proving difficult for DCI Isaac Cook and his team at Challis Street Homicide to find the guilty person – not that they'll cease to search for the truth, not even after one suspect confesses.

Six Years Too Late – A DCI Cook Thriller – Book 11

Always the same questions for Detective Chief Inspector Isaac Cook — Why was Marcus Matthews in that room? And why did he share a bottle of wine with his killer?

It wasn't as if Matthews had amounted to much, apart from the fact that he was the son-in-law of a notorious gangster, the father of the man's grandchildren.

Yet the one thing Hamish McIntyre, feared in London for his violence, rated above anything else, was his family, especially Samantha, his daughter. However, he had never cared for Marcus, her husband.

And then Marcus disappeared, only for his body to be found six years later by a couple of young boys who decide that exploring an abandoned house is preferable to school.

Grave Passion – A DCI Cook Thriller – Book 12

Two young lovers out for a night of romance. A shortcut through the cemetery. They witnessed a murder, but there was no struggle, only a knife through the heart.

It has all the hallmarks of an assassination, but who is the woman? And why was she beside a grave at night? Did she know the person who killed her?

Soon after, other deaths, seemingly unconnected, but tied to the family of one of the young lovers.

It's a case for Detective Chief Inspector Cook and his team, and they're baffled on this one.

The Slaying of Joe Foster – A DCI Cook Thriller – Book 13

No one challenged Joe Foster in life, not if they valued theirs. And then, the gangster is slain and his criminal empire up for grabs.

A power vacuum; the Foster family is fighting for control, the other gangs in the area aiming to poach the trade in illegal drugs, to carve up the empire that the father had created.

It has all the makings of a war on the streets, something nobody wants, not even the other gangs.

Terry Foster, the eldest son of Joe, the man who should take control, doesn't have his father's temperament or wisdom. His solution is slash and burn, and it's not going to work. People are going to get hurt, and some of them will die.

The Hero's Fall – A DCI Cook Thriller – Book 14

Angus Simmons had it made. A successful television program, a beautiful girlfriend, admired by many for his mountaineering exploits.

And then he fell while climbing a skyscraper in London. Initially, it was thought he had lost his grip, but that wasn't the man: a meticulous planner, his risks measured, and it wasn't a difficult climb, not for him.

It was only afterwards on examination that they found the mark of a bullet on his body. It then became a murder, and that was when Detective Chief Inspector Isaac Cook and his Homicide team at Challis Street Police Station became interested.

Phillip Strang

The Vicar's Confession – A DCI Cook Thriller – Book 15

The Reverend Charles Hepworth, good Samaritan, a friend of the downtrodden, almost a saint to those who know him, up until the day he walks into the police station, straight up to Detective Chief Inspector Isaac Cook's desk in Homicide. 'I killed the man,' he says as he places a blood-soaked knife on the desk.

The dead man, Andreas Maybury, was not a man to mourn, but why would a self-professed pacifist commit such a heinous crime. The reasons aren't clear, and then Hepworth's killed in a prison cell, and everyone's ducking for cover.

Guilty Until Proven Innocent – A DCI Cook Thriller – Book 16

Gary Harders' conviction two years previously should have been the end of the investigation. A clear-cut case of murder, and he had confessed to the crime and accepted his sentence without complaint. But now, the man's conviction was about to be overthrown, but why? And why is Harders not saying that his confession was police coercion? His prints are on the murder weapon, but Forensics has found another set.

Not only is there proof of either the Forensics department's error, incompetency or conspiracy, but Commissioner Alwyn Davies is getting tough on crime, draconian tough.

Detective Chief Inspector Isaac Cook and Chief Superintendent Richard Goddard are under pressure to take sides, aware that a positive return ensures promotion, but at the cost of their respective souls.

Davies has powerful backers, persons willing to make a deal with the devil. To allow violent putdown of those who disrupt the streets and removal of those who cause unsolicited and anti-social crime.

The plan has merits, a return to the safe society of decades past, but where will it stop. Who will say it's time to ease off, and then, what's the Russian mafia got to do with it? Too much from what DCI Cook can see, but he's powerless.

Devil House – A DCI Cook Thriller – Book 17

'I thought they used virgins,' Sergeant Wendy Gladstone said. She thought she had seen it all, but a naked man spreadeagled on a bare floor in a suburban house in London was a first for her.

Wendy surmised middle-class affluence, pagan worship, and human sacrifice. She had read fiction and watched the occasional late-night horror movie, but to be confronted by reality made her feel uneasy.

'He might have been,' Inspector Larry Hill said, responding to Wendy's initial comment.

He had seen more of man's depravity than his sergeant, but she thought his remark was flippant. Although Wendy knew, as any police officer did, especially in Homicide, that flippancy often defused the situation. It was for them to be dispassionately professional, not to be melancholy or disheartened by humanity's ability to inflict terrible actions against another.

Detective Chief Inspector Isaac Cook, the senior officer in Homicide at Challis Street Police Station, arrived within the hour. He took one look at the body and walked outside the house. 'It's a murder; that's all we need to know,' he said.

Murder Without Reason – A DCI Cook Thriller – Book 18

DCI Cook faces his greatest challenge. The Islamic State is waging war in England, and they are winning.

Not only does Isaac Cook have to contend with finding the perpetrators, but he is also being forced to commit actions contrary to his mandate as a police officer.

And then there is Anne Argento, the prime minister's deputy. The prime minister has shown himself to be a pacifist and is not up to the task. She needs to take his job if the country is to fight back against the Islamists.

Vane and Martin have provided the solution. Will DCI Cook and Anne Argento be willing to follow it through? Are they able to act for the good of England, knowing that a criminal and murderous action is about to take place? Do they have an option?

Sergeant Natalie Campbell Thriller Series

Dark Streets – Book 1

A homeless man, Old Joe's death was not unexpected. Not until it was found to be murder.

This was Darlinghurst Road, Kings Cross, once a hub of inequity, of strip joints and gentleman's clubs, of licensed premises and restaurants. But now, the area is changing, going upmarket, another enclave for those that can afford it, not a place for the homeless, nor is it a place of murder, but then there is another murder in Point Piper, upmarket and exclusive; a woman, her throat cut.

Deadly Secrets

Detective Gary Haddock's a seasoned hand in Homicide, but he's baffled by the murders that continue. Statistically, Sydney's Eastern Suburbs doesn't have murder, but after four, are they serial or random, and if they are serial, why?

Sergeant Natalie Campbell from Kings Cross Police Station is wet behind the ears when she pairs with Haddock but soon learns she is more astute than he is, although she's a risk taker. He has to protect her, but she will take the investigations forward.

Pinchgut – Book 2

An old fort in Sydney Harbour – the body of a woman missing for seventeen years. It's murder, but after so long, can it be solved?

Sergeant Natalie Campbell and Inspector Haddock are resolute that it can. But then, there's the complication of the murdered woman's father, the bombastic, bullying Bernie Cornell. One of Australia's richest men, but he's closing in on death due to old age and ill health.

There's no shortage of intrigue, no shortage of potential murderers.

Island Shadows – Book 3

The island was a prison in colonial days, then a shipbuilding facility, and now it's a venue for concerts and tourists, with some camping overnight and others wandering around the engineering workshops or the prison ruins.

Death wasn't uncommon in the island's earlier, more violent days, but not in the present, and not at a heavy metal concert.

Lead singer Alan Greenworthy is reclusive and mysterious except when he's on stage, but now he's dead.

Was the murderer the woman he had just made love to or a jealous paramour, or was the motive more obscure? And would others die?

It's another challenging case for Sergeant Natalie Campbell and Inspector Haddock.

Steve Case Thriller Series

The Haberman Virus – Book 1

A remote and isolated village in the Hindu Kush Mountain range in North Eastern Afghanistan is wiped out by a virus unlike any seen before.

A mysterious visitor clad in a spacesuit checks his handiwork, a female American doctor succumbs to the disease, and the woman sent to trap the person responsible falls in love with him – the man who would cause the deaths of millions.

Hostage of Islam – Book 2

Three are to die at the Mission in Nigeria: the pastor and his wife in a blazing chapel; another gunned down while trying to defend them from the Islamist fighters.

Kate McDonald, an American, grieving over her boyfriend's death and Helen Campbell, whose life had been troubled by drugs and prostitution, are taken by the attackers.

Kate is sold to a slave trader who intends to sell her virginity to an Arab Prince. Helen, to ensure their survival, gives herself to the murderer of her friends.

Prelude to War – Book 3

Russia and America face each other across the northern border of Afghanistan. World War 3 is about to break out and no one is backing off.

And all because a team of academics in New York postulated how to extract the vast untapped mineral wealth of Afghanistan.

Steve Case is in the middle of it, and his position is looking very precarious. Will the Taliban find him before the Americans get him out? Or is he doomed, as is the rest of the world?

Standalone Novels

Malika's Revenge

Malika, a drug-addicted prostitute, waits in a smugglers' village for the next Afghan tribesman or Tajik gangster to pay her price, a few scraps of heroin.

Yusup Baroyev, a drug lord, enjoys a lifestyle many would envy. An Afghan warlord sees the resurgence of the Taliban. A Russian white-collar criminal portrays himself as a good and honest citizen in Moscow.

All of them are linked to an audacious plan to increase the quantity of heroin shipped out of Afghanistan and into Russia and ultimately the West.

Some will succeed, some will die, some will be rescued from their plight and others will rue the day they became involved.

Verrall's Nightmare

Historians may reflect on what happened, psychoanalysts may debate endlessly, and although scientists would attempt to explain, none would conclusively get the measure of all that had occurred.

Others, less knowledgeable, aficionados of social media, would say that Benedict Verrall was mad, or else the events in a small hamlet in the south of England never occurred and that it was a government conspiracy. That Samuel Whittingham was a figment of Verrall's imagination and the storms and their devastation, unprecedented in their scope and deaths, were freaks of nature, not of evil.

The truth, however, was more obscure, and that Verrall was neither mad nor was he malicious. Although he was responsible for instigating what was to happen, that hadn't been his intention.

He did not believe in the paranormal or the metaphysical, but then, he had not considered the brain tumour pressing down on his brain.

Or was it Verrall's madness, either the dream or the nightmare? That will be for the reader to decide.

ABOUT THE AUTHOR

Phillip Strang was born in the late forties, the post-war baby boom in England; his childhood years, a comfortable middle-class upbringing in a small town, a two hours' drive to the west of London.

His childhood and the formative years were a time of innocence. Relatively few rules, and as a teenager, complete mobility due to a bicycle – a three-speed Raleigh – and a more trusting community. It was the days before mobile phones, the internet, terrorism and wanton violence. An avid reader of Science Fiction in his teenage years: Isaac Asimov, and Frank Herbert, the masters of the genre. Still an avid reader, the author now mainly reads thrillers.

In his early twenties, the author, with a degree in electronics engineering and an unabated wanderlust to see the world left England's cold and damp climes for Sydney, Australia – the first semi-circulation of the globe, complete. Now, forty years later, he still resides in Australia, although many intervening years spent in a myriad of countries, some calm and safe – others, no more than war zones.

Printed in Great Britain
by Amazon